The Flight of Peter Fromm

The Flight of Peter Fromm

MARTIN GARDNER

The Noonday Press
Farrar, Straus and Giroux
New York

Library of Congress Cataloging in Publication Data
Gardner, Martin
   The flight of Peter Fromm.
   I. Title.
PZ4.G23124Fl [PS3557.A714]   813'.5'4   73-1932

Grateful acknowledgment is made to Alfred A. Knopf,
Inc., for permission to reprint "Seven Stanzas at
Easter" from *Telephone Poles and Other Poems*,
copyright © 1961 by John Updike

And there followed him a certain young man, having a linen cloth cast about his naked body; and the young men laid hold on him: and he left the linen cloth, and fled from them naked.

Mark 14:51–52

Contents

The Flight of Peter Fromm

Foreword

When I was an undergraduate at the University of Chicago, from 1932 through 1936, the university was in the throes of its now-famous "Hutchins-Adler" period. Robert Maynard Hutchins had been lured from the Yale Law School, where he had been dean, to become the country's youngest, handsomest, wittiest, and most arrogant college president. Hutchins in turn had lured to Chicago his friend and mentor, Mortimer Jerome Adler. A great hue and cry went up from these two men about the deterioration of the higher learning in America, the importance of the Great Books, and the need for a return to metaphysics and theology. No one who was not at Gray City on the Midway during this clangorous period can appreciate the shock waves that rattled the academic community when it first discovered that its president, invoking the name of God in commencement speeches, actually meant what he was saying.

It was also the time of the University of Chicago's so-called "New Plan." A student could proceed at his own speed, take final exams whenever he felt like it; class attendance was noncompulsory, and one could audit, without credit, as many extra courses as desired. As a philosophy major with vague yearnings to become a writer, I took the utmost advantage of these freedoms. One of the most rewarding of the many courses which I audited was Dr. Homer Wilson's introduction to the psychology of religious belief. I can still remember the bewildered divinity school students, shifting positions uncomfortably on their chairs, listening intently to Wilson's measured, sonorous tones as he slowly, inexorably undermined the foundations of their faith.

Several years later, when I was working in the university's department of press relations, I became personally acquainted with Wilson and his wife, and with Wilson's young protege and friend, Peter Fromm. In the late forties, after I had settled in New York City to pursue a writing career in earnest, I lost contact with all three, though occasionally I would come across an article or book review by Wilson, usually in a scholarly journal, or see a notice of the publication of a new book by him.

Homer Wilson died in June, 1971, a few days after the passing of Reinhold Niebuhr. Wilson was 86. A year later his widow, searching his files, came upon the typed manuscript of a book which he had titled *The Flight of Peter Fromm*.

Incredibly, Mrs. Wilson had not known that her husband had written it. No one else, it seems, was aware of the manuscript's existence except Peter himself. Although the book's first chapter makes clear that Wilson intended to publish his book, there is not a scrap of correspondence to suggest that it had ever been submitted to a publisher. I do not know why. Perhaps he felt it was too personal a story to make public until many years had intervened between the narrated events and the book's publication. Perhaps he was never satisfied with what he had written, for the manuscript was cluttered with revisions in penciled longhand on almost every page.

Mrs. Wilson wrote to me in October, 1972. Would I, she wanted to know, be willing to read her husband's manuscript, to tell her candidly whether I thought she should make an effort to get it published? I read the pages with mixed emotions. The Wilson who tells the story of his strange, in many ways inexplicable (at least to me), friendship with Peter comes through the lines as stuffier, more pedantic, certainly more opinionated than the Wilson I remember. At times his lengthy, rambling discourses on theology—the Barthian theology in particular—are annoyingly tedious and tendentious. Peter, as I recall him in the thirties, was not nearly so straightforward and guileless as Wilson makes him out to be. And Mrs. Wilson, an attractive, vivacious woman, remains curiously in the shadows. It may be that Wilson considered it unseemly to write about his wife in depth and detail. He was, after all, not writing a novel.

If personalities in Wilson's narrative, including himself, are slightly caricatured, as it seems to me they are, I do not think that Wilson consciously intended it that way. I am convinced that every incident and conversation is as accurate as he could recall it or reconstruct it from what he was told by Peter and other participants in the story. If distortions are there, they are surely understandable. Small, seemingly irrelevant facts have a way of slipping from an old man's memory. Events shed their ragged edges, their loose ends. They take on sharper outlines, more vivid colors.

The thousands of corrections and marginal insertions scribbled on Wilson's battered manuscript testify, as I mentioned before, to his constant efforts to polish his text and bring it up to date. It is a pity he did not live to add some pithy comments about the recent revival of fundamentalism and the young Jesus People with their upward-pointing index fingers, their Pentecostal fervor, and their quaint prophecies of doomsday. One wonders, too, what Wilson would have said about the exploitation, by the Broadway money-changers, of the life of Jesus. Hard rock of ages, amplified for me. It is difficult to say if he would have liked or disliked *Jesus Christ, Superstar,* or been utterly indifferent to it.

And there is that latest Protestant fad, the "theology of hope." As though hope were something new in Christianity! What would Wilson have thought, I sometimes wonder, of the recent Protestant emphasis on singing, dancing, laughing, playing, with Jesus as the great super-clown of history and the crucifixion as the climax of God's vast super-comedy staged with such brilliant light and sound effects on a hill outside the ancient city of Jerusalem. (See Harvey Cox's, *The Feast of Fools,* Sam Keen's *To a Dancing God,* and a dozen other recent books with similar ploys.) There is, we all know, not a single reference in the New Testament to Jesus as having smiled or laughed. As I write, one can buy a "Jesus wristwatch" bearing the face of a grinning Savior (he comes in two racial colors, white and black) and a rotating crimson heart.

On the surface *The Flight of Peter Fromm* is the story of a young man who, to the end, never shares an old man's conviction that God does not exist. Below the surface, the clash between these two irreconcilable ways of viewing the mystery of our existence generates an elaborate counterpoint of conflicting ideas. Wilson was writing about a theme deeper, older, and more permanent than perhaps he fully realized. The battle between atheism and theism is as ancient as humanity and unlikely to subside as long as the human species, with its unimaginable progeny in the millenia that may lie ahead, is on this old earth or flourishing in colonies on other planets. Who can say that the conflict is not one that divides all thinking creatures on billions of other planets in this monstrous universe of ours? Who can say that it is not a conflict that will last until the end of time?

But it is best to say no more. At Mrs. Wilson's request, I have edited her husband's manuscript only in the most superficial way. It is a privilege to have played a small role in its publication.

Martin Gardner
Hastings-on-Hudson, N.Y.
1973

Part I

BEFORE THE WAR

If one could only know what really happened in Judea! How immensely would matters be simplified, if anyone but knew the truth about You, Man upon the Cross!

—JURGEN

Part I

BEFORE THE WAR

1

Peter

If you were living in Chicago in the spring of 1948, and if you read one of the city's newspapers on the Monday following Easter, you may have seen the story. A divinity school student named Peter Fromm had been preaching an Easter sermon, his first Easter sermon, at the Midway Community Church in the Hyde Park section of Chicago's south side. Toward the end of the sermon Fromm suddenly lost control of his speech. After collapsing on the floor of the pulpit, he had been rushed to the University of Chicago's Billings Hospital, a few blocks west of the church. If you saw the story, perhaps you paused for a few seconds of genuine compassion. Or a few seconds of sardonic amusement? More likely you read it quickly, wondered for a fleeting instant what had been wrong with the poor fellow, then promptly forgot about him.

Except for one garbled story in the *Chicago American*—even Fromm's last name was misspelled—the newspaper accounts were brief and accurate. Fortunately, it was not until Sunday evening that the City News Bureau, which then supplied local stories to city papers, heard about the incident. Their account of Peter's collapse had been based on nothing more than one telephone conversation, late Sunday night, with Dr. Homer Wilson, pastor of the Midway Community Church where Peter Fromm had been invited to preach. Wilson did not tell the reporter on the phone that young Fromm had first interrupted his own sermon by bursting into wild, mirthless laughter. He did not explain how the sermon had degenerated into nonsense words, or describe the unfortunate assault suffered by Beulah Schwatzer, the church organist. No Chicago paper printed a single line about the chaotic physical struggle which took place in the pulpit or reported that Fromm had finally been subdued by a blow on the side of his skull. When the pastor answered the reporter's questions he had not, to be sure, exactly lied. He had merely omitted. The lurid, slapstick details spread rapidly by word of mouth through the University of Chicago area. Miraculously, they never reached the city's newsrooms.

This is a book about what happened in the Midway Community Church on that crazy Easter morning, why it happened, and what happened afterward to Peter Fromm.

I am Homer Wilson.

I first met Peter in 1938, three years before Japan's little toy bombs dropped gently down on Pearl Harbor. I was then in my early fifties. For fourteen years I had been pastor of the Midway Community Church; for twelve years I had been a part-time teacher at the University of Chicago's Divinity School. Peter had been one of my students.

A teacher's first impressions of a student are often so wide of the mark that he learns to guard against them. Every new face is a fresh encounter with a young, hopefully malleable mind, but I had been teaching too long to suppose that I could predict on the opening day of a class which minds would react favorably to my radical brand of Christianity. Most of the students, I knew, would be disturbed by my approach. They would conceal their disagreements, avoid controversy in their questions, but I would sense the hostility in their eyes. As the months galloped by, two or three who were receptive to my views would become personal friends; my "disciples," I sometimes called them. They would take other courses from me. I would follow their academic careers with interest and, after they left Chicago to become ministers in other cities, I would exchange letters with them about their problems.

But the majority of students in my classes would remain permanently nondescript. Week after week I would see their cherubic, unlined faces arranged in rows in front of me, eyes watching me warily, not quite sure of how to take my phrases. Was I or was I not an atheist? Occasionally one of them would nod in agreement or frown slightly with disapproval, yawn or cough or scratch his nose, or smile at one of my stale, time-tested jokes. I would find it difficult to memorize their names. Even their faces, as soon as they left the classroom, would blur in my memory. Unless they spoke first, I seldom recognized them when I passed them on the campus or met them in an elevator.

From the start, Peter Fromm was an exception. Although he disagreed strongly, sometimes violently, with almost everything I said, I found it impossible not to take an instant liking to him. On the first day of my class—it was a course listed in the divinity school's catalog as "Problems of Applied Christianity"—I was sitting behind a desk in a second-floor

room of Swift Hall, in the middle of my opening remarks, when the door
on my left burst open and Peter hurried in.

"I'm sorry," he said, a bit out of breath. "I got lost. I hope you're
Dr. Wilson."

"So do I," I replied.

Polite laughter rippled around the room and Peter grinned as he
took one of the few remaining empty chairs in the front row. I can close
my eyes now and see him sitting there, looking incredibly boyish,
watching me intently, waiting for me to resume speaking. His eyes were
large and clear and blue. A faint scar slanted across his forehead,
above his left eye, and there was a slight, barely perceptible twist to his
nose that gave him the appearance of a good-looking young pugilist.
Indeed, I learned later, he had been the top middle-weight boxer on his
high school team. It was in a high school boxing tournament that his
nose had once been broken.

Peter was never a brilliant student in the academic sense. Not that
he lacked intelligence. He simply had a low threshold of impatience
with the minutiae of scholarship. He was too eager to get finished with
one book and on to the next. But he had one rare, refreshing trait, a
constitutional inability to accept any form of intellectual evasion.

To be a Protestant minister today, in the typical church of a prosperous suburb, one must be as skilled as a politician in the rhetoric of
ambiguity, circumlocution, and double-talk. I am not referring now to
those fashionable "in" terms that vary from year to year in the nation's
leading seminaries: *estrangement, kerygma, didache, hermeneutics,
agape, demythologizing,* or such Germanisms as *Angst, Wissenschaft,* and
Redaktionsgeschichte. At the moment, at divinity school teas, phrases
most often heard are those that Dietrich Bonhoeffer invented when he
was in a Nazi prison—*cheap grace, religionless Christianity, holy world-
liness*—and Harvey Cox's *Christian secularization.* When, however, the
student becomes a minister he obviously has to bottle up this esoteric
jargon. He must talk plain language, though in such a way that no lis-
tener can take offense. He may attack race prejudice, but it must be
done obliquely so that no one in the congregation imagines it refers to
him. He may attack business ethics, but it must be in such a manner that
no businessman who listens will think that *he* is implicated. The minister
can, indeed must, use the old doctrinal phrases, but always so cunningly
that conservative listeners will take them one way, liberal listeners
another. In brief, he must learn to preach without saying anything.

One of the great functions of a liberal divinity school is to train its
students in just these skills. It is amusing to watch a student slowly

acquire them as he moves closer and closer to his graduation. But Peter
would have none of it. He insisted, at all places, at all times, on calling
a spade a spade. He struggled perpetually to get down to brass tacks, to
the nitty-gritty. Other students in my classes, who also did not share my
radical views, would remain discreetly silent. Not Peter. We collided
openly and head-on. It was not hard to see, however, that behind his
blustering confidence, behind his brash dogmatism, his mind was in a
typical ferment of seminarian uncertainty. He knew so little. He had
so much to learn.

One afternoon, a few weeks after the class had begun, I mentioned
—too casually perhaps—that not many Protestant ministers today, outside fundamentalist circles, believe in a physical Resurrection of Jesus.
A deep flush came over Peter's face.

"But how," he said, interrupting my remarks in a loud voice, "could
such a person accept Saint Paul's remark in First Corinthians, Chapter
fifteen, verse fourteen: 'And if Christ be not risen, then is our preaching
vain'?"

A deathlike silence sat on the classroom. I must have looked startled.
It is not the sort of question that students at the University of Chicago
Divinity School often ask their professors.

"Mr. Fromm," I said, trying to keep my face solemn, "I agree with
you that Paul thought of the Resurrection of Jesus in a literal, physical
sense. But Protestant Christianity has never been a fixed, unchanging
set of doctrines. There are all sorts of things we can see more clearly
today than Paul could. Old wine must be put into new bottles. The old
dogmas have to be reinterpreted. They have to be given fresh meanings,
meanings relevant to our secular, scientific age."

"But," insisted Peter, oblivious of the smiles around him, "suppose
you have a church. Suppose the people in your church all believe in the
Resurrection the way Saint Paul did. Wouldn't it be dishonest to be their
pastor if you didn't believe it, too?"

"In a way," I said. "Surely, though, it's a trivial and justifiable kind
of dishonesty. In the first place there are many Protestant congregations
in which only a small handful of members take the Resurrection story
literally. And even if they *are* a majority, a minister has the responsibility
of holding his congregation together while he liberalizes it. He doesn't
want to split it down the middle into two warring factions. He has a
choice"—and here I threw out an alliterative aphorism I had stolen
years before from one of my older colleagues—"of being a truthful
traitor or a loyal liar. If he's too explicit in making his doctrinal views
known to his congregation, he's not likely to remain long at that church
as pastor. If he wants to continue his ministry, to work inside the frame-

work of an ongoing, viable denomination—in short, if he wants to remain a loyal Protestant—he can't avoid a certain amount of deception. After all, Jesus himself side-stepped a lot of embarrassing questions by answering them ambiguously."

Peter didn't agree. He had just challenged me to cite an example when the class bell rang like the gong that closes a round of a boxing match. After the other students had left the room, he was still standing by my desk and arguing.

"I really can't stay any longer," I said, checking the time on a watch I always carried in an upper vest pocket. "I have another class on another floor."

As Peter followed me out the doorway and down the hall, I found myself making an impulsive suggestion. It surprised me. Never before in all my years of teaching had I made such a proposal to a student I had so recently met.

"Why don't you come over to my house tonight? It's hard to discuss things like this briefly. If you have the evening free we can talk as much as we like."

Peter was delighted. I gave him my address, in the fifty-seven hundred block of Harper Avenue, and suggested he drop around at eight. It was the beginning of a series of similar evening sessions that continued until they were interrupted by the war and Peter's enlistment in the Navy. When the war ended, in the shadows of those two malevolent mushrooms, Peter returned to Chicago to complete his studies, and I began to see a lot of him again.

Over the years my wife and I grew extremely fond of Peter. Our own son, had he not died a few weeks after his birth, would have been about Peter's age. The complications of delivery had left my wife unable to bear more children. We had one older child, a daughter, now married to a physicist and living in Pasadena, California. As for Peter, he had been a small boy when his father died. There was clearly a strong component, unrecognized by either of us at first, of a father-son attitude toward each other during those early formative months of our friendship.

Although I carefully followed the constant twists and turns in Peter's thinking as he stumbled away from his boyhood beliefs (twists and turns for which I myself was partly responsible), it was not until after his mental breakdown that I began to attach a mythic, archetypal quality to his development. I do not want to minimize his unique traits. Peter was very much an original. But there was a general sense in which his history seemed to me more and more a paradigm of the mental growth of thousands of young men who come to the University of Chicago Divinity School from the small towns of the Midwest, bringing with them the shabby, disintegrating baggage of their narrow sectarian backgrounds. My long affiliation with the school had kept me in close touch with the minds of these young men and with the problems that most tormented them. In Peter I could see those problems heightened, intensified, dramatized by the impulsive candor of his personality.

Like his namesake in the Gospels, Peter was impetuous in both speech and action. While other students kept a diplomatic silence, he never hesitated to voice his doubts, express his convictions, ask the foolish questions. Where other students accepted compromises, soaked up the comfortable, other-directed attitudes of the university's religious community, Peter plunged recklessly into the very core of things until he found an answer that satisfied him in the deepest recesses of his soul. It was Simon Peter who did not pause, as John did, at the entrance to the open tomb. He ran inside. It was Simon Peter who did not hesitate to step out on the waves or draw his sword in quick defense of his Master. It was Simon Peter who wept bitterly when the crowing of a rooster reminded him of his proud boast and cowardly denial. And when the risen Christ appeared on the shore of the Sea of Tiberias, the wonderful old myths tell us, it was the naked and impatient Peter who put on his fishing coat and cast himself from the boat into the sea.

In a loose, fragmented way, the story of Peter Fromm parallels the history of Protestant theology. His adolescent conversion was, as we shall soon see, to a type of primitive Christianity indistinguishable from the childlike, apostolic faith described in the Book of Acts. As Peter matured, his views inevitably grew more sophisticated. During his second year in the divinity school, he was deep in the study of Augustine and Thomas Aquinas. He plunged with enthusiasm into the dusty writings of Luther and Calvin. Then came the gnawing doubts of the Enlightenment, the Higher Criticism, a fatal flirtation with Karl Barth's abortive attempt to go "beyond modernism" and back to the theology of the Reformers. The analogy must not, of course, be pushed too far. Nevertheless, as Peter boxed his way nimbly down these spiritual corridors, there were few major periods in the evolution of Christianity with which he did not have at some time, in his rough, intuitive way, an insider's understanding.

None of these thoughts occurred to me until after Peter's breakdown. "Of all the forms of genius," Thorton Wilder wrote in one of his early books, "goodness has the longest awkward age." I thought of Peter as a student and a friend who I was helping through an awkward age. It was not until I learned more about his history, before he came to Chicago, that I realized how rocky and twisted had been the road he had traveled.

There is a poem by Stephen Crane that goes:

> The wayfarer,
> Perceiving the pathway to truth,
> Was struck with astonishment.
> It was thickly grown with weeds.
> "Ha," he said,
> "I see that none has passed here
> in a long time."
> Later he saw that each weed
> Was a singular knife.
> "Well," he mumbled at last,
> "Doubtless there are other roads."

Peter was as incapable of taking easier roads as most Protestants are incapable of walking the hard pathway to truth. They do not even *look* for such a path. Outside the "Bible Belt" a churchgoer seldom asks himself what he really believes about any central doctrine of his faith. It is true that in recent years a small number of young Protestant liberals have become active in such causes as civil rights, peace, the wars on poverty and drug addiction, and the currently fashionable "ecumenical dialog." But activism in those areas, admirable though it be, is quite a different thing from activism in theology. The typical American Protestant today is in a state of unprecedented metaphysical indifference. His theology has the shape and substance of a fog-bank.

Question him about his deepest religious convictions and what will you discover? You will find him believing vaguely that Jesus is somehow the son of God, but in precisely what sense he neither knows nor cares. He may tell you, if he has thought about it at all, that the Bible is a unique document. In exactly what way it is unique he isn't sure. If he has read any part of the Bible since he went to Sunday School, the chances are high that he is some variety of fundamentalist: Pentecostal, Seventh-Day Adventist, Jehovah's Witness, or any of a dozen other sects that bemuse the poor and poorly educated. If he is not a fundamentalist, he may still insist that the Incarnation and Resurrection are the foundation dogmas of his faith; but ask him what exactly those dogmas mean, and you find him strangely ill at ease. He stammers gray phrases. He parrots fusty platitudes. Do you really think, he will counter, that those are *important* questions?

For most Protestants today their "religion" is little more than a weekly ritual which they endure for reasons which have nothing to do with God. The ritual is familiar and comfortable. It reminds them of their childhood. And their children in turn must not be sent morally rudderless into the world. After all, a child must write *something* in those blanks on school questionnaires which ask for his religious affiliation. Church membership confers social status. (The church of highest status in a community is, of course, the one with the highest proportion of lawyers, doctors, and wealthy businessmen, plus one or two families of well-educated blacks, preferably light-skinned, to prove that the congregation is racially progressive.) The church is a place to meet friends on Sunday morning, listen to good music, and (hopefully) to hear a sermon that arouses a warm feeling of piety without suggesting—God forbid!—that one alter a single prejudice or behavior pattern. The ancient doctrines—sin, salvation, atonement—float high overhead like distant, misty clouds, utterly irrelevant to daily life.

Nor does the average upper or middle-class Protestant care one rap about what his pastor or any of his Protestant friends believe. He would sooner ask Mrs. Jones, sitting next to him at a church dinner, her opinion about clitoral versus vaginal orgasm than to ask her what she thinks about the Trinity. Theological questions are invasions of privacy. They are upsetting questions, annoying questions, *de trop* questions.

Americans do not even ask such questions of their political leaders. To be sure, our country still considers itself a Christian nation ("In God we trust"), and voters still insist that their political leaders belong to a church. Because Protestants outnumber Catholics and Jews, the church of choice for the president is Protestant, but it is only his attendance at church that matters, not what he believes.

It would be hard to find a Protestant troubled in the slightest by Richard M. Nixon's naval career or his bombing of North Vietnam, even though he knows that Quakers are traditionally and steadfastly pacifist. Nixon plays golf with fundamentalist Billy Graham, has appeared on the platform of Billy's revival meetings, and has even (in November, 1962) written an article on "A Nation's Faith in God" for Graham's magazine, *Decision*. In that article he tells of his high school conversion in Los Angeles by Chicago evangelist Paul Rader, then one of the Windy City's windiest and most ignorant fundamentalists.

On the other hand, when Nixon lived in New York City, he attended the liberal (in the religious sense) Reformed Church of Norman Vincent Peale, and it was Peale who performed the marriage ceremony when Julie Nixon married David Eisenhower. By having himself photographed with both Peale and Graham, Nixon works both sides of the Protestant street and strengthens his image along the entire spectrum of WASPs who elected him. As to which direction he leans in his private convictions, toward Peale or Graham or neither, most WASPs couldn't care less.

With respect to John F. Kennedy, the situation seems at first to have been altogether different. Was it? Arthur Schlesinger, Jr., writes in his biography of Kennedy that the president had an essentially "secular mind." He was, Schlesinger tells us, a Catholic in the same sense that Franklin D. Roosevelt was an Episcopalian. This isn't much help. It only raises the equally puzzling question: In what sense was F. D. R. an Episcopalian? Kennedy was the first American president to be a Roman Catholic, Schlesinger continues, but he was not the first Roman Catholic president. What does *that* mean? The words are discreetly evasive. Was Kennedy a believing Catholic, or was he Catholic in name only, like the machine-controlled mayors of so many big cities with large Catholic populations? Had Kennedy broken early with his Catholic upbringing he would have had no political future in Catholic Massachusetts or, for that matter, anywhere else. A Catholic will vote for a Protestant or Jew, never for an ex-Catholic. But there is another point to consider. Had Kennedy talked much about his Catholic beliefs, assuming he had some, he would probably have lost the presidential election to Nixon. And so, like Episcopalian Roosevelt and Quaker Nixon he kept his inner religious life concealed.

Let us sharpen the question mercilessly. Did John Kennedy, in the private sanctuary of his mind, believe that the mother of Jesus was born without sin, remained a virgin after giving birth to the Son of God, and did not die a natural death but was transported bodily into heaven? It is possible that not even his wife, Jacqueline, knew precisely what John Kennedy believed about his church's major doctrines.°

The point I want to make, however, is not that no one knows what a president of the United States really believes about religion, but that

---

°When I originally wrote this section about Kennedy's religious beliefs there was still a sort of gentleman's agreement among journalists not to ask such questions. The agreement was broken by William F. Buckley, Jr., himself a devout Catholic, in his review of *John F. Kennedy and American Catholicism*, by Lawrence Fuchs. (See the *New York Times Book Review*, May 14, 1967.) Buckley's opinion is that the great religious event which supposedly occurred in 1960, the election of the first Roman Catholic to the White House, actually was a pseudo-event.

In contrast to Kennedy's perpetual evasions, Buckley quotes a delightful rejoinder by Hilaire Belloc. Belloc had been running for a seat in the House of Parliament when a woman asked him if it were true that he was a "Papist."

"Madam," said Belloc, taking a rosary from his pocket, "do you see these beads? I say them every morning when I rise, and every evening when I go to bed; and if you object to that, madam, I pray to God that he will spare me the ignominy of representing you in Parliament."—H. W.

no one is even curious. We are a nation of Laodiceans. The typical Protestant churchgoer—young activists who join freedom marches and peace demonstrations are *not* typical—is neither cold nor hot, believing nor unbelieving. He attends church regularly or irregularly, drones though recitations of the Apostles' Creed, sings the dreary, antique hymns, occasionally eats the Bread and drinks the Wine. Do not ask him what he thinks the ritual is supposed to mean.

In every age, in every society, there has always been a small band of men and women of a different breed. They are blessed, or cursed, with a compulsion to take religion seriously. If they are atheists, they will have no part in religious ritual. If they believe in God, they hunger to know as much as they can about what God would have them believe and do. Such was Peter. He was too honest with himself to suppose that the "good"—what one should do—can ever be separated from the "true." If nothing is true, said Nietzsche, everything is permitted. If something is true, some things are good, some bad. Is it true, is it *really* true, that God, through the agency of an historic faith, is calling on us, His children, to do this and this, to *not* do that and that? And if God has in truth revealed a strategy of living, what sort of Revelation is it? A book, a creed, a living church? How does the child of God extract from the Revelation a way of distinguishing this from that?

The more I thought about Peter, after his fantastic Easter sermon, the more I thought about the knife edges along the weedy road he had traveled, the stronger my desire grew to write a book about him. I began to carry a notebook in which from time to time I jotted down recollections of events and conversations. For more details I went to Peter himself. I spoke to his friends. I called on several girls with whom in one way or another he had once been intimate. Finally I set to work in earnest, shaping the material as orderly as I could into what I suppose is best called a spiritual biography.

Twenty years passed before I convinced myself that this confusing narrative could be published without harm to Peter and to others. Peter himself has read the manuscript. On his insistence I removed several episodes which he considered too uncharitable to the participants, but otherwise I have told the story as fully and faithfully as I can. I cannot add that Peter has approved its publication. The most I can say is that he did not vigorously disapprove.

Had Peter been an imaginary character in a work of fiction I doubt if I could have invented for him a name with more suitable overtones. I have already spoken of his temperamental likeness to Simon Peter. His less familiar surname is a German word for "pious." In Danish it is spelled "from," and it is interesting to learn that one of Sören Kierkegaard's satirical sketches is about a theological student named Ludwig From. Young Ludwig imagines he is seeking the Kingdom of God when actually his ultimate concern, to use Paul Tillich's still popular phrase, is for the comfortable, secure life of a parson. Kierkegaard himself, in his youth, was not wholly free of this conflict. In a later chapter we shall see how a form of it was involved in Peter's emotional crisis.

It is also singularly appropriate that Peter's surname had been used by Kierkegaard because, at the end, the final question Peter asked himself was the same final question that Kierkegaard shouted into the complacent ears of Danish Protestantism. Is it possible to be a Christian in any honest sense without believing heart and mind and soul in the orthodox view of the divinity of Jesus, in what Kierkegaard called the great Incognito of God?

"There has been much that is strange," Kierkegaard wrote, "much that is deplorable, much that is revolting about Christianity; but the most stupid thing ever said about it is, that it is to a certain degree true."

In this, as in many other respects, Peter Fromm's mind and tastes, though not his temperament, resembled those of the Danish thinker. They shared a fondness for the hot-cold cleavage of either/or. They shared an abiding hatred for the tepid mixture of both-and.

Finally, Peter's surname conveys an essential fact about his spiritual Odyssey. He was fleeing "from" the superstitions of his childhood. Is he also on a pilgrimage? It is possible. But it is only with the "from" that this book will be concerned.

2

Pentecostal Power

While Peter was under heavy sedation in the psychiatric ward of Billings Hospital, I wondered if I should get in touch with his mother and step-father. The psychiatrist assigned to Peter thought I shouldn't. It would be best, we both agreed, to wait until more was known about the nature and severity of Peter's illness before one of us tried to explain to his parents (how could anyone then explain?) exactly what had happened.

Peter's deceased father, Matthew Fromm, had been the eldest son of a large German family which came to America and settled in Pennsylvania in the early 1870's. Young Matthew had worked as a roustabout in the Pennsylvania oil fields until the large oil deposits of Oklahoma, discovered in the first decade of the new century, drew him like a magnet to the vicinity of Tulsa. After working several years as a driller in oil fields around the state, he became a foreman—the vernacular term is "tool pusher"—for a large drilling company that had its home office in Tulsa.

Oklahoma's southern boundary is a river, the Red River, a dreary, rusty-silted river that snakes its way through the shallow valley celebrated in the familiar old song. It was in this valley that Peter's mother, part German and part Irish, had spent her childhood. Hilda Yates was sixteen when the drilling of a wildcat well on her father's farm, in Bryan County, south of Durant, brought Matthew Fromm into the Red River Valley. They met at a revival meeting sponsored by a Pentecostal Church of God. The well proved to be dry, and Matthew was shifted to a new location; but, as the old ballad goes, he must have missed Hilda's blue eyes and sweet smile. They were married a year later in 1918. A few months after Peter was born, in 1919, they settled in Sand Springs, a small Oklahoma town on the north bank of the Arkansas River, bordering Tulsa on the west.

I have mentioned before that Matthew Fromm died when Peter was just a boy. There was one other child, a girl named Gabrielle. She was a year old at the time of her father's death. Four years later Peter's mother married Gregory Brown, a widower who owned a plumbing shop in Sand Springs. There were no children by her second marriage. Brown's previous marriage also had been childless.

In the early spring of 1941, when Peter was in his third year at the University of Chicago Divinity School, I had an opportunity to visit his parents. Reverend Alexander Wilkes, one of my former students, invited me to Tulsa to preach at his First Unitarian Church. (The church's name has always amused me. Its founders no doubt expected it to be the first of several Unitarian churches in the rapidly growing "Oil Capitol of the World," as Tulsa then liked to call itself. To this day it is the only Unitarian church in the Greater Tulsa area.) Wilkes offered to reimburse my travel expenses and to put me up for a stay of several days.

"Why don't you visit my folks while you're there?" Peter suggested. "Sand Springs is only a fifteen-minute drive from downtown Tulsa."

He had written so much about me to his mother, he went on to say, that he knew she would enjoy seeing me in the flesh, and he added that she was one of the best cooks in Oklahoma. My immediate inclination was to tell Peter I would not have time to see his parents. I knew that both of them were fundamentalists. They would regard me, a Unitarian, with grave suspicion. On the other hand Peter had told me almost nothing about his family or his childhood. To my surprise I was intensely curious. Did I know then, in the dark substratum of my mind, that some day I would write a book about Peter? Did I sense then in some dim way the mythic quality of his flight?

I do not know. All I can say is that I heard myself telling Peter I would indeed like to meet his family. Please inform them, I said, that I would telephone them Sunday afternoon, after my sermonizing, and arrange to see them the following day.

As my plane glided down toward Tulsa's Will Rogers Airport on a late Saturday afternoon, I could see ahead the small cluster of office buildings sparkling in slanted April sunlight. Twenty years earlier, when I had been offered the pastorate of Tulsa's First Unitarian Church, I turned it down. Had it been a wise decision? How could one tell? Wilkes apparently had been happy there. He was an ambitious fellow, a bit conservative in his political views but with a flair for comedy, showmanship, and publicity. His church had featured jazz concerts and folkscng fests long before it became fashionable to sponsor such events in more traditional churches. It would be relaxing to see him again. His congregation, he had written, was enlightened theologically. I could speak freely on any religious question. As for political and social topics, he sounded a cautionary note. Many of his church members, he warned me, including the publisher of Tulsa's evening newspaper, reflected the city's strong Republican sentiments.

My sermon was well received. If any of the wealthier listeners were offended by my temperate remarks on the evils of unregulated capitalism, they said nothing about it when they shook my hand on their way out.

Wilkes drove me to Sand Springs the following afternoon and deposited me, as Mrs. Brown had requested when I telephoned, in front of the fire station on Main Street. He had no desire to meet the Browns. "See you in the sweet bye and bye," he singsonged through the car's open window as he quickly drove away. Mr. Brown had promised to get me back that night to Wilkes' house where I intended to stay a few more days before returning to Chicago.

A thin, prematurely gray-haired woman—I guessed her to be in her early forties—walked toward me smiling. "I'm Peter's mother," she said.

We shook hands. "How in the world, Mrs. Brown, did you recognize me?"

She gave a quick, embarrassed laugh. "Peter told me you were real tall and had white hair. And he sent me a story from a newspaper once. It had your picture in it."

Mrs. Brown's narrow face and birdlike features wore a pale, faded look, but her blue eyes, behind rimless bifocals, were bright and penetrating. I could see a strong resemblance to Peter around the eyes.

"And is this Gabrielle?" I asked. A pretty girl of fourteen or fifteen had walked over to join us.

"Yes, this is Gabrielle," Mrs. Brown said proudly.

The girl smiled and said shyly that she was pleased to meet me. Her face was free of cosmetics, young and innocent and hard to improve on. She had blue eyes like her mother and soft yellow hair.

We walked along Main Street, past the dismal, dusty-windowed shops. Even in daylight, before the awful red and blue neon tubes begin to glow, is it possible to tell the business street of one small Midwestern town from the business street of another? We turned off the pavement to climb a gently sloping dirt road.

"You don't know how happy I am, Mrs. Brown," I said, "to meet you at last. Peter has told me so many good things about you."

There are millions of Christians like her, I thought, scattered through the nation's vast farming areas: gentle, self-sacrificing, loving of neighbor. She would practice the golden rule with all the light she had. But she would have a low opinion of the Jews (did they not execute and refuse to accept their own Messiah?), and the notion of taking communion next to a black-skinned neighbor—well, it would simply be unthinkable. Has an organized religion ever failed to sanction its culture's mores? For the majority of believers is it not always God's will that social patterns be pretty much the way they are? As I grow older, though, I find myself becoming more charitable toward simple souls who can hardly be expected to rise higher than the prejudices of their habitat. One can and must condemn their beliefs. It is more difficult to condemn their hearts. How can you condemn a set of conditioned reflexes?

The house where the Browns lived was an old, ramshackle two-storied colonial, but its white clapboard siding was freshly painted. Gabrielle excused herself at the porch steps and sauntered off up the road. "Be home by six!" Mrs. Brown called out. The girl turned and bobbed her head.

"I'm so glad you can stay for supper," Mrs. Brown remarked over her shoulder as I followed her up the steps and into the house.

The living room was like a dozen others I had seen before in the homes of Midwestern fundamentalists. An upright piano with well-worn hymnals on the rack, assorted pieces of ancient furniture, a brick fireplace with a large picture of Jesus in a frame above its high mantel. It was a reproduction of Heinrich Hofmann's popular painting: Christ praying in the Garden of Gethsemane. A shaft of supernal light bathed his sad, effeminate profile. Scriptural quotations lettered on large slabs of colored cardboard hung here and there on the walls.

Come unto me all ye that labor and are heavy laden, and I will give you rest.

Cast thy burden upon the Lord, and He will sustain thee.

Underneath are the Everlasting Arms.

God so loved the world, that He gave His only begotten Son.

They looked as if they would shine brightly in the dark.

Mrs. Brown seated herself on a creaky wooden chair and motioned me into a sofa backed against two open windows.

"I know you must be very proud of Peter," I began. "He's working hard this year. I expect him to pass his finals with flying colors."

Mrs. Brown had been sizing me up carefully through the tops of her bifocals. "I pray every night for God to bless my boy," she said, "and protect him from false teachings. I've heard a lot about the University of Chicago, Dr. Wilson. There are so many professors there who are the servants of Satan."

I nodded imperceptibly.

"For the time will come when they will not endure sound doctrine," she went on, tapping a bony finger on the arm of her chair while she recited Saint Paul, "but after their own lusts shall they heap to themselves teachers, having itching ears; and they shall turn away their ears from the truth."

I made no reply. My own left ear began to itch. I scratched it thoughtfully. Through the windows behind me I could smell the oil refineries and hear the sound of heavy trucks rolling on the highway. The sofa's cushions were hard and uncomfortable. A cool breeze caressed the back of my hot neck.

We chatted for a while about inconsequentials. Suddenly, without warning, she leaned forward. "Dr. Wilson," she said, looking me straight between the eyeballs, "have you accepted Christ? I mean, have you accepted him as your personal saviour?"

I must have jumped visibly. It had been thirty years since anyone had asked me that.

"You don't have to worry about me, Mrs. Brown," I said smiling. "I was saved when I was a small boy in Wisconsin. I've been preaching the old, old story ever since."

Solemn-faced, cheeks flushed, she leaned back in her chair, searching my eyes. I had a feeling she did not believe me. But I was not questioned again about my status among the elect.

"I've been so afraid Peter would learn more than what was good for him," Mrs. Brown said finally. "That he'd read too many books. Remember how the Saviour prayed? 'I thank thee, O father, that thou hast hid these things from the wise and prudent, and hast revealed them unto babes.' "

"I remember," I said, nodding piously.

Mrs. Brown seemed to be examining the pink flower pattern on her print dress. "Peter has changed since he went to Chicago," she said, almost in a whisper.

"In what way?"

"I don't know as I can rightly say. He used to go to prayer meetings with us every Wednesday night and give such wonderful testimonies. The last time he was home he wouldn't go at all. He just sat around the house and read books and looked out the windows. He used to laugh and talk all the time. But last summer. . . ." Her voice trailed off. I could see moisture in her eyes.

It was a good moment to change the subject again. While she cleaned her glasses on the hem of her dress, I asked, "What church do you and your husband attend, Mrs. Brown?"

"We go to Holiness Tabernacle. It's just a short piece down the road. The minister's such a fine man."

Peter had told me that his fundamentalist upbringing had been of the Pentecostal kind. "Holiness" is a favorite word of these noisy, ignorant little congregations. They differ from most other fundamentalist sects by their belief that certain "gifts" on the day of Pentecost—healing, prophecy, speaking and interpreting the Unknown Tongue, the power to pick up serpents or to drink poison without harm, and so on—were given for all time to congregations of true believers. Other fundamentalist groups maintain that the Pentecostal gifts were withdrawn by the Lord after they had played their necessary role in strengthening the early church, although in recent years there has been a curious, unexpected revival of faith healing and glossolalia even in the more respectable churches, Catholic as well as Protestant.

Saint Paul had a good deal to say about the gifts. "I thank my God," he wrote, "I speak with tongues more than ye all." I have often reflected that if Paul were to return to earth today, his original beliefs unchanged, it would be the Pentecostal movement with which he would instantly affiliate. There and there only would he find an authentic Pauline theology combined with the emotional enthusiasm that characterized the early "awkward age" of Christianity which he knew so intimately. I must admit, however, that Paul would surely be shocked by the movement's fiery female preachers. ("Let your women keep silent in the churches," Paul wrote, "for it is not permitted unto them to speak.")

"Does your congregation practice the taking up of serpents?" I asked. The injudicious question slipped out before I could stop it.

Mrs. Brown adjusted her glasses to give me a long, cold stare. "We don't believe in tempting God," she answered, tight-lipped. "But we do say that if a Christian has sufficent faith in the Lord, *nothing* can harm him unless it be God's will." It was an admirable answer, and I did not pursue the matter further.

Our talk returned to Peter. I told a few innocent anecdotes about him that seemed to amuse her, and was relieved to see that apparently she had no intention of grilling me about changes in her son's beliefs. Perhaps she had made up her mind that I was to be counted among the false teachers, that it would be profitless to discuss these things with me.

Something she said touched on Peter's conversion, and I asked her if she would mind telling me about it. No, she did not mind. Although Peter had been brought up in the Pentecostal faith, she explained, he had not taken it seriously until he was in his first year at the township high school. A cowboy evangelist—this worthy gentleman preached in spurred boots, black-string tie, and ten-gallon hat—had been conducting a tent meeting a few miles out of town along the highway.

"He had such power then," Mrs. Brown said wistfully. "But a few years ago he took to drink and terrible sins." I did not press her for the details.

It was midsummer at the time, and the revival was well attended. There was a great outpouring, she said, of the Holy Spirit. In my youth in Wisconsin I had been to country meetings like these, and while Mrs. Brown talked about them I could picture the scene vividly in my mind. Hot summer night, suppressed sexual excitement in the air, the smell of woods, sawdust, perspiration. There would be group-singing from grimy hymnals, solos by shapely young farm girls with guitars, breasts, and nasal voices:

> Would you be free from your burden of sin?
> There's pow'r in the blood, pow'r in the blood;
> Would you o'er evil a victory win?
> There's wonderful pow'r in the blood.

The evangelist, red of face, sodden of shirt, would take off his jacket when the Power seized him. He would slam it against the back of a chair, knocking it over with a resounding crash. "Praise the Lord!" "Thank you, Jesus!" The shouts could be heard for miles.

Slowly the preacher's delivery would increase in volume and tempo as his sermon pumped its way toward an orgiastic climax of athletic oratory. Then the altar call and the plaintive invitation hymns:

> Come home . . . come home . . .
> Ye who are weary, come home.
> Earnestly, tenderly, Jesus is calling,
> Calling, O Sinner, come home!

The clapping of a thousand hands, beating out a slow jungle rhythm, has a curiously hypnotic effect on any crowd. Rock-and-roll is old-fashioned music to these Pentecostal congregations. The beat gets faster, cries and moans grow louder. The chanting and clapping and tapping of feet reach a crescendo of uninhibited frenzy. Shouting. Weeping. Everyone praying at once in a great babble of confusion. People rise, heads thrown back, arms upraised, neck tendons swelling. They shake with the Power. They scream with the Power. The sick are healed. The blind see. The deaf hear. The dumb talk. Cripples throw away their crutches. "Thank you, Jesus!"

> *There is pow'r, pow'r,*
> *Wonder-working pow'r*
> *In the blood*
> *Of the Lamb!*
> *There is pow'r, pow'r,*
> *Wonder-working pow'r,*
> *In the precious blood of the Lamb!*

Some poor creature, eyes rolling, armpits wet, stands and jabbers in the tongue of angels. . . .

Peter had gone through it all. He was fourteen when the Holy Spirit called him, an age when pent-up sex drives explode in the most intense conversion experiences. I listened with embarrassment while Mrs. Brown told me how her son had wept miserably for his sins, how he had shouted his response to the altar call, how he had knelt trembling and groaning at the toes of the evangelist's black and silver boots. He had been roped and tied like an Oklahoma steer. Yes, Peter had been through it all.

Do you smile at this, O my gentle Christian reader? Are your refined spiritual sensibilities offended by these twentieth-century American counterparts of the ancient Bacchic rites? Then take in hand your Bible and read—or read again—the fourteenth chapter of First Corinthians or the second chapter of the Book of Acts, and ponder well the revival techniques of Simon Peter, the Rock of Faith upon which Christ built your holy church.

"It was that very night," Mrs. Brown said, her eyes glittering through her glasses, "that Peter gave his life to the Lord. It was then that he decided to become a great preacher. He wanted to win millions of souls for Christ. He wanted to start a big revival up and down the land."

She spoke of the diligence with which her son had studied his Bible. Five times in one year he had read it through, verse by verse, word by word. (I slid a handkerchief across my forehead. Yes, Peter knew his Bible well.) He taught Sunday School at Holiness Tabernacle. He preached at prayer meetings. One summer, between his junior and senior high school years, he hit the sawdust trail. I did a double-take. Peter had never told me *that*. Billed as Oklahoma's boy evangelist, he had howled and pounded on the pulpit at tent and tabernacle meetings throughout Oklahoma, Texas, Missouri, Arkansas, Kansas. . . .

Mrs. Brown handed me a badly centered, out-of-focus snapshot taken during Peter's senior year. He was scowling into the sun. A large shock of dark hair hung over his forehead.

"How old was Peter when his father passed away?" I asked as I returned the picture.

She walked over to a table on which a large leather-covered Bible was resting. "I think he was eight, going on nine." She opened the Bible to slip the snapshot between its pages. "Yes, that must be right. It was in nineteen twenty-eight that my husband was killed. Peter was almost nine."

"Killed?"

"Didn't Peter tell you?"

I shook my head.

"Peter was with him when it happened. It was terrible, terrible." She walked slowly back to her chair, shaking her head, and sat down again.

It had been an accident. The derrick of a drilling rig, a rig on which Mr. Fromm had been working, had collapsed. All the drillers had been killed but one.

"Is that man still living?"

"Oh yes. He's made lots and lots of money since he was a driller. He's president now of some kind of company of his own. They make machinery for drilling oil wells. He lives in a big house in Tulsa."

"Do you know the company's name?"

She couldn't remember.

"What was the man's name?"

"Howard. Howard Richter. He and Matthew were right good friends. But we never see him any more."

She was watching me with a slight frown, puzzled as to why I wanted to know all this. She started to ask me something, but the sound of the front door opening made her stop and turn her head.

Gregory Brown, a large chunky man, moon-faced and bald, came into the living room. He gave me a hearty handshake, apologized for the black grease stains on his hands, asked me how the weather was in Chicago, and chuckled loudly when I told him it had been windy and cold on the day I left.

Mrs. Brown excused herself and was on her way to the kitchen when Gabrielle rushed into the house. The girl gave us a quick, worried nod as she hurried into the kitchen to help her mother. Brown and I talked for twenty minutes or so about nothing of importance, then Mrs. Brown summoned us all to the dining room.

We stood around an oval table, behind our chairs. Mrs. Brown asked me to give the blessing.

Heads lowered. I cleared my throat. I was not caught unprepared.

"Father in Heaven," I began, in my best stained-glass voice, "we thank thee for all the good things thou hast granted us today. We thank thee for this wholesome food. Bless it and consecrate it that it may nourish and strengthen us. We pray that thou wilt watch over Peter. Protect him from the wiles of Satan as he studies to show himself approved unto thee, a workman who needeth not to be ashamed, rightly dividing the word of truth. Bless us all and fill us with thy Spirit. We ask it in the holy name of our Lord and Saviour, who shed his precious blood that we might be cleansed from all sin. Amen."

There was a chorus of muted "Amens" around the table. As we sat down I noticed that Mrs. Brown was gazing at me intently. My appetite was ravenous. Peter was right about his mother's cooking. It was the best meal I had had in years.

3

The Invisible Hand

When I visited Peter's family I did not question his mother in any detail about her son's childhood. I did not even keep an accurate record of the few things she did tell me. Why, then, was I so interested in her disclosure that Peter had witnessed his father's death? I can answer this best by first giving a brief account of my own history and religious point of view.

Although I am a Unitarian minister, working in a tradition that had its origins in Protestantism and Catholic heresy, I do not consider myself a Christian except in the widest, most humanistic sense. I do not, for example, believe in God.

Ten years ago this admission surely would have surprised more readers than it does today. Now that the Trojan horse of humanism has opened within the walls of Protestant seminaries, and the death-of-God theologians have climbed out, a Unitarian's profession of atheism is unlikely to raise a single eyebrow. Nietzsche's famous proclamation that "God is dead" is an old cry to our movement. We have been wittily described as a church whose members believe there is *at most* one God. It is not an unfair description. No Unitarian accepts the Trinity, but there are some Unitarians, albeit a minority, who do believe in God. In opposition to the theists in our ranks, or rather in cooperation with them (it is the essence of our creedless faith that we do our best to be tolerant of one another's views), are the atheists and agnostics. We prefer to call ourselves by the more positive term of humanist. It is the point of view elaborated so beautifully by George Santayana in his *Reason in Religion*, so succinctly by John Dewey in *A Common Faith*. It is the theme of Charles Swinburne's *Hymn of Man*. The poem is close to doggerel, but when I was young its final stanza strangely stirred my blood:

> By thy name that in hell-fire was written,
>   and burned at the point of thy sword,
> Thou art smitten, thou God, thou art smitten,
>   thy death is upon thee, O Lord.
> And the love-song of earth as thou diest,
>   resounds through the wind of her wings—
> Glory to Man in the highest!
> For man is the Master of things.

During my childhood in Appleton, Wisconsin, I believed in Jehovah for the simple reason that my parents had taught me to believe. My mother and father were both of Scotch descent, their ancestors having settled in the rural areas surrounding Green Bay in northeast Wisconsin. My father owned a prosperous dairy and livestock farm not far from Appleton where he and my mother faithfully attended a Presbyterian church of rigidly orthodox persuasion. The doctrine of hell, when it was first explained to me by my father, later by a Sunday School teacher, terrified me by day and in the night troubled my dreams. Fortunately, and to my father's everlasting anger, I was able to break away at an early age from such monstrous pieties. After two years at the University of Wisconsin, in Madison, I decided to become a Unitarian minister. With the aid of a scholarship, I enrolled at Meadville Seminary, a Unitarian theological school now affiliated with the University of Chicago.

After completing my ministerial training, I returned to Madison where for many years I was pastor of a small Unitarian church near the university. It was during this period that I wrote my first two books (*The Vitality of the Christian Process* and *The Dynamics of Religion in a Changing World*) and acquired a wife.

Edna Phillips was 22, four years my junior, when we first met in 1911. She was of medium height, though more than a foot shorter than I, with enormous brown eyes and almost jet black hair. Her high cheek bones and dark coloring were inherited from an Indian great-great-great grandmother (of the Sioux tribe) on her mother's side. She had come to the University of Wisconsin from Waukesha to major in anthropology. At the time we met she was working for her master's degree. We became acquainted at a picnic sponsored by my church—to this day neither of us can recall who invited her—and quickly discovered that we shared similar theological opinions (or rather a similar lack of them) and a freedom from sexual hangups that seems mild by today's college standards. She had little interest in philosophy, religion, or politics, but the patterns of primitive cultures, especially in music and art, endlessly fascinated her. We were married in my church, by a member who was a local judge, in the fall of 1912.

I was an ardent pacifist during the first World War. For that I paid the modest price of six months in prison. After the war I was invited to Chicago to become assistant pastor of the Midway Community Church, even then one of the city's largest Unitarian congregations. I was 39 when I became its pastor in 1924. Two years later I took on the additional duties of part-time teaching at the University of Chicago Divinity School.

One reason Peter and I got along so well, even when we disagreed, was that both of us were repelled by the shapeless compromises of modern Protestant theology. I shared his passion for the either/or, the stark line that separates, that makes for clear outlines. Nothing seems to me more deserving of contempt than the half-gods spawned by recent theologians: the "personality producing forces," and the "creative cosmic urges," and the "ultimate ground of being" of those verbal contortionists who dabble one toe timidly in the waters of theism while they keep their other foot firmly planted on the pragmatic rock of John Dewey. I do not like to talk of God when all I mean is a cosmic Uncle Sam. To turn upside down a famous remark by Karl Barth, I do not like to talk of humanity by talking about God in a small voice.

I make these confessions now because they help one to understand my interest in the psychoanalytic approach to religious faith, to understand my lifelong preoccupation with those unconscious, deeply buried needs which are, I am persuaded, the underpinnings of theism. More than twenty years before I knew Peter I wrote a book called *The Psychological Frontiers of Religious Belief*. In a recent revision it is still used today as a textbook in several of the nation's leading seminaries. On the title page of this book I quote the following passage from William James's *Varieties of Religious Experience* (Lecture III):

> *In the metaphysical and religious sphere, articulate reasons are cogent for us only when our inarticulate feelings of reality have already been impressed in favor of the same conclusion. . . . Our impulsive belief is here always what sets up the original body of truth, and our articulately verbalized philosophy is but its showy translation into formulas.*

James Stephens, in his incomparable fantasy *The Crock of Gold*, says the same thing more simply: "The head does not hear anything until the heart has listened. . . . what the heart knows today the head will understand tomorrow."

Unfortunately, my book was written when my knowledge of the analytic movement was severely limited. In later years I became increasingly convinced that Sigmund Freud was stating a simple, empirically demonstrable fact when he described religion (in the supernatural sense) as the "universal obsessional neurosis" of mankind. Every man and woman longs for the comfort and security of childhood. As a substitute for this unobtainable satisfaction, adult mankind has acquired what the German theologian Friedrich Schleiermacher called a sense of "creaturehood." Unconscious memories of the real father, who was both loved and feared, are projected on the skies, out of space and out of time, as an image of infinite goodness and power. Our Father who art in Heaven. . . . In the childhood of the human race such projective systems may have been socially useful. Today they are a burden. They divert our energies from the great cooperative task of building a Kingdom of Righteousness on earth.

At the time of my visit to Tulsa I had been doing an enormous amount of reading and hard thinking along such lines. The conviction had grown upon me that obsessive theism is always an expression of a more-than-normal hunger for a father image. (Interested readers will find this argued at length in my paper on "The Neurotic Foundations of Theism" in *The Journal of Depth Psychology*, Volume 5, Number 3, Autumn, 1943.) Peter had studied carefully the traditional "proofs" of God and found them all, without exception, shot through with logical *non sequiturs*. He had no interest in the shabby pseudo-evidence of Spiritualism, those puerile messages which mediums are forever transmitting from loved ones behind the veil. He no longer believed that God had revealed himself in a special book or person or church. Yet that curious, Quixotic tour-de-force that we call "faith in God" persisted. Why? Had there been in Peter's childhood an event so traumatic that it stamped indelibly upon his unconscious an abnormal craving for a father substitute?

It seemed to me that seeing his father killed was just such an event. The fact that Peter had never spoken to me about it made it even more significant. I was intensely anxious to hear the details of the tragedy, to learn how Peter had reacted to them.

Only one Howard Richter was listed in the Tulsa telephone directory. I called his office Tuesday morning and soon had him on the line. He was surprised by my reason for wanting to see him, though his tone was cordial. He asked about Peter's mother and expressed regret that it had been so long since he had last visited her. I accepted his invitation to lunch on Wednesday.

Richter owned a factory west of Tulsa that manufactured parts for drilling equipment, but his office was in downtown Tulsa on the twelfth floor of the Philtower Building. When I walked into his office, he bounded out of his chair and came over to pump my hand. He seemed about my age, not quite as tall as I, but considerably broader. His tanned, leathery face was creased with a network of canals.

"So, you're a Unitarian minister, eh?" he said, grinning. "Well, well, well! Have a cigar?" He pulled one suddenly from his shirt pocket.

"Thanks," I said.

He took out another cigar, broke away the cellophane, bit off the end and spat it toward an enormous brass spittoon near the windows. It missed. "You a Communist?" he asked. He pronounced it "Commonest."

When I assured him I was not, he slapped me on the back and roared with laughter.

During our lunch, at a private businessmen's club, we chatted mostly about President Roosevelt and the prospects of America's entry into the European war. His distrust of Roosevelt (he assured me in confidential tones that the man was hopelessly insane) and his strong isolationist sentiments were unbelievably naive, but it was amusing to hear him talk and I made no attempt to argue.

"Will Japan attack us?" He answered his own question with a vigorous shake of his head. "Ain't got the guts. All they got the guts for is hara-kiri."

I smiled faintly at his feeble joke while he used the prong of a fork to mark on the tablecloth a rough, indented outline of the United States. Around it he drew an oval. "If the Krauts cross that line, we let 'em have it. Wham! If the Japs cross it—Bam! If they stay on their side, why the hell should we fight 'em?"

After we finished eating, he produced two more cigars. I shoved back my chair to get into a more comfortable position and, after lighting up, hung my thumbs in the lower pockets of my black-and-gold-checked vest. (Outlandish vests are one of my few extravagances.)

"Tell me about the accident," I said.

"Ah yes," he replied, mumbling the words around his cigar. "What you looked me up about. Almost forgot."

I have no inclination to retell here, in Richter's clipped explosive sentences, everything he said. He had an irritating habit of rambling off into unrelated topics, and I would have to yank him back again. Eventually I managed to piece together a fairly clear account of what had happened.

The oil well where the tragedy occurred was in Eastern Oklahoma near a little town call Sallisaw. The well was being drilled with old-fashioned cable tools.

"You know the kind," Richter explained. "The kind that go up and down like a Yo-yo." He doubled his hand into a massive fist and moved it up and down several times. "Pounds through the rock. Other kind rotates. Drills through." He moved a stubby forefinger in small circles above his coffee cup.

Matthew Fromm had been the tool-pusher of the drilling crew. Richter was one of the drillers. "Fine fellow, Matt," he said. "Best goddam tool-pusher I ever worked for. Really knew his business. Knew all there was to know about how to drill an oil well."

The cable stuck one afternoon when they were coming out of the hole. The producer of the well, a prosperous oilman from Oklahoma City, happened to be on the floor of the rig at the time. The hole had almost reached "pay sand," where oil was anticipated, and he had made a special trip to Sallisaw to watch the men "bring in the well." Fromm was operating the engine. The cable refused to shake loose and the producer became more and more irritated by the delay. He asked Fromm to increase the power.

"No safety gauges back in them days," Richter said between heavy puffs. "No way to tell how much your engine was pullin' except by the sound of the motor. Matt stepped her up so far, then stopped. The producer yells, 'Whatcha scared about, Matt? Think you're gonna pull down the derrick?' Matt shouts back, 'If we pull any harder, we sure as hell will!'"

"Where was Peter?"

"He was standin' there on the floor of the rig. Just a little fellow about so high." Richter put out his hand, palm down.

Matthew Fromm pointed to a raised spot of turf about a hundred yards away and told Peter to go over to it. The boy didn't want to go. His father insisted.

As soon as Peter was off the wooden floor, Matt and the producer began to argue again. Fromm finally threw down an oily rag he had been holding and refused to step up the engine any further. The producer threatened to have him fired. Matt shook his head, said nothing.

As I got the picture, the engine could be controlled in two ways: by a lever on the drilling floor near the cable or by a small wheel called the telegraph wheel at the opposite end of the engine, just outside the rig. The producer strode over to this wheel. He began to turn it slowly.

"When that old steel derrick began to strain and creak," Richter said, "Matt yells to the crew to get the hell off the floor. He starts to run.

I start to run. I don't see it happen, but I hear an explosion. Like a big clap of thunder."

When Richter looked back, the ground was a mass of crumpled, spidery steel. A cloud of dust was rising. . . .

"It was like an invisible hand had reached down from the sky," he said, "and smashed that derrick flat."

Richter illustrated his metaphor by smacking the palm of his left hand on the table with such violence that a dozen heads in the room spun around. One leg of the derrick, he explained, had been weaker then the others. Instead of crumpling directly on top of the floor, the derrick had pulled slightly to one side. The Oklahoma City oilman, who had been standing by the engine, was untouched. Richter was the only member of the crew lucky enough to run in the right direction. The other three had followed Fromm. The steel girders crashed directly on them.

Richter and the producer had been too concerned with the men to pay attention to Peter. The terrified youngster watched them drag the mangled bodies from under the twisted metal. Peter flung himself screaming on his father's body. Richter had difficulty pulling him away. A small piece of jagged steel had struck the boy above his left eye. Blood was pouring down his cheek. Richter bound Peter's forehead tightly with a towel. Later, a doctor in Sallisaw stitched up the wound.

While Richter rambled on, it seemed impossible to me that anyone could see in an accident like this anything but the utter indifference of the universe, of that great ground of being, to any man's destiny. (If Someone's eye is on the sparrow, what difference does it make?) Santayana once wrote that if the command "Thou shalt not kill" were a divine command, nature would long ago have been arrested. When Franz Kafka was a clerk in the Workers' Accident Insurance Office, at Prague, he handled the records of hundreds of deaths as absurd as that of Peter's father. They seemed to him like slapstick comedies. If Kafka did believe in God (which I have always doubted), he certainly must have been persuaded that God's behavior toward humanity displays all the traits of a bumbling, absent-minded sadist.

Peter had loved his father. I am convinced that seeing his father killed added immeasurably to his need in later life for a faith in God. Only a trust in a higher, incomprehensible Benevolence could ease his memory of such meaningless cruelty.

(In fairness to the theists I must add that my own relationship with my father had been the opposite of Peter's. It was closer to that of Kafka or even Freud. I hated my father. When I was a child he would punish me, with ill-concealed pleasure, for the most trivial offenses. He was a narrow-minded, self-righteous, Presbyterian bigot. His tyrannical abuse of my mother led finally to their divorce. She never recovered from the disaster of the marriage. The Freudian sword is a versatile weapon. Its double edge, as Freud himself recognized, often cuts equally well in opposite directions.)

Before we left the dining room, Richter told me an anecdote about an argument that had taken place the morning after the disaster on a farm about four miles from the well. A young boy who liked to hang around the rig had told it to him a few days later.

The boy and his grandfather had risen early to do their morning chores. News of the derrick's collapse had not yet reached them. The lad looked off toward the rig and was amazed to observe that the top of the derrick, usually visible above the trees, was nowhere to be seen. He called this to his grandfather's attention.

The old man squinted off over the wheat and corn. "Joey," he said, "you must be needin' a pair of spectacles. Why I can see the thing as plain as all get-out."

They had argued about it with some heat, and the grandfather had finally stomped off in disgust. He did not want to admit his failing eyesight. He could no more conceive of the derrick *not* being there than my father or Matthew Fromm could have conceived of the collapse of Christianity.

A strong belief can play strange tricks on one's perception. Perhaps that old Oklahoma farmer actually fancied he could still see the tall steel frame silhouetted against the bright blue of the morning sky.

4

The Guiding Fiction

When Peter finished high school in 1936, there were hundreds of well established fundamentalist colleges and Bible institutes around the country that he could have attended. They ranged from narrow, sectarian schools to such nonsectarian institutions as Wheaton College, in Illinois, soon to be the *Alma Mater* of Billy Graham. Why did Peter not go to one of them? How did it come about that two years later Peter, still firmly persuaded that God had rescued Jonah from the belly of a whale, turned up at the University of Chicago Divinity School where the professors did not even believe that God had rescued Jesus from the tomb?

To understand Peter's decision to come to Chicago one must first know the incredible, almost paranoid, goal that had taken shape in his adolescent mind. In Alfred Adler's useful terminology, one must know the "guiding fiction" of Peter's "life plan."

"I must have been a colossal egotist in those days," Peter once remarked, sitting in my living room and shaking his head incredulously as he thought about it. "But you see, Homer, I really was a little smarter than most of my friends in high school. I certainly knew more than they did about the Bible. I was sure my beliefs were right and that anybody who disagreed with me was wrong. I couldn't see how anyone who claimed to be a Christian could possibly think otherwise. It seemed to me it would be an easy thing to go to a great modern seminary and expose the errors Satan had put into the heads of so-called Christian professors. So," he smiled and spread his hands, "here I am!"

The goal, the guiding fiction that young Peter had set for himself as he sat dreaming in the classrooms of his senior year in high school, was nothing less than the starting of a new Protestant Reformation. The churches, he was certain, had moved too far away from God's truth. They had betrayed their divine heritage. It was the hour of decision for America, the historic moment for a great revival to sweep the nation. In his adolescent fantasies he saw himself as chosen by the Lord to lead this new awakening. And to carry out this stupendous undertaking he conceived a brazen plan. (Did not the Lord once tell his disciples that although they should be as gentle as doves they must also be as wise as serpents?) He would enter the very citadel of the enemy. He would master all the science and modern learning that a great secular university has to offer. Every false and infernal argument would be examined and exposed. He would probe the diseased heart of twentieth-century theology, dissect it nerve by nerve, artery by artery. He would lay bare its corruption. It would be necessary, of course, to become an effective public speaker. His oratory would reverberate around the globe. He would use the radio to reach audiences vaster than any previous evangelist would have thought possible. He would write persuasive books. He would establish Bible schools.

It is possible that I am describing all this in more grandiose terms than Peter would have used at the time, but that was essentially how he saw himself in the years ahead. He kept this "life plan" strictly to himself. His pastor at Holiness Tabernacle, even his mother and stepfather, knew nothing about those wild, megalomaniacal dreams.

The first step in Peter's secret strategy was to select the most liberal of liberal seminaries. He wrote here and there for catalogs and spent hours poring over their statements of policy and descriptions of courses. "Words like eschatology and ecclesiology and soteriology and hermeneutics really threw me for a loss at first," he recalled. "But I looked them up at the library, in dictionaries and religious encyclopedias."

Eventually he eliminated all schools but two: Union Theological Seminary, in New York City, and the University of Chicago Divinity School. He settled on Chicago. Based on vague stories he had heard from Pentecostal ministers, and from a careful reading of the catalogs of the two schools, he concluded—with astonishing insight for one so ill-informed—that Chicago had gone a step or two beyond the New York seminary in its departure from the Pentecostal faith.

Before Peter was eligible to enter the Chicago Divinity School it was necessary for him to complete two years of college. Tuition rates at the University of Chicago, where he would have liked to go, were far beyond the reach of his parents' meager savings, and Peter's mediocre high school grades prompted a quick rejection of his application for a scholarship. Even Wheaton College was too expensive. Besides, it did not fit into his strategy of invading enemy ranks as quickly as possible. The state college at Norman, near Oklahoma City, with its low tuition for state residents, seemed the best choice. He enrolled there as a freshman in the fall of 1936.

I know little about Peter's two years at the University of Oklahoma. From his scattered remarks I have concluded that the only significant change in his beliefs during this period was a scuttling of the Pentecostal point of view for a slightly less eccentric type of fundamentalism. No living person or group of people seems to have been responsible. The change came gradually as the result of his own reading and thinking. For a high school graduation gift his parents had given him a *Scofield Reference Bible*, the notes of which he studied with intense interest, and somehow he had accumulated a large supply of books, pamphlets, and tracts from the Moody Bible Institute in Chicago. It was this literature, he once told me, which convinced him that the gifts of Pentecost had been withdrawn from the church after serving their initial purpose. He did not tell his parents about this subtle shift in his beliefs.

The stocky, bearded figure of Dwight L. Moody dominated Peter's thinking at this time. No other native evangelist, Peter believed, had lived a life so completely dedicated to the task of winning souls. In a paperback collection of Moody's sermons, *Calvary's Cross*, published by the Moody Bible Institute, he found Moody's famous sermon on "The Blood." Peter considered it the greatest sermon he had ever read.

"Some time ago a very solemn thought came stealing over me," Moody had said, in that easy, conversational way he had of addressing large audiences, "and made a deep impression on my mind. The only thing that Christ left of His body on the earth was His blood. His flesh and bones He took away, but when He went up on high, He left His blood down here. What are you going to do with the blood? . . . If you read your Bible carefully, you will see the scarlet thread running right through every page. The blood commences to flow in Genesis, and runs on to Revelation. That is what God's Book is written for. Take out the scarlet thread, and it would not be worth carrying home."

Moody preached a simple either/or that would have delighted Kierkegaard. Christ was either what he said he was, God's Incognito, or he was an impostor. Take out the scarlet thread, the doctrine of the blood atonement, and the Bible is not worth carrying home. Those were precisely the sentiments that Peter longed to hear and preach. He told me he had been so emotionally shaken by Moody's sermon that he had thrown himself on the narrow bed of his dormitory room, weeping and praying for the ability to speak some day with Moody's simple eloquence.

It is easy to understand how Moody's rough-hewn honesty, his impatience with pious humbug, would have appealed strongly to Peter's uncompromising spirit. Long after he had abandoned fundamentalism, he liked to tell the story of how Moody, during one of his revival services, had interrupted a prayer of interminable length by standing up and saying, "While our good brother is praying, let us all join in singing hymn number. . . ." It was characteristic of Moody to let nothing, not even common courtesy, interfere with the efficiency of his public meetings.

At the time of Peter's interest in Moody he also became acquainted, perhaps through references in Moody Institute literature, with the geological theories of George McCready Price. A Seventh-Day Adventist and amateur geologist, Price was the last of a long line of American anti-evolutionists who were not totally ignorant of modern science. His monumental work, *The New Geology*, is a remarkably ingenious defense of the medieval view that the earth was created six thousand years ago, in six literal days, and that fossils are simply the buried forms of plant and animal life which flourished before the great Deluge. To Peter's scientifically illiterate mind, Price's worthless arguments seemed overwhelmingly convincing. He even took an introductory course in geology during his freshman year at the University of Oklahoma. For the first few weeks he so annoyed his professor by bringing up Price's clever objections that one day the professor took him aside after class and begged him to keep his mouth shut.

"It's a funny thing," Peter told me, "but the man who taught that course didn't know quite what to say about *any* of Price's arguments. One day in class I asked him how a worker bee could have evolved. Worker bees are sterile, you know. They don't leave descendants. So if there's a genetic change in a worker bee it never gets passed on. He really didn't have a good explanation. It was embarrassing for him. I gave him my copy of *The New Geology* to read. He handed it back to me the next day and all he said was, 'The man's as nutty as a fruitcake.'"

When Peter finished the course he was more certain than ever that Price had given the theory of evolution its *coup de grace*.

Peter was active on both the debating team and the boxing team. In the ring, I would suppose, he fought calmly, courteously, without a trace of anger. But outside the ring his temper was hard to control, and there was one occasion on which it almost got him into serious trouble. An open-air meeting had been arranged on the Oklahoma campus by the local chapter of a student Communist-front group calling itself the American League for Peace and Democracy. It had formerly gone by the name of the American League against War and Fascism; but Hitler had just signed a ten-year non-aggression treaty with Stalin, and Communist parties throughout the world had instantly lost all enthusiasm for strong action against the growing Nazi menace. The principal speaker at the meeting, a tall, gangly youth from Brooklyn, shouted the familiar platitudes about Capitalist imperialism and the horrors of a new world holocaust. He read a statement called the "Oxford Oath." It was a solemn pledge of refusal to support the United States if it embarked on another war. Everyone was asked to raise his right hand and repeat the words.

At that moment Peter, standing near the front of the platform, called out "Traitor!" An angry exchange between Peter and the speaker took place; then Peter climbed up on the platform and punched the speaker on the nose. A small riot followed. There were a few nosebleeds and blackened eyes, but no one was seriously hurt. OKLAHOMA STUDENTS TROUNCE REDS was the *Chicago Tribune* headline the following morning.

Peter was called before the dean. He had expected to be expelled. To his surprise the dean shook his hand, congratulated him warmly on his patriotism, and hinted that the university would welcome a repetition of the incident if similar meetings took place again.

Peter's social life at the university was, he later told me, nonexistent. He formed no permanent friendships. He did not smoke, drink or dance. He had no dates with campus girls. In jacket pockets he carried at all times a midget New Testament and a supply of Moody Bible Institute tracts entitled "Are You Certain Your Soul is Saved for Eternity?" He would leave these terrifying leaflets on seats in classrooms, surreptitiously thumbtack them to hallway bulletin boards, occasionally hand one to a classmate. There were embarrassing episodes involving students whom he tried without success to "win for Christ."

On Sundays he attended a small Baptist church in Norman where he taught Sunday School and occasionally preached. My impression is that Peter, the spell of conversion still strong upon him, was very much a loner. He lived almost wholly within the guiding fiction of his dreams. I can picture him moving about the campus, keeping to himself, wary of the temptations of tight-fitting sweaters and bouncing behinds, reading his *Scofield Bible*, praying, thinking, planning the great evangelical work he was sure God had called upon him to undertake. He lived like a foreign agent. His role of student was a kind of cover for a top-secret mission within the borders of an alien land.

At the end of his sophomore year Peter applied for a tuition scholarship to the University of Chicago Divinity School. He had been working at part-time restaurant jobs around the Oklahoma campus, trying to save money. There was a good chance, he knew, of not getting the scholarship, and he was prepared to drop out of school altogether until he could earn enough to pay for his first year at Chicago.

To his delight and astonishment the scholarship came through. God was indeed guiding him! His college grades had been excellent. Even his geology professor had given him a B. The dean and the other faculty members he had listed as references on his application had apparently been favorably impressed by his clerical prospects.

Peter spent the summer with his family in Sand Springs. In the fall of 1938 he hitchhiked to Chicago along Route 66, young and zealous in faith, ready to do battle with Goliath.

•

5

Gray Towers

The University of Chicago is a miniature city of gray Gothic towers that
flank the sides of a broad and busy thoroughfare called the Midway. In
1893 the street was the Midway Plaisance of the World's Columbian Ex-
position, the most impressive, most successful of all world's fairs. It was
on this strip of land that the gigantic Ferris wheel and the belly of Little
Egypt rotated. The great carnival on the Midway is still going on:

*Come right in and see next year's model of the universe! Press a button
and watch a nuclear chain reaction occur before your very eyes! Step this
way and see how quickly—three balls for a dollar—you can knock over
last year's economic theory! Hear Professor Footnote explicate the fourth
thunderword in* Finnegans Wake! *Listen to the Reverend Wilson prove
that Christianity and Buddhism are very much alike, especially Buddhism!*

The university's massive, pseudomedieval fortresses grew slowly, wall
by wall, arch by arch, gargoyle by gargoyle, on a tract of prairie mud
provided by Marshall Field in 1890, and with funds from the coffers of
John D. Rockefeller. The money carried a Protestant proviso: the Baptist Union Theological Seminary, a small sectarian institution in the area,
must (said Baptist Rockefeller) become the new university's divinity
school. "Praise John from whom oil blessings flow," sang the seminarians
on Sunday morning, according to a joke that must be as old as the university.

William Rainey Harper, who had once taught Hebrew at the little
Baptist seminary, was persuaded by Rockefeller to leave a teaching post
at Yale to become the new university's first president. Like so many
Protestant administrators of the higher learning, then and now, he was an

amusing mixture of vague Christian commitment and shrewd business acumen. On one occasion, a story about him runs, a visiting banker was asked by Harper if he wished to attend a faculty prayer meeting. The purpose of the meeting, Harper explained, was to ask the Lord for funds with which to establish a Law School building.

"You mean to tell me," said the astonished banker, "that you actually expect the good Lord to listen to your prayers and provide those funds?"

"Oh, yes," replied Harper, smiling and patting a bulge in his jacket. "I have the signed checks here now."

Most of the scholars who were drawn by high salaries to the new divinity school were men of liberal or, as it was then called,"modernist" persuasion. They quickly became known as the "Chicago school" of theology. Shailer Mathews, dean of the divinity school from 1908 to 1933, probably did more than any one man in America to free Protestant thinking from the shackles of old-fashioned orthodoxy. He was the country's foremost fugleman for the "social gospel," a point of view that stressed the need to understand the great Christian doctrines in terms of the social milieu in which they arose, and the necessity of expressing them in terms of the social milieu of today. Environment, interaction, change, process—those were the great shibboleths of the Chicago school. You can see the emphasis in the titles of Mathews' books: *Jesus on Social Institutions, The Growth of the Idea of God, Christianity and the Social Process, The Church and the Changing Order, The Atonement and the Social Process.*

In 1938, when Peter entered the University of Chicago Divinity School (where I had taught for twelve years), three other schools of theology were flourishing in the shadows of Gray City: The Chicago Theological Seminary (Congregationalist), Meadville Theological School (Unitarian), and The Disciples Divinity House (nonsectarian). This was several years before the four schools federated to form a common faculty and curriculum. They were, however, already affiliated in a loose way, and students from all four schools commingled in classrooms and at social functions. At the time Peter arrived, not a single faculty member of any of the four seminaries believed in such doctrines as the Virgin Birth or eternal punishment for the wicked. There were, of course, deep divisions of opinion on all sorts of broader doctrines. The majority of the faculty, I suspect, believed in some type of God, but many of them had redefined the term in so private a way that it had little in common with the God of Moses and Jesus.

Consider, for instance, the "theology" of Henry Nelson Weiman, then on the divinity school's staff. "God," Weiman announced, "is that kind of interaction between things which generates and magnifies personality and all its higher values." Note the "which" instead of "who." The definition automatically converts everybody to theism. Who can be an atheist if *that* is all one means by "God"? Weiman liked to call himself a "naturalistic theist." He had a neat little syllogism for proving that God is not a "person":

> All "persons" are members of a society.
> God is not a member of a society.
> Therefore, God is not a "person."

Alas, no one can pray to a principle of interaction. "Pitiable rearguard actions" was Freud's admirable phrase for these smudgy semantic stratagems of theologians in full retreat before the steady advance of modern science. "One would like to count oneself among the believers," declared Freud, in an often-quoted passage from *Civilization and its Discontents*, "so as to admonish the philosophers who try to preserve the God of religion by substituting for him an impersonal, shadowy, abstract principle, and say, 'Thou shalt not take the name of the Lord thy God in vain.'"

But there were honest giants in those days on the faculties of the four seminaries of Gray City. I think in particular of Edward Scribner Ames, head of the Disciples Divinity House, and Albert Eustace Haydon, dean of the University of Chicago's department of comparative religion. To be sure, both men conceded the poetic value of the term "God" when it was spoken by a minister to his congregation, but to avoid confusion they themselves preferred not to use the word.

"When man at last assumes responsibility for the creation of the values he desires," Haydon beautifully wrote in his *Biography of the Gods*, "and finds the plastic stuff of reality yielding readily to his molding intelligence and will, some day he will look up from his work, surprised to find that God has taken the opportunity to disappear."

It was into this atmosphere, the atmosphere of a bedroom in which God was slowly dying, that Peter strode like an angry sheriff of the old West, gun on hip, looking for the varmints who had shot his Father.

No one, of course, had shot Him. The American people were simply busy with other things, and God was taking the opportunity to disappear. Peter couldn't see it that way. It was the Devil's work, and he wasted no time in rounding up a little band of loyal deputies. By putting up notices on fifty bulletin boards around the campus, he actually flushed out of hiding, in obscure recesses of Gray City, about twenty other fundamentalists, most of them studying in the physical sciences or in the business school. They formed an organization called the Chicago Christian Fellowship. I would not be surprised to learn that it was the first group of its kind on the Chicago campus since the days of William Rainey Harper. Members gathered once a week, on the second floor of Ida Noyes Hall, for prayer and Bible study.

I find in my files some yellowed clippings from the *Daily Maroon*, the student newspaper, indicating that on one occasion the Fellowship sponsored a public lecture that drew several hundred listeners. The speaker was J. Gresham Machen, former professor of New Testament at Princeton University and then the leader of a fundamentalist splinter group within the Presbyterian denomination. Machen deserves to be remembered as the last of the scholarly fundamentalists. Peter had just discovered two of his books: *The Virgin Birth* and *Christianity and Liberalism*. The second book had impressed no less a pundit than Walter Lippmann. Not that Lippmann was a Christian—he always considered himself a humanist—but Lippmann believed, and I agree, that Machen was on firm ground when he accused his liberal colleagues of having abandoned the heart of the Christian gospel. In his widely read *Preface to Morals*, Lippmann spoke of *Christianity and Liberalism* as a book in which Machen won a complete victory over his opponents.

"It is an admirable book," wrote Lippmann. "For its acumen, for its saliency, and for its wit this cool and stringent defense of orthodox Protestantism is, I think, the best popular argument produced by either side of the current controversy. We shall do well to listen to Dr. Machen."

But of course no Protestant leader paid the slightest attention to Dr. Machen. I myself was not sufficiently curious even to attend his lecture. According to the *Maroon*, Dr. Ames had arisen to ask the speaker if he thought that Plato and Aristotle had been under the curse of Original Sin, and Dr. Machen replied that indeed he did.

On Sunday mornings Peter steadfastly refused to enter either the University of Chicago chapel, where Charles W. Gilkey had been dean since 1928, or my own nearby Midway Community Church. He regarded the services of both churches as insipid and uninspired. Instead, he crossed the Midway and walked to Sixty-third Street where he took the "El" to Chicago's near north side to attend services at Moody Memorial Church. Now and then a group of Chicago Christian Fellowship members would make the long trek with him. It gave them a chance to worship with others of their persuasion, to bellow the old hymns they knew so well, to hear a rousing evangelical sermon.

"You must have felt lonely and isolated during your first year here," I once remarked to Peter.

He considered a moment, then shook his head. "No, that's not quite how it was, Homer. Of course I didn't have much in common with the students in the divinity school, but I did have some good friends in the C.C.F. I think we were drawn together by the feeling that we were in a hostile environment. When we met at Ida Noyes we thought of ourselves as like the disciples who met in an upper room or the little bands of Christians who gathered in the Catacombs." He grinned. "I know it's hard to believe now. But that's the way it was."

In the 1939 *Cap and Gown*, the university's student year book, there is a picture of the fourteen members of the C.C.F. Several Orientals are in the group, one of them a beautiful Eurasian girl who was, Peter once told me, studying for a degree in anthropology. (How long did *her* fundamentalist faith hold up, I wonder?) Peter is standing in the front row, legs slightly apart, hands behind his back. His trousers are unpressed and baggy at the knees, his tie askew. The slight twist of his nose throws a crooked shadow on one cheek. Sturdy, broad-shouldered, he looks as if he might have played on the football team if President Robert Maynard Hutchins had not just abolished the football team.

Aside from Peter, the only student in the picture whom I later came to know personally was a charming little Methodist girl with fluffy hair and a tantalizing figure. She came, as I recall, from some hamlet in Iowa. Active in the Epworth League of her home church, she had been seized with an impulse to become some sort of church activist, perhaps a missionary. Like Peter she had completed two years of college elsewhere and had entered the divinity school on a scholarship.

Shortly after she arrived on the campus, one of Peter's bulletin board notices about the C.C.F. caught her eye and she began attending meetings. Her orthodoxy eroded at a fast clip, much faster than Peter's, but she had an interest in Peter that kept her in the Fellowship until the end of her first year. In the middle of the next school year she vanished from the area, having married a law school graduate who had just passed his bar examination. She had been a good student in one of my classes. During the second World War, when she and her husband were in the university area (I cannot recall now why), she dropped by my office on the fourth floor of Swift Hall to say hello. Somehow Peter's name came up, and she told me a revealing story about him.

It seems that one evening in May, after a meeting of the C.C.F., Peter had offered to escort her back to her dormitory. It was a warm windless night. They decided to take a walk to Lake Michigan, the shore of which is only a short distance from Gray City, and they found a place to sit on one of the large boulders that form a rocky rim around a small promontory near the eastern end of Fifty-fifth Street. A fat yellow moon floated low over the water. On the underbellies of clouds in the southeast they could see the flickering rosy light from the open furnaces of the steel mills in Gary, Indiana.

"I wanted him to make love to me," she said. "I squeezed his hand. I put my head on his shoulder. I lay on my back with my head in his lap."

"Yes?" I said, amused that she would tell me this.

"Can you guess what he did?"

I shook my head.

"He talked for two hours about what he thought Jesus meant by the unpardonable sin!"

I shuddered. Then both of us were convulsed with laughter.

"Peter has changed," I said.

"I'm so glad," she said. "I knew he would."

6

The Mustard Seed of Doubt

Peter's religious views altered very little during his first year at the divinity school. He worshipped regularly at Moody Memorial Church, his social life was restricted to friends in the Chicago Christian Fellowship, and he had not yet been exposed to me or to any of the school's other faculty "radicals." On the other hand, the intellectual climate of Gray City, and his conversations with other seminarians, were building up subtle doubts and conflicts in his mind. Then, near the middle of his second year, his fundamentalism was dealt a mighty death blow.

Curiously, the blow did not come from any course in the divinity school, certainly not from my harmless class in applied Christianity which Peter was then attending. It came from an extracurricular class that Peter had decided to audit. He had been disappointed by the way his geology professor at the University of Oklahoma dismissed the views of George McCready Price. Price's *New Geology* had convinced Peter that the theory of evolution rested on shaky evidence, yet at the same time he felt uneasy about many of Price's arguments. After all, Price was a Seventh-Day Adventist, and Peter knew that the Adventists advocated a variety of strange doctrines—ultimate annihilation of the wicked, for instance, and soul sleeping until the day of judgment—doctrines he regarded as in conflict with the plain teachings of Jesus.

Moreover, the *Scofield Reference Bible*, in its notes on the first chapter of Genesis, suggested that fossils were not a record of life obliterated by the great Flood (as Price maintained) but a record of an earlier creation that had preceded the present one, a creation which God had destroyed by a great cataclysm. "Relegate fossils to the primitive creation," declared Reverend Cyrus Ingerson Scofield, "and no conflict of science with the Genesis cosmogony remains."

Like Teilhard de Chardin, whose writings he later read with great excitement, Peter had convinced himself that evolution, more than any other single theory of modern science, had become a stumbling block to orthodox Christian faith. He wanted to get his own mind clear on the subject, and he had enough humility to realize that he could not get it clear until he knew more about the evidence on which Darwin had based his theory. The course in geology that he had taken at the University of Oklahoma had been diffuse and superficial. No more than a week or two of lectures had been devoted to the fossil record. Peter studied the University of Chicago catalog carefully. He finally decided that the quickest way to the heart of the matter was to audit a course called "Introduction to Historical Geology," taught by the distinguished geologist J. Harvey Blitz.

Peter's decision to attend this class was no small act of courage. I often wonder why leading fundamentalists—Billy Graham, for example—seem incapable of realizing how they commit the sin of pride when they refuse to acquire the kind of scientific knowledge necessary for a thorough understanding of certain doctrines of their faith. One can forgive medieval Christians for crowding into churches to pray that a plague be abated, thereby spreading the disease more rapidly, because none of them knew about microbes. One can forgive Luther and Calvin and Wesley for believing that God created the earth and all living things in six literal days, because science did not then have the evidence to dispute it. Today, when a self-styled Christian resolutely refuses to inform himself about scientific truths which bear upon his faith, why is it that he cannot see his refusal as an insult to the very God of Truth he fancies he is serving?

Peter always had the courage to search for truth wherever he could find it. On the first evening that he came to see me at my home, the topic of evolution entered our conversation—we had been discussing original sin—and I urged him to read a good modern book on the subject. I was surprised when he told me he had already enrolled for Blitz's course. A few weeks later I found myself sitting next to Blitz during a lunch at the faculty's Quadrangle Club.

"One of my students is attending your introductory course in historical geology," I began. "I'm curious. . . ."

Before I could finish, Blitz deposited his fork noisily on his plate and said, "What's his name?"

"Peter Fromm."

Blitz slapped his forehead.

"You know him?"

"Do I know him! My God, Homer, he's the first student I've had in fifteen years who thought God made the world in six days then sat down on his divine ass and rested!"

"I know," I said, smiling. "Peter comes from a small town in Oklahoma. Give him time, Harvey. He's really anxious to learn."

Blitz resumed his attack on a slice of blueberry pie. "As a matter of fact, Homer, the boy has a first-rate mind."

Peter had raised his hand in class one day, Blitz told me, to ask if it were possible that all the sedimentary rock on the earth had been deposited at the same time. "You mean," said Blitz, intending to be funny, "by the big flood described in the Old Testament?" Everyone in the class laughed except Peter who nodded gravely.

"I was dumbfounded," said Blitz. "I didn't want to embarrass the kid by arguing with him in front of the class, but I spent the rest of the hour going over all the evidence I could think of that proves sedimentation has been going on for hundreds of millions of years. The boy listened without batting an eyelash. After class he came up and asked if he could see me sometime in my office."

Blitz pushed away his empty dessert dish and blotted his mustache with a napkin. "When he came to see me he had a big book with him called *The New Geology*. It was by some knucklehead named Price."

"I know the book," I said. "Price is a Seventh-Day Adventist who lives in Walla Walla, Washington. He must be as old as Methuselah. You know, he was the scientific authority William Jennings Bryan kept referring to during the Scopes trial in Tennessee."

"It figures," said Blitz. "I borrowed the damn book and stayed up half the night reading it. I had no idea anyone like Price still existed. Why, he has the notion that. . . ."

"You don't have to tell me about Price," I said. "I've read his book."

Blitz lifted his bushy eyebrows. "Sometimes you amaze me, Homer. Is there anything you *haven't* read? Have you seen my latest paper, 'Vadose and Phreatic Features of Limestone Caverns'?"

I laughed and shook my head.

"I was so fascinated by Price," Blitz went on, "that next day I took his book to class with me. For three days all I did was talk about Price and the man's priceless stupidities. When I gave the book back to Peter, do you know what he did?"

"He still wanted to argue about it?"

"*Au contraire.* He shook my hand and thanked me. He told me those were the most important lectures he'd ever heard."

I felt relieved. Peter meant, of course, exactly what he said—he always meant what he said—even though he could not then have been aware of how sharp a corner he had turned. To change the metaphor, Blitz had driven the point of a geological hammer into the rock of Peter's fundamentalism. He had opened the first tiny fissure through which the waters of modern science could begin their slow erosion. Now the metaphor breaks down. It may take a million years for a boulder to crumble. A religion can crumble in a few centuries. A man's faith can crumble in less than a year.

Peter threw away his copy of *The New Geology*.

My wife and I listened to him one evening in our living room while he told us about his new point of view. Evolution, he had decided, was here to stay. He had been reading other books that Blitz had recommended—H. G. Wells' *Science of Life* was one of them—and he had come to the conclusion that a Christian who tried to oppose the theory of evolution was fighting a hopeless battle which in the long run could only damage his faith. He had been rereading Genesis in the light of this new conviction. Saint Augustine had surely been right, he said, in suggesting that each "day" of Genesis actually was a vast stretch of geologic time. Evolution was God's method of creation. Isn't it remarkable, he asked us, that the order in which the animals were created, as recorded in the first chapter of the Old Testament, parallels so closely the order of evolution?

"What about the Fall?" I said. "Doesn't the doctrine of Original Sin imply a sharp discontinuity between man and beast?"

Peter agreed. He took the position Teilhard took, indeed, the position most modern Catholic philosophers now take, that at some point in history, millions of years ago, a miracle occurred. A mysterious gulf was crossed by a divine mutation. The first human souls were infused into the evolutionary process.

My wife and I exchanged amused glances. "But Peter," she said, and I knew what was coming because we had raised the point so often before with other students, "doesn't that mean that little Adam and Eve must have been reared and nursed by a mother who had no soul?"

Peter seemed momentarily transfixed, the blood slowly coloring his cheeks. "I. . . .I never thought of it quite that way, Edna," he said with an awkward laugh. We could see that the thrust had gone home. Edna eased the tension by going to the kitchen for some coffee and sweet rolls, and our conversation drifted off to nonreligious topics.

I have stressed this rotation point in Peter's interpretation of the first chapter of Genesis, not only because it marked the first signs of his tottering faith in the Bible's scientific accuracy, but also because it symbolizes in so many ways a similar rotation point in the history of modern Protestantism.

Darwin once wrote in a letter: "At last gleams of light have come, and I am almost convinced. . . .that species are not (it is like confessing a murder) immutable."

Darwin did commit a murder, or rather several murders. His great book was a death blow to the literal interpretation of the Bible and also a mortal blow against the doctrines of Original Sin and Atonement. Were not Darwin's opponents exactly right in contending that the central doctrines of Christian orthodoxy hang and fall together? "In Adam's fall we sinnéd all," was the way the old Puritan school readers put it. Knock over the doctrine of the Fall, and the others, including Jehovah himself, topple like the proverbial row of dominoes.

Peter's new way of interpreting the Bible's story of creation was quickly reflected in a more elastic interpretation of other parts of the Old Testament. He was willing to admit, for example, that perhaps the story of Jonah should not be taken literally. He was still reluctant, however, to question the historicity of any incident in the Gospels.

One wintry evening at my house, when he and I were sitting in front of a roaring log fire, we got into a discussion about the conflicting New Testament accounts of the Resurrection of Christ. Peter insisted that they could be harmonized if one assumed that *two* groups of disciples, instead of one, visited the empty tomb. The first visit, he argued, is described by Matthew, Mark, and John. Luke speaks only of the second. That is why, he said, there are two angels in Luke's account and only one angel in the others.

I took a King James Bible from a shelf and read the four accounts aloud while Peter broke in between verses to give a running reconstruction of exactly what he thought had taken place. His clever chronology was essentially as follows:

At sunrise, Mary Magdalene and a group of ladies go to the sepulchre to annoint Jesus' body with spices they had prepared on the Sabbath. They were the last to leave the Cross, now they are the first to visit the tomb. When they arrive they are astonished to find that the stone is rolled away. Has the body been stolen? Mary Magdalene, tremendously excited, leaves the group and runs back to tell Peter and John. The two men had apparently been living apart from the other disciples—Peter because of his denial, John because he was taking care of Jesus' mother. Meanwhile, the other ladies enter the sepulchre where a single angel tells them that Christ is risen.

While the ladies are returning, Peter and John (having heard the news from Mary) run to the tomb. John, the younger of the two, gets there first but does not enter. Peter rushes inside. They see the burial clothes and headpiece lying apart, suggesting (Fromm pointed out) that the body had not been stolen.

As John and Peter are returning to join the other disciples, Mary Magdalene goes back to the tomb, still believing the body stolen. She looks inside, speaks with two angels, then Christ appears to her outside the entrance. He appears also to the original party of ladies as they are on their way to tell the disciples.

And now a second party of ladies (of which only Luke gives an account) goes to the tomb. This time there are *two* angels inside. The conversation differs from that of the first visit. The women of this second group return to the disciples "and to all the rest." True, Luke 24:10 seems to name the ladies of this group, and they are the same as the names which the other Gospels apply to the women of the first group. But, insisted Peter, Luke does not specifically say that these are the names of those who had just returned. They are merely the most important women present among "all the rest." They are the ladies who had earlier returned from visit number one. And because Luke 24:9 speaks of all eleven disciples as there, we know that Peter and John also had returned.

I told Peter that I greatly admired the ingenuity of his reconstruction. It seemed to clear up all conflicting details except one. Luke 24:12 reads as follows:

> Then arose Peter, and ran unto the sepulchre: and stooping down, he beheld the linen clothes laid by themselves, and departed, wondering in himself at that which was come to pass.

How, I asked Peter, did he fit this into his scheme? In the first place, Luke clearly asserts that Peter's visit occurred after the second (two-angel) visit, whereas John's account just as clearly has Peter's visit occur before the second group of ladies go there; indeed, even before Mary Magdalene returns to the sepulchre. In addition, Luke 24:12 conflicts with John's account by saying nothing of John being with Peter and by telling us that Peter merely *looked* inside. I let Peter thrash vainly about until he finally conceded that he could think of no plausible way to fit Luke 24:12 into his complicated tableau.

"It may interest you to know," I said, "that Luke's troublesome verse is considered an interpolation by most New Testament scholars."

"What do you mean?"

"I mean that it was probably added later to Luke's Gospel. The verse doesn't appear at all in the earliest New Testament manuscripts. Goodspeed's translation, for example, leaves it out entirely."

Peter was ecstatic. "Don't you see, Homer?" he exclaimed, leaping out of his chair and bounding to one side of the fireplace. "Don't you see how beautifully everything fits together now? And the very fact that the accounts *seem* to disagree really makes them even more reliable."

He turned to face me. "If the four accounts agreed in every little detail," he said, trying to keep down the excitement in his voice, "we'd suspect collusion among the writers, wouldn't we? Or that one had copied from another. But they're *not* alike. They're different. They disagree just the way you'd expect eyewitness accounts to disagree. Each writer emphasized a different part of the story. Yet they all interlock, like a . . . ."

"Jigsaw puzzle," I said.

Logs crackled in the fireplace. I did not inform Peter then that Saint Chrysostom in the fourth century had used this identical line of reasoning. I did not remind him of how easily resurrection stories had been believed in ancient times before the spirit of scientific inquiry led even the most gullible Christian to demand better evidence for such a miracle. I did not ask him what he thought of the Old Testament accounts of how Elijah and Elisha had each raised a boy from the dead, or the story of how a corpse flung into the tomb of Elisha had, as soon as it touched Elisha's bones, stood up and lived. I did not ask him if he believed that Jesus had raised Lazarus and the daughter of Jairus and the widow of Nain from the dead, or if he believed the statement (Matthew 27:52-53) that when Christ died "the graves were opened; and many bodies of the saints which slept, arose, and came out of the graves after his Resurrection, and went into the holy city, and appeared unto many." I did not ask him if he believed that his namesake Peter, as reported in Acts 9:36-42, had raised a woman of Joppa from the dead.

Nor did I send him to Frazer's *Golden Bough* where he could learn about the Syrian god Adonis, the Phrygian god Attis, and the Egyptian god Osiris—all of whom became men of flesh and bone, died, and rose again. I did not tell him of the inscriptions on the walls of pyramids built more than two thousand years before the time of Christ, inscriptions that promised eternal life to every believer because, "as Osiris lives, so shall he also live; as Osiris died not, so shall he also not die; as Osiris perished not, so shall he also not perish."

I did not ask Peter if he believed the countless stories recorded in the middle ages of persons who had been raised from the dead by saints, many of these stories better attested than the New Testament records. Saint Augustine, in Book 22 of his *City of God,* speaks of numerous revivals of the dead by the miraculous power of the relics of Stephen the Martyr, but he mentions only those for which he has "indisputable evidence." I did not refer Peter to Brewer's *Dictionary of Miracles* where he could find accounts of decapitated saints who walked about carrying their own heads.

I did not suggest to Peter that one or two of the more emotional disciples, Mary Magdalene for instance, could have had an hallucination of the risen Christ and how, in the electrically charged atmosphere of the moment, it would have become a mark of status to have been visited by the risen Lord. Would not Jesus appear to those who loved him best? Some would have visions, some would see a vague shape in the darkness, and their imagination and hope would do the rest. Others would exaggerate; a few would lie. The mania among the devoted would increase. It is all so easy to understand.

I knew that these thoughts would come to Peter in due time. For the present it was enough that he had not been entirely satisfied with his ingenious reconstruction of the events of that Resurrection morning. The Gospel texts had to be strained considerably at several spots to make everything fit, and I had managed to get across to him that at least some verses of the King James version of the New Testament were not to be completely trusted.

During the spring quarter, at the end of Peter's second year, difficulties of Bible exegesis began to trouble him more and more. Big doubt, like big faith, can grow from a tiny mustard seed. The puzzles came at him from all directions, from his friends, from his reading, from his teachers, and from me. They were the same old questions that had precipitated the "higher criticism" in Germany, that distressed the Roman Catholic "modernists," that helped produce the deists and the broad church movement in England. They were the problems that Bishop John William Colenso had faced so courageously and which led to his shameful excommunication by the English Church. In Revolutionary America they gave substance to Thomas Paine's *Age of Reason* and a century later to the eloquent lectures of Robert Ingersoll. They are questions which today's emancipated Roman Catholics have long since put behind them but which would still torment any average Catholic who took the time to read his Bible.

It is hard to realize that these enigmas were once such violent storm centers of controversy. They seem so comic when repeated now. Where did Cain get his wife? Did the sons of God actually marry the daughters of men as Genesis 6:2 so unambiguously asserts? Did the God of Israel really command his people to enter villages, massacre entire populations, and keep the virgin girls as slaves? Did Lot's wife become a pillar of salt, did the Red Sea divide, did the sun and moon stand still?

And the New Testament riddles! How should one harmonize the two conflicting genealogies of Christ? Was it one or two blind men whom the Lord healed on the road to Jericho? When Jesus cast the devils out of the naked wild man (Matthew, Luke) or the two wild men (Mark), what did the devils gain by entering into two thousand pigs (Mark 5:13) and drowning them in the sea? Why did Jesus plainly declare that he would return to earth before a generation had passed and that some standing before him would not taste of death until they saw the Son of Man return to set up his kingdom? Was Jesus mistaken about the date of his second coming?

These and a hundred other dreary questions began to beat incessantly on the inside of Peter's forehead. It was obvious, he finally realized, that many verses of Holy Writ cannot be statements of historical fact. But where in the name of the Almighty does one draw the line? If Christ did not curse a fig tree and cause it to wither, if he did not turn water into wine, if he did not walk on the surface of the sea, how can we be sure that he raised Lazarus from the dead? And if he did not call Lazarus back from the grave, why should we believe the story, told in the same documents, that Jesus himself rose from the dead? The doctrinal dominoes were starting to fall. I can imagine Peter, alone in his dormitory room, struggling with these ancient perplexities, kneeling and praying, "Lord, I believe! Help Thou my unbelief!"

A few days before the end of the spring quarter, Peter attended a Sunday evening service at Moody Church. Years later he told me about the shattering effect it had on him. The speaker, from some little Bible Institute in California, had devoted many years of study to the prophesies in the Book of Revelation. He had convinced himself that Russia, with its Godless Communism, was none other than the Beast that John tells us would appear during the earth's last days. On a large blackboard this learned scholar solemnly demonstrated how the number 666, the "mark of the Beast," could be derived from the name of Joseph Stalin by applying a complex cipher system.

Peter stood up abruptly in the middle of the sermon. He had been sitting near the center of one of the front rows, and the huge auditorium was jammed to capacity. It was with great difficulty, he told me, that he restrained himself from shouting something at the speaker. He managed, however, to control himself and make his way to the aisle without causing too much commotion; then he tramped furiously out of Moody Memorial Church and straight into a warm June night. He felt like walking. Instead of taking the El back to the south side, as he usually did, he decided to walk south down Clark Street to the Loop.

North Clark Street! Only a Thomas Wolfe could do it justice, but Wolfe never got to know Chicago. To the east, the wealthy Gold Coast along Lake Michigan. To the west, Italian and Black slums. Between the two worlds, yet part of neither, runs North Clark Street. A street of noisy bars, sleazy cabarets and stripjoints, garages, bleak shops, cockroach-infested apartments, decaying office buildings. A street of pushers, pimps, and whores. Peter walked the length of it, from North Avenue to the Loop, past the Red Star Inn, past Newberry Library, past Bughouse Square.

The soapbox orators of Bughouse Park, in front of the library, were out in full force. One speaker was informing a small circle of listeners that the only way to solve their problems was to join the Communist Party and work for the overthrow of the whole rotten capitalistic system. Twenty feet away another speaker was telling *his* clump of listeners that the only way to solve their problems was to take them all to Jesus.

Peter stopped and listened to the second speaker with a detached attitude of professional criticism. "He was saying the same things," Peter told me, "using the same phrases, quoting the same Bible verses that I had quoted back in the days when I preached at Pentecostal meetings. But his gestures and timing were all wrong. There was no fire in his voice, no oratorical tricks to whip up enthusiasm. I knew I could find myself a crate, stand on it, and draw a larger audience in three minutes than any other speaker in the park."

Peter did not look for a soapbox. A strange lethargy had gripped his soul. He listened for a while to the sad, irrelevant pieties, then moved on until he came to the bridge where North Clark Street arches over the Chicago River, just before it intersects the Loop. For an hour or more he stood on that desolate structure, leaning against its iron parapet. Not a soul was in sight. It was not late, but traffic was sparse near the Loop on a Sunday night, and not a single car crossed the bridge while he was there. The Wrigley Building, that monstrous monument to chewing gum, gleamed stark white in the beams of its giant arc lights.

The sermon still angered and frightened him. He had suddenly seen the members of Moody Church in a new, disquieting light. They were not the vanguards of a new faith. They were just the tired, simple-minded, superstitious refugees from earlier ages of ortnodoxy. The thought had come to him, while the visiting speaker at Moody Church was chalking his prophetic numerals on the blackboard, that God was watching it all with tolerant mirth. A night wind rippled the sluggish black water below the bridge and disheveled his hair, for Peter never wore a hat even in midwinter. As he rested his elbows on the railing, gazing at the mammoth, smoky city, his thoughts drifted back to that hill of skulls where three men, one of whom Peter still believed to have been God himself, were hammered to wooden crosses and left to die. How small and remote Calvary seemed!

His thoughts were jarred by the sound of a girl's voice behind him. "Excuse me, honey. You got a match?"

He spun around. There were no lights at the center of the bridge, and it was difficult to make out the girl's features. He could see that they were heavy with make-up and that her dark hair had been elaborately coiffured. The air had previously held a faint odor from the Chicago stockyards—the wind was blowing from the south—but now that odor was masked by a scent of strong perfume. He could not tell if the lady was young or early middle-aged. An unlit cigarette projected from her lips.

"Sorry," Peter said. "I don't smoke."

"Never you mind," she said, reaching into a small handbag. "I just found some."

She handed Peter a folder of matches. He struck a light, but the wind immediately extinguished it.

"Let me," she said, taking back the folder. She scratched a match, then carried the spurt of flame quickly to the cigarette while she drew air through it. In the momentary yellow glare, before the flame blew out, he could see that she was much younger than he expected.

She inhaled deeply to make sure the cigarette stayed lit. "I could use a drink."

"Do you live near here?"

The girl nodded. "I got me a nice room on Ohio street."

"How much do you charge?"

She shrugged. "We can talk about that later, honey. Let's get a drink first."

Not for one moment, I regret to say, was Peter seized by the slightest impulse to take this young lady up on her kind invitation. Instead, he reached into his trouser pocket and produced a five-dollar bill. Then he reached into the top pocket of his jacket and produced a tiny copy of the New Testament. He handed both items to the girl.

"And what did the lady do then?" I asked, when Peter first told me about the incident.

"Well, Homer, first she gave me a long, funny look. Then she laughed a high-pitched crazy laugh, shoved the money and the New Testament into her handbag, said 'Thanks,' and walked off."

Peter said he stood there, leaning against the bridge's iron railing, watching the girl walk north, cross the street, and enter a tavern. There was a sudden blare of jukebox jazz, then the door closed and Clark Street was silent again. The perfume faded. The old Chicago smell returned. I can imagine Peter closing his eyes for a moment while he offered up a silent prayer for the girl, perhaps also for himself.

He resumed walking south across the bridge and on to Randolph Street. He turned left, then continued along Randolph until he reached the Illinois Central Station where he caught the next train back to Gray City.

7

Chesterton

Throughout Peter's second year at the divinity school he came to see me in the evening about twice a month. It was not just that my wife and I had grown to like him, and he us. There was more to it than that. He was going through a difficult transition and we provided a sympathetic pair of older friends who did not laugh at what he wanted to talk about. Edna and I had long ago learned that the best way to ease a young seminarian's doctrinal anxieties is to listen much and argue little. Our tactics were to chat informally about the dilemmas he brought up, to explore alternatives, to suggest helpful books. In our earlier sessions he had a tendency to raise his voice and wave his arms. After a time he grew more relaxed, less sure of himself, more open to points of view that differed from his own.

"Perhaps it's a good thing, Homer," he remarked one evening, "that the Bible is such a *human* document, that it has so much bad history, so much bad science, and so on."

"Why would that be good?"

"Well, suppose the Bible were absolutely accurate in everything it said. The book itself would be a great miracle. It would be obvious it came from God."

"And that would be bad?"

"Yes, I think it would. Everybody would be *forced* to be a Christian. Belief in the Bible wouldn't be an act of will. It wouldn't be faith. It would be compulsion."

Peter, you see, still looked upon the Bible as a unified, God-inspired work even though he had learned to distrust its history and its science. He was moving away from the Bible-centered fundamentalism of the

Moody Institute and Wheaton College toward a broader kind of ortho-doxy. Although it surprised me at the time, I can understand now how it was, at this point in Peter's developing sophistication, that he would see the Roman Catholic Church in a way that he had never seen it before.

By insisting on the right to interpret the Bible as it sees fit, to continu-ally shape and alter Christian doctrine, the Roman Church has suc-ceeded in preserving orthodoxy within a distinguished intellectual and literary tradition. Today it is slowly accommodating itself to evolution—not to mention a dozen other things!—just as it managed several centu-ries ago to accept slowly the cosmology of Galileo. Give it a few more decades and it will be warning its members of the threats of world over-population and urging zero population growth. The Church is much too huge and complicated to move rapidly. Nevertheless, to paraphrase that remark which recent scholarship tells us Galileo never made, the Church *does* move.

Oddly enough it was Robert Maynard Hutchins, president of the Uni-versity of Chicago, who first stimulated Peter's interest in Rome. I write "oddly" not because the university is a secular institution of long-forgot-ten Baptist origin but because Hutchins himself is the product of a con-servative Presbyterian background. (In one of his published speeches he speaks of his habit while shaving of "moaning third-rate hymns.") There is no stranger period in the history of Gray City than the period in which its president, entranced by the revival of Neo-Thomist theology, be-haved for all the world like a potential Catholic convert.

Exactly what internal and external forces were then shaping Hutchins' religious beliefs I would not presume to guess. Was he, like Peter, going through his own confusing awkward age? At any rate the Neo-Thomist phrases became more and more conspicuous in his public utterances. He even quoted occasionally from that once much-admired Catholic apologist, Gilbert Keith Chesterton. Several of his appointments to the faculty (notably his friend Mortimer J. Adler whom he made "professor of the philosophy of law" after the philosophy department refused to make room for him) were men similarly preoccupied with the thought of medieval schoolmen. He invited Jacques Maritain, the distinguished French Catholic philosopher, to Gray City for a series of lectures which were published in 1933 by the University of Chicago Press. The book is affectionately dedicated (in Latin) to Hutchins. Its frontispiece is a portrait of Maritain sketched by Hutchins' wife.

Even the Great Books program, in which Hutchins and Adler later took such active roles, was warmly applauded by the nation's leading

Catholic educators. Modern Thomists are forever stressing the virtues of the "classics," forever attacking the emphasis in secular education on teaching narrow "facts" instead of broad "ideas." Nine-tenths of what Hutchins had to say about the higher learning came straight out of John Henry Newman's *The Idea of a University*. Catholic journals praised and flattered Hutchins in much the same way that Communist journals praised and flattered any college president who had kind words for Karl Marx or Joseph Stalin. Enthusiastic Catholic laymen played no small role in the early growth of the Great Books movement, especially at the grass roots level where they often were prime movers in organizing Great Books discussion classes in their home towns.

I remember the astonishment with which Peter reported to me his discovery, one winter afternoon, that Hutchins really did believe in God. He had heard Hutchins speak somewhere—I have no record of the time or place—and the president had referred to God in such a way that one could not doubt his sincerity. Peter's curiosity was so aroused that he immediately obtained copies of Hutchins' two published books, *No Friendly Voice* and *The Higher Learning in America*. Later he discovered—it may be that I called it to his attention—the introduction Hutchins had written for a book called *The Case for Theology in the University*.

The author of this book, a Presbyterian cleric named William Adams Brown, maintained (as did Cardinal Newman) that a university with theology as its ordering principle is superior to a university organized around what Hutchins persisted in calling metaphysics. Hutchins said in his introduction that he agreed. Metaphysics, he explained, includes natural theology. When he wrote in one of his books that "to look to theology to unify the modern university is futile and vain," all he meant was that a secular school like Chicago had to permit within its walls a diversity of beliefs. Then came the following incredible passage:

> Nor have I meant to imply that we should forget that we are living in a Christian world and return, via metaphysics, to the Greeks. There are a Christian philosophy, a Christian metaphysics, and a Christian natural theology which in all their central points are a great advance over the Greek accomplishment. I should hope that if universities attempted to achieve intelligibility through metaphysics they would arrive at the best. The best, as far as I know, is the Christian achievement.

Those sentences tantalized Peter as much as they did all of us on the divinity school faculty who read them at the time. What did Hutchins mean by "Christian natural theology"? Did he mean the natural theology of Aquinas as distinct from, say, the natural theology of Augustine, Anselm, Bonaventure, or Scotus? And what about the natural theologies of the great Protestant theologians? What "central points" of Christian natural theology could be common to the rational proofs of God by Thomas Aquinas and the moral proofs by Immanuel Kant? And what about Karl Barth, for whom all natural theology was an abomination? "What manner of God," Barth once asked, "is He who has to be proved?"

In a later speech, a convocation address given shortly before he left Gray City to raise and dispense millions of Ford Foundation dollars, Hutchins declared that the "brotherhood of man rests upon the father-hood of God," that humanitarianism without theism is doomed to fail, and that only a spiritual revolution can stay the collapse of civilization. "It is very late; perhaps nothing can save us." Like the exhortations of an ancient Hebrew prophet, Hutchins' unfriendly voice fell on ears that heard him not. In the name of which Christian God did the president deliver those prophetic warnings?

In many ways the Chicago Neo-Thomist movement resembled the earlier cult of Neo-Humanism that flourished during the twenties under the leadership of Irving Babbitt, Paul Elmer More, Norman Foerster, and the University of Chicago's own Paul Shorey. Both groups faulted modern education for its neglect of metaphysics, the humanities, the great books; for its overemphasis on science, isolated facts, the elective system, vocational training, and the pragmatic naturalism of John Dewey. Both groups drew inspiration from Greek philosophy and were linked (through certain members) to Christianity, though the New Humanists were closer to Plato and Protestantism than to Aristotle and Catholicism. Both groups belonged to what George Santayana in a famous essay called this country's "genteel tradition," a tradition in which he said one could sniff the unmistakable odor of "fustiness and faggots."

There were, of course, all sorts of differences between the two movements. To my mind one of the most significant was that the New Humanists made no attempt to hide their religious light under bushels of elliptical phrases. Babbitt was outspoken in defense of Buddhism. More was equally frank about his Anglicanism. Indeed, he was not ashamed to devote an entire book to his Christology. Did Jesus rise from the dead? We know exactly where More stood on this question. Hutchins? No one in the divinity school to this day has the slightest inkling of what the president believed then or believes now about any "central point" of Christianity.

"It's not fair," Peter once complained. "If Hutchins thinks Christianity is a great advance over Greek philosophy, why doesn't he tell us which Christianity he means?"

I told Peter that I had once approached Hutchins at a cocktail party, and asked him if he would mind telling me something about his theology. "Yes," he said, then turned his back and walked away.

"Why," asked Peter, "didn't you kick him in the pants?"

On Monday evenings, seated at the head of a large table in a room of the Classics Building, Hutchins and Adler led a Great Books discussion class. Peter slipped into the room one night as a visitor to hear a spirited discussion of one of Saint Thomas Aquinas' treatises. This sent him scurrying to the philosophy department's library to pore over long sections of the *Summa Theologica*, then to books on Thomas by Maritain and Etienne Gilson. He found the Saint droll, dull, and often incomprehensible. The terminology was strange and the arguments frequently centered on fantastic issues totally foreign to Peter's background. I remember how amused he was by the Saint's sober explanation of why Eve had been made from Adam's rib rather than from Adam's foot or head, and his demonstration that women would have been born to the human race even if there had been no Fall. The books by Maritain and Gilson were too technical for Peter to get much out of except a vague impression of the enormous architecture of the *Philosophia Perennis*. And then he came upon Chesterton's lively little book, *Saint Thomas: the Dumb Ox*.

I myself have never been an admirer of G. K. Chesterton. I find his writing flawed by verbal sleight-of-hand, subtle antisemitism, excessive paradox, and occasional intellectual dishonesty. For Peter, the discovery of the rotund British Catholic convert was one of the milestones of his intellectual development. The gorgeous rhetoric blew through his brain like the great wind that blows through the opening chapters of Chesterton's *Manalive*. It was a wild, humorous, existential, poetic approach to Christian faith, unlike anything he had encountered before, and all of it suffused with Chesterton's childlike wonder at the miracle of the world and his feeling of gratitude for the privilege of existing. Chesterton's book on Aquinas did not send Peter back to Aquinas, but it sent him to Chesterton. For the next six months Peter devoured every book by Chesterton he could get his hands on.

It was during this period, his Chestertonian period as he likes to call it, that Peter met an attractive Italian girl named Angelina Provocino. The time was late March, in Peter's confusing second year, a few months before he abandoned Moody Memorial Church and the Chicago Christian

Fellowship. There had been a burst of unusually balmy weather. Peter and a classmate had decided to spend the morning playing tennis.

The public tennis courts on the southern side of the Midway were crowded, and they had to wait almost an hour until one was free. Two girls had also been waiting about the same length of time. There was some confusion as to which pair had been there first. It was quickly resolved by a decision to play a game of doubles. They spun rackets to decide partners, and Peter found himself paired with Angelina, the smaller and prettier of the two girls. Her father was Italian, but she had inherited the coloring and features of her Irish mother: fair skin, blue-green eyes, dark red hair (pulled back in a knot), small up-tilting nose, and freckles that dotted her nose and cheeks.

"You have a smudge of dirt on your forehead," Peter remarked as they walked to their positions on the court.

Angelina glanced up at him and frowned. "Are you kidding? Today's Ash Wednesday."

Peter's face reddened. "I'm sorry. I didn't know."

The four were well acquainted by the time the set was over. When Peter suggested a walk to Reader's Campus Drugstore, at Sixty-first and Ellis Avenue, the girls were quick to agree. While they sat in a rear booth drinking Cokes, Peter began to question Angelina about the meaning of the ash on her forehead. This led to other questions concerning the symbols and rituals of the Lenten season. Peter had been reading a great deal about Catholicism, but Catholics were a rare breed back in Sand Springs and not once had he ever set foot inside a Catholic church. The details of the Mass, so commonplace to Angelina, were fresh and fascinating to him.

"If you'd like," the girl said, "why don't you come to Mass with me Sunday? I'll explain what everything means. At least everything I can remember."

Peter said he would like to do that very much. He penciled her name and address carefully on a paper napkin and promised to come by for her Sunday morning at ten-thirty.

8

Angelina

Angelina lived with her parents, an older sister, and three younger brothers in a drab, low-rent area which extended on either side of East Fifty-fifth Street. Her father was the superintendent of a small apartment building on Kimbark Avenue, a few blocks north of the Church of Saint Thomas the Apostle. (The building was later replaced by a high-rise apartment hotel during the district's big slum clearance program of the late fifties.) The Provocino family occupied an apartment in the basement. For the past two years, following her high school graduation at the Saint Thomas parochial school, Angelina had been working in the kitchenware department of the Boston Store, a large department store in Chicago's Loop.

Every Sunday during the Lenten season, and some of the Holy Days as well, Peter accompanied Angelina to services at the Church of Saint Thomas. The solemn chants, the violet robes, especially the somber atmosphere of the last two Sundays when the cross and statuary were draped with purple veils, must have been for Peter an impressive introduction to Catholic ritual.

I remember Peter telling me how deeply stirred he had been during a Tenebrae service on Holy Thursday. He had studied the liturgy beforehand, in a prayer book Angelina had given him, so he knew the meaning of the symbolism and most of the Latin phrases. After the last burning candle disappeared behind the altar, leaving the church in total darkness, the sudden chant of "Christ was made obedient for us, even unto death," set his heart pounding. Invisible fingers drummed on his spine when, after a lengthy silence, the priest intoned "Lord, have mercy." The great crash that symbolizes the opening of the sepulchre, followed by the reappearance of the candle and the triumphant chant of "Christ, the Lord, is risen," lifted him into a state of exultation such as he had not

experienced since the days when he had preached at tent revival meetings.

"One feels," wrote William James, ". . . as if in presence of some
vast incrusted work of jewelry or architecture; one hears the multitudi-
nous liturgical appeal; one gets the honorific vibration coming from
every quarter. Compared with such a noble complexity, in which as-
cending and descending movements seem in no way to jar upon stability,
in which no single item, however humble, is insignificant, because so
many august institutions hold it in its place, how flat does evangelical
Protestantism appear, how bare the atmosphere of those isolated religious lives whose boast is that 'man in the bush with God may meet.'"
(*The Varieties of Religious Experience*, Lecture XIX.)

Peter was struggling desperately to get himself into the frame of mind
of a believing Catholic. "It is not enough," declared Giovanni Papini, an
Italian anarchist who later became a Catholic, "even in the field of philosophy to *know* a theory. One must live with it and feel it with all one's
soul, must fill one's thoughts with it, must make it, for the time being,
the content, the coloring, and the significance of one's whole life." Oxford linguistic philosophers like to speak of a metaphysical system or a
religious system as a kind of language game. There is a set of posits—
basic emotional commitments—and a set of rules for elaborating those
posits into complicated ways of talking and behaving. Unless you are
willing to play the entire game, according to its posits and its rules, you
will never really understand the satisfactions the game provides its
players.

In my student days at Meadville Theological Seminary, when I took a
course on the religions of ancient Greece, I once tried playing such a
game with Greek mythology. For several weeks I mumbled little prayers
to whatever Greek deity was most appropriate. If I wanted to get to
class on time, I prayed to swift-footed Hermes. If I was cramming for an
examination, I sought the aid of blue-eyed Athene. When my cigarette
lighter flared on the first flick of my thumb, I breathed a quick word of
thanks to Hephaestus. I even arranged a small altar in my room, surrounded by tall white candles, to the goddess of love. If a girl responded
to my overtures, I tried to imagine that Aphrodite was assisting me as
she had once assisted Paris in abducting Helen.

Is all this so far removed, my patient reader, from the language and
behavior of millions of Catholics and Protestants who believe that God
seriously listens to their prayers? Do not pious Christian farmers, in every country of the world including Russia, still pray for rain? I once
heard Billy Sunday explain on the platform, as he ran across the floor and

leaped high into the air, how God had helped him catch a hard-hit base-ball at a crucial moment when he was playing outfield for "Pop" Anson's famous Chicago White Stockings.

Playing the "Greek religion game" was an illuminating experience. Something close to the religious mood of the ancient Hellenes actually began to permeate my heart and mind. I found myself thinking seriously one evening of catching a pigeon and taking it in the dead of night to some suitable marble slab where under a full moon I would slit its throat as a blood sacrifice to Artemis! To this day I cannot walk by marble statues of the Greek deities without seeing what Lord Dunsany once de-scribed as "something very wistful in the faces of fallen gods, suppliant to be remembered."

Peter was not, of course, consciously aware that he was playing the "Roman Catholic game." He took it all with as much seriousness as a newly converted Catholic novice. Unlike most Protestants, when they find themselves trapped into attending Mass with a friend, Peter refused to remain seated during the ceremony. He was eager to participate in everything, and Angelina was happy to prompt him with whispers when-ever he missed the proper moment to rise or kneel. On Good Friday he trailed her to the altar steps and knelt beside her to kiss the crucifix. On Easter he insisted on taking Holy Communion. I can close my eyes and see him, hands clasped, walking solemnly back to his seat, doing his best to imagine what it would be like to believe, to truly believe, that he carried in his mouth the actual substance, the divine essence, of the Lord's body.

After the Easter service he asked Angelina to take him on a tour of the Stations of the Cross. He tried to meditate, as he was supposed to do, on each of the fourteen scenes. Then he led Angelina to the altar of the Blessed Virgin where he paused to inhale the rich fragrance of the lilies and to attempt to pray to God through Mary's intercessory power. It was at this point that his Protestant heritage shattered the spirit of the game.

"I just couldn't do it, Homer," he told me later. The statue was beau-tifully sculptured, not the usual painted plaster monstrosity, and the im-pulse to pray had been strong. But he kept thinking, he said, of that episode recorded in the eleventh chapter of Luke, verses 27 and 28:

> And it came to pass, as he spake these things, a certain woman of the company lifted up her voice, and said unto him, Blessed is the womb that bare thee, and the paps which thou hast sucked.
> But he said, Yea, rather blessed are they that hear the word of God, and keep it.

The steady growth of Mariolatry—first the Gospel myths of the Virgin Birth, then the non-Biblical doctrine of the Immaculate Conception (even Thomas Aquinas vigorously opposed it), and finally the church's recent declaration that Mary did not even die a natural death—has never ceased to annoy me. The intent of Christ's rebuke to the woman who praised his mother is surely unmistakable. So it seemed to Peter. For almost a year he continued to play the Catholic game. Not once was he able to manage a genuine, heartfelt prayer to Mary.

Peter did not return to Sand Springs during the summer following his second year in the divinity school. He was anxious to get on with his ministerial training, to finish it as quickly as he could, and to this end he enrolled for courses during the school's summer quarter. He was still reading vast quantities of Chesterton. I do not believe that he had forgotten his old "life plan" of revitalizing the faith of America, but he was in a state of great spiritual confusion and the plan got filed away in a back compartment of his mind. He was too busy trying to outline the contours of a new orthodoxy.

And, I must add, he was preoccupied with the contours of Angelina. During the hot summer months of July and August, Peter and Angelina spent Saturday and Sunday afternoons together on the beach of Lake Michigan. One sweltering Saturday, while I was taking a stroll along the Lake front, I passed them lying on their backs on a flat ledge of rock, eyes closed, soaking up the rays of a blazing sun. They were a picturesque pair. Peter: deeply tanned, muscular, wearing a pair of lavender shorts. Angelina: her trim and tiny figure wrapped in a white beach robe to protect her skin, large dark green sunglasses, her wet hair flaming and flowing back, and dripping over an edge of rock.

Peter leaped to his feet when I spoke. Angelina sat up and extended her hand while Peter introduced us. Did I detect a slight discomfort in his manner? We chatted briefly. I asked Peter to bring Angelina to the house sometime.

He was not, I guessed, too happy about this invitation, but a few evenings later Angelina was with him when he came to see us. It did not take long for Edna and me to discover why Peter had not brought her before. She had no interest whatever in any of the topics we usually discussed. I don't mean that she was not intelligent. She was bright and self-possessed, a normal, unassuming girl who did not question any aspect of her faith or bother her pretty head with theological hairsplitting. She took the truth of Roman Catholicism for granted the way one takes for granted the existence of the sky and clouds. Conversation with her was pleasant enough, though difficult to raise above the level of triviality. Edna finally hit on a topic that saved the evening. Cooking.

When I first began to pull together my scattered notes for this book, I realized with a shock that it would be incomplete if it did not include something about the girls who had played important roles in Peter's life. I was struck by the curious fact that three of the most sharply defined later periods in his development (of which the first was his Catholic game-playing) had coincided with periods of interest in girls who more or less shared the point of view which then dominated his thinking. It was hard to say which was cause and which effect. Did Peter's interest in Angelina, for example, intensify his interest in Catholicism? Or was it the other way around? Whichever way it was, I convinced myself that to round out my records of this phase of Peter's history it would be good to speak to Angelina.

The parish office at the Church of Saint Thomas put me in touch with Angelina's parents. From Mrs. Provocino I obtained her daughter's address and telephone number. Angelina had married an Italian boy who was then managing a liquor store in Oak Park, a western suburb of Chicago. I had little difficulty reaching her by phone. She was surprised, of course, to hear from me. I told her something about Peter's recent mental illness and said I was helping his psychiatrist gather information about his behavior and mental attitudes during the past ten years. This was not strictly true, but I could think of no better way to make my visit appear plausible. She seemed genuinely concerned. Yes, she would provide whatever help she could.

I went to see Angelina on the morning of a week day, knowing her husband would be at work and that we could talk alone. When she opened the front door of her home, a modest split-level house in a new development, she looked exactly as I remembered her. Her face had the same freckled charm, and her red hair was drawn back and knotted in the way she used to wear it. A baby boy with curly black hair was sitting in a playpen near the front window. When I entered the living room he pulled himself up on his feet to stare at me silently, thumb in mouth, with big, solemn eyes. I could hear an infant crying in a back room.

Angelina excused herself to attend the baby. When I asked if I could come along, she smiled and led me to the bedroom. It was another boy. Watching the little fellow gurgle and flap his arms, while Angelina expertly changed his diaper, reminded me of how anxious Edna and I were to have a grandchild. I made a mental note to include another tactful hint in my next letter to our daughter in California.

When we were back in the living room and seated, I gave Angelina a brief account of what had happened to Peter since she had last seen him. She had not known of his naval service during the war nor had she heard about his Easter sermon. I described most of what had taken place in my church, leaving out only Peter's final act but including details about how it all had ended. She listened with growing incredulity, frowning and shaking her head in sympathy.

Yes, she said, she had been very attached to Peter, though I noticed that she was careful not to say she had been in love with him. I waited for an appropriate moment and then—abruptly and awkwardly I'm afraid—I asked if Peter had ever made love to her.

Her face was strangely neutral. "No, not really. I used to think he didn't want to. Then I realized it was because he was so shy."

I was astounded. Peter had always been, it seemed to me, anything but shy.

"One night," she said, "we were sitting on a bench in Jackson Park. It was late. No one was around. Peter put his arms around me and kissed me. Right away he said he was sorry. He said he hadn't meant to do it."

Why, Angelina asked, was he apologizing? Because, he explained, he wasn't sure he was in love with her. I couldn't keep from chuckling. Even Angelina smiled. Yes, that sounded more like Peter. For several weeks he continued to apologize. I could hardly believe it. It was the only time they had so much as kissed.

"It *was* funny," she agreed, "for him to be so upset over just one little kiss." She turned to glance at the boy in the slatted pen. He was playing with a rubber duck that quacked each time he squeezed or bit it. "But Peter was like that. He worried about everything."

Peter's break with Angelina had come with the same suddenness with which he stopped attending Mass. Was there an element of subconscious cruelty in his tactics or had he decided that a sudden break would be less cruel in the long run?

"He just told me one day he wasn't in love with me," Angelina said with a shrug. "It was just like that. He said he could never be a Catholic or bring his children up as Catholics. He said he couldn't marry me. Since that was how things were, he thought he should let me know."

It was not quite that simple. For several weeks they tried to discuss their relationship with one another and what they should do about it, but the discussions were confused and indecisive. Then they stopped seeing each other altogether. She never heard from him again.

Before I left, Angelina told me about one of the last occasions on which they had been together. What she had to say made my trip to Oak Park worth the trouble.

Peter had taken her to a Friday dinner at a seafood restaurant on Lake Park Avenue, a block north of Fifty-fifth Street. The time was late

November in the beginning of Peter's third Chicago year. On the walk home they passed the gate in a high brick wall surrounding the Kimbark Street side of the Church of Saint Thomas the Apostle, the church they had so often attended. Peter lingered for a moment to peer through the gate's iron grillwork at the large stone statue of Saint Thomas that stands in front of the church's entrance.

It was dusk and the Saint's face was in deep purple shadow. A powdery snow was clinging to his head and shoulders and to the arm outstretched as if to touch the wounds of Christ.

"I am his brother," Peter said in low tones.

"What do you mean?" Angelina had never read the Gospels. If someone had asked her who Saint Thomas was, she would not have known how to answer.

"He refused to believe the Lord had risen from the dead," said Peter. "He refused to believe until he could put his finger in the nail prints or rest his hand on the wound made by the soldier's spear."

"Did he ever do it?"

"No, when he saw Jesus he believed. That was when Christ said to him, 'Thomas, because thou hast seen me, thou hast believed. Blessed are they that have not seen, and yet have believed.' " Peter's voice had a curious ring. "It was the last of the beatitudes."

Puzzled and a little frightened, she studied the statue more carefully through the softly falling flakes. "Why are you like him?"

"Because," Peter answered desolately, his words blowing clouds of whiteness into the freezing air, "I'm not sure I believe the story about Thomas."

Although he did not notice, Angelina crossed herself unobtrusively with a mittened hand. They gazed at the dark stone figure for several minutes, neither of them saying anything. And then, through the falling snow and fading light, Peter walked her slowly home.

9

The Flames of Hell

In the early fall of 1940, before Peter stopped playing his Catholic game, the University of Chicago's New Testament Club sponsored a symposium on "The Unity of the Bible." I was one of its three speakers.

The symposium was held in the Chicago Theological Seminary's Commons Room, a spacious, richly furnished lounge with panelled walls of dark oak, an enormous fireplace, large comfortable sofas and deep leather chairs. The topic had generated so much advance excitement among students of the four federated divinity schools that extra chairs had to be taken from the dining room to accommodate the guests. Peter nodded to me when he came in late, during the moderator's introductions. I watched him find a chair against the rear wall under a large oil portrait of one of the seminary's trustees.

Dr. Heinrich von Cloven, a professor of theology at Chicago Theological Seminary, was the first speaker. He was a portly gentleman with small eyes that diminished almost to invisibility behind the thick concave lenses of his horn-rimmed glasses. He spoke with a thick Teutonic accent. Like Karl Barth, who had been his teacher, he had left Germany because of the Nazis, and he was widely regarded as a world expert on the Barthian movement. He spoke rather well, better than I had anticipated, emphasizing his points with a relaxed wave of his hand, occasionally bending his knees slightly, then rising up on his toes to deliver a climactic line.

He defended, as everyone expected, the neo-orthodox view of Barth, Emil Brunner, and their lesser Continental sympathizers. The Bible, he conceded at once, was a human document. It was filled with historical error, inaccurate science, and all the superstitions of the Hebrew culture in Old and New Testament times. Nevertheless, he said, it was in and through this culture that God had chosen, for reasons we cannot now and perhaps will never fathom, to manifest Himself in a special way. The Bible was the written record of this extraordinary Revelation. It differed in kind, not just in degree, from the sacred books of other cultures. Beneath its diversity, its mythology, its often crude, unliterary language, there was one basic, unifying theme: God calling man to repentance through the mediation of a Savior.

In the Bible, von Cloven declared, we encounter what Barth, in one of his earliest and best sermons, had called a "strange new world." It is a world in which men have caught the "epidemic of standing still and looking up." Like the pointing finger of John the Baptist, in Matthias Grunewald's grim altar painting of the Crucifixion, the Bible points to Jesus Christ. His life is the pivotal event of history, yet not part of history for it was the intersection of the eternal, wholly other world of God with the finite, space-time world of man. The Old Testament points forward to the Incarnation. The New Testament points back to it. It is this event, this collision of God with history, that gives the Bible its divine unity.

Von Cloven closed his address by reading the following passage from Douglas Horton's translation of Barth's sermon:

> *It is not the right human thoughts about God which form the content of the Bible, but the right divine thoughts about men. The Bible tells us not how we should talk with God but what he says to us; not how we find the way to him, but how he has sought and found the way to us; not the right relation in which we must place ourselves to him, but the covenant which he has made with all who are Abraham's spiritual children and which he has sealed once and for all in Jesus Christ. It is this which is within the Bible.*

Von Cloven bent his knees then rose slowly in height to deliver Barth's punch line on his tiptoes. "The Word of God is within the Bible."

Although Horton's translation of eight sermons by Barth had been published as early as 1928 (under the title, *The Word of God and the Word of Man*), and several of von Cloven's books on Barthian theology had been translated into English, Barth's point of view was then still relatively unpopular in American seminaries. I had a feeling that von Cloven's speech bewildered his listeners more than it enlightened them. The students applauded politely, however, and Peter seemed impressed.

Shailer Mathews, at that time professor emeritus of the Chicago

Divinity School, was supposed to have been the next speaker, but an illness prevented him from coming. In his place, to flutter the banner of the social gospel, was the Most Reverend Abel Claxton Powys, pastor of the Halsted African Baptist Church, the largest and wealthiest church in Chicago's Black Belt. Powys was a friend and former student of Mathews and the city's most influential Black religious leader. Tall, handsome, light skinned and faintly moustached, he spoke with an easy charm and without the slightest trace of a Negro dialect.

The unity of the Bible, Powys gently informed his audience, is the unity of a steadily developing quest. It is *not*, Barth notwithstanding, a record of God's search for man. It is plainly a record of man's search for God. To view it as von Cloven had recommended, as a special Revelation written, so to speak, by the finger of the Almighty, is to return to a Biblicism which enlightened Protestantism long ago happily abandoned. We must, he said, look upon the Bible as a chronicle of the growth of spiritual awareness within the Hebraic tradition. To be sure, it is in many respects a unique record. No two cultures conduct their quest for religious values in the same language, with the same myths and symbols. But it is foolish to look to the Bible for doctrinal unity, or for truths qualitatively superior to those of other religious traditions.

He was defending, of course, the view of the German higher critics and the liberal theologians of the nineteenth century. In England it had found its finest expression in the writings of Matthew Arnold. In twentieth-century America the most effective purveyor of this way of looking at the Scriptures had been Harry Emerson Fosdick during that long stretch of years when he was pastor of the Riverside Baptist Church in New York City. The Reverend Powys referred many times to Fosdick's then-still-popular *Guide to Understanding the Bible*.

The Old Testament's oldest documents, Powys reminded his listeners, depict God as a tribal Yahweh, easily moved by jealousy and anger, a deity only a cut or two above the Zeus of Greek mythology. He was a God who could be placated by the blood of sacrificial animals. He was a God who could order Abraham to sacrifice his own son just to see if the old man was willing to obey him. As we read the later Hebrew documents we find this cruel deity slowly changing to a God of love and mercy. Of course it is not God who changes. It is our concepts of God that change. Just as Nature remains always the same, while scientists alter and improve their theories, so God remains eternally the same while humanity grows in its understanding of God's nature.

Think of the Bible, Powys said, as a series of still photographs of a growing rose. Some of the pictures are fuzzy. Others are sharp and clear.

First we see only a tiny green bud. But it is not a lifeless bud. As we turn the sacred pages we see the bud slowly unfold its petals. Powys held up his fist and slowly opened his fingers. Finally the bud blossoms forth in the beauty and wisdom of the teachings of Jesus, the Rose of Sharon. The unity of the Bible is like the unity of a growing flower. It is the unity of unfolding insight into higher and higher spiritual truths, and so on and so on. Need I say more? I paraphrase, though I do not believe I have distorted Powys' central theme.

The chairman, I suspect, had asked me to speak last because he guessed that I would have the most explosive things to say. I decided not to disappoint him. I would, as Peter liked to put it, pull no punches.

Yes, I began, resting my thumbs comfortably in the lower pockets of my maroon-colored vest, there *is* a unity of sorts in the Bible. But it is a superficial unity. It derives solely from the fact that all its documents are the products of one single isolated culture. It has the same trivial unity that ancient Greek religious literature would have if you bound it all together in one volume. It is a unity of language and customs and tradition. Homer tells us absurd and bawdy anecdotes about the gods of Olympus. Plato speaks of them more metaphorically. In Aristotle they all but vanish. The Old Testament is a similar mix of attitudes, from the anthropomorphic theism of Genesis to the despairing atheism of Ecclesiastes. And there are books in the Bible, like the erotic Song of Solomon, that have no religious meaning at all.

"Rose of Sharon indeed!" I said, turning to glance at Dr. Powys. "The Rose of Sharon, the lily of the valleys, is a young Jewish girl who sings one of Solomon's songs about the beauty of her boy friend and how he comes to her at night like a wild stag in the springtime, when the voice of the turtle-dove is heard in the land. And what do we find when we turn to the New Testament and take a cold, hard, objective look at its chapters? Can we say in all honesty that we find a greater poetry than we find in the Old Testament, that its religious ideas are more advanced than those of the earlier Hebrews?"

The rest of my speech developed, I suppose, what can be described as an invidious parody of Fosdick's book. I emphasized, no doubt exaggerated, those areas in which it seemed to me that the New Testament displays a degeneration of spiritual values. In the Old Testament, I said, we find a strong and healthy expression of man's obligation to society. To be sure, it is a small tribal society, ruthlessly ethnocentric. Nevertheless an admirable sense of social obligation is clearly present in its tribal ethics. Compare this with Christ's indifference to cooperative, politically constructive efforts. "Render unto Caesar the things that are

Caesar's." Can this advice be called anything except a plea for placid submission to every sort of political oppression?

Pre-Christian Hebrews, I continued, had a vivid concept of Utopia, of a New Jerusalem that could and would be built upon the earth. Compare this to Christ's wild, apocalyptic vision of how he would soon return to earth, accompanied by great thunder and lightning, to destroy the world and supervise a final judgment. Can anyone really believe that the book of Revelation, the last book of the Bible, is superior to the prophetic chapters of Daniel? Does not the New Testament "rose" finally unfold its petals to disclose at its center a nightmare vision of the future so eccentric that it has no religious relevance whatever?

Old Testament ethics, I insisted, places right and wrong on a solid pragmatic base. The good man is he who does good. The evil man is he who does evil. But in Pauline theology, the last stage of Biblical unfolding, we come straight up against the harsh declaration that "there is none righteous, no not one." Goodness is contingent *not* upon doing good but upon a mysterious transformation of the soul, a transformation that occurs if, and only if, one believes that Jesus is God. The older Hebraic view of salvation by works became in the fifth century the Pelagian heresy. Indeed, we can say that the only doctrine by which Christianity can be judged truly unique among the great religions of the world is just *this* view, this bizarre view that a mere act of faith, a single effort of will, suddenly and miraculously obtains forgiveness for one's sins and changes the sinner from a child of darkness to a child of light.

"Please do not suppose," I went on, tracing a large vertical circle in the air with the tip of my forefinger, "that this somersault of the soul is dependent on no more than a heartfelt rush of love for God. Perhaps it was so regarded by Jesus. But by the time of Paul a narrower, much uglier doctrine had unfolded. Conversion had become dependent on a set of beliefs about the nature of Christ and the meaning of his death. It certainly involved, for instance, a belief in the Resurrection. Paul is quite explicit on this point. 'If thou shalt confess with thy mouth the Lord Jesus,'" I said, quoting Romans 10:9, "'and shalt believe in thine heart that God hath raised him from the dead, thou shalt be saved.'"

I looked toward Peter, sitting in the back row of chairs. He was watching me with an odd smile. "'Neither is there salvation in any other,'" I continued, shifting to Acts 4:12, "'for there is none other name under heaven given among men, whereby we must be saved.'"

"Is this doctrine of salvation through faith in Christ, and *only* through faith in Christ, broader or narrower," I asked, "than the earlier Jewish doctrine of simple love toward God and man, a doctrine which the Lord himself told us was a summary of the entire Law and Prophets?"

From these thoughts I plunged directly into a discourse on the New Testament doctrine of hell. "It's really astonishing," I said, "how smoothly the Reverend Mr. Fosdick, in his famous guide to the Bible, slides over this scandal in Christ's teaching. He admits that Jesus didn't oppose the current Jewish belief in eternal punishment for the wicked, but he argues that Jesus did not stress the doctrine. Nothing could be further from the truth. Jesus stressed it as much as he stressed any aspect of his teaching, and he did so with his usual picturesque imagery. He described the rich man in hell calling from the flames to Abraham, begging him to ease his torment by sending the righteous beggar Lazarus to cool his tongue with a finger dipped in water. He bitterly upbraided the great cities of Israel—Chorazin, Bethsaida, Capernaum—because they had not responded to his preaching. He spoke opaquely of a sin that would not be pardoned in this world or the world to come, and he prophesied that those three wicked cities would go down to hell with a fate worse than that which befell ancient Sodom."

"In his Sermon on the Mount Jesus said that if your hand or eye offends you, cut if off or pluck it out. Better to go through life maimed or half-blind than to suffer with your whole body in everlasting fire. The doctrine of eternal punishment is implicit even in that most quoted of all New Testament verses, John 3:16, 'For God so loved the world, that he gave his only begotten Son, that whosoever believeth in him should not *perish*, but have everlasting life.'"

Peter had stopped smiling. I could see him at the back of the room, nodding grimly.

I lowered my voice to a more conversational tone. "Let's reflect a moment about this doctrine of eternal punishment. Is it really an improvement, an unfolding of the rose of spiritual truth, when compared to the religious beliefs of the ancient Jews? Does it really suggest a transmogrification of the old Yahweh into a God of mercy? Old Testament scholars tell us that the early Jews did not believe in soul survival at all or else they believed in Sheol, a vague, shadowy place not unlike the Greek hades to which all men, good and bad alike, would go. Are we not justified in saying that either of these views is more merciful than the belief that God will punish some poor creations of his forever? In the mind of Christ, apparently, only the wicked deserve such fate. But in the letters of Saint Paul it is not the wicked but every person who does not believe in Christ, in a *risen* Christ, who loses his soul for eternity!"

I took a sheet of paper from my inside jacket pocket and read from it an epitaph by the Scottish poet George Macdonald:

> *Here lie I, Martin Elginbrodde;*
> *Hae mercy o' my soul, Lord God,*
> *As I wad do were I Lord God,*
> *And ye were Martin Elginbrodde.*

"In those four whimsical lines," I said, "It seems to me that we have a final, crushing answer to the doctrine of hell. Surely we must think of God as having qualities of mercy that are higher, not lower, than our own. Even the stern Allah of the Moslems gives a second chance to sinners in hell if they beg sincerely for forgiveness. But the God of Paul offers *no* second chance. It is no good trying to hide the cruelty of hell behind the phrase 'God's justice.' What kind of justice is it which is less admirable than our own? In Plato's *Republic,* Socrates criticizes Homer for portraying the gods as having the baser emotions of mankind. Does not Socrates' indictment apply even more strongly to the God of the New Testament? Is he really an improvement over the God of Moses?"

"I don't know," I said, stealing a glance at the gold watch in my vest, "whether anybody reads James Fenimore Cooper any more these days. I remember that as a boy, when I first read *The Deerslayer* for a high school class, there was a scene in the novel that made a strong impression on me. It may have had a lot to do with the direction my thinking took later when I was a young theological student here at Meadville. One of the characters in *The Deerslayer* is a pious girl named Hetty. She tries to convert an Indian to Christianity by showing him the Bible and telling him that every chapter in it comes straight from the throne of God. I've never forgotten the simple question the Indian asked. I think it says all that need be said about the notion that the Bible is a unified, unique repository of spiritual truth."

I paused a moment to build suspense. Then I said: "The Indian asked— and I quote exactly—'Why Great Spirit no send book to Injin, too?'"

The students applauded enthusiastically when I sat down. Professor von Cloven clapped listlessly, his round face enigmatic. The Reverend Powys scowled while he tapped his manicured and bejeweled fingers together lightly at their tips. Peter, his blue eyes smoky with meditation, took no part in the brief question-and-answer period that followed (brief, I suspect, because most of my listeners were too stunned to think of anything to ask). He stayed until almost everyone had left.

"Well, Peter," I said, buckling my briefcase, "where were your sympathies?"

"With you and von Cloven," he replied without hesitation. "If his approach or something close to it isn't right, then I think yours is."

We had some coffee and sweet rolls at a restaurant on Fifty-seventh Street. I was careful not to bring up any of the topics I had spoken about. Peter, too, avoided them. It was not the time to push or prod. It was a time to wait. In my living room a few weeks later, when Peter made a weak attempt to defend his tottering orthodoxy, I fired my heavy guns again.

Peter had just finished telling me that he had been talking with one of the younger priests at the Church of Saint Thomas, and the priest had assured him that no modern Catholic believes any more that all non-Catholics are destined for eternal damnation.

"Hallelujah!" I exclaimed. "Yes, the population of Dante's inferno has been steadily declining ever since he wrote about it. And Catholic obstetricians no longer keep at hand those long syringes they once used for baptizing infants who might die in the womb. But *some* sinners still arrive in hell, don't they?"

"Only those who consciously and wilfully turn against God."

"Does anybody do that? And even if they did, should they suffer forever? Wouldn't it be kinder just to let their wretched souls fade out of existence?"

"But," Peter countered, "we shouldn't think of hell as duration in time. Heaven and hell are part of eternity. How can we know now what eternity means? Hell is just a crude symbol for something outside of space and time, something we can't understand."

"I know exactly what you mean," I said. "It's the last defense. But even if the true nature of hell is beyond our comprehension, that doesn't make the idea less offensive. Isn't it easier, more respectful to God in fact, to assume the concept developed because it gave believers an outlet for their unconscious feelings of revenge and self-righteousness? Do you know what Saint Thomas Aquinas wrote about the suffering of the lost?"

He shook his head.

I got up and took a book down from a shelf. After locating the passage I had in mind, I read aloud: "In order that nothing be wanting to the happiness of the blessed in Heaven, a perfect view is granted them of the tortures of the damned."

Peter, his face coloring, tightened his lips and did not reply. We shifted to other topics. It was two in the morning (my wife had long since gone to bed), and both of us were getting sleepy. Again and again

Peter came back to the notion of the finite symbol that points to a transcendent, inconceivable truth. Satan, for instance. Obviously he is not a personality like Milton's admirable angel or Dante's three-headed monster. Nevertheless, Peter argued, isn't something valuable lost when the concept of the Devil is dropped altogether?

"The Devil symbol puts evil outside of God," he said, "but lower and less powerful. It treats evil as something real, something that has to be fought and conquered. That's why Chesterton, in *The Man Who Was Thursday*, picked for his Satan symbol the only true anarchist in the story. He was the man who really wanted to blow up the world."

Peter tried the same approach with Original Sin. He was willing to admit there had been no actual Garden of Eden, with its strange trees and thornless roses and persuasive serpent. Still, there must be a profound truth of some sort lurking behind the myth of the Fall, though he wasn't sure exactly what it was.

"How can you be saved unless you're saved *from* something?" he asked.

"Look, my dear boy," I said (it is the only time I can recall when I almost lost my temper with him), "why don't you stop fooling yourself? Blood sacrifices and atonements have long, long histories. They go back far beyond the death of Christ. You can read all about them in James Frazer's *Golden Bough*. The atonement myth keeps popping up in so many forms, in so many cultures, precisely because it expresses so poignantly man's feeling of loneliness, his sense of guilt, his hunger for the love and protection of a supreme Father. The myth, to be sure, is beautiful. It's profound. Don't cheapen it by believing that it's true. The story of Leda and the swan is a charming Greek fable unless you think it really happened. Oz is a delightful place in a child's imagination unless he begins to think Oz actually exists. The Virgin Birth and the Resurrection are marvelous fairy tales. Let's keep them that. Let's not degrade God to the level of a magician who made a miraculous entrance on the stage of history two thousand years ago, disguised as a Jewish prophet and faith-healer, to perform a carnival trick of dying for the sins of humanity, then sprang back to life again, like Houdini escaping from a locked trunk, and finally left the scene by floating up into the clouds."

Peter was looking at me strangely. "I thought you didn't believe in God."

"I don't. But if I did, I'd try to believe in a more dignified deity than one who went about engaging in such drolleries."

"The Crucifixion isn't droll."

"No. Did you ever think, though, how droll the Virgin Birth would have been if only it were true? Poor old Joseph the carpenter, building a house and trying to make up his mind whether his pregnant young wife is telling him the truth about Gabriel and the Holy Ghost! No wonder the Gospels tell us so little about him."

A year ago I would not have dared to talk this way to Peter. It would only have made him angry.

It is best not to spend more time on Peter's short-lived interest in Catholicism. Let me say merely that he did not find in Rome the authority he was seeking. He spoke sadly one evening about the church's evasion of the higher criticism. Catholic Modernism had been quickly liquidated by the famous 1907 *Pascendi Dominici Gregis* encyclical of Pope Pius X which branded it a "synthesis of all heresies." Rome had met the challenge of the modernists, not by answering them but by excommunicating them. Even the implications of evolution, Peter concluded, were still so carefully avoided that it was difficult to find a Catholic textbook on biology that dealt forthrightly with the topic.

"How many times," Peter later remarked, "did I sit in church with Angelina, trying to feel in my bones the miracle of the Mass, trying to believe that the wafer and the wine were really turning into the body and blood of the Lord!"

He couldn't do it. As a Protestant he had been taught that the Atonement had taken place once and for all on the hill of Calvary. It was impossible for him to suppose that amid the chanting and the incense and the slow ballet of the priest and his acolytes it was occurring again, in a mysterious, unbloody fashion, before his very eyes.

As for Gilbert Chesterton, Peter's attitude toward him eventually settled into a double one. He was disappointed by Chesterton's ridicule of evolution in *Everlasting Man,* the antisemitism that occasionally surfaced in his books, and his early, naive admiration for Italian fascism. But he never stopped reading and rereading him, especially his fiction and his poetry, and his writings on topics not peculiar to Catholicism. To this day he continues to admire him.

And for the Roman Church he always retained the same double attitude he had for Chesterton. He could say of both what Robert Browning said about the Catholic Church in his poem *Christmas Eve:*

> *I see the error; but above*
> *The scope of error, see the love.*

It is a feeling I cannot share. Where Peter finds an inner core of truth, I find only superstition. H. G. Wells, in *Mr. Blettsworthy of Rampole*

Island, hit on the perfect metaphor. The Roman Church is like a pre-historic megatherium, a grotesque, gigantic sloth that somehow managed to survive extinction. It crawls clumsily around the world, getting in eveybody's way, refusing stubbornly to die.

10

Karl Barth

Dr. Heinrich von Cloven's address on the Bible, which I summarized so briefly in the preceding chapter, made a stronger impression on Peter than I had realized at the time. As I look back on it now, this is not hard to understand.

Peter had abandoned fundamentalism, but he had not abandoned orthodoxy. Jesus was still for him the Son of God in a way that had no parallel with Moses, Mohammed, or the Buddha. For a short time he had turned to Catholicism, hoping to find a more intellectually respectable support for the Incarnation. It, too, had failed him. He found the Roman Church to be little more than a gaudy, pretentious variety of fundamentalism. It asked him to accept doctrines—the Immaculate Conception for example—which seemed to him even more preposterous than doctrines such as the Virgin Birth which he already had abandoned. Now, as the waves of doubt rolled higher, Karl Barth extended a hand. Poor sinking Peter did not hesitate to grasp it.

The reader may find it strange, if he knows anything at all about the theology of Barth, that a point of view so out of step with the great secular surge of western Protestantism could interest *any* United States seminarian. I suspect, however, there were many young men in America, with backgrounds similar to Peter's, who discovered Barth at about this time and found him speaking to them in words that thundered with authority.

Consider the writer John Updike. Who would guess that *he* had a Barthian past? Yet I was surprised to read, in Updike's introduction to a collection of his essays, the casual remark that there had been a period in his youth when the only thing that sustained him was the Barthian theology. These young men to whom Barth spoke were searching desperately for a way to save the foundation doctrines of their faith. They saw the church rolling down the grassy slope to humanism and, like a dropped ball of yarn, the farther it rolled the smaller it became. It seemed a clearcut either/or. Either a turn in the direction proposed by Barth or an honest abandonment of traditional Christianity.

Barth saw the rolling ball of yarn and put out his foot to stop it. It struck his toe, bounced over it, and continued rolling. At the time of the symposium described in the previous chapter, von Cloven was the only faculty member of the four federated seminaries who was in sympathy with Barth. Even he was critical of many aspects of the Barthian theology. A few of von Cloven's students developed a mild interest in Barthianism, but by and large the university's religious community dismissed the movement with a shrug. It was a German "failure of nerve," a product of the disillusionment and economic chaos that followed Germany's defeat in the first World War. Liberal theology, with its bland faith in science and progress, had suddenly seemed superficial and hollow. What could be more natural than that German Protestant leaders would cast a nostalgic backward look at the old grim doctrines.

Here and there in American liberal seminaries the Barthian rhetoric found an echo, but among the great mass of ordinary churchgoers Barth had no influence whatever. Occasionally they might see his photograph in *Time*, but that was only because Henry Luce, a devout Presbyterian, was one of Barth's great admirers. In March, 1962, when Barth made his first and only visit to the States, his face even made *Time's* cover. His oldest son, Markus, was then a professor of New Testament in the University of Chicago Divinity School. None of us on the faculty hesitated to speak of Karl Barth as the most distinguished living Protestant theologian. Yet one could count on the fingers of one hand the theologians in the States who were willing to call themselves Barthians.

Although I never was in sympathy with any of Barth's religious views, I am convinced that his theology offers the last and only hope for Protestant orthodoxy. So it seemed to Peter then. So it seems to both of us today. In any case, my history of Peter would be incomplete if I did not try to sketch as sympathetic a picture as I can of what Barth had to say. It is not an easy task. My own humanist stand was regarded by Barth as the ultimate in religious pride. (There is a curt footnote in one of the later volumes of his *Dogmatics* in which he dismisses all my books as the irrelevant scribblings of a Yankee journalist.) Yet attempt it I must. If the reader finds it boring, he can skim what follows, perhaps skip it altogether. In a later chapter I shall return to Barth in a more critical mood.

Karl Barth (pronounced "Bart") was born at Basel, Switzerland, in 1886. After studying theology at several German universities he became the pastor, in 1911, of a small German Reformed Church in the Swiss village of Safenwil. His views were liberal. It was not until after the war that he began to realize, to his great embarrassment, that as a liberal he really had nothing at all to say. He spoke of the "grotesque situation" that confronts every minister when he enters his pulpit on Sunday morning:

> When they come to us for help they do not really want to learn more about living: they want to learn more about what is on the farther edge of living—God. We cut a ridiculous figure as village sages—or city sages. As such we are socially superfluous. . . . Why do they come to us, when they must long since have made the discovery that they cannot expect the same service from us as they do from an attorney or a dentist, for instance, and that if the truth must be told we can answer their questions no better than they themselves?

Then something happened to Barth that rotated his orientation by 180 degrees. In 1919, in the aftermath of the first World War, he published his first important book, Der Römerbrief, a commentary on Paul's Epistle to the Romans. Its full impact on German theology was felt in 1921 when it was reprinted in a greatly revised and enlarged edition. Barth later described the book's effect in the following fable. A man climbs the tower of a church at night. Reaching out for support, his hand grabs a bell rope and the resulting clang awakes everyone in the village. Written with a strange blend of Platonic and Kantian terms, and a heavy borrowing from Kierkegaard and Dostoevsky, the book was less a scholar's commentary than a series of impassioned sermons. Barth spoke as one who had just discovered in Paul's letter an explosive, incredible secret.

The secret? It is simply to take the Bible seriously and recognize its God as God. He is not a projection of human hopes and fears. He is not another name for the universe but the creator of the universe. In Rudolf Otto's famous phrase he is the totaliter aliter, the Wholly Other, separated from the world by an infinite gulf. Barth's entire theology, Paul Tillich once wrote, is contained in the first of the Ten Commandments.

In the blinding light of God's transcendence, how can the poor faltering minister speak to his congregation about ultimate questions? It was not, Barth said, that he had found in Paul's letter a way out of this predicament. "Exactly," he said, "not that." To understand the predicament itself was the core of his message, his "corrective," as he called it, his "marginal note" to twentieth-century theology. To ministers already aware of their predicament, of their obligation combined with their inability, to speak about God, Barth said: "I have really nothing essential to say. You are already introduced to 'my theology.' "

Barth's influence on Continental theology grew rapidly during the next ten years. His voice, especially in its written form, seemed the voice of a new prophet calling Christianity back to the forgotten theology of Luther and Calvin. In 1933 he was suspended from Bonn University for his opposition to Nazi controls over German churches. Two years later he became an exile, settling in Basel, the city of his birth.

From 1932 onward Barth's chief task was the writing (in ironic contrast to his early "marginal note") of his *Kirchliche Dogmatik* (Church Dogmatics). It is a sort of Protestant *Summa Theologica*, a vast, erudite elaboration of what Barth regards as the basic ingredients of Revelation. He was able to complete twelve enormous volumes before his death in 1968. It has been called (though not by me) the greatest work of its kind since Calvin's *Institutes*.

Six years before Barth died, when he lectured at Chicago's divinity school and received an honorary doctorate, I sat in the audience and listened with admiration and dismay. He was then 76, a tall man in a rumpled suit, with scraggly gray hair and bushy black eyebrows. His pale blue eyes squinted at his audience through spectacles slightly askew. He mispronounced so many of the English words in his prepared address that it was difficult to understand him.

The Barthian movement has been called by many names: the Swiss school, dialectical theology, crisis theology, neo-orthodoxy, neo-Lutheranism, neo-Calvinism, neo-Reformationism. I prefer to call it (following H. J. Paton in his book, *The Modern Predicament*), "theological positivism." Like the logical positivists of the Vienna Circle, Barth and his friends were uncompromising foes of metaphysics. Barth early recognized his affinity with positivism by siding with Ludwig Feuerbach, the great German materialist, in regarding all natural theologies (whether based on reason or emotion) as no more than fantasies born of human desires. Barth was as ruthless as Rudolf Carnap in dismissing all the great metaphysical systems of the past as poetry and nonsense. It is through Revelation and Revelation only, he insisted, that we can go beyond the knowledge of science and mathematics.

Barth's early theology was dialectic in a way closer to the principle of complementarity in quantum physics than to the dialectic of Hegel and other philosophers. Contradictions of thesis and antithesis come together in a higher synthesis only on God's side of the infinite gulf. On our side there is no resolution. There is only the dialectical tension, the shuttling back and forth between "yes" and "no." Is my will truly free or is my future known to God? I must affirm both and learn to live with this unavoidable paradox, as with all the other paradoxes that arise when we try to comprehend the incomprehensible.

God himself must be viewed in a paradoxical double way. The liberal theologians of the nineteenth century stressed his immanence, his dwelling in the world and in our hearts. Now it was time, said Barth in his younger days, to "reinstate the distance" between God and man. (In his later years Barth wrote much about God's humanity to "correct" his earlier emphasis on God's transcendence.) We must tremble and stammer when we talk of God, as little Franz Kafka trembled and stammered in the presence of his awesome human father. To be sure, the demands of our spirit make it necessary for us to think of God as a "person," but we must never forget how feeble this symbol is. The deeper question is whether *we* are persons. *"Cogitor, ergo sum,"* Barth wrote. "I am thought about, therefore I am."

The reader with some knowledge of the history of theology may recognize this way of talking about God as a modern formulation of what once was called the *via negativa*. We cannot say what God is. We can only say what he is not. It is a "no" that was first expressed in the *Parmenides* of Plato, and echoed by almost every theist since whose God is more than nature. It is certainly present in the theology of Thomas Aquinas who pointed out (as others did before him) that we do not even know what "existence" means when we ascribe the property to God.

Much has been written about Barth's early fondness for a passage in which Kierkegaard speaks of "the endless yawning qualitative difference" between our world of time and the eternal world of God. The Barthian God, like the God of Plato, Augustine, Aquinas, and Kant, is outside of time. "The ribbon of time," wrote Barth, "which to our eyes is unwound endlessly, is in God's view rolled up into a ball, a thousand years as a day. *Together* he calls Abraham and us and our children's children." From the standpoint of eternity the Kingdom of God is identical with the Paradise man lost and the Paradise to be ushered in by the Parousia or Second Coming. It is here *now* in the sense that it lies above, below, behind the world we know. It is the Omega point of Teilhard de Chardin, the day of judgment when, in what Paul called the "twinkling of an eye," history crashes into the nonhistorical, timeless *other* world.

Karl Heim, whose views were close to Barth's in many respects, liked to dramatize God's transcendence with a geometrical metaphor. God's world is to ours as a space of four dimensions is to our space of three. "He thought," wrote Thomas Wolfe, "that he could twist his hand a certain way, or turn his wrist, or make a certain simple movement of rotation into space . . . and that by making this rotation with his hand, he would find the lost dimension of that secret world, and instantly step through the door that he had opened." Wolfe was writing about his youth in New York, his search for a door to Paradise. I remember Peter telling me one day that he had discovered the key to what Wolfe called his "unutterable loneliness"—in today's fashionable jargon, his "sense of estrangement." He had found it, he said, in a marvelous commentary on Wolfe's novels. The "commentary" was Barth's sermon, "Paradise Lost," in a collection translated under the title, *God's Search for Man*.

"God's search for man." The phrase goes to the heart of Barthianism. There *is* no way that man by his own efforts can find a path to God. (This is the issue on which Barth and Emil Brunner clashed so bitterly, attacking each other in what seemed to English and American spectators such an un-Christian spirit.) The God who stood at the end of some human way, declared Barth, would not be God. He is not to be found in a sunset, a starry sky, the music of Mozart (which Barth loved passionately), or even in the voice of conscience. Kant was right in saying that there is no proof of God by pure reason. He was wrong in thinking God could be proved by practical reason. The gods of the philosophers, of primitive cultures, of all non-Christian religions are not the God of the Bible. They are idols to be studied by psychologists and anthropologists.

"No man," said Christ, in a statement Barth liked to quote, "cometh unto the Father but by me." The infinite, yawning gulf between time and eternity is crossed only by the action of the God of Moses who revealed himself to us through Jesus Christ. We may stretch our arms upward toward God, but the contact is made only when God reaches down.

And until this contact is made, every person remains "lost," outside of Paradise, estranged from God. This is the meaning of the Fall, of Original Sin. We are separated from God's Kingdom, trapped in a world of time in which we find ourselves moving inexorably toward our death. There is a curse upon mankind. It is the white whale of Melville, the unseen courts of Kafka's *Trial*, the fatal illness on *The Magic Mountain*.

And as long as we are under this curse we have within ourselves an uncontrollable propensity for malevolence. The myth of Satan's rebellion tells us that sin is somehow, exactly how we cannot know, bound up with the freedom which God has given to those whom he has created in his own image. Sin is a demonic misuse of will. It is not ignorance as Socrates taught. It is not bad conditioning as Rousseau and B. F. Skinner have assured us. It is not a genetic defect of our animal heritage. It is a flaw of the soul, a weakness of the highest component of our nature.

When a person becomes aware that he is lost, aware of his sin, aware of his separation from God and the inevitability of his death, he has reached the Barthian state of "crisis." It is the moment at which he can either throw himself upon the mercy of God or resign himself as courageously as he can to what he believes to be a Godless cosmos from which he soon will disappear. The choice that he makes is his response to what Barth calls the Word of God, for it is precisely at this critical hour that God speaks and offers the gift of faith.

And what is the Word of God? It is any means whatever by which God chooses to speak to man. The Bible is the supreme instance because it is the record of God's plan of salvation through the appearance in history of himself. Not that every word of the Bible is of sacred origin— the Bible for Barth was not what he called a "paper Pope"—but the "word behind the words" comes straight from God. In addition to the Bible, God also speaks through the creeds of the churches, the sermons of ministers, the writings of theologians, or through any other means that convey the Word at a given time and place. "God can speak," Barth once wrote, "through Russian Communism, through a flute concert, or a blossoming branch, or a dead dog."

A nagging question arises. How does one know when it is really God who speaks? How does one know that the Bible does in truth contain the Word of God?

The startling answer is that one cannot know in the way that he knows the truth of a mathematical theorem or the probable truth of a scientific statement. He knows in a more direct way, a way analogous to what philosophers have called knowledge by direct acquaintance. A man who sees the sun cannot doubt that the sun exists. The believer, confronted by a transcendent "object," God, is unable *not* to believe. The object is simply *there.* Proofs become irrelevant and absurd. It is foolish for the man of faith to try to convince a doubter by *any* sort of argument. He can only proclaim the Word of God and hope that the doubter hears it. In his *Dogmatics* Barth puts it this way:

> This is a conviction which needs no proof, a knowledge which has its ratio in itself, an experience which derives from revelation and from nowhere else. . . . The Bible is known as God's word because it is God's word. If one tries another proof, one will prove something else. . . . It is

a circle into which one cannot come from without and out of which one cannot go from within. One can only be either within or without. There is no neutral position, in which one might think over the possibilities of being within or without and arrive at the appropriate conclusion.

The justification of faith, for Barth, is unabashedly circular. "In thy light shall we see light" (Psalm 36:9). Revelation is self-authenticating. God proves himself. He calls to us from outside. Within us he hears and answers. Transcendence is apprehended by the transcendent eyeballs of our soul. God fills the hollow he himself has placed inside our hearts.

11

Situation Ethics

It is not surprising that Barth's stern, uncompromising views, which I summarized uncritically in the previous chapter, would have a strong appeal for Peter at a time when he was searching for a new and firmer ground for his beliefs. Barth was not a fundamentalist. He had no quarrel with modern science or the results of Biblical criticism. He cared not a rap for the latest theories of evolution or cosmology, or whether a new scroll from the Dead Sea might contradict something in the Gospels. The higher criticism was a controversy over and done with, to be accepted and put behind.

On the other hand, neither was Barth a liberal. His theology did not abandon or explain away the central dogmas of the Reformation. Brunner, the second most influential figure in the German neo-orthodox camp, once described precisely the two roads which he and Barth and their friends were careful to avoid. Fundamentalism, he said, is the "petrifaction" of Christianity. Liberalism is its "dissolution."

Peter had, of course, heard of Barth before Professor von Cloven's speech aroused his interest, but he had postponed reading Barth while he was occupied with Angelina and Chesterton and playing the Catholic language game. Now the Barthian promise of a new Protestant awakening, without doing violence to the old doctrines, rekindled the smoldering embers of Peter's "life plan." Once more he began to see himself as someone who might play a role in this revival. With characteristic energy he began to read all the books by Barth that he could find in English. Where translations were not available he even struggled with the original German, a language he was studying at the time. After Barth he turned to Brunner, reading, rereading, trying his best to fathom exactly where the two giants agreed and disagreed.

He tried also to read Paul Tillich and Rudolf Bultmann—this was before anyone had heard of Dietrich Bonhoeffer—but he soon decided that both men were too far outside of orthodoxy to have anything important to say to him. Tillich then had only a small following among American seminarians. Many years would pass before he would complete his three-volume *Systematic Theology*, edge out Reinhold Niebuhr as the best known American theologian, and appear on the March 16, 1959, cover of *Time*. He was teaching at the University of Chicago Divinity School when he died at Billings Hospital in 1965.

Peter agreed with Barth (and me) in finding Tillich's system "ultimately uninteresting" and his God a "frigid monstrosity." Tillich was a Christian only in the vaguest, mushiest sense. He wrote that the Protestant Principle—the only respect in which Protestant Christianity is superior to other religions—is that it possesses the Cross symbol. Tillich takes this to mean that no symbol (except perhaps the Cross?) is completely true. When Christ in his moment of final agony cried, "My God, my God, why hast thou forsaken me?" he was, Tillich assures us, recognizing at long last that the God to whom he had been praying all his life was not really God at all. He was just another idol, a partial symbol of the "God behind God" or Being-itself. How pleasant to learn, Peter once said with heavy sarcasm, that before Jesus died he finally achieved an insight into Tillichian theology!

The plain fact is that Tillich was a secular philosopher in the pantheistic tradition. If his brand of idealism, deriving from Friedrich Schelling, appeals to you, you may find what he has to say (if you can understand it!) significant. As for his relevance to the future of Protestantism, Peter could see nothing of enough value to justify the labor of mastering the complex pseudo-Christian terminology and translating the foggy sentences into plain English. Tillich's "ultimate ground of being," his "God behind the god of theism," turns out finally to be nothing more than the old Hegelian Absolute, not *a* being but Being-itself, devoid of personality and related to the historical Jesus in a way that no minister could ever make clear to the ordinary mortals in his congregation.

Since even a humanist believes the world exists, he too believes in Tillich's God. He becomes a theist by a Tillichian trick of definition. Shall I prove to you that all women have beautiful figures? It is easy. In my language system I declare that all shapes possess beauty. Since every woman has a shape, she has, by definition, a beautiful shape. Shall I prove to you that all visible objects are green? It is easy. I define "green" as the property of reflecting light. All visible objects reflect light, therefore all visible objects are green. For the impregnability of such assertions, however, I must pay a heavy price. Not only have my statements become vacuous, but because my language departs so widely from common speech my assertions are sure to cause more confusion than enlightenment. Of course I then can have the pleasure of explaining to my critics how they misinterpret me.

Arguing with Tillich, Sidney Hook once declared, is like "punching an eiderdown or fencing with a ghost." Whenever Hook, an honest atheist, tried to disagree with him, Tillich would reply with complete sincerity, "I agree with everything you have said." And when Pope Pius XII announced that Mary's bodily ascension into Heaven was true doctrine, Tillich said he saw no difficulty in accepting this because all doctrines of Christianity are, after all, just symbols. Terms like "grace" and "Will of God," Updike once wrote (reviewing one of Tillich's books), "walk through [his] pages as bloodless ghosts, transparent against the milky background of 'beyond' and 'being' that Tillich, God forbid, would confuse with the Christian faith."

For the most devastating criticism of Tillich on this score let me recommend Paul Edwards' article, "Professor Tillich's Confusions," in *Mind*, April, 1965, pages 192-214, and the section on Tillich in Edwards' marvelous discussion of "Atheism" in *The Encyclopedia of Philosophy*. Edwards' thesis is that Tillich's theology is safe from all attacks because it is "compatible with anything whatsoever" and therefore little more than a collection of empty tautologies expressed in pompous phrases. Tillich's description of faith as an awareness of the "depth" of existence turns out to be compounded of such insights as that there is more to Being than what we experience, that only the ultimate is ultimate, and that Being embraces non-Being. This last notion, so puzzling to the uninitiated, simply means that to describe the structure of a doughnut you must also describe its hole.

"Tillich is like the peace of God," Peter said one day in exasperation after reading one of Tillich's sermons. "He passeth all understanding." My own favorite application of a Biblical passage to Tillich is I Corinthians, Chapter 14, verses 8 and 9, where Paul points out how unedifying it is to speak the unknown tongue: "For if the trumpet give an uncertain sound, who shall prepare himself to the battle? So likewise ye, except ye utter by the tongue words easy to be understood, how shall it be known what is spoken? for ye shall speak into the air."

Reinhold Niebuhr had yet to make his mark as a serious theologian, with his *Nature and Destiny of Man*, and although Peter knew about him he did not read him carefully until after the war. Bultmann, however, captured his interest for a time because, unlike Tillich, he seemed at first to be a genuine Barthian. He had the same dialectical approach, the same double vision of a transcendent-immanent God, the same conviction of the uniqueness of God's revelation in Jesus Christ. But when Peter finally grasped the full import of Bultmann's program of demythologizing, it struck him, as it did me, as a colossal joke which Bultmann had played unwittingly and humorlessly on neo-orthodoxy. He had set out along the Barthian highway and then, in his compulsion to be as scientific and secular as possible, had simply followed Tillich and the nineteenth-century liberals in purging Protestant orthodoxy of all those alleged historical events that provide its necessary support.

In an earlier chapter I told about an Oklahoma farmer with fading eyesight who imagined he could still see in the distance the oil derrick that actually had collapsed and killed Peter's father. Bultmann can be likened to a man in charge of a wrecking crew. Quietly, in the middle of the night, he and his men demolish an entire oil derrick and all its drilling equipment. Beam by beam, piece by piece, they load it on trucks and cart it off to the junkyard. Next morning Bultmann returns. The drilling crew and a crowd of curious spectators have gathered at the spot to find out what has happened. Bultmann mounts the bare wooden platform.

"Dear brothers and sisters," he begins, "I see by your faces that you are astonished and perplexed. What on earth has happened, you ask yourselves, to the derrick? Let me assure you, nothing *authentic* has been removed. The real derrick, the transcendent, spiritual derrick is still here. It is true that you cannot see it with your eyes or feel it with your hands, but to the eyes and hands of faith it is grander, more beautiful, more incorruptible than ever before. We have purged it of its gross, material substance. See how it points upward like a church spire toward the eternal? Back to the rig, my faithful roughnecks! Let the drilling for God's oil go on!"

So great is Bultmann's eloquence that a few drillers actually climb up on the floor and make a feeble effort to continue their work. Unfortunately, they find it difficult to operate with an invisible engine and invisible tools. Eventually they become disillusioned and leave. Is not this precisely what is now happening to Protestant theology in the liberal seminaries? The road from Barth and Bultmann is a road that continues on (with little side detours by way of Niebuhr and others) to Tillich and Bonhoeffer, then inexorably into the camps of those theologians who are not ashamed to proclaim that God is dead.

Peter did not smoke or drink during his first two years at Chicago. In his third year, when he began to play the Barthian language game, these and other restraints began to loosen.

One of the ways that Protestant neo-orthodoxy has adjusted to modern secularism is by accepting the humanist view that moral laws constantly change to meet new cultural conditions. To be sure, the Bible tells us to love God and man, perhaps even provides a few broad ethical commands. Alas, it fails to spell out in detail how to go about the practical tasks of loving God and man. From a Barthian point of view it is blasphemy to identify the Wholly-Other with any man-made set of moral rules. Christ's commands are transcendent. They apply only to the Kingdom of God, to a Paradise in which no concession is made to sin. Be ye perfect, resist not evil, take no thought for the morrow, turn the other cheek. . . . The Sermon on the Mount preaches a love too absolute to be achievable on earth. It provides no clues for solving the peculiar, pressing problems of everyday life and politics.

To all such moral questions, Barth once declared, Jesus has only one answer: "What interest have I in your practical life? Follow *me*." Barth has no quarrel with the cultural anthropologists, forever reminding us that mores vary from one culture to another and alter with time. The believing Christian may have an inner love for God and man, but on all moral and political issues his approach must be relative, tentative, pragmatic. He can never be certain that his decisions reflect God's will. That is a knowledge God alone possesses. The most he can do is bring to bear on such questions all the knowledge and intelligence and love that he can. There is a sense in which he is beyond good and evil as defined by the standards of his culture.

Does this mean that a Barthian is a cultural relativist unwilling to make value judgments? Far from it! Barth did not hesitate to condemn the moral values of Nazi Germany. He did not hesitate to condemn the moral values behind the iron curtain or the values he saw flourishing behind what he once called the "gold curtain" of the United States. But he did not pretend to have found those condemnations in the Scriptures.

Let me be more explicit. We do indeed learn from the Bible, say the Barthians, that we must love all men including our enemies. But this absolute command does not help us decide if a given war is just or whether capital punishment is desirable or what our foreign policy should be or whether abortion should be legal or what the answer is to a thousand other questions that must be answered. Christ did indeed tell us to consider the birds of the air and the lilies of the field and like them to take no thought for tomorrow. But this impossible ideal does not and should not inhibit any person, group or nation from planning for the future. It does not tell us that insuring cars and houses and lives is the work of Satan, or that a man is a fool to put money aside for old age or for the education of his children. It does not tell him when to marry or when to divorce or how many children to have or where to go on next year's vacation.

The truth is that the Scriptures contain no blueprints for individual or national conduct. On all such matters they are, said Barth, "strangely silent." The Bible, he declared, has a way of saying, "My dear sir, those are *your* problems. You must not ask *me!*" Perhaps I put it extremely. Brunner, I recall, argued that there are "creative ordinances" such as the family and the state which rest on Biblical foundations and provide a society with necessary Christian norms. But Peter, reacting no doubt to his Puritanical adolescence, leaped quickly to the more extreme position. Barth convinced him that in a sense there *is* no morality in the Bible. There is only that blinding vision of the "other, new, greater world" in which we are commanded to love God and man. "Love," said Saint Augustine, "and do what you will."

As usual, modern Protestant theologians are fond of dignifying their belated insights by giving them new technical names. The pragmatic, relativistic approach to ethics, so old and commonplace in secular philosophy, is now called "situation ethics" in the seminaries. In this country its leading proponents were Tillich and Richard Niebuhr; on the Continent, those four great B's—Barth, Brunner, Bultmann, and Bonhoeffer. Only *love* is absolute and intrinsically good. On the level of everyday affairs there are no binding rules. The Christian's way of expressing love is subject to endless variations depending on the context. You can read all about this in a paperback book, *Situation Ethics*, written by Episcopalian Joseph Fletcher and published in 1966. One quotation will be enough to convey the book's profundity: "Is adultery wrong?. . . . One can only respond, 'I don't know. Maybe. Give me a case. Describe a real situation.'"

Peter began to experiment hesitantly and in little ways with situation ethics. One evening when he and I were discussing something in my sitting room he took a package of cigarettes from his shirt pocket. Astonished, I flicked my lighter and held the flame toward him just as my wife walked into the room.

"Good heavens!" Edna shouted, staggering and pretending she was about to faint. "When did you start the filthy habit?"

Peter tried to conceal his discomfort, but his face was flushed and he held the cigarette clumsily. "A few days ago," he said. He took small puffs, blowing out the smoke without inhaling.

A week later, at a social gathering of the New Testament Club, he accepted a martini.

Did Peter, under the influence of his new moral freedom, calmly decide that there would be no "sin" in sexual play under circumstances that had not the remotest connection with love or marriage? Or was it that his long repressed sex drives, no longer held in tow by the ethics of fundamentalism, were propelling him into experiences for which situation ethics provided a convenient rationalization?

12

Room X

As I assemble my notes for this chapter I find a recent clipping, from the *Chicago Tribune*, about an interview with the dean of one of the best known eastern colleges for girls. No longer, says the dean, does the school automatically expel a girl if she is caught with a boy in her dormitory bed. "Our practice," the dean explains, "is to study carefully the couple's *motivation* [my italics]." If they are in love, if they have been going together for a while and their relationship is "meaningful," the episode is considered inoffensive.

My own attitude is not quite the same. When two college students are experimenting with sex, it seems to me that a meaningful relationship is usually undesirable. The "situation" is especially fraught with peril when one is serious and the other is not. Of course if they are actually planning to get married, and each is mature enough to have made a wise choice, that is a different matter. But how often is this the case in those golden early years? In the absence of such an unlikely "context," an *eros* uncontaminated by *agape* seems to me the desideratum. Better by far that the relationship on *both* sides be an "I-it" than an "I-thou." (We divinity school pedagogues, writing on such matters, must always demonstrate our familiarity with the dull terminology of Martin Buber.)

Naturally there should be consideration for one another in taking desirable precautions. *Here,* rather than in the area of meaningful love, is the proper place to draw the thin wavy line between good and evil motivation. A boy and girl with nothing more in mind than a sexual romp, but with enough respect for each other to exercise care in contraception and hygiene, are surely more to be praised than honorably intentioned, passionate lovers who are too stupid or lazy to bother.

But enough of moralizing. I make these remarks only to explain my admiration for the care, the alert presence of mind, displayed by Peter when he conducted his first experiment in careless college love. Of course he did not discuss this "situation" with me at the time (many years passed before we were on intimate enough terms to talk about such things), although my wife and I gathered from his behavior, and from remarks we overheard at student-faculty socials, that some sort of hanky-panky was going on. This partial reconstruction of the episode is based on what Peter told me more than ten years after the event. The episode is not of great significance in my narrative, but perhaps it will provide a moment of comic relief after the heavy theological slogging of the two previous chapters. At the time of its performance the act of love may be drenched with solemn beauty for the actors, but (as Mary McCarthy has observed) when viewed from outside—through the keyhole, so to speak—how can it be described except as comedy?

A few blocks east of the University of Chicago, in an empty space that is now above a school playground, there once stood a humble eatery called the Maid-Rite Sandwich Shop. It was a restaurant that overflowed at noon with teen-agers from a nearby high school and during the dinner hour with students from the university community. Peter worked there for his meals. A scholarship in the divinity school was still in effect, but it covered only his tuition and residence in a campus dormitory. By manipulating a soda fountain for an hour at noon and busing dishes for an hour in the evening he eliminated, without sacrificing study hours, a heavy drain on the small supply of cash from home.

Of the two full-time waitresses at the Maid-Rite, one was a slightly (very slightly) plump, blonde Danish girl named Olsen. Peter was never able to recall her first name. Everyone called her Queenie. Peter guessed her to be a few years older than himself and about two inches taller than his five-feet-ten. He could not remember the color of her eyes. She had a sunny disposition, smiled all the time, enjoyed her work, and flirted with every man she waited on.

"She had a way," Peter told me, "of talking in Barthian dialectic. There was always a 'yes' contained within her 'no'."

For several weeks after Peter started working at the Maid-Rite, Queenie subjected him to a steady barrage of winks, smiles, and whispered pleasantries whenever she passed close to him.

"It's a funny thing, Homer," Peter said later, "but what I remember best about her is how delightfully she *smelled*."

"Did she know you were studying to be a clergyman?"

"She did, she did. It was my chief attraction."

The two of them usually ate their evening meal together in one of the rear booths, and their conversation often drifted toward sexual topics. Peter had recently acquired—my eyebrows went up when he first told me this; it was a sidelight on his reading that had escaped me at the time—a four-volume set of Havelock Ellis. As a result he was a mine of curious, exotic, and (I suspect) largely unreliable information. Queenie's eyes would widen with wonder whenever Peter discoursed learnedly on these arcane matters.

"I must have given her the impression," he said, wincing, "that I was wise and experienced in the ways of the wicked world."

Queenie lived in the Homestead Hotel on Dorchester Avenue near Fifty-sixth Street. Fifty years ago it had been converted from a once-fashionable brownstone mansion to a place of cheap furnished rooms. A few graduate students usually inhabited the building, but it was filled mostly with old ladies on relief who lived there with their mothers. Oddly enough, there were exactly 26 rooms which were labeled from A to Z. Queenie had rented Room X, one of the three rooms (X, Y, Z) on the attic floor. One mild spring evening Peter found himself walking Queenie home. She invited him in.

Her room, as Peter later remembered it, was large and untidy. There was a faded rug on the floor, worn through in several spots, a radio on a chair beside the bed, and a loud-ticking alarm clock on the dresser. Clothes and toilet articles were scattered here and there. On the cracking plaster above the painted iron bed hung a framed print of Hope (or is she Despair?), blindfolded, head lowered, seated on the globe of earth and plucking the single string on her broken lyre while one star glints feebly in the firmament. (It is hard to believe that George Frederick Watts, the pious Anglican artist who perpetrated this Victorian allegory, once rated five laudatory columns in the *Encyclopaedia Britannica* and that Chesterton wrote an entire book about him.)

As soon as they entered, Queenie closed the door, kicked off her shoes, and took a bottle of red wine from a closet shelf. She moved the radio to the floor so she would have a place to sit while they drank and talked. Peter sat on the edge of the bed. After half the bottle had been consumed, the girl abandoned the chair to sit beside him. There were some moments of amorous wrestling, then Queenie stood up, removed her underpants and pulled the cord that dangled from a single naked bulb in the middle of the ceiling.

If I had written this five years ago, I would have been obliged, in the interest of Protestant propriety, to leave Room X in gentle darkness. Who can be shocked today if I continue?

The click of the light triggered a click in Peter's brain. Loyal to his Barthian ethics he had suddenly reminded himself that the "situation" was pregnant with the possibility of pregnancy. Queenie had just reached down and unzipped his trousers.

"I think we'd better stop," he said, "unless you're wearing a diaphragm."

"I'm not," said Queenie. "I never got one. Don't you have a rubber?"

"No," Peter said hopelessly. To tell the awful truth he had *never* owned any.

The girl stood up, pulled down her skirt, and turned on the light. "You'd better go and buy some."

Red-faced and shaken, Peter sat on the edge of the bed and closed his fly. "Okay, Queenie. I'll be right back."

When he returned he half expected to find her undressed and in the bed. To his surprise she was still fully clothed and was busy writing a letter to her mother. She put down the pencil and smiled when he came in.

They embraced and moved back to the bed. Peter took off his shoes and pulled the light cord. Queenie pulled the zipper. She waited. Nothing happened. Sounds of fumbling hands and dark mutterings from Peter. Another minute zipped by before it must have dawned on her that Peter was totally inexperienced. Queenie took charge of the "situation" with admirable tact.

She got up and turned on the light. Peter had the wrong side of the condom toward him and was having difficulty getting it to unroll.

"She didn't say a word," said Peter. "She just snatched it out of my hands, turned it around, and rolled it on."

He had been sitting on the side of the bed. She pulled him down on top of her and with one hand guided him smoothly in. No one bothered to turn off the light. Queenie's hips moved up and down a few times, but no sooner had she started to rotate her pelvis than Peter was finished. He overflowed with apologies and self-recrimination.

"Don't worry about it, sweetie-pie," Queenie said, patting him on the head. "You just stay there like a good boy and take a nap while I finish my letter."

Peter remembered lying on the bed, a bit frightened, his ego shattered and his eyes closed to shut out the incessant glare of the burning bulb. The moving pencil wrote and having writ moved on. In the distance he could hear an Illinois Central freight train clatter down the tracks. A car honked. Wind was somehow blowing into the flooring of the closet and up through the cracks, rattling newspapers that the girl had spread on the floor to keep out the Chicago soot. On the wall above him Hope twanged her string.

Queenie finished her letter, turned off the light, and tiptoed from the room. He heard her slippered footsteps going down the creaky stairs as she headed for a bathroom on the floor below. When she came back he pretended to be asleep, but between his eyelids he watched her quietly undress.

She slid into bed beside him. "Wake up, sweetie-pie, and take off your pants," she said.

Peter meekly obeyed. His second performance was much better than his first.

They decided they were hungry. At Queenie's suggestion they dressed, descended from Room X, and walked to the drugstore on Fifty-seventh. A middle-aged man behind the cash register—the same gentleman from whom Peter had earlier made a purchase— said hello when they entered. Peter, enormously embarrassed, assumed the greeting was for *him*. But Queenie said "Hi, Freddie," and then Freddie winked at Peter as he followed Queenie to the fountain.

On their way out, after sandwiches and coffee, Peter was relieved to see a woman working the register while friendly Fred waited on a customer in back. Peter paid the bill. Queenie bought a postage stamp. She popped her letter into a mailbox on the corner, then they returned to the Homestead Hotel and ascended to Room X.

This time, at least as Peter told it, Queenie was ecstatic.

They were lying half asleep on the rumpled bed when there came a sudden pounding on the door. Peter's heart flipped over. Was the door locked? Yes, Queenie had locked it. The knob rattled. The knocking was repeated. The girl pressed her hand over Peter's mouth. A few minutes later he could hear the thud of footsteps growing fainter down the stairway.

"Who was that?" he whispered.

The movement of her hair against his face told him she was shaking her head. "I don't know. Maybe it was Steve."

He didn't ask who Steve was.

If Peter had any guilt feelings about this episode, or about the bouts that followed in Room X on other days, they must have been short-lived. A few months later Queenie stopped working at the Maid-Rite, moved out of the Homestead Hotel, and vanished without a trace into the city's asphalt jungle. She was, I gathered, like a million other lonely, rootless young women who service tables in the crowded metropolitan centers of our land; warmhearted, amoral, moving restlessly from job to job, getting married, getting divorced, sometimes having children.

Peter saw Queenie only once after she left the Fifty-seventh Street area. It was five years later. World War II ha d ended and Peter, back in Chicago, was walking through the Loop one afternoon when she passed by without noticing him. He called out to her and she turned around. There was a moment of frowning perplexity before she broke into a wide grin and crushed him with a bear hug.

She had lost some weight, Peter recalled, and this had much improved her figure. Her face was skillfully made up, her hair set in the latest fashion. She was working, she informed him, as a 26-girl at a nightclub on the near-north side. (For readers unfamiliar with Chicago, 26 is a dice game that has been popular in the city's bars and cabarets for three-quarters of a century.) They moved to a less congested spot on State Street and chatted for a while about what each had been doing during the past few years.

Queenie was engaged to be married. She raised her left hand to display an enormous, glittering diamond. Her fiance, she said, had several business enterprises, one of them the manufacture of pinball machines.

The last time I questioned Peter about this he told me how his conversation with Queenie had begun.

"You haven't changed much," Peter said. "You're as pretty as ever. Maybe prettier." He sniffed the air. "And you smell marvelous."

"You haven't changed much either," she replied, reaching out and straightening the lopsided knot in Peter's tie. "You have the same naive little-boy look."

And then, while Peter smiled sheepishly and managed a few synthetic chuckles, Queenie leaned back her head and roared with laughter.

13

Marx

It is something of a scandal that German Protestant leaders of this century have been so sharply divided in their political loyalties. Before the first World War many of Karl Barth's liberal friends supported (as he did not) the Kaiser. Before the second World War some of Barth's friends, Emanuel Hirsch and Friedrich Gogarten for instance, supported Hitler. Barth himself, as I mentioned earlier, despised the Nazis. Bonhoeffer even participated in a plot to *murder* Hitler. After the war, Brunner became a militant anti-Communist while Barth remained neutral with respect to the cold war.

Not that Barth was a Communist! "Whoever," he once declared, "wants a political negation from me against this system and method can have it immediately." He was convinced, however, that today's confrontation of America and Russia does not call for a church condemnation of Communism comparable to its earlier condemnation of Nazism. It calls for patience. He advised Protestants in Balkan countries not to oppose their Communist regimes. Throughout the Hungarian revolt he maintained a thunderous silence.

"The message from Christ is as repulsive and painful to the West as to the East," he said in 1959. Then he added: "Who knows? Perhaps it is *more* painful and repulsive to the West than to the East."

It was Barth's refusal to side with the West that so irritated Reinhold Niebuhr and other Western theologians who had praised him for his stand against Hitler. Ironically, Barth's attitude toward the Soviets strongly resembled the attitude taken by some of his old enemies, the American liberal theologians, in the depression years before World War II. Niebuhr himself, though never a Stalinist, had at one time called himself a Marxist. His early political writings were filled with arguments that could easily have been used for justifying the crimes of Stalin. The best possible political action, Niebuhr taught us, is always a compromise between good and evil in a world where all governments, including one's own, are to some degree malevolent. It necessarily calls for acts, sometimes violent acts, which clearly contradict the absolute ideals of the New Testament.

It is a small step from reasoning such as this to the means-ends arguments by which the Stalinists justified their atrocities. In the thirties a small but vocal group of Protestant leaders (what is gained by denying it?) made such steps. The church, said Niebuhr, should move right theologically and left politically. By "left" he did not mean toward Communism, but in the thirties "left" was commonly confused with "East." Was not Communism the extreme left end of a spectrum on which the New Deal liberals occupied a position only slightly to the left of center? If a Christian should move left politically, why stop at the New Deal?

A few of the politically radical Protestant leaders of the thirties, in America and England and Europe, did not stop. Together with so many secular intellectuals similarly smitten by the Soviet mystique, they looked upon Russian Communism as a great, constructive experiment in economics and politics. It seemed not unreasonable to suppose that its official atheism was a temporary phase, a childish but understandable reaction against the degenerate Christianity of Czarist times.

"Atheism is often a form of striving for a better religion and life," wrote my friend James Luther Adams, then a professor at Meadville Seminary, in an article on Communism. It can, he went on, "be inspired by a sort of religious fervor and be motivated by a religious impulse." I myself published a small book in 1938, now happily out of print, that bore the title, *What Can American Protestants Learn from Soviet Atheism?* Among students of the four federated divinity schools, fellow-traveling was almost as fashionable as it was among the other inhabitants of Gray City.

In his fundamentalist days Peter had been totally uninterested in political action. He took patriotism and loyalty to his country for granted, but politics was for politicians, not for vicars of the Lord. In Albert Schweitzer's famous phrase, New Testament ethics was an "interim ethics," the ethics of a small band of believers who waited for Armageddon. When Peter took the Second Coming seriously he, too, lived in a similar state of expectation. Why work for economic and social reforms when the Bible assures us that the world will steadily grow more wicked until the Devil and his cohorts are banished forever in the fiery lake?

For this crude Biblicism Peter had now substituted the more enlightened Biblicism of the Barthians. Barth and Queenie Olsen had convinced him that the Sermon on the Mount could (in Barth's words) "be applied neither to modern nor to any conceivable society." It proclaimed "men blessed who do not exist." It preached "a morality that presupposes that morality is no longer necessary." Peter now found himself faced with the agonizing task of translating the divine *agape* into whatever political action would most effectively, in the long run, move a fallen world toward the ultimate Kingdom of Righteousness.

And, as always, the times were crying for such action. The Western World was in the grip of a great depression. On every side one could see the follies of unregulated capitalism. Millions of Americans suffered from poverty not because the United States lacked food and goods but because its creaky system of production and distribution had gotten out of kilter. Was it God's will that the business cycle fluctuate eternally between boom and bust? The notion seemed absurd. Business cycles are man-created. Why should they not be man-controlled? The courses Peter took in the social sciences, his reading, his conversations with me and with Edna—above all, the subtle, pervasive, intellectual climate of Gray City—slowly did their work. Peter found himself caught up in a riot of new and disturbing ideas that had no direct bearing on his evolving religious views.

Christ's world, I tried to make clear to him, bore no resemblance to the complex, industrialized, interdependent society of modern America. In ancient Judea the only way a man could express his love for neighbor was by personal acts of kindness toward individuals with whom he chanced to come in contact. The Good Samaritan bound up the wounds of the man he found bleeding by the roadside. What Christian today, walking the streets of Chicago, considers himself responsible for the drunken bum he sees prostrate on the sidewalk? His responsibility goes no further than notifying the nearest policeman, perhaps not even that far. Poverty and alcoholism and drug addiction have complicated economic and psychological causes. Today's Good Samaritan knows that he can best help a sidewalk drunk by supporting those agencies that do whatever can be done. Better still, he works for legislation designed to remove the economic, social, and racial pressures that create human misery.

In the modern city, I told Peter, your "neighbors" are not the people who live in the apartment above you, people you may not even know.

They are the East Indians and the Chinese and the Africans who die every year by the millions because their countries are overpopulated and their food supplies inadequate. Charity is no longer the private, personal little affair it was in earlier times. It is bound up with governments and foreign policies, with political and economic theories, with sociology and psychology. The Christian today who wants to work for the ideals of Christ has no way to do so without involving himself in political causes.

Before the end of 1941's summer, Peter had adroitly fused in his mind the dialectics of the two Karls—the dialectical theology of Karl Barth and the dialectical materialism of Karl Marx. He became a Christian Marxist. Although he did not discuss it with me at the time, his "life plan" was undergoing radical modification. No longer did he see his future role exclusively as that of a great evangelist, a modern Dwight L. Moody who would address mass meetings and persuade millions of lost sheep to enter the fold. He began to see himself more in the role of a religious leader who would arouse Christians to the need of combining their faith, their conservative faith, with political activism.

Peter still had not in any essential way abandoned the central dogmas of orthodoxy. Nevertheless, entangled as he was in the hour's political ferment, his theological speculation took a holiday, his energies detoured along other roads. Peter was never one to go halfway. The University of Chicago then, as now, was an arena in which dozens of student political groups were forming, dissolving, and reforming again. Many of these groups were dominated by non-Communist liberals and socialists, even by Trotskyists, but the more boisterous ones were fronts for the tightly disciplined band of young Communists on the campus. They were quick to spot Peter as a potential convert, at the least a valuable ally. He was an experienced public speaker with an engaging platform personality. He was a tireless worker. Above all he was a divinity student! Everyone knows a Communist doesn't believe in God. What could be better cover for a Moscow-manipulated meeting than to have it chaired by a local seminarian?

In Peter's home state of Oklahoma, Robert Wood, state secretary of the Communist Party, his wife Ina, and several of their associates had recently been arrested and sentenced to ten years in the state prison.° Their crime: operating a bookstore that sold literature advocating a

---

°The prison sentence for the Woods was never carried out; a higher court overruled. Ten years later (see *Time*, April 2, 1951) Robert Wood was formally expelled from the Communist Party for "panic in the face of the fire of the class enemy, for acts endangering the party. . . for acts of white chauvinism, and conduct unbecoming. . . his post."—H. W.

violent overthrow of the government. Although the conviction had been appealed and the defendants were out on bail, funds were needed to carry their case through higher courts. Peter was approached by a group of students calling themselves the Campus Civil Liberties Committee. Wood was going to be in Chicago the following month, they told Peter, and they had arranged for him to speak on the campus. Since Peter came from Oklahoma, would he be willing to chair the meeting?

No, they assured him, they were not Communists. They were loyal Americans. But they knew that American freedoms could not survive in a country that did not respect the rights of free speech for everybody. The "witch hunt" in Oklahoma was only the beginning of a native fascism. As someone (Huey Long?) had said, when fascism comes to America it won't be called fascism. It will be called Americanism. It was this fascist form of American patriotism that had persecuted the Woods. Would Peter help?

The person in the group who spoke the most persuasively was a slim, black-haired girl named Lois Green. Her earnest, flashing dark eyes were impossible to resist. When Peter consented to be chairman of the meeting she threw her arms around him and kissed him on the cheek.

Peter asked me to give a short preliminary speech at the meeting before Wood delivered the main address. I was happy to oblige. Peter acquitted himself well as chairman. After that, the local Stalinists gave him top priority. He was flattered and fawned upon. He found himself chairman of this rally, president of that organization, speaker at this and that meeting. He was invited to chummy little parties in smoke-filled basement apartments on the fringes of the campus. There would be beer and dancing and group singing of worker songs. Attractive girls of all shapes and colors swarmed over him. And especially Lois Green. His advice was sought solemnly by the local C.P. hacks, and if his answers coincided (as they usually did) with the Party Line, he would be made to feel as if *his* decisions had formulated the policy of whatever front organization was involved. If it failed to coincide? Well, there would be quiet arguments with Lois and her friends, and the marshaling of many facts until Peter saw the light. This rapid inflation of Peter's social conscience was admirable enough, though it must be said that, as in the case of so many noisy young radicals, the expansion was not accompanied by any strenuous effort to understand modern economic theory. To be sure, he tried to read *Das Kapital*. Alas, this weighty tome was then as out of date and unreadable as Newton's *Principia*. The name of John Maynard Keynes would have meant nothing to Peter at this time, even though the Keynesian revolution was already under way and inspiring much of Roosevelt's New Deal. You must understand that although Peter still believed in the power of the blood, the blood of the Lamb had become so diluted that he no longer was able to sing and shout about it. His heart hungered for a fresh commitment. And did not Communism present itself in those dark depression years with all the emotional trappings of a modern Pentecost?

There was the same initial act of decision. There were the new Scriptures to read (Marx, Engels, Lenin, Stalin), the new Saints and Martyrs to emulate. There was the sense of belonging to a small, persecuted elite who possessed the secret keys to the Coming Kingdom. Many of the stirring worker songs were no more than new words for revival hymns that Peter had sung as a child. The power of the blood was replaced by the power of the proletariat, the "wretched of the earth." The bursting of the workers' chains, the triumphant construction of the New Jerusalem in Russia, soon throughout the world, gripped Peter's starved imagination in the way it had once been gripped by the vision of God crucified. It was not that he gave up the old vision. It was that he found a way, incredible as it now may seem, to sing both *The Old Rugged Cross* and *The Internationale,* and see no conflict between the two! He was like clay in the hands of the Party functionaries. He was their best catch of the year.

But Peter, bless his confused young soul, never actually joined the Party. Something held him back. Was it his recent disenchantment with the Moody type of Christianity that made him hesitate to throw himself too quickly into another cult? Was it a private, gnawing suspicion, in some back corner of his skull, that he should keep his freedom to think as he pleased and not become another robot activated by buttons pushed in the Kremlin? I wonder if he himself knows today why he refused to take that final step. He could have taken it. It would, indeed, have been characteristic of him to take it. Perhaps the main reason—this is only my opinion—is that he was repelled by the metaphysics of dialectical materialism. It is, after all, materialistic. And its weird blend of humanism with a muddy variety of Hegelian idealism left Peter unmoved. In the end, I suspect it was his Christian faith that held him back.

Like the Very Reverend Hewlett Johnson, the "Red Dean" of Canterbury—later like Henry Wallace—Peter began to play the game of finding Marxian allegories in passages of Holy Writ. Did not Amos write (8:4), "Hear this, O ye that swallow up the needy, even to make the poor of the land to fail"? And did not Jesus declare that it was easier for a camel to go through a needle's eye than for a rich man to enter the Kingdom of Heaven? It opened up for Peter a fascinating new style of

Biblical exegesis. In his Moody days he had taken the passage, "The stone which the builders refused is become the head stone of the corner," (Psalms 118:22) to be a prophecy of Christ. Now he saw it also as a symbol of the oppressed proletariat who would some day become the foundation of a Kingdom of God on earth.

"The treatment of the Negro is America's greatest sin," he said to me one evening when he and Lois were visiting us, and of course I agreed. "Can you imagine how Jesus would feel if he were on earth today and saw black people in the South meekly stepping off the curb every time they passed a white man? If Christ lived in the United States today, he would be the greatest revolutionary in our history. He would be lynched in the South by the same sort of bigots who nailed him to the Cross."

"Yes," I said, "and unless we can give the Negroes their freedom and dignity and education, the time will soon be ripe for a charismatic Negro prophet to come along. He'll combine fundamentalism with the notion that the white church has abandoned the true faith. He'll tell his people that in these last days, before God destroys the earth, God's entrusting the true faith to a black remnant."

This was twenty years before the rise of the Black Muslims. With a little more insight I might have guessed that a non-Christian religion would have a stronger appeal than Christianity for militant young blacks, impatient with results, sick of the hypocrisy of our self-styled Christian power structure.

I remember one occasion on which Peter suggested, half in jest, the project of an elaborate modern commentary on the Bible. It would ignore the usual theological interpretations to concentrate on social and political implications.

"Take the story in Daniel," he said, "the story about the hand that wrote nonsense words on the plaster wall at Belshazzar's feast. Do you remember how Daniel interpreted the words? God had doomed Belshazzar's kingdom. It had been weighed in the balance and found wanting. It was to be divided and given to the Medes and Persians. What a beautiful allegory about the fall of capitalism! The local sooth-sayers, who couldn't understand the writing, are the conservative economists of today. They're the men who do nothing but think up excuses for the bankers and businessmen."

"Who is Daniel?" I asked, smiling.

"Me," said Peter. He raised his hand and wrote in the air with an extended forefinger while he slowly recited, "*Mene Mene Tekel Uphar-sin.*"

"And who are the Medes and Persians?"

He lowered his hand. "The farmers and the industrial workers." Then his face broke into a grin. "Don't take me seriously, Homer. I know the Bible story doesn't mean all that. But it's amusing to interpret it that way."

Peter's knowledge of the Soviet Union, I must admit, was then as thin as his knowledge of modern economics; indeed, it was almost as watery as his knowledge of geology had been back in his diluvial days. He considered *Soviet Communism*, that monumental hoax by Sidney and Beatrice Webb, the "definitive reference" on the subject. He praised the writing of Anna Louise Strong. Perhaps he felt a special kinship with Miss Strong because of her own fundamentalist background and because she had done her graduate work at Chicago.

Miss Strong had been born in Friend, Nebraska, 1885, the daughter of a Congregationalist minister. Her doctor's thesis (University of Chicago, 1908) was "A Study of Prayer from the Standpoint of Social Psychology," her first job that of associate editor of *Advance*, a fundamentalist magazine published in Chicago. "For me," she later wrote, "the Party combines all the early gods of my youth."

When I first drafted this chapter, I assumed Miss Strong was dead. A year later I read in the Sunday *New York Times* (October 16, 1966) that she had just been made an honorary member of the Red Guards, Communist China's revolutionary youth movement! She was then approaching her eighty-first birthday. "Miss Strong said she fully embraced Mao Tse-tung's philosophy," the *Times* reported, "and looks forward to the 'fine days' when revolutionaries will be putting up posters in New York."

I clipped the story and mailed it to Peter, recalling how enthusiastically he had once read Miss Strong's autobiography, *I Change Worlds*. His return comment was: "Poor, weak Miss Strong! Still changing worlds! The Chinese Reds will probably have to deport her, too." Peter was alluding to Miss Strong's expulsion from the Soviet Union in 1949. After she had lived in Russia for thirty years, Stalin's agents had arrested her as an American spy and booted her out of the country. [Wilson penciled in the margin of his manuscript, at the end of this paragraph: "Miss Strong died in Peking in 1970, age 84. See *N. Y. Times* obit, March 30, 1970."—M. G.]

The great black spots of Soviet history—Stalin's starvation of the kulaks, his horrendous purges, the hideous labor camps, the suppression of civil liberties, the antisemitism, the iron hand over the arts and sciences—all were either justified by the Party hacks and their fellow hackers with elaborate means-ends arguments or dismissed as the fabrications of America's red-baiting press.

"Sure, the Soviet government has made mistakes." Peter admitted once when Edna and I were arguing with him. "But you've got to see those mistakes in perspective. Russia's at war, at war with herself. The old bourgeois elements are still there. Stalin can't afford to relax an instant. Naturally Hearst and Colonel McCormick and Henry Luce are going to play up and exaggerate everything they can find wrong about Russia. But you have to judge Russia *now* in contrast to what she *was* under the Czars. Is there any other nation that has made so much progress in such a short time?"

"There's Japan," Edna said.

"You can't compare the two," Peter responded. "In Japan the progress is just an industrial progress. It's inside a totalitarian, reactionary system that makes puppets out of everybody. In Russia the progress is inside a progressive system. Stalin is building freedom and democracy among the masses, working for a day when everyone will cooperate voluntarily, and the police and even the government won't be needed."

Thus spake Peter, the young Daniel, in those awkward days when he played the Soviet language game.

I remember another occasion, when I chided him for his tolerance of Russian atheism while at the same time attacking my own program of humanism as the direction in which I wanted American Protestant churches to move.

"But the situation isn't the same, Homer. In Russia, before the revolution, its churches were evil and corrupt. They were infection centers of reaction. They would have done everything they could to block the revolution. It's easy to see why Lenin and Stalin had to make a clean sweep of the old religion."

"I still think America needs it, too," I said.

Peter gazed off into space, then surprised me by saying: "Perhaps you're right. Maybe the whole world will have to go through a catharsis of atheism. Maybe it's the only way God can purge the churches of superstition, the only way he can bring them back to the simple message of the Gospels. You know, Homer, I wouldn't be surprised if Russia wasn't the first country in the world to experience a big new revival of Christian faith."

"I would be," I said, shuddering.

The divinity school took a dim but forbearing view of Peter's left-wing enthusiasm. On only one occasion did the school's patience stretch almost to the snapping point. The time was late May, a few days before Hitler attacked Russia. An open-air peace rally was being held in the center of Stagg Field. Peter and Lois, each wearing a large button that said "The Yanks are NOT Coming!", were among the speakers.

I was not there, but according to the newspapers several local R.O.T.C. boys, aided by two members of the American Legion, tried to overturn the small wooden platform on which the speakers were standing. As the floor began to tilt, a burly Legionnaire reached up and yanked the microphone out of Lois' hand. Peter leaped to the ground, his face dark with fury, and laid the ex-soldier flat with a short jab to his chin. Numerous scuffles and fist fights were underway when the Hyde Park police arrived and ended the brawl.

The fracas was page-one news. DIVINITY STUDENT PUNCHES PATRIOT said a four-inch banner headline on Hearst's evening paper. For the second time in his life Peter found himself summoned to an accounting before school authorities for his part in a minor riot. I and several colleagues intervened on his behalf. Eventually the divinity school let the matter quietly subside.

Ten days after the riot Russia was at war with Germany, and no one was louder than the campus comrades in urging the Yanks to enter the fray after all. I find it painful to record the speed with which Peter and I made similar about-faces. During the period of the Hitler-Stalin non-aggression pact, both of us had taken a pacifist, hands-off attitude toward the European war. Even Norman Thomas, who loathed the Communists, took the same position. I recall how annoyed I had been with the new Protestant journal, *Christianity and Crisis*, founded a few months earlier by Reinhold Niebuhr and his associates at New York's Union Theological Seminary. The "crisis" was, of course, nothing less than the possible destruction of Western Europe. The magazine had been urging America's entrance into the conflict with all the vigor with which it urged, twenty-five years later, the nation's withdrawal from the war in Vietnam. Not until Hitler turned on Stalin did Peter and I decide that Niebuhr and his friends had been right all along.

Peter, who was never under Party discipline, made the switch a few days before Lois did. Years later he told me with amusement about the occasion when they were alone in her apartment and the Word of Stalin was revealed to her.

The press had been printing rumors about an impending Hitler break with Stalin. Lois was convinced those rumors were imperialist lies designed to drag America into the war. Peter tried to persuade her that the war had reached a point at which it was no longer prudent for the United States to remain neutral. Hitler was going too far. He was mad. Nazism would have to be destroyed.

No, insisted Lois, it was still a dirty capitalist conflict. Hitler might be crazy, but not so crazy that he would dare attack the Soviet Union. The

Yanks were still *not* coming. The phone rang while they argued. Lois picked up the phone, and Peter saw her frown while she conversed in low monosyllables. She hung up, glanced at Peter, smiled brightly and said, "You know, I'm beginning to think you're right."

Perhaps, gentle reader, you are wondering why I, Peter's older friend and mentor, did not try to dampen his pro-Soviet passions? Surely you have guessed the reason. I myself was then the faculty sponsor for three of the Communist Party's most vigorous campus fronts. Although I was never quite the enthusiastic fellow-traveler that Peter became, it would be fair to say that I fellow-traveled with the fellow-travelers. To put it in a jargon that became fashionable in certain Gray City circles after World War II, I did not discourage Peter because I was not at that time opposed to anti-anti-Communism.

14

Lois

Lois Green was a graduate student in the University of Chicago's School of Social Service Administration. I have already mentioned how she and Peter met. As head of the Campus Civil Liberties Committee, she had approached him to ask if he would chair a fund-raising rally. When Peter began to play the Marxist political game, Lois seemed to be everywhere. She was at every campus left-wing meeting that Peter attended, at every off-campus left-wing party. One Friday afternoon he made a long trip by street car to the west side of Chicago to support a factory strike. There was Lois walking in the picket line!

They liked each other. Peter made an opening move. Lois responded. A new sex game began.

I found Miss Green attractive in a dark, exotic way: black hair, black eyes, and a thin but erotic figure. There were faint, almost imperceptible lesbian signals in her gestures and clothes, in the inflections of her low whispery voice. A gauzy smile perpetually clung to her lips, vanishing only when something annoyed her, as it frequently did. Her eyes when she was angry flashed bolts of lightning. When something amused her, she would cup her mouth with her left hand (perhaps to conceal a slight space between her two front teeth) and emit a girlish giggle. Her father owned a large clothing store in the Bronx. Both parents were of Hungarian Jewish descent.

The few conversations I had with Lois (Peter visited me less often during this period of Marxist-sex play) were confined almost entirely to political and economic issues. Lois was intelligent and articulate, burning with enthusiasm for all things Soviet, contemptuous of all opinions that did not mesh with her own. In many ways, I thought to myself as she rattled on excitedly about various causes, she resembled Peter himself when he first came to Chicago. She was on the inside of a fundamentalist sect. I guessed her to be an actual Party member, under strictest discipline, but I was not sure and I did not ask. Such a question was considered bad taste at the time in Gray City, just as it was considered bad taste to ask if Mortimer Adler or some other local Thomist had joined the Catholic Church.

In 1965, when I reviewed my sparse notes for this chapter, I decided it would be worth the effort to locate Lois Green and talk to her. I remembered Peter telling me in a recent letter that she was working part-time for one of the city's welfare agencies, although she still lived in the university area and was taking occasional courses in psychology and the social sciences. During World War II, while Peter was in the Navy, she had returned to New York City where she was married for a time to a Party functionary whom I shall leave nameless. (He is now an editor at one of the country's largest book publishers.) After the war Lois returned alone to Gray City to get her master's degree.

She was still working for it. I had the impression that she had joined the ranks of that shabby, immobile little group of perpetual graduate students unable to break the umbilical cord of Alma Mater. Sherwood Anderson's *Memoirs* contains an amusing reference to the female of this species. Anderson's sister had attended the University of Chicago. "She became a kind of fixture there," he writes. "The years passed and it went on and on. About every college and university there are such women. They stay until they become old women, they remain graduate students for life."

I found Lois living in a small, inexpensive, spotlessly clean and neat basement apartment on Fifty-fourth Street. Some framed prints of pictures by Mondrian and Jackson Pollock hung on the walls. A low, two-tiered bookcase made of unpainted shelving lumber, the shelves supported by glass building bricks, ran the length of one side wall.

Lois took my overcoat. When she saw the scarlet vest I was wearing she shielded her eyes with her left arm and said, "Your waistcoat's blinding me!"

"If it pains you too much, I'll turn it inside-out. The other side's a muted blue-green paisley."

"Thanks a lot. Don't bother."

She stuffed my scarf part way into the armhole of my overcoat, and while she was hanging the coat in a closet, I walked to the bookshelves and genuflected to read the titles. There were volumes by Freud, Horney, Reik, Alexander. . . .

"No Jung or Adler?"

She shrugged and made a face. "I've read them but I don't think they have much to say. They stole parts of Freud and distorted what they stole." She walked back across the room to retrieve a cigarette burning in one of those huge ceramic ashtrays that resemble an amoeba. "What was it Freud said? Jung changed the hilt of psychoanalysis then he put in a new sword? Is Jung still alive?"

"I think so. I haven't heard much about him since the war."

Lois had aged. She had been thin before though hardly flat chested. Now she was thin and flat. She wore no make-up, and her large dark eyes contrasted strongly with her pale, tightly drawn face. Her short hair was trimmed like a man's.

"Would you like a highball?"

"Fine, thank you."

"Water or soda?"

"Water."

She mixed the drinks on the counter of a small kitchen in back while I leaned against the humming refrigerator and brought her up to date on Peter. I quickly sketched his Navy career. I told her about his Easter sermon. She had heard about the sermon. Who in Gray City hadn't? It had passed into folklore, and she was glad to get the details straight. When I described what happened at the end, she broke into screams of laughter.

"I know I shouldn't laugh," she said. "Has Peter been to an analyst?"

I shook my head.

"It's the only thing that will help him."

She told me about her "marriage" and "divorce" (there had been no official ceremonies) in a toneless, matter-of-fact voice as if she were talking about the case history of one of her welfare clients. There had been no children. She had quit the Party.

I feigned surprise. "I didn't know you'd been a member?"

"Dear old Peter," she said with a twisted smile. "I never told him."

"Was that your strategy or was it the Party's strategy?"

She considered for a while, her fingers nervously turning the glass in her hands. "Both, I think. We decided that pushing Peter into the Party wouldn't work. It would only push him the other way. But there was more to it than that." She hesitated, inhaling deeply and letting the smoke drift out through narrow nostrils.

"If you were in love," I said, "you probably didn't want Peter to think your interest in him was just a recruiting maneuver."

The twisted smile again. "Love? What's that?"

For two years Lois had been going to a lady psychoanalyst in down-town Chicago. Everything she told me about her relationship with Peter was elaborately embroidered with Freudian speculations. The Marxist neologisms of her pre-war years had been replaced by Freudian neol-ogisms. Peter, it seems, had blue eyes like a younger brother of whom she was particularly fond. Would that not introduce an unconscious element of incest? She assured me—there was no doubt about it—that Peter suffered from an "inverted Oedipus." It had led him to identify her with his mother, creating a classic love-hate ambivalence. And so on. Her speculations impressed me as amateurish. She had read a lot of analytic literature but not enough. I spare the reader further details.

One thing, however, was obvious. The two of them had bedded down regularly for almost a year. Lois lived then in a kitchenette apartment on Woodlawn Avenue, a block south of the Midway. After an evening of political action—speaking at a meeting, picketing, pre-election door-bell ringing, envelope licking, or some other dreary ritual of dedicated do-goodism—they would retire to Lois' apartment for the night. The possibility of a permanent liaison seems not to have entered either of their heads. Lois, I suppose, could no more imagine herself the wife of a Protestant minister than Peter could imagine himself married to a devout Communist.

On the morning after their first night together, while they were having breakfast, Peter said something that so startled Lois that she had never forgotten it. She spoke about it now with wry amusement.

"When you first met me, Peter," she had said, touching his arm, "did you guess something like this would happen?"

He was spreading jam on a slice of toast. "To tell the truth, Lois, I not only hoped it would, I prayed to the Lord it would."

Lois had been drinking coffee. She put her cup down so suddenly that it missed the saucer and turned over. Peter, cheeks flaming, jumped up to get some paper towels.

"I shouldn't have said that." He wagged his head in dismay as he blotted the table. "It slipped out before I thought."

Ah love! Ah *agape*! Ah *eros*! Ah situation ethics! Above all, ah youth! I felt old and tired. It was hard to believe Lois had been shocked. I can only suppose that the coupling of God with traditional moral codes is so much a part of our culture that it is taken for granted even by those who fancy they are atheists.

I would guess that Lois knew nothing at all about Peter's religious convictions at the time or the difficult transitions he was making. She would not have been curious enough to ask, and Peter would have been too confused to talk about them. "As this passionate rapture absorbed me more and more," wrote another Peter, Peter Abelard, after he began a famous sex game with his teen-age pupil, Heloise, "I devoted ever less time to philosophy and to the work of the school." Surely that is one of the great unintentionally funny remarks in the history of theology. Did Abelard pray for God's help in practicing the art of love?

I doubt it. Yet Peter Fromm did. He believed, you see, that there was no "situation" which did not come under divine judgment. He wanted to make his decision about Lois prayerfully. He wanted it to reflect God's will. It was just like him. He was still a Puritan.

Their Marxist sex game began in the spring of 1941. The first six months, I gathered from what Lois told me, had been great fun on both sides. Toward the end of the game the situation started to corrode. "Latent hostilities emerged" was how Lois put it. "We both wanted to stop. At the same time we didn't want to. You can understand that, can't you?"

I nodded. Half-forgotten faces of girls I had known in my youth flitted vaguely through my mind. Yes, I could understand.

They had begun their game in the lengthening shadow of the European war. Before Hitler attacked Russia, on June 22, 1941, both Peter and Lois had trumpeted a vigorous pacifist line. As I indicated earlier, it was not only the Communist line. Norman Thomas, for instance, was busy making speeches against American involvement in the war. On the University of Chicago campus he debated philosopher T. V. Smith, then a U.S. congressman at large, on this very topic. I attended the debate with Lois and Peter. We clapped whenever Thomas scored a point, sat silent during Smith's irreverent sallies. A few months later Thomas was back again for a similar round against economist Paul Douglas, at that time a Chicago alderman. Charles Lindbergh—remember?—was addressing mass meetings around the nation, urging Americans to sit this one out. Even Robert Hutchins our president (and a personal friend of Lindbergh) added his voice to the chorus of isolationism and America Firstism. On January 23, 1941, Hutchins began a radio address (it was later published) with the following warning:

> I speak tonight because I believe that the American people are about to commit suicide. We are not planning to. We have no plan. We are drifting into suicide. Deafened by martial music, fine language, and large appropriations, we are drifting into war.

On May 22, a month before Germany's attack on Russia, Hutchins had this to say on NBC's Town Meeting of the Air:

The United States cannot serve humanity by making the totalitarian revolution world-wide. Yet if Hitler is really devoted to the totalitarian ideal, and is prepared to undergo personal defeat to realize it on a world scale, he should pray for America's entrance into this war. For it would follow as the night the day that a totalitarian banner would be raised over the Western Hemisphere.

I quote these passages not to embarrass Hutchins, whose ego I think is unembarrassable, but to convey to younger readers a sense of the intellectual confusions of the time. I myself was as confused as Hutchins. My sermons in the Midway Community Church resounded with purple flourishes against the war that would seem just as absurd if I were to quote some of them now.

Although the United States was not yet officially at war—Pearl Harbor was not hit until December 7—a military draft was already under way. Peter was exempt because he was a seminarian; nevertheless, he had written a long letter in early June to his draft board explaining why he wanted to register as a conscientious objector. Peter let me see the carbon of that letter. It was a curious document. He made clear that he was preparing for the ministry, that he believed in God and Christ, but he did not wish to claim a C.O. status on religious grounds. He was not opposed to all wars. He believed some wars were just. It was *this* war he objected to. In the total context, adding up the pros and cons, weighing probable good and evil consequences, he was convinced that he would serve God best by doing all he could to prevent his country from being drawn into the maelstrom.

When Hitler broke his pact with Stalin there was no visible sign of bewilderment in Party ranks. The faithful toddled along with the new line as they always do, and Peter and I trailed after them. In the fall of 1941 Peter sent his draft board another letter, even longer than the first. It explained how profoundly the "situation" had altered. No longer did he feel that America should sit the conflict out, now that it threatened to engulf the world. No longer, he said, did he consider himself a conscientious objector. No longer did he wish to be excused from the draft. They could summon him at any time. The draft board had not replied to his first letter. It did not reply to his second.

After Pearl Harbor, when America was at war with Japan, Germany and Italy, Peter debated with Lois and himself for several tortured weeks about what he ought to do. The draft board apparently had no intention of calling him. After all, he was about to become a legitimate man of the cloth. Should he enlist? He asked for my opinion. I honestly did not know what to say. I evaded his question. It was, I said, a decision he would have to make alone.

Peter must have prayed long and earnestly about it. And while he was trying to make up his mind, his affair with Lois began to develop terminal complications. There were increasingly frequent, sometimes violent arguments. On one occasion she had blackened one of Peter's eyes. He was dumbfounded and furious, Lois said, giggling behind her left hand while she described the scene. But Peter had controlled his temper and turned his other cheek. There had been a tearful, albeit temporary, reconciliation.

The game ended much more neatly than such games usually end. Peter terminated it late in January, 1942, by the simple expedient of enlisting in the Navy. It must have been a great relief to both of them. They corresponded for a while, then Lois returned to the Bronx, "married" a comrade, and stopped writing altogether. Her husband, who had a punctured eardrum, was exempt from service. They supported the war as best they could.

Lois' break with the Party, she said, came rather late, not until two years after the war ended. Even so, it preceded her husband's disenchantment. Failure to synchronize on this score had been the major reason—or so it seemed to Lois then, now she was not so sure—for their separation. He had moved out of their apartment in Greenwich Village to take up residence with a still dedicated comrade.

American ex-Communists (in Europe perhaps it is not the same) are by and large an unhappy, lonely breed. Some of them fill the void by returning to the religion of their childhood. Some, like Frank Meyer who had been the Party's educational director in the University of Chicago area before the war, move to the right [Meyer was senior editor of William Buckley's *National Review* when he died in April, 1972. —M. G.] to thump the drums for conservatism as loudly as they once had thumped them for Communism. A few become liberal democrats or democratic socialists (is there any difference?), finding an outlet for their altruism in the labor movement, in racial causes, in organizations like Americans for Democratic Action and the New York Liberal Party.

Some are proud of their past. They defend it self-righteously on the grounds that they were wrong for splendid reasons while their opponents were right for stupid reasons. They feel that they should still be considered experts on all economic, political and international questions, apparently on the strength of having once made a colossal blunder. A few muster the courage to say kind words for those (John Dewey, Bertrand Russell, H. G. Wells are the first three that come to mind) who were right for right reasons.

I like the honest way Granville Hicks has put it: "For some of the persons who joined the Communist Party in the thirties, I have great admiration. For some of those who stayed out, for what seems to me the wrong reasons, I have no regard whatever. But for the persons who saw through Communism when I was taken in by it, I have nothing but respect."

Ignazio Silone, Italy's most respected ex-Communist (he helped establish the Italian party), once said to Palmiro Togliatti, "The final struggle will be between the Communists and the ex-Communists." The statement is often quoted by writers who do not know that Silone spoke in jest. Ex-Commies, like defrocked Catholic priests, are an ineffectual, befuddled little group. They have no power, no influence, not even a common set of attitudes. If there ever is a final conflict (which I doubt; the Cold War will most likely whimper to its end like the great Protestant-Catholic conflict of the past), who would bother even to ask an ex-Communist for advice?

"What are your political opinions now?" I asked Lois, sneaking a glance at the big watch on the gold chain that looped between the upper pockets of my scarlet vest. Edna was expecting me home by six. "Are they left, right or center?"

Lois crushed out her cigarette. She wasn't sure exactly what those three words meant. She was bored with politics. The Democrats and Republicans, she said, were like Tweedledum and Tweedledee. She was trying to help in a small way the city's poor, especially the poor in Chicago's Black Belt. She wanted to get her master's degree and go into psychiatric counseling. She hoped to find out through her analysis why she was so unhappy, why Gray City seemed so gray.

She got up wearily to refill her glass and get my overcoat when I told her I could not stay for another drink.

Part II

THE WAR

Oh ye! who have your eye-balls vex'd and tired,
Feast them upon the wideness of the Sea.

—KEATS

15

Boots and Sparks

Why did Peter enlist in the Navy? Why not the Army? I once asked him this, and he said it was because he wanted to avoid as much as possible any direct contact with the act of killing. I am not sure this was an honest answer. There were other reasons: the romantic tradition of the sea, the relative cleanliness of Navy life; above all, the increased likelihood of not coming in contact with his *own* death. Whatever the reasons, conscious or otherwise, Peter decided on the Navy. This called at once for a second decision. Should he seek a commission?

The dilemma seemed real at the time. The higher pay, I'm sure, meant nothing to him. He was objective enough, however, to know he was good "officer material," and that as an officer he would maximize his contribution to a cause which he believed was just. Ten days after Peter made his application a well dressed, well scrubbed young man showed up at my office in Swift Hall and informed my secretary that he wished to see me about a private matter. As he entered my study I greeted him with, "Ah, naval intelligence, I presume?"

He looked taken aback. "How did you know?"

"Elementary, my dear Watson. For one thing, I've been expecting you. For another. . . ."—I pointed my cigar toward his feet—"I perceive that you're wearing black regulation Navy shoes."

We had an amiable conversation. I was diplomatic, perhaps a bit evasive. It was apparent from the man's questions that his home office was well informed about Peter's left-wing activities and also mine. I learned later, from a friend who worked in the Chicago office of naval intelligence, that our dossiers, in what the Navy called its "Red file," were indeed thick ones.

When the commission was denied, Peter was relieved and pleased. He wanted to experience Navy life on its humblest levels, he recoiled instinctively from the officer caste system, and he was happy to be relieved of high responsibilities. He lost no time in enlisting. Papers were signed. Physical examinations were passed. I let him store several large cartons of books and a trunk filled with clothes in the basement of my house. He wrote a long letter to his parents. After his swearing in, at a recruiting office in the Loop, he and some thirty other boys and young men were herded into the back of a large open truck and driven to the Great Lakes Naval Station at Waukegan, north of Chicago.

As the truck rattled down a narrow side street, through a slum section of Chicago, a street game of touch football was momentarily halted. A smiling black boy tossed the pigskin to Peter. And Peter never forgot it. "It was a gesture of confidence, of respect, of love," he said, telling me about it many years later. He caught the football, grinned, spun it back.

During the next four years I saw Peter only for one brief period, during a leave that preceded his assignment to sea duty, but throughout the war we corresponded regularly. His letters were a therapeutic outlet for the tensions and conflicts that churned through his mind during the war years. Taken altogether they provide a fairly complete documentation of his Navy career.

It was an ordinary, mostly humdrum career. He did not see much action. There were no heroics. Nevertheless it was an important four-year hiatus in Peter's spiritual Odyssey. It was a period of marking time, a period in which he allowed the vexed, bloodshot eyeballs of his mind to stop plowing furrows of black type on narrow, unmoving, rectangular white pages and to feast them on the surging blue-gray wideness of the sea. The clean salt air blew vast quantities of dust out of his skull. It was a broadening, maturing experience, one that I can best communicate by letting Peter speak directly, in his own voice.

I have made a careful selection of his letters. They are about half of almost eighty that I received and have preserved. In many of the letters printed here, when Peter referred to topics of little interest to anyone except ourselves or to something that could be made clear only by lengthy footnotes, I have made excisions. Some of the missing passages concern technical philosophical and theological arguments that would be meaningless unless I included, as I prefer not to do, long excerpts from my side of our correspondence. To further compress and smooth this nautical midsection of my book, this pause between Peter's youth and manhood, I have omitted all dates of letters and, on all except the first and last, the conventional closings in which Peter asked to be remembered to my wife and signed his name after a "cordially" or "faithfully" or some similar phrase.

Peter's first letter, written from the Great Lakes Naval Station, arrived a week after he began his "boots" training:

Dear Homer:

I'd hoped I could get back to Chicago over the weekend so you and Edna could see how ridiculous I look in a sailor suit, but no "liberties" are allowed until we finish boot camp. After that, maybe I can make the trip.

I still find it hard to believe I'm actually in the Navy. Things happened so fast! Here at Great Lakes the war seems infinitely far away. The station is immense. Most of the sailors look like kids who have just finished high school. They're completely unconcerned about any ideological aspects of the war. Most of them seem to be enjoying it. They're like children at a summer camp, eager to start the fun and games.

The sailor suit is surprisingly comfortable, though there's not much pocket space. I've learned how to carry my handkerchief inside my jumper, over a shoulder, and there's a spot at the back of the pants, behind the lacing, where you can stick a pocket comb. The thirteen buttons on the front flap, so says an old chief in charge of our barracks, are supposed to represent the first thirteen states of the union. Apparently Uncle Sam wants every sailor to honor them every time he goes to the "head" (that's Navy slang for bathroom).

This afternoon I saw a platoon of about fifty boys being marched across the snow toward the station's main gate, all of them wearing baggy, unpressed civilian clothes and large, funny-looking caps. Someone told me they were boys who had been "surveyed out" of the Navy for psychiatric reasons. The practice seems to be to keep a supply of misfitting clothes on hand for these psychological misfits to wear when they're sent back home. You'd think the Navy would spare them the humiliation of marching them across the base. Why can't they take them to the train in a bus? Most of them looked unhappy as they galumphed by. A loudspeaker on top of one of the buildings was blasting out the song, *The Hills of Idaho*. It's a record they play constantly. I'm sick of hearing it.

Thanks again for storing my books and trunk. Give my love to Edna and my best to any friends you see.

Faithfully,
Peter

After taking an aptitude test at the end of his boot period Peter was assigned to a radio training school at the University of Wisconsin, in Madison. It is a town I once knew well. My wife and I (as I mentioned earlier) were students at the university there, and from 1911 to 1918 I was pastor of the All Souls Unitarian Church on Langdon Street, only a few blocks from the campus.

Peter went directly to Madison from Great Lakes and so was unable to make the visit to Chicago that he had planned. What follows is part of a long first letter I received from him after he began his radio training. It is followed by excerpts from other letters that he sent from Madison.

Dear Homer:

. . . The Navy has decided to make a radioman out of me. This means I'll be assigned to a ship or naval base where I'll work in the "radio shack" with headphones over my ears and a typewriter in front of me. Several hundred of us sit most of the day in a large garage the Navy has taken over, listening to the dots and dashes that come from a sending key on the instructor's desk.

They're starting us out slow. We're learning the touch system on the typewriter at the same time we learn the code. I can already type pretty fast with my three-finger system (first and second finger of my right hand, first finger of my left), but of course that's not allowed. It's surprising how quickly you build up reflexes. The dots and dashes skip your brain and go right down to your fingers. You can type the code without ever thinking about what it means.

A few hundred WAVES are also here to learn code. When we march out of the garage several platoons of WAVES march in. We're not allowed to speak to them, but I've been exchanging notes with a WAVE who uses the same typewriter I do. We write them on slips of paper and stash them inside the machine. She hasn't told me yet what her name is. . . .

Dear Homer:

I certainly don't have to tell you and Edna how beautiful the campus looks when it's covered with a foot of snow and the lake is frozen for several hundred yards out. It probably hasn't changed much since the days when you both lived here. I hadn't realized that the church where you held forth is so near by.

I bought a pair of ice skates and spent last Sunday afternoon skating on one of the tennis courts that the university has flooded, and I got acquainted with a girl from Passaic, New Jersey. She was bundled up in winter sports clothes and looked like she wanted a skating companion. When I asked if I could take her to dinner (we have weekends free) she shook her head and told me she was the assistant physical education officer at the WAVES school! No fraternizing, you know, between officers and enlisted men.

However. . . .

Dear Homer:

Is it my imagination or are the students here healthier and less neurotic than students at Chicago? Is it possible that certain neurotic types are attracted to the University of Chicago? The girls I've met at mixer dances in the Student Union Building seem—how shall I put it?—refreshingly normal. I suppose the girls at the University of Oklahoma when I was there were pretty much the same, but *I* was different then, as you know, and I saw them in a different light. Chicago students are certainly brainier—I've not heard any discussions of Aristotle in the Student Union's Rathskeller!—but the girls do seem happier and better adjusted. . . .

I remember one time when you spoke in class about Freud's views on the correlation between neurosis and mental achievement. It does make sense. A maladjusted high school intellectual would want to go to Chicago instead of a university like this where he or she would feel out of place in the fraternity and sorority life and all the enthusiasm for the football team. Has anyone ever made a study along such lines? I mean a statistical survey of I.Q.'s and the kinds of neuroses among undergraduates at different American colleges?

Dear Homer:

Remember Jack Elder, one of Notre Dame's football players a few year's back? Well, he's just arrived on the base to take over the phys ed program. We spend an hour every afternoon doing calisthenics and then jogging around the university's field house track. He's organized a boxing tournament in which I'm entered. The final matches take place next week at a Happy Hour show. (What childish names the Navy uses! But they go, I suppose, with the little-boy suits they make us wear.) I'll be fighting another trainee for the middleweight crown. There wasn't any competition getting to the finals. None of the sailors here have done any serious boxing before. I'll let you know how it all turns out.

Lieutenant Elder, by the way, is one of the few officers here who is universally liked by the trainees. The average officer, especially if he's been to Annapolis, seems to have a built-in sense of superiority toward all enlisted men, even toward older chiefs who are far more experienced than he is. The officers most respected by the men are those who don't blame the enlisted man for not respecting most officers. Maybe I'm being unfair. Maybe I'd see it differently if I'd gotten a commission. . . .

Dear Homer:

I won the middleweight bout. I really should have disqualified myself. The boy I fought was so incompetent I could have knocked him out in three minutes, but I didn't want to humiliate him. He's a good guy, and I knew he had a girl friend watching. 1 just sparred around and got the decision on points.

Lt. Elder presented me with the prize. It's a waterproof wrist watch donated by a Madison department store. As Lt. Elder said, if I'm ever on a ship that goes down I'll always know what time it is while I paddle around in the salt water. . . .

I enclose a funny document. It's the mimeographed form we use for recording hourly events when we stand a night watch at the Gate House. The executive officer, a lawyer from Detroit, wrote the complicated instructions. Aren't they hilarious? So far nobody, not even any of our division chiefs, has been able to figure them out.

Dear Homer:

Does the *Capital Times* go back to the days when you and Edna lived in Madison? Someone told me that William Evjue, the editor, is one of the old Bob La Follette Progressives. Did you ever know Evjue personally? He really keeps the town on its toes. I've been reading his paper regularly. It's surprisingly liberal. It's as far left, it seems to me, as New York's *P.M.* The editorials are excellent.

Which reminds me. I've become a journalist of sorts myself. The base has just started a thing called the *Badger Navy News*. It's supposed to be inserted once a week in the student newspaper, the *Daily Cardinal*. Each division of sailors and WAVES has a "reporter" who's expected to write a kind of gossip column about the persons in his or her division. My division chief asked me—well, he *ordered* me—to take on this chore.

The yeoman who edits the Navy paper is named George Groth. He's a skinny fellow with bushy black eyebrows and a sad expression. I met him yesterday when I brought him my first column. It turns out that before he enlisted he was working for his master's degree in philosophy at the University of Chicago! He told me that three years ago he took your course in religious psychology. Do you remember him? He says you probably won't because he attended class irregularly and didn't join much in the discussions.

Dear Homer:

. . . I've had several bull sessions with him [Groth] over coffee in the Pine Room. He's a shy, odd sort of person with lots of curious views. He's a great admirer of William James, and he keeps telling me I should read a Spanish writer named Unamuno. I thought at first he was pulling my leg, but he says there really was someone with that name. I've never even *heard* of Unamuno. Who is he?

Groth agrees that Hitler has to be stopped but he has a very low opinion of Stalin and Russian communism in general. We haven't talked much about politics, but I think he must be some kind of socialist. Whenever I say anything about Russia, he just stares at me and smiles. He says I should read a new novel call *Darkness at Noon* by someone whose name sounded like Kessler. Do you know anything about this book?

Dear Homer:

A frightening thing has been happening here. For the past week there's been big "scuttlebutt"—that's Navy slang for gossip—about the next division coming from Great Lakes being a division of Negro sailors. No one knows how the rumor started. I suppose some trainees had seen some Negro enlisted men at the Lakes and just assumed that some of them would be sent here to the radio school. The division chiefs said they knew for a fact that the next division would be all white, but that didn't stop the rumor.

I was having coffee in the Pine Room with Groth a few days ago, and two WAVE storekeepers (part of the school's Ship's Company) were sitting at the same table. "I can't believe it," one of them said. "I just can't believe they'd send niggers up here. Why, where would they put 'em?"

Groth asked her where she came from, and she said New Orleans. He told her he'd heard that the Navy would be recruiting Negro WAVES next year. I thought the storekeeper would have an apoplectic fit!

Later that afternoon, when my platoon was marching across the campus, we passed another platoon of trainees tramping the other way. The boys were singing words to the tune of *John Brown's Body*. This is what they sang:

> *Oh, it's John Brown's Navy,*
> *Soon the niggers will be here.*
> *It's John Brown's Navy,*
> *Soon the niggers will be here.*
> *It's John Brown's Navy,*

Soon the niggers will be here.
They will, like hell, they will!

Dear Homer:

The new division arrived yesterday on schedule. It was the usual assortment of palefaces, fresh out of boots, some from farming areas in the Middle West, some from the big cities. That killed all the scuttlebutt.

It was a revelation to me, seeing how intense the feeling had been. Good Lord, one reason we're fighting Hitler is *supposed* to be because he wants to impose his nutty racism on the world. It's so easy for us to see the motes in the eyes of other nations and overlook the beams in our own. . . .

I've become more friendly with Groth, the yeoman in the public relations office. We get along fine as long as we don't talk about Russia! He has a girl friend who's a nurse in the University of Wisconsin Hospital. And his girl friend has a girl friend—another nurse. Groth introduced me to her last Saturday and the four of us went to the Jolly Roger, a beer and dance spot on the outskirts of Madison. She's a very pretty girl and. . . .

Dear Homer:

I thought the recent outburst of anti-Negro feeling on the base had disappeared. I was wrong. An ugly incident took place a few days ago. Your faithful correspondent, I regret to say—no, I'm proud to say—was involved.

A colored student at the university was walking up State Street last Saturday night. He was with a white girl. They passed a couple of radio trainees who had just come out of a tavern. Both sailors were slightly drunk. One of them made an insulting remark to the girl, and the Negro boy had the guts to answer back. A fight started.

I happened to be about a block away when I heard the shouting and saw a crowd gathering. I ran to the scene and got there just in time to break up the fight before the colored boy got badly hurt. The smaller of the two sailors quit swinging as soon as I pulled him away and gave him a shove. I had just started on the bigger one, and got in a few blows on his ribs, when a shore patrol wagon pulled up to the curb. Both sailors dived into the crowd and vanished.

Result? The shore patrol arrested *me*! Fortunately the onlookers verified the story told by the Negro boy and the girl with him. The patrolmen gave them both, and me, some dirty looks, then finally let me go after taking down my name and serial number.

I thought that would be the end of it. But next day the *Capital Times* played up the incident and demanded that the Navy take action and punish the two trainees. The Commanding Officer called me into his office. He seemed relieved when I told him I wouldn't recognize either sailor if I saw him again. That was true. The fight happened at a poorly lighted spot in the middle of the block. Besides, I was so mad I didn't pay much attention to what they looked like.

The C.O. ordered one of his ensigns to get together with the division chiefs to see if they could find out who the two trainees were. Groth told me later that when the chiefs reported no success the ensign congratulated them. "You did a splendid job," he said. "You did your best to find the men, and you didn't."

There's more! A few days later a naval intelligence officer from Milwaukee arrived to investigate the incident. It turned out that his real purpose was to investigate me! The suspicion was that the colored boy and I had gotten together and provoked the whole thing. The officer questioned me for several hours. Did I know the boy? Did I know the girl? Had I attended any meetings of left-wing campus groups? And on and on. I think I finally convinced him that I'd never seen the boy or girl before. I have no idea whether either of them is involved in any radical activities. (The officer wouldn't tell me anything about them.) I had the impression that naval intelligence hasn't discovered yet that the Commies are *supporting* the war. . . .

Dear Homer:

. . . so nothing came of the investigation, although the story does have a kind of anticlimax. Yesterday about dusk I was on my way to the Student Union's Rathskeller, walking along a wooded path that winds along the shore of Lake Mendota. A sailor approached, headed the other way. He stopped a few yards in front of me.

"You don't remember me, do you Mac," he said in a heavy Southern accent. I told him no, I didn't. "I'm the guy you punched the other night," he said. And then he said, "Now I'm going to beat the shit out of you."

He walked closer and started a long, clumsy swing at my nose. It was easy to dodge. He tried again. I dodged again. "Goddam it, you sonofabitch, hold still!" he shouted.

He grabbed the lapels of my pea-jacket and started shaking me. I hit him a couple of times on his chest—not hard but just enough to make him let go. Then I tapped him gently on the chin. That staggered him a bit. I popped another light blow to his belly. He dropped both hands, and I was just about to land a good solid right on the point of his chin when the situation suddenly struck me as preposterous. I checked my fist in midair.

You'll be happy to know, Homer, that for once I got the best of this lousy temper of mine. Maybe I wasn't really mad. Here he was, a sailor from the South, an obvious victim of his upbringing. Being what he was, how could I blame him for feeling the way he did? I knew that nothing I could do or say could make him see things any different.

I picked up his hat, dusted it off, and handed it to him. "No hard feelings, Mac," I said.

He took the hat and didn't say anything. I continued on to the Student Union. A few days later I noticed him marching in a platoon of trainees who had arrived about two weeks ago. He pretended not to see me.

Well, that's the story. It set me thinking a lot about race prejudice. Is free will really involved? If it's all a matter of conditioning, how can we, how can God, put any moral blame on a Southern racist? Or *is* it all conditioning?

I think that here we come up against the mystery of will. I have a feeling—it's hard to put into words—that the human will is the mystery of all mysteries. If God tried to explain it to us, he could no more make it clear than a mechanic could tell a year-old baby how the engine of a car works. . . .

Dear Homer:

Spring in Madison has finally sprung. It's even more beautiful than I expected. Last Sunday I rented a canoe and spent the day paddling around Lake Mendota in my bathing trunks and getting started on a suntan. The lake was like a big blue mirror, hardly a ripple on it. In a month or so I may be seeing some real waves—ocean waves, that is, not WAVES.

Today's the first Sunday I've missed church. I don't think I've mentioned before that I've been going every Sunday to a different church. You'll be pleased to know that the only service I've attended that I liked was at the Unitarian Church where you once were minister and your old friend Patton now holds forth. He never mentioned God in his sermon, but there were Negroes in the congregation and the sermon was a stirring appeal for expressing love through social action, especially in civil rights and race relations. I had a stronger sense of God's presence *there* than at any of the large Protestant churches I've been to.

I know you don't like my saying this, but I think that you and Patton, and the other Unitarians who are working for a better world, really believe in God without realizing it. . . .

Dear Homer:

My division graduates next Tuesday. I'll get my "sparks"—an arm insignia with one "V" and an electric spark. It will make me a third-class petty officer and give me a nice raise in pay. I have a ten-day leave before I report to wherever I've been assigned. I hope it's a ship. . . .

I'm planning a trip to Oklahoma to see my folks, but first I'll be in Chicago on Wednesday morning. Could you put me up for the night? The sofa will do fine.

It will be wonderful to see you and Edna again.

16

USS Montgomery

Peter's two-day Chicago visit, before he went to Oklahoma to see his parents, was the first time I had seen him since his enlistment. He seemed in excellent spirits. The blue sailor suit and the white hat made him look younger than he was, and although he made a number of remarks about the stupidity of the uniform, I suspect he secretly enjoyed wearing it.

Our conversation was mostly political. Russia was of course a war ally, and we were both pleased with the favorable articles about Stalin that had been appearing in mass-circulation magazines. Even American movies—*Mission to Moscow*, for example—were portraying Stalin as a wise and kindly "Uncle Joe." Peter looked forward, as did I, to a postwar period of Soviet-American friendship. Would not the ideal state combine the political democracy of the West with the economic democracy of Russian Marxism? The two giants would move closer together, cooperating in comradely rivalry, each correcting its faults in the light of the other's virtues. This old "convergence theory" is a hope, I suppose, that many still cherish. I was surprised to find it expressed in the following poem by the Russian poet Andrei Voznesensky (my quote is from a translation by Anthony Austin which I clipped from the *New York Times Book Review* on May 14, 1967):

> *In the world ring two wrestlers,*
> *gasping, clung in an embrace,*
> *One orange and one black,*
> *joined chest to chest.*
> *But oh horror! on an orange back*
> *Great menacing spots of black*
> *Appear, the seepage has begun!*

The orange one strains and twists
his rival's ear
And howls with pain. The ear is his.
It has flowed over to his adversary.

Not all the trainees in Peter's graduating division were made third class petty officers. Peter was one of the few honor students who got the rating. He brought a supply of "crows" (as he called the cloth insignias) with him, and Edna sewed them on the left sleeves of all his jumpers.

After his trip to Oklahoma, Peter reported to the Navy's classification center at Lido Beach, Long Island, New York, where he was assigned to a destroyer escort called the *USS Montgomery*. It operated with five sister ships and, on rare occasions, with a small aircraft carrier. The six ships were what the Navy called a "killer group." It had one single purpose: destroying German U-boats. Each DE carried the Navy's new (then top secret) sonar equipment for underwater submarine detection. The group wandered over the Atlantic, sweeping the ocean with its sound waves, looking for the big fish on which to drop its "cans."

From Lido Beach, Peter was sent to the base at Norfolk, Virginia, to join the crew of the *Montgomery*. Unfortunately the ship left Norfolk a few days before he got there. After a week or two at Norfolk, he was sent to Jacksonville, Florida, but by the time the paper work involved in *that* transfer had been completed, the *Montgomery* had sailed again. He finally caught up with her at Portland, Maine. I did not hear from him again until he had been at sea for several weeks.

This chapter is a selection from letters I received from Peter during his first year on the Atlantic. Most of them were typed with all letters in upper case because he used the special typewriters in the radio shack. As before, I have chosen only portions which seem to me of special interest.

Dear Homer:
  . . . I've just recovered from a really violent attack of sea sickness. We had a calm sea the first week after I came aboard, then a storm blew up and the ship began to rock like a cork. To *me* it was a storm. The men on the ship tell me that the earlier period of calm was the exception and that what I call a storm is just the usual choppy North Atlantic! A few months ago, they said, the ship went through a *real* storm. One wave—it must have been forty feet high— ripped a search-light off the signal bridge and smashed a port lookout station like it was cardboard.

But the waves looked big to me, and the nausea flattened me on the sack for about five days. I began eating slowly and finally managed to keep some food down, then suddenly, *mirabile dictu*, the nausea disappeared! The ocean has been a lot rougher since, but I feel marvelous. We have a strap in our bunks that keeps us from getting tossed out while we sleep. Most of the men carry large knives which they jab into the mess hall tables to keep their food trays from sliding around. Coffee pots are suspended from the overhead on long ropes. They hang straight while the ship tilts. It takes a bit of doing to pour yourself a cup of "Joe" without spilling it.

The first day on board I did a stupid thing. I left my wrist watch (the one I got as a boxing prize at Madison) on my bunk while I went to the head. It was gone when I got back. Some sailors standing nearby swore they hadn't seen anybody take it. It's a mistake I won't make again!

Dear Homer:

I'm amazed at how complicated life can be on such a small ship! I've finally learned the difference between the fo'c'sle and the fantail, what "ladders" to climb and what hatches to go through to get where you want to go, the names of the officers, and so on. . . .

The profanity shocked me for a while but you soon understand that it's just the way men naturally talk on a ship. It doesn't mean anything, and it sets you apart from the others if you speak any other way. I'm actually getting quite proficient in using all the four-letter words.

Some of the expressions are little masterpieces of vulgarity: "blow it up your ass," for instance, and "fuck that shit." Isn't that last one a beauty! Another delightful phrase is "bring all this shit to a focus." A bunch of gunner's mates were reorganizing a compartment where our ammunition is stored. "All right, youse guys, get the lead outta your ass," the chief said. "We gotta bring all this shit to a focus." We have one old-timer on board, a boatswain's mate with five hashmarks on his sleeve, who puts four-letter words between *syllables*. I asked him the other day if he was sure something was right and he said, "Pete, my boy, I guaranfuckintee it!"

My boss, the chief in charge of the radio shack, is named Sam Hall. He comes from Alabama. I'll tell you more about him in my next letter.

Dear Homer:

I postponed writing again until the ship docked and I could mail a letter that wouldn't be read by the officer in charge of censoring mail.

I don't have anything to say that violates security regulations, but I do want to tell you more about Sam Hall, our chief radioman. You'll realize why I didn't want any of the officers to read this.

Sam is probably a Communist. If he isn't, he's close enough to be indistinguishable from one. I imagine he's been wondering the same thing about me. I don't intend to ask him, partly because it doesn't really matter, partly because he might tell me something it would be best for me not to know. As you can appreciate, Communism isn't something one discusses openly on a Navy ship, and the less I know about Sam's party connections the less likely I'll let something slip that might get him in trouble. I suppose he feels the same way about asking me questions. But we've had lots of long discussions about Russia. So far as I know, we're the only two men on the ship who have any knowledge or sympathy for what the Soviets are doing.

Also, Sam's the only person on the ship I've told that I was preparing to be a preacher. He was very much interested in hearing about my campus political activities, and he tells me he knows Frank Meyer. Remember Frank? I'd wondered what happened to him. Sam says he enlisted in the Army. I think you'd like Sam. He feels as you and I do that a socially conscious minister can perform a great service in leading his congregation into more liberal political views. I've told him a lot about you. He says he hopes we can all get together sometime after the war.

Sam grew up in a small town in Alabama and went to work as soon as he finished high school. . . . He's never been to college, but he's done a fantastic amount of reading. Before the war he was putting out a small weekly paper with a left political slant. He distributed it to Alabama Negroes and farmers and sharecroppers. There were two occasions on which he almost got himself killed. . . .

This will amuse you. Sam's in charge of preparing a news report that I thumbtack every day on a bulletin board on the bulkhead outside the radio shack. He does a careful job of editing and selecting, so the crew gets a daily dose of news edited in a progressive direction. It's not enough to be obvious, but enough to start the men thinking. Of course the Old Man doesn't know Sam's doing this. He thinks the report is a verbatim transcription of what the Navy sends. . . .

Dear Homer:
A shocking thing happened last week. Our executive officer was escorted off the ship by two Marine officers who came aboard and politely arrested him! I'd heard some scuttlebutt about the exec, but

I didn't believe it. Now Sam tells me the background on the whole thing.

The exec apparently had been giving money to a couple of young seamen in the deck force. Whenever the ship pulled into port for a few days, the exec and those two boys would shack up in a hotel room. The Captain knew about it but hadn't been able to persuade either boy to talk. Then something must have happened because one of the sailors spilled the whole story. The episode is wrapped in obscurity. All I know is that about three weeks ago the two sailors were transferred off the ship, and last week the exec. We're supposed to get a replacement for him before the ship pulls out. "Buck" Harden, our chief yeoman, told Sam that the boys were only interested in the money and are *not* homosexuals (hard to believe!). They will probably get light prison sentences. Buck predicts that the exec will get a medical discharge.

It's hard to know how much homosexual activity goes on on the ship. The men involved naturally don't talk about it, but the scuttlebutt singles out three of the petty officers. They're called "pogues" by the other men. Do long periods at sea bring out repressed homosexual drives, or did the men just slip through whatever screening methods the Navy uses? It never occurred to me until now that life on a ship could be highly satisfactory for a homosexual. Was Melville a homosexual? Now that I think about it, I can't remember anywhere in *Moby Dick* that Ishmael ever thinks about women. And there was that cannibal buddy of his, Queequeg. Did Melville mean Queerqueg? What about famous pirates like Captain Kidd? I used to think of the seafaring man as a rugged masculine type. But why would such a person choose a career that forces him to spend most of his life on a ship where all his companions are men?

Of course the present Navy is a good deal different from the regular. We have only about a dozen regulars aboard. The rest (there are about 200 men altogether) are here only because of the war and anxious to get the hell out as soon as it ends. It is heterosexual sex that dominates the thoughts of almost every sailor when he leaves the ship. There are usually two or three enlisted men getting shots in sick bay for gonorrhea. The standard question everyone asks when you get back from a liberty is, "How did you make out?" Meaning, of course, how did you make out with the girls.

Here in Norfolk the prowling section for the enlisted man is several blocks along Main Street. The most popular spot is a bar called the American Garden. Sam and I are going there tomorrow night to see what it's like. I'll give you a report next time.

Dear Homer:

The American Garden is a depressing place. I can't make up my mind whether I approve or not. It's one enormous room with a bar that serves nothing but beer and bottles of cheap champagne (cheap in quality, not price!). The place is jammed every night, including Sunday, with sailors, soldiers, and marines—but mostly sailors. There's usually a fight or two before the place closes at about three in the morning.

The waitresses are a spooky lot. They're all under twenty, and most of them are attractive in a crude, animal sort of way. They carry on a steady stream of obscene chatter that's indistinguishable from the language of the ship. I noticed one peculiar thing. Every girl, when you see her up close, has some sort of physical defect. A bad complexion or an odd nose or a poor figure or a good figure but ugly face. There's always *something* wrong.

They *seem* happy. Most of them wear tight sweaters and Navy dungarees rolled up to their knees. They slither in and out between tables, exchanging profanity with the patrons and letting themselves get patted on their behinds. There are no other girls in the place. I've no idea whether the waitresses hustle on the side or whether they just give the impression they do. My guess is—I could be wrong—that they're just simple-minded, not-very-attractive teen-age girls from low-income backgrounds who enjoy the noise and excitement of the place and a life of nonprofessional promiscuity.

The girl who waited on Sam and me was a dark-skinned creature named Arabella. She looked like an Oklahoma Cherokee, but more likely she's part Negro. Her face would have been lovely except for one eye that's slightly cocked and a hideous red scar that runs from the corner of the bad eye down her cheek. Her hips are wider than they should be, and her breasts are huge. She has a small blue anchor tattooed on her left tit. She pulls up her sweater to display this on request.

She told us she lived in a trailer camp on the edge of Norfolk. Sam asked if we could take her home after the place closed. She shook her head and said her boy-friend was meeting her. "Ask me some other time," she said, patting Sam on his crotch. We later decided that that was probably a well-rehearsed maneuver intended to persuade customers to come back again.

We stayed a couple of hours, then a commotion started in a rear booth. A sailor had poured a glass of beer over the head of a fat waitress that everybody called "Big Bag." She tried to hit him with a beer bottle, then she sat down, buried her face in her hands, and began to cry. My heart went out to her. Several sailors were standing around and shouting at each other. It looked as if there might be a fight, but someone called the shore patrol and they got there before any trouble started. Sam and I grabbed our change and ducked out. . . .

Dear Homer:
We've got a fundamentalist aboard! Didn't you tell me once that Mencken had written that if you toss an egg out of a train window anywhere in Tennessee you'll hit a fundamentalist? Anyway, this fellow is a baker from Nashville. He joined our crew last month when we were in Norfolk, and already he's decided that what the USS *Montgomery* needs most is a worship service on Sunday! Two Sundays ago he actually rounded up about a dozen sailors and took them into the mess hall for hymn singing and a Scripture lesson. He tried it again last Sunday.

I went to his first service. Believe me, Homer, I had a funny feeling sitting there and listening to him talk a language I hadn't heard since I belonged to Holiness Tabernacle. The baker tells me he taught Sunday School at a Pentecostal Assembly of God church in Nashville. He wasn't quite sure why I was there. I made the mistake of singing the first hymn, *The Haven of Rest* (he'd picked it because of the sea angle), all the way through without using the hymnal. (He had found about twenty hymn books on the bottom shelf of the ship's book locker.) I saw him watching me out of the corners of his eyes while I was singing.

After the service was over he asked me if I was saved. I told him I was. Then he asked me what church I belonged to. I didn't want to get involved in helping him at other services, and while I was trying to think of what to say I remembered something I'd read in Upton Sinclair's novel *Oil*. Did you ever read *Oil*? Whenever the oilman in that book wanted to avoid talking about religion to a farmer, he'd tell the farmer that he belonged to a sect called the Church of the True Word and that members weren't allowed to talk about their beliefs to anybody except other members. That's what I told our baker. It puzzled him no end. Every time I bump into him on the ship, he tries to get me to tell him something about the Church of the True Word. I smile like a Sphinx and shake my head.

His second service was a complete bust. Nobody showed up. As soon as he left the mess hall, with his arm load of hymn books, a group of seamen moved in and started a crap game.

It's hard to believe I ever shared his views, yet I must have been very much like him six years ago. I thought about talking to him seriously sometime about evolution and the Bible and so on, then I decided it wouldn't do any good. I can remember myself too well to expect that anything I could say would have any meaning for him. You must have realized that when you first knew me. I can't remember that you ever tried to argue, really argue, with me about anything. . . .

Is anybody *ever* talked out of a religious belief?

Dear Homer:

Our baker's attempt to stir up some religious enthusiasm on the ship has got me thinking again about the great doctrines of Christianity and how Barth interprets them. Last night I had the midwatch in the radio shack. It's four long hours from 2400 (midnight) to 0400 (four in the morning). Nothing was being transmitted, so I had lots of time to meditate.

God still seems as real to me as ever. Here on the ship where we're so close to the elements, He seems particularly real. Yet I'm astonished at how dim Calvary and the Cross have become. Fanny Crosby's old hymn, *Jesus Keep Me Near the Cross,* used to be one of my favorites. I sang all the verses to myself, and it was like singing *The Wreck of the Old Ninety-Seven.* Jesus died a bloody death on the Cross. The engineer in the ballad was scalded to death by the locomotive's steam. It seemed to me as if neither death had anything *special* to do with God. How I would have been ashamed of such a thought two years ago!

I've moved a long way, Homer, toward your humanism. There's a growing rift in my mind between faith in God and faith in the Christian mythology. I feel sure that if the ship were hit tonight by a torpedo and I were to die, I would die in God's good graces. But what does this sense of being "saved" have to do with the life and death of Jesus? At the moment I don't really know how to answer that. Maybe the size of the Atlantic has something to do with it. It makes the Sea of Galilee seem so small. . . .

I sometimes wonder: Would I have my faith, my feeling of being saved, if I hadn't gone through an old-fashioned conversion? It's hard to say. If I hadn't had such an intense experience, such a strong feeling that God had reached down and started my soul moving in a new direction, would I be believing in God today?. . . .

Dear Homer:

. . . The big problem for me now is what to make of Jesus Christ. In my fundamentalist days it was no problem. From *your* standpoint

it's no problem. But for someone like me, hoping some day to be a
Christian minister, it is *the* problem. I always assumed that Barth's
Christology is the same as Luther's and Calvin's. Now I am beginning
to wonder.

I don't think I ever admitted to you before—I now freely confess it!—
that I never fully understood Barth's distinction between the historical
and nonhistorical events in the life of Jesus. The same goes for Bultmann.
I used to get a strange feeling when I read the German theologians. It
was a feeling that someday in Heaven I might meet the Christ, and he
in turn would introduce me to a former carpenter called Jesus whose
body and mind he once had inhabited. Surely the Barthian Christology
doesn't reduce to *that*! But if it doesn't, what *does* it reduce to?

The orthodox Christ who was the paradoxical union of God and man—
the Christ of Saint Paul and Saint Augustine and Thomas Aquinas and
the Protestant Reformers and Kierkegaard and Moody and Chesterton—
that Christ is easy to understand. At least *I* never had any difficulty
with it. But Bultmann's Christ? When the war's over, if I'm still alive,
I must study these German Christs more carefully. Maybe I've misunderstood. Maybe there are subtleties I haven't yet grasped. . . .

Dear Homer:
We're tied up in Norfolk again for minor repairs. Sam and I went
back to the American Garden last night. I'd hoped Arabella would wait
on us, but the girls told us that she'd quit working there several months
ago. None of them seemed to know or care where she'd gone.

Have I mentioned Coleman's Tattoo Parlor before? It's on Main
Street a few blocks from the American Garden. Sam and I spent some
time hanging around inside to watch Coleman work. He's a thin, middle-
aged man with a crucifixion scene, complete with the two thieves and
Mary, tattooed on his back. It was a hot day, and Coleman was wearing
nothing but a pair of shorts. A big sign on the wall says, "We do not
tattoo intoxicated sailors." Another sign says, "How to Remove Tattoo
Marks." When you walk up close you see that the directions are in
Chinese!

There's a funny story about Coleman and a boatswain's mate on our
ship. When we were last in Norfolk, this boy had gone to Coleman to
get the words "port" and "starboard" tattooed in blue ink on the left
and right sides of his ass. It's a common thing to have those words
tattooed on the body, but usually on the arms or chest. Coleman was
used to putting "port" on *his* right because the sailor always faced him.

It didn't occur to him while he was decorating this poor fellow's tail that the boy was facing the other way and that this would reverse his left and right sides. So Coleman put "port" on the sailor's right cheek and "starboard" on his left!

It gets funnier. When he finished, the sailor inspected the job in a mirror. But a mirror reverses left and right so everything looked okay! It wasn't until a week later, while he was taking a shower on the ship, that one of his buddies noticed the mistake. Is he pissed off! He tells me he plans to go back to Coleman and make him change both words into large blue roses.

Dear Homer:

We're back at sea. I'm writing this in a new spot I've found on the ship where I can sneak off and hide when I want to read in private. It's the extreme aft compartment called "after steering." The wheel in the pilot house is connected electrically with a mechanism in here that operates the big gears and rods that move the rudders. There's a large flat place on top of one of the rods where you can sit. It's pleasant to be rotated slowly, first one way then the other, as the rudders keep changing positions. I'll mail this letter later after we get to port because I want to get some things off my chest that I don't want the officers to read.

There's one sense in which the gulf between officers and enlisted men is greater on a ship like this than at a shore station, and another sense in which it's less. The sense in which it's *less* is that on a ship as small as a DE most of the rules of etiquette are suspended. There are no salutes on deck, for instance. The officers wear work clothes. Most of them are young. On our ship they're all reservists. (The only Annapolis man ever on the *USS Montgomery* was the first exec who is no longer with us.) For all these reasons there's a much more informal relationship between the two castes than at a shore base.

I haven't been on any ship except this, but I'm told by other enlisted men who *have* served on other ships that we're lucky in having better-than-average gold braid. The Captain, who used to manage a drugstore in Montana, is an admirable fellow. So is the new exec. On the whole the officers are well liked by the enlisted men, especially the first lieutenant who himself dislikes the caste system, and we all know he feels that way.

The main thing wrong with the system, as I see it, is that the separation between the two classes is hardly ever based on merit. It's based on the accident of having been or not been to college. The result is that a man of mediocre abilities is often giving orders to chiefs who are older than he and with more expertise. I sometimes think that if all the officers on our ship were tossed overboard, except for the Skipper and one or two others, the ship's fighting efficiency might actually improve. Incompetent officers would no longer have to mediate between the Skipper and the chiefs who really run the ship. What the Navy needs most, it seems to me, is more promotion from the ranks. It needs more officers who know their jobs and who understand how to handle enlisted men even though they may not know the etiquette of how to handle a knife and fork.

On a small ship like ours, the incompetent officer just retreats into silence and inactivity where he can't cause any harm. He lets the chiefs run his division. All he does is sign the papers the yeomen bring him and stay out of everybody's way by hiding in the officer's lounge where he can play solitaire, drink coffee, and listen to the radio. It's a sad thing on a ship when the enlisted men know an officer is no good, and he not only knows it, too, but he knows the men know.

The main way that the gulf between the two castes is *greater* on a DE is in the living conditions. The sailors wait in long lines for low-grade chow which they eat off metal trays. The officers have excellent food specially prepared for them in a separate galley by special cooks who are on board just for that purpose. The food is served on a table-cloth, set with elegant china and polished silverware, by Negro steward's mates. The enlisted man sleeps in a crowded, smelly compartment, with no sheets, and locker space that's no more than a few cubic feet. I don't know how it is on other DE's, but on ours the lockers crawl with cockroaches. Every now and then, when we're taking on fuel, the "snipes" (the men in the engineering division) get careless and the entire after crew's sleeping compartment is flooded with diesel oil. It flows into the lockers, and everything you own has to be cleaned or thrown away.

The officers are paired two to a stateroom. Each room has a wash basin, bookcase, and two dressers. A Negro steward's mate keeps the room clean, makes up the bunks, and changes the linen. The officers' lounge has a sofa, easy chairs, radio, and an always-hot pot of coffee. There's no lounge for the crew. In fact there's not a single chair on the ship where an enlisted man below the rank of chief can sit when he's not on duty. Even the benches in the mess hall are backless. If you have a spare hour to "crap out" (rest), you're not allowed to unhook your bunk. You have to lie on top of the metal lockers under the bunks or crap out in some out-of-the-way corner. I'll spare you the scatalogical details about our head.

The old Navy, I suppose, was even worse. Sam tells me he's spent some time studying the Soviet military system and that in Russia the commissions are now given strictly on merit and experience. He says that officers and enlisted men all call each other "Comrade" and that most of the regulations that emphasized caste in the days of the Czars have been abolished. Maybe that's one reason why Stalin's army has been doing so well against the Nazi invaders. . . .

Dear Homer:

In case you've wondered why you haven't heard from me for so long, we've been at sea more than six weeks and this is the first chance we've had to get mail off the ship. One of the carrier planes is flying the mail to the states. The big news is that two weeks ago we ran into the first real action that's happened since I came aboard. I can't give you any details, for security reasons, but I *can* say that at last I'm feeling as if I'm really in the war.

I've often wondered how our crew, me included, would behave in a battle situation. It's amazing how a sudden need for cooperation will seize a group of men and give them an efficiency you never dreamed they'd be capable of. We were at our battle stations for 70 hours without sleep. The cooks were kept busy doing nothing except bringing us sandwiches and coffee. And what a feeling when it's all over! Everyone laughing and slapping each other on the back. A common danger is a great promoter of human brotherhood. Everybody loves everybody, including the officers!

I've wondered, too, how I'd feel if I had to take a more direct part in killing. I'm not so naive as to think that noncombat military service is less wicked than combat service. Like the Army, the Navy operates as one enormous, complicated *thing*. The enemy, at least for the Navy, is almost always invisible. No one has the experience of seeing him or hitting him directly, the way soldiers do in hand-to-hand combat. It takes six men to operate one of our three-inch guns. No single man in the gun crew feels that he *personally* is doing the shooting. Even the fire control man who trips off the blast is only obeying a command from an officer on the bridge. And the entire ship couldn't function without hundreds of men and women at shore stations who are involved in its operation and maintenance. Every person in the Navy, even if he's training carrier pigeons or playing a trombone in a Navy band, is contributing something to the operation of the *thing*.

And yet there's no escape from the emotional feeling of personal responsibility when the time comes that your acts are part of a chain of causes and effects, scarcely a minute long, that ends with sending fifty living souls into eternity. Believe me, Homer, it was a shattering experience! Was I obeying God's will? I think I was. I hope I was. But how can one ever know for sure?

Our only casualty was one of the cooks. We could see his hands shaking when he brought us coffee. He kept his lifebelt inflated throughout the action—not very smart because that makes it harder to swim away from a sinking ship—and he had *two* Saint Christopher medals on a chain around his neck! After it was all over he had such a bad attack of stomach ulcers that we had to send him to a shore hospital as soon as we docked.

Our Pentecostal baker held up splendidly. He knocked himself out preparing sandwiches and handing them out, and he always had a cheerful remark when he gave you one. Yesterday he tried to interest the crew in a prayer meeting to thank God for the outcome. It met with a chilly response.

It's not that the men aren't religious. I doubt if there were ten men on the ship who didn't pray at some time during the action. But those who did kept it to themselves. That's how it should be. At least, under the circumstances, considering the total situation, I think that's how it should be.

17

The Ship Becomes a She

It was not until after the war that I got from Peter the full story of the military operation to which he had alluded in his letter at the end of the previous chapter. The USS *Davis*, one of the six destroyer escorts in his killer group, had suddenly been blown in half by a German torpedo. The ship sank quickly and within sight of Peter's ship. Ironically, most of the survivors of the torpedo were killed moments later by shock waves from their own depth charges. There had been no time to set the safety devices. When the ship sank to the proper depth, the cans exploded.

Peter had been assigned to a battle station on the flying bridge where he was able to watch the terrible scene through binoculars. Did his mind leap back to memories of the accident that had killed his father? Perhaps. At any rate it was clear to me, as I listened to him tell the story, that the hideous deaths of these men had no more disturbed his faith in God than the death of his father had disturbed his mother's faith. For the true believer such tragedies are easily rationalized. No matter how monstrous, are they not essential episodes in some mysterious, incomprehensible, far-off Plan? I can imagine Peter standing at his lookout post, gazing out over the heaving water, praying for the men he saw floating and bleeding in the sea, and for the safety of his own ship and the others.

One of the DE's had the sad task of picking up the dead and wounded. The other four ships, including Peter's, began an immediate search for the U-boat that had scored the lucky hit. A sonar contact was made in a few hours, and after a long, wearisome chase the submarine was finally trapped and destroyed. Peter himself, standing on the bridge, activated some of the depth charges. On orders from the Captain, his thumbs had pressed two buttons, one red, one green, that fired the cans off the port and starboard sides of the fantail. "These are the thumbs of a strangler," he once said to me, holding up his hands.

Peter became much more security conscious after this event. Although his ship participated in several other battle operations, he did not mention them in later correspondence.

The letters that follow in this chapter were all written during Peter's second and third years aboard the USS Montgomery. He had advanced to radioman second class. I was pleased to observe at the time that his letters were singularly free of theological pettifoggery. The salt sea air was continuing to scour and ventilate his mind. If I believed in Divine Providence, I might suspect that Peter's four years of service had been a gift of grace to prevent him from going mad. His brain cells had been working overtime in the year before he enlisted, and the changes in his beliefs had been coming with ominous rapidity. Now his energies were channeled into the secular here-and-now task of keeping a small ship afloat, of keeping it operating at peak efficiency as a killing machine.

Readers who know Samuel Butler's great religious novel, The Way of All Flesh, may remember how Ernest Pontifex's six months in prison gave him just the period of rest and reflection he so desperately needed to make his transition from the prison of his orthodoxy to intellectual freedom. Was it Samuel Johnson who called a ship a floating prison with the extra feature that one might be drowned? I suspect that Peter's physical confinement, the hard work and discipline of Navy life at sea, the shoulder-rubbing contacts with two hundred ordinary boys and men, provided just the kind of group and work therapy that he needed. Above all, he had no access to scholarly books. There were no lectures to attend. When there was time to stand and stare out over the ship's railing, there was nothing to see except water and sky and at night the stars.

The third letter of this chapter, in which Peter describes his emotions while sitting alone one midnight on the ship's bow, should be of special interest to readers who have experimented, vicariously or otherwise, with psychedelic drugs. It was written many years before Aldous Huxley published his Doors to Perception, and of course the term LSD would then have meant nothing to Peter or myself. There is, however, much in Peter's language to suggest that he experienced, without the aid of drugs, something close to that intense awareness of existence which users of LSD, especially those who have prior religious beliefs, are writing about these days in the psychedelic publications.

Dear Homer:

We've had an unusually long period at sea. It was long enough for us to go many weeks on our emergency rations of miserable dehydrated food and to shower with ocean water to conserve our fresh water supply. A few days ago we finally pulled into port to take on new supplies.

I'm writing this at a USO center where I've been enjoying a comfortable chair. How good it feels to sit on something with a back to it! I've been reading a little paperbound collection of English sonnets. There's one by Rossetti that begins: "Tread softly, all the earth is holy ground." Isn't that a marvelous line? It says *exactly* how I felt when I stepped off the ship and on to something firm that didn't sway eternally back and forth.

Yet, strangely, I find that after several days in a dull port I'm anxious to get to sea again!

In the mail waiting for me here was a small package from a Catholic neighbor of my parents. She had sent me a Saint Christopher medal. I carried it around all day wondering whether I ought to keep it or throw it away. It seems to me such a childish superstition. On the other hand the lady's a dear and sweet old friend who was very kind to me when I was a child. Her gift was one of love. She'll probably ask me about it someday, if this war ever ends. I certainly can't tell her I'd thrown the medal away. I'll compromise. I'll drop it into a corner of my locker. . . .

Dear Homer:

. . . One of our signalmen, a Kansas City boy named Muschietty, pulled a crazy stunt a few weeks ago. Some of his buddies got to talking late one night about how cold the water must be. Muschietty volunteered to jump in and find out. His friends thought he was kidding. One of them bet him five dollars he wouldn't do it.

But he did! His buddies set up a cry of "Man overboard!" The officer at the conn had to stop the ship, reverse engines, and find Muschietty with searchlights. Fortunately there were no German subs in the area. They finally fished him out of the drink. Muschietty told the Skipper he'd been coming down the forward ladder from the signal bridge when his foot slipped. . . .

I'm still distressed over FDR's death. Did the *Chicago Tribune* manage to find any kind words to say about him?

Dear Homer:

I'm typing this in the radio shack during a midwatch. I want to get down in words, before I forget, an experience I had tonight just before starting my watch. I give you fair warning—I'm in a poetic mood! I'm going to type rapidly then revise the letter and retype it with a carbon for myself. It's something I think I'll be glad to have, to read again twenty years from now—assuming of course I get out of this war alive.

I hit the sack early, hoping to get some sleep before the watch, and keeping on my dungarees and socks to save myself the trouble of having to dress completely again. I finally dozed off for a while, then suddenly woke with a start. I had dreamed that the chief on duty had just punched my ribs to get me up. I looked around but the chief was nowhere in sight. My eyes were sticky. I squinted off through the dark tangle of bunks, ventilating pipes, stanchions, and projecting feet, trying to see the hands of a clock near the forward hatch.

The clock is lit by a tiny red bulb. It's the only light in the compartment. (Last year someone scraped the paint off the bulb so we could see better at night. When the exec found out about it he was furious. I asked him why. "Because," he shouted, "if a torpedo ever blew a hole in the side of this compartment, the Germans could see that light for miles!") The bulb throws a crimson glow over the faces and arms of the sailors who sleep close to it. The hands on the clock were near 2300. I had another full hour to sleep.

But I couldn't sleep. I was irrevocably, unaccountably wide awake. I dropped to the deck in my stocking feet and groped around under the lower bunk until I found my shoes. The ventilating shafts were roaring unusually loud, I thought, but not doing their job too well. The smell of perspiration and stinking feet is hard to remove from a sleeping compartment when the weather is hot. One ingenious sailor, sleeping alongside a bulkhead, had fastened a pair of white trousers over an air duct and stretched it out with ropes in such a way that the air blew through one of the pants' legs and directly over his bunk. He was snoring happily. I turned my shoes upside down, gave them a shake in case some cockroaches were inside, and pulled them on.

In the head, while I was urinating, the ship seasawed slowly. We had an unusually quiet sea. My eyes were getting used to the darkness, and I could make out the shape of the metal trough in front of me. The air was warm, and the head smelled like . . . well, it smelled like the head. A small blob of phosphorescent plankton floated like a glow worm down the trough of salt water and vanished through the drain at the lower end. I buttoned my fly, slapped some cold water on my face, and dried my hands with toilet paper.

I walked through the shower room down a passageway, through the empty machine shop, along another narrow corridor, then down a hatch to the mess hall. A Negro steward's mate (they sleep in a spot near the galley where they are isolated from the rest of the crew) groaned in his sleep. I drew myself a cup of scalding coffee from the machine available to those on watch. The eerie red light from the small bulb near the machine, and the black shadows, made a scene that seemed unreal, like a color dream of hell, yet at the same time a scene that was sharp and vivid. I could hear the engines pounding in the ship's bowels. I could feel the deck vibrating under the soles of my shoes. I could smell the diesel oil.

I climbed out of the mess hall, pushed open a hatch, and stepped out on the weather deck. It was the most magnificent night I'd ever seen. There was not a single cloud, and the sky was saturated from horizon to horizon with tens of thousands of bright, glowing stars. A white, quarter moon swung low on the port side. The air was cool and salty and fresh. The sea was in a benevolent mood. No waves. Just long low swells that rocked the ship gently.

For a minute or two I stood there transfixed, inhaling huge breaths of sea air and watching the water churn by the side of the ship in billowy foam that shone with unearthly whiteness. Then I walked forward to the extreme tip of the fo'c'sle and sat down near the anchor chain. Its enormous links glittered like gold in the dim light of the moon and stars. They were clean links. They were *honest* links. They were an essential part of the ship. They were not something added to the ship for killing purposes.

The tip of the fo'c'sle (there must be a name for it, but I've never heard it called anything) is a fine place to sit and meditate. The deck curves steeply upward so you are on a sort of raised spot from which you can look back and see the entire ship. Or you can face forward with the wind and spray stinging your face and see nothing ahead except black sea and sky. The bow comes to a sharp point. It makes the area small and cozy.

The ship's forward speed creates a strong and steady wind. I sat facing the pilot house, my back against the wind. There was not the slightest sound of the engines, only the rhythmic swish of water past the bow. The ship's mast, topped by the rotating radar loop, swayed slowly back and forth against the velvet backdrop of stars. Through the portholes of the pilot house I could see the violet and green glows of vacuum tubes.

I know, Homer, that you don't believe in God, and I don't want to bore you with an account of the emotions that surged through my head, or rather, as it seemed, through the blood and fibers of my entire body. But I want to have a record of what I felt. The majesty and the power of God seemed overwhelming. I could understand, for the first time I think, why the ocean has always been such a gigantic religious symbol even to unbelievers. It's because it stretches off like space, in all directions, to what seems like infinity. "So lonely 'twas," says Coleridge's ancient mariner, "that even God scarce seeméd there to be."

To me, though, it seemed that God was everywhere. Not only behind the stars in some higher dimension of space-time, perhaps beyond space and time, but also closer to me than my breathing. My mind expanded to the outer limits of human thought, to the edges of that ultimate mystery, the mystery of being, the mystery of why anything should exist at all. At the same time, and this is the curious thing, I was aware of that mystery in such a way that there was not the slightest trace of anxiety or dread. There was no fear of God or death. There was only a calm acceptance. I accepted the unbelievable fact that here was a universe. And here was I, miraculously alive in it, conscious of it, conscious of my being conscious of it, and (like dear old Chesterton) grateful for the privilege of existing.

Below me, in the inky depths, swim the White Whales and the Black U-boats. But tonight I did not worry about the mystery of why God permits these monsters to roam the sea. The ship caught up with, or they with us, a school of wonderfully friendly porpoises. For twenty minutes they followed the ship, playing about the bow, cutting the air in graceful arcs, their wet shiny backs glistening in the moon and starlight. They made soft whistling sounds. I swear, Homer, they saw me sitting there and knew that I was watching them. They were trying to tell me something. I whistled back to them. Like the ancient mariner when he saw the water snakes, I blessed them, but not "unaware."

Then suddenly, for the first time since I've been at sea, the ship itself took on a graceful, feminine, almost human aspect. It became a Thou, a person to be loved. It was an astonishing emotion. I've never before been able to capture that feeling, so common to men on the old wooden sailing ships, of the vessel as a "she." The USS Montgomery had always struck me as woefully deficient in personality. The DE's in our group are so much alike that one night in port our quartermaster, "Pop" Swenson, came back drunk from liberty and hit the sack in the right bunk but on the wrong ship! Then, too, the ship is so obviously built for war. Her gray lines are strictly functional, her body a thing of cold, colorless steel—crude, awkward, with as much beauty as a guillotine or an electric chair.

Tonight she cut the swells as gracefully as the dolphins, with a smooth, erotic, undulating motion, and the milky light from the sky rounded and softened her harsh outlines. She lost her metallic ugliness, became something soft and womanly, something more than just a hunk of steel plates welded together for war purposes. It's hard to put into words. I had a feeling of attachment, of belonging. And not just to the ship but also to the ocean and to the stars.

The stars! Surely there must be life out there, on other planets, and maybe far ahead of us in intelligence and knowledge. And in theology? What gods do they worship? What revelations, if any, have they had? I felt a sudden sympathy for all the great religions of the earth, even for the crude mythologies of lost cultures and primitive tribes. I know that to you and Haydon it's all a patchwork of superstition. But to me tonight, as I sit here typing, all the religions of humanity seem *true!* Their myths and symbols transmit little beams of light from suns that decorate like gems the throne of the Almighty, suns that would blind the eyes of faith if we could see them any better.

But I've already written too much, and midwatch is about to end. Through the half-open hatch of the radio shack I can smell bread baking. The marvelous aroma is rising from the galley. In a moment I'll go down there and the baker, our Pentecostal preacher, will hand me not a stone but a large chunk of warm fresh bread. (What kind of bread can I someday give *my* congregation?) Believe me, Homer, at 0400 in the morning, in the middle of the Atlantic, it tastes like the manna of the Exodus!

Dear Homer:

Are we approaching the end of the war with Germany? My guess is we are. Close enough, anyway, for false reports of surrender. This evening I was on the flying bridge chatting with one of the lookouts when "Ace" Hudson, standing watch as the talker, came over and said, "The Old Man just called up to say he's heard a radio report that Germany's surrendered."

"You're not shitting me?" I said. "No," said Ace, "that's the straight dope."

I walked over to Lieutenant Hollingsworth who was at the conn. Yes, he said, Germany had surrendered unconditionally. I asked him what we should do if we got a sub contact. He said that as far as he was concerned he was hard of hearing and hadn't heard the announcement yet.

The muffled words of Payne, one of our sonar men, came through a voice tube. "Can I secure the sound gear, sir?" Hollingsworth grinned, put his lips to the tube and said, "Negative."

Ace had already given the news over the phone to all the men on watch. When I walked past him on my way to the hatch he stopped me and said, "Smitty wants to know what unconditional surrender means." I told him and he relayed the information. Someone on watch must have asked for the time because Ace moved his head so he could see the luminous dial of the clock near the voice tubes. Then he said into the mouthpiece of his phone: "At the sound of the musical tone it will be exactly. . . ." He gave the time, paused, then blew a loud Bronx cheer.

I descended the spiral ladder to the radio shack. Sam Hall was at the controls. When I walked in he took off his headphones and said, "It's a false alarm, Pete. President Truman just came on the air and said so." I asked him where the rumor came from. "The Associated Press," Sam said. "I can't understand it. The AP doesn't usually make mistakes like that."

We talked a while, then I went back to my bunk in the after crew's compartment. Several men stopped me on the way to ask what the dope was. I told them what Sam told me. Their faces were blank. They made no comments. If the Atlantic war does end soon, the Mighty M will probably be sent to the Pacific. You can't blame the men (me too) for not getting too worked up about it.

Dear Homer:

This letter comes to you direct from Norfolk. We tied up here yesterday after escorting to the base one of the surrendered German subs. As you know, all the U-boats have been ordered to surface and surrender. We happened to be the ship that was closest to where one popped up—off the coast of Iceland.

We sent a boarding party to the sub to take it over. Our men ran down the U-boat's two black flags of surrender and ran up an American flag. Then we called the *Pillsbury* to join us and help us take the submarine to Norfolk.

We left enough Germans on the sub to operate it. The others in the U-boat crew were divided between us and the *Pillsbury*. We got the captain, another officer, and seventeen men. It was amusing to watch their reactions when they first came aboard. A mixture of fear and curiosity. One of the sailors patted a depth charge as he walked by.

It was amusing, too, to see how quickly our crew changed its feelings about the Germans. Some of our men had been saying that they wanted a chance to stand the machine-gun watch. They hoped, they said, that one of the prisoners would start something so they'd have an excuse to shoot him. But it was soon obvious to everybody that the German sailors weren't much different from ours. They were just simple, decent fellows who believed what they were told and went to war because they had to and were relieved now that it was over. We put them to work on cleaning and sweeping jobs which they did efficiently and without complaining. In a few days our men were playing cards with them and swapping souvenirs.

That course I had in German came in handy. One of our snipes, whose parents came from Austria, and I were the only persons on the ship who could communicate with the sailors who didn't know any English. Of course he speaks much better German than I do, but if a German sailor spoke slowly and used simple words I could get most of what he meant. And he could understand me!

I found out from one of the men that only their captain was a Nazi party member. He had—I must admit it surprised me—all the arrogance of a Hollywood version of a Nazi officer. He even wore a monocle when he came aboard, but one of our seamen swiped it from his bunk during the night. (He told me later that it was just ordinary window glass.)

The only time the sub's captain approached me was when he pointed to one of our storekeepers and asked in fairly good English whether the man was Jewish. When I said yes and that two of our *officers* were also Jewish he said, "Ach, unglaublich!" and stalked away. The Old Man was greatly amused when I told him this. For the rest of the trip he gave our two Jewish officers the job of taking care of the prisoners!

Someone on the ship had a recent issue of *Time* (one of those miniature "pony" editions that they send us) with a story in it about the snorkel. You know, the new German invention that let's a submarine recharge its batteries without coming to the surface. The U-boat that surrendered to us had a snorkel but the crew scuttled it before we got to them. I showed *Time's* diagram of how the snorkel works to the officer who wasn't the sub's captain. He laughed and said in broken English, "Ja. Almost right." He wouldn't tell me what was wrong.

Did the Chicago papers report all the crazy fanfare that Navy public relations cooked up for us when we got to Norfolk? There were two blimps, three airplanes, and two helicopters overhead. Six ships carrying photographers, reporters, and newsreel cameramen clustered around us. A dozen grim-faced marines, with loaded rifles in hand, rushed aboard the sub as soon as it docked! This made no sense at all because the ship was completely under our control, but I'm sure it made great newsreel pictures.

The Skipper tells me he has no idea what the Mighty M's next assignment will be. We go into dry dock next week at the Brooklyn Navy Yard. That just might give me a chance for a ten-day leave. If it works out I may be able to get to Chicago. . . .

18
Mothballs

The *USS Montgomery* tied up at the Brooklyn Navy Yard for extensive repairs, as Peter had expected, though he failed to obtain the leave he wanted. Judging from a letter posted in New York City he spent his evening liberties listening to Dixieland jazz at a spot called Nick's in Greenwich Village. (Was there ever really a trombone player there with the name Miff Mole?) The ship's next assignment was flagship for a group of DE's that escorted a convoy to Liverpool. It was the last convoy of the Atlantic war and the first to sail with navigation lights burning.

Peter had several liberties in Liverpool. He did not get to London. In one of two letters from Liverpool he commented on how young and lewd-mouthed the hookers were on Lime Street, and on a second-hand bookstore where he bought a copy of William James' *The Will to Believe* from a pretty girl whose upper teeth were missing. In his other letter he spoke of a Sunday morning effort to attend a temple on the outskirts of Liverpool where (he had somehow learned) the service was based on August Comte's attempt to establish a religion of positivism.

The temple, I have been told by a former student now living in London, was then the only survival in Europe of what had once been a flourishing cult in Paris. The nineteenth-century French philosopher had actually tried to establish a God-is-dead church, a "Catholicism minus Christianity" as it was called, complete with its own trinity (Humanity, Earth, Space), its own saints (mostly scientists), its own calendar (thirteen months), its own hymns to man, and its own elaborate rituals for public worship. Unfortunately the Comtean temple in Liverpool had closed for the war's duration. Peter found its doors locked and no one on the premises. "Perhaps," he wrote, "the pastor, too, is dead."

After returning to the states, the *USS Montgomery* was assigned to several routine operations in the training of pilots for aircraft carriers. The first two letters that follow are from this period. Then the war in the Pacific came to its apocalyptic end, and the *Montgomery* headed for sleep in the mouth of the St. John's River, at Green Cove Springs, Florida. Several of Peter's letters from Green Cove Springs, written while his ship was being decommissioned, seem to be of sufficient interest to include. Peter had by then been promoted to a first class petty officer. The final letter here, written just after Peter's discharge, was the last I received from him before he returned to Chicago to complete his work for a doctor of divinity degree.

I was anxious to see Peter again. His thinking had steadily matured during his life at sea, and I had great hopes for his future as an enlightened, influential pastor. Give him a few more years, I told Edna, and his old illusions about a transcendent "throne of the Almighty" will vanish, and he will find himself committed to the ideals of secular humanism, unhampered by lingering dreams of Christian orthodoxy.

Dear Homer:

Pietz, our new chief yeoman, told Sam and me last week that two Negro electrician's mates have been assigned to the ship. We're to pick them up in a few days when we dock at Gitmo [the vernacular expression for the U.S. Naval Station at Guantanamo Bay, Cuba—H. W.].

This is truly surprising news! The Navy's program of racial integration is moving faster than I'd have thought possible. Until now, as you know, the only Negroes on the ship have been the steward's mates, the personal servants of the officers. . . .

Dear Homer:

. . . As Sam and I anticipated, our southern boys did a lot of loud and angry bellowing before and after the two electrician's mates came aboard. The Navy surely expected it because the two men were well briefed on how to behave. They ignore the threats and insults, say nothing back, and just keep working hard and quietly at their jobs. Both are men of the highest competence, courage, and good humor.

Sam and I are doing everything we can to be friendly with them, to make them feel welcome on the ship, and to convince the Southerners —most of them are youngsters on the deck force—that there's no cause for panic. We've been afraid some of the more violent and unstable ones might try to provoke a fight. . . .

Dear Homer:

. . . [the electrician's mates] have been with us three weeks now. To the great astonishment of both Sam and me, the Southern sailors have calmed down completely! There's been no violence. One of the boatswain's mates who comes from Arkansas—he was the most outspoken in his fury when the colored boys first arrived—has now made friends with the younger Negro who also comes from Arkansas. Last night they went out together on liberty!

I wonder if our ship is typical of what's happening on other ships. And is it possible that people in the South (the North, too!) would lose their prejudice if they ever had to live for a while in an integrated community? It's hard to believe, but something like this seems to have happened on our ship.

It occurs to me—I weep to say it—that the Navy (I don't know what the Army's doing) seems to be trying harder to get rid of racial discrimination, at least on the enlisted man's level, than the Protestant churches of America. Come to think of it, even organized baseball is doing more. Are the Catholics doing anything?

It seems to me that eliminating racial prejudice should top the list of moral crusades for every Christian in the country. We've just won a war against a nation whose leaders regarded Jews as low-grade humans, yet I think you'd agree that more than half the white Christians in the United States, Protestant and Catholic, feel the same way about Negroes. Not that they hate colored people the way the Nazis hated Jews. It's subtler and more insidious. It's a tacit, unspoken assumption that Negroes are inferior—intellectually, morally, and in almost every other way.

Most Christians, I suspect, seldom think of Moses and David and other Old Testament characters as "Jewish." And the leading figures in the New Testament, from Jesus to Saint Paul, are even less Jewish. Only Judas was a Jew! Perhaps antisemitism of a sort is built into the foundations of Christian orthodoxy. If Christ were truly the Son of God, how could a Christian believer look upon Jews with anything less than pity for having failed to recognize God himself when he appeared in their midst, born to one of their own women?

As for Negroes, an American white Christian doesn't even have the rejection of Christ to fall back on as an excuse. As you know, Negroes have flocked to the white Protestant denominations. Even in slavery days the old-time gospel gave them hope and peace in their bondage. Yet where can you find a whiter gathering today than on Sunday morning in the white churches of America?

Oh, I know you've preached many times about this and served on a dozen committees in Chicago to promote racial brotherhood. But you're a Unitarian minister. You're not typical. I'm thinking of the thousands of white Protestant ministers in the South. What are *they* doing? Nothing! The racial revolution is sure to come. Of that I'm certain. And I'm beginning to think that when it does it will come from outside the churches. The ministers will be trotting along behind as usual, out of breath, trying to catch up with God's work which they should have been doing.

After I'm ordained I intend to make this a major content of my preaching. I'd feel like a traitor to God and Christ if I didn't. . . .

Dear Homer:

We're back on the Brooklyn Navy yard after a month of pilot training maneuvers. I learned today for the first time (from a story in the *New York Times*) about how Earl Browder was booted out of the C.P. What a strange twist of events! I can understand why, now the German war is over, the Party might want to swing back to a policy of noncooperation with capitalism. But to make the swing so soon! To make poor Browder the scapegoat! It seems not only cruel but also not very smart public relations. . . .*

Sam's taking it hard. He told me yesterday that he'd gone to the Party's headquarters in Manhattan to get a supply of back issues of the *Daily Worker* so he could bone up on all the details. Sam has always been one of Browder's great admirers. We've talked many times about how the end of the war would find Russia anxious to buy American goods and American businessmen anxious to sell. We had a vision of the two great countries working together, each benefitting the other while working for its own good, within its own political and economic systems. All this now seems a futile hope.

I'm puzzled and depressed. Do you have any opinion on the matter? Do you know what Haydon's attitude is? What is Reinhold Niebuhr saying?

---

*For readers too young to recall this famous reversal of the Party line it may be of interest to mention that the first official sign of the switch was a furious attack on "Browderism" by the French Communist, Jacques Duclos. The possibility of conquest by Hitler had made it necessary for Stalin to collaborate for a time with the United States. When the threat of Nazi conquest vanished, the need for this collaboration vanished also. Browder was caught flat-footed. He was the fall-guy, replaced by William Z. Foster, a long-time Party hack who had never been happy with the Party's soft attitude toward the Roosevelt administration.—H. W.

While I was discussing the Browder-Foster controversy with Sam, I finally got around to asking him point blank if he's a Party member. He smiled and said no. I'm certain he was lying, and I think he knows I know it. I can understand, though, why he'd still be reluctant to tell me. I don't intend to ask him about it again. . . .

Dear Homer:

Well, it's all over. My God, what a climax! We were cruising near Bermuda when I first heard the news. I think I must have been the only person on the ship who really got excited. I rushed around trying to tell everybody what had happened, that we had just cracked the atom and entered a new age! They must have thought I'd gone crazy.

I had the advantage, of course, of having been at the University of Chicago when the project to make the bomb first started. Remember the time that Mrs. R., after she got her job as a secretary in the "Metallurgy Department," told Edna that the physicists were trying to split the atom? And how ridiculous it all seemed? . . . . I used to see Enrico Fermi peddling his bicycle along Kimbark Avenue. It never occurred to me that anything would ever come of the project. I don't think I've given it a single thought from then until now.

To everbody else on the ship, from the Skipper on down, the atom bomb is just another bomb, larger and bigger than most but not qualitatively different. Even Sam is curiously unmoved. I suppose he's miffed because Russia didn't build it first. He probably doesn't want to commit himself until we get back to the States and he can read what the *Worker* has to say about it.

Everyone's excited about the prospects of getting home. Everybody's asking Pietz if his yeomen have started yet to type discharge papers. A coxswain named Schnepp just stuck his head in the radio shack and said to me, deliberately using civilian language, "I'm going *downstairs* to get a drink at the *drinking fountain.*"

What's the reaction around the divinity school to the Big Bomb? Has Hutchins said anything about it? What's *your* reaction? I haven't made up my mind yet whether we should or shouldn't have dropped it. At the moment I'm inclined to think Truman did the right thing, but I may change my mind after I learn more about the circumstances. . . .

Dear Homer:

We—or rather the tugs—finally got the Mighty M up the St. John's River to Green Cove Springs. The five DE's in our group are anchored alongside each other in what the base calls a "nest." As soon as we tied up we were boarded by an officer from the base who came into the radio shack and carried off our electrical code machine. It's the typewriter Sam used for coding and decoding messages.

The Navy is often confused, but never have I seen such confusion as prevails here. Sam said the other day that the motto of the base is: "Wait, there's a harder way!" I told him I'd heard a funnier one: "The Navy moves in mysterious ways its blunders to perform."

Ten days ago the ship had orders to cover the entire weather deck with some new kind of fiberboard. It was supposed to be glued down. After about half the deck had been covered, a new order came through canceling the previous one and ordering removal of the fiberboard. This proved to be almost impossible because the glue was so strong, but our first lieutenant started a detail of men chipping away at it. Fortunately, they hadn't made much headway before a third order arrived that canceled the second one and restored the first. The first lieutenant is holding off action for two weeks to make sure the base doesn't change its mind again.

I suppose the Navy will put most of its DE's in mothballs. Our little pop-guns are being sprayed with some kind of plastic stuff that looks like white cloth when it dries. The job will probably take six months because no one is working hard except the yeomen They're complaining about the tons of new paper work they have to do each day. Everybody's taking it easy until he accumulates enough "points" to get out. . . .

Dear Homer:
Now that the five ships are tied together I've been able to raid the "libraries" (small book lockers) of the other four ships and pick up some new reading matter. Pickings are slim. Mostly old books of the sort you see on ten-cent tables outside the old bookstores in Chicago, and about fifty paperback mysteries and sex novels. I'm getting a good tan reading on the fantail and wearing only my underwear shorts. No liberties yet for any of us. All is still confusion. I understand that Green Cove Springs is nothing more than a USO center, one small restaurant, and a drugstore, but I'm looking forward to visiting Jacksonville and Saint Augustine. They're both only an hour or so away by bus.

According to how the yeomen figure my points, I won't be eligible for discharge until next March. It seems years away. The Captain and the Exec were transferred off the ship as soon as we anchored. Our new Skipper is an earnest young fellow who joined the Navy a few months ago. He knows less about the ship than Seaweed. [Seaweed was a mongrel dog that was the ship's mascot throughout the entire war

—H. W.] But no one can blame him for that. He has sense enough to stay out of everyone's way.

Thanks for that pamphlet of Hutchins' speech about the bomb. [*The Atomic Bomb Vs Civilization*, a speech published in 1945 by Human Events, a Chicago organization.—H. W.] I'm not sure I agree with Hutchins that we used the bomb when, as he puts it, "we did not need to do so," but I certainly agree that our number-one task now is to work as hard as we can for a world community and, after that, for a world government. And I agree with him that we must keep the good will of Russia by sharing atomic knowledge with her. . . .

Dear Homer:

. . . We have only a skeleton crew aboard. Half the men have been transferred to discharge centers. Sam left last week. He gave me the address of a friend in Birmingham through whom he said he could always be reached. He told me he had no special plans but if my suspicions are correct he's going back to Alabama for an assignment to C. P. work.°

I've enjoyed knowing Sam. His heart's in the right place. But there's something sad about him. He's too much of a political idealist and too naive and uninformed about most things. I suspect he's in for rough times. I argued with him a bit before he left. I'm sorry now I did. I brought up some of the evils of Russian totalitarianism just to see how he'd react. I mentioned Stalin's treatment of the kulaks and the awful famines that resulted. Sam was distressed and annoyed. He was hurt that I would say such things. I must try to keep in touch with him. . . .

Dear Homer:

One of the sailors on the USS *Pillsbury*, the ship that's tied to our starboard side, asked me if I'd like to buy his trombone. It's an old battered piece of junk that he doesn't want to bother taking home. I said yes and gave him ten dollars for it. There are long hours now with nothing for me to do. I take the trombone down into one of the empty

---

°Peter's suspicions were borne out. When eleven Communist leaders were on trial for conspiracy in New York City in 1949 one of the witnesses was Samuel J. Hall, Jr., age 39, chairman of the Communist Party in Alabama and Party organizer for Alabama, Tennessee and Mississippi. Hall said he had not joined the Party until January, 1946, but admitted that he became state chairman six months later in spite of the Party's constitutional provision requiring two-year membership before holding such an office. See the *New York Times* and *New York Herald Tribune*, August 5, 1949. Peter recognized Sam immediately when I showed him Sam's picture in the *Herald Tribune*, and was not in the least surprised. Neither Peter nor I know anything about Sam's subsequent history or even if he is still alive.—H. W.

storage compartments where I can close the hatch and blow as loud as I want without disturbing anybody.

I know absolutely nothing about a trombone. I've always liked hearing it played, though, and I've managed to figure out how to produce a scale. I'm probably doing it all wrong, but I *can* play recognizable versions of *Shall We Gather at the River, Almost Persuaded,* and *Tell Mother I'll be There.* I'm working now on a Pentecostal hymn I used to like when I was a boy. It's called *Anchored in Jesus.* I'm sure you've never heard it. It has a simple melody with a powerful beat and awful lyrics. . . . Don't be surprised if I join the Salvation Army when I get back to Chicago. . . .

Dear Homer:

I managed to get off the ship yesterday for my first liberty since we anchored here. It was too late in the day for a trip to Jacksonville or Saint Augustine. There was, as I'd been told, nothing of interest in Green Cove, but just outside the town the local American Legion chapter was trying to raise money with a sleazy little carnival. It had only a few concessions—a couple of wheels, the wooden milk bottles, and a cat rack (that's what the carnies call the booth with those stuffed cats you try to knock off ledges with baseballs). No Ferris wheel. No rides of *any* kind. °

The main attraction and the biggest moneymaker was at the back of the lot. You guessed it—the girlie show. I paid my fifty cents and followed some sailors into a small tent with a raised stage at one end. There were two girls. They took turns coming out and going through a tired routine of bumps and grinds while the other stayed somewhere behind the scene to play a scratchy Glenn Miller record.

You can imagine my surprise when the second girl to dance turned out to be Arabella! Didn't I once write to you about her? She was the dark-skinned gal with the scar on her face who used to wait tables at the American Garden in Norfolk. I didn't recognize her at first because her hair was dyed yellow and her scar was covered with make-up. When she exposed her breasts—they're really enormous—I saw that blue anchor tattooed above the left nozzle. I looked more carefully at her face. Yes, one eye was slightly off, and I could see the scar under the face powder.

Have I mentioned before that I've grown a moustache? It's big, black and bushy. Arabella noticed it. She smiled in my direction, rubbed a

---

°One summer in his early teens (before he became "Oklahoma's boy evangelist") Peter joined a small carnival called the Riley Shows and traveled with it for a season. He helped a cousin of his father sell hot dogs and ice cream in what, he tells me, the carnival people still call a "grab joint."—H. W.

finger over her upper lip, then blew me a kiss. Her dancing wasn't much —about as graceful as an inebriated cow. After stripping to high heels and a G-string, she wriggled over the stage, flapping her udders, while the sailors shouted such brilliant bon mots as "How long did it take to grow those?" and "Which side gives chocolate milk?"

When the record stopped, Arabella instantly quit gyrating. She popped the gum she'd been chewing and started to walk off stage. One of the sailors standing in front reached up and grabbed her ankle. Arabella squealed. He gave a pull. Down she went on her bare ass. Thump! The sailor tried to drag her off the platform.

Well, I won't bore you with a blow-by-blow account. I can't say I lost my temper. There did, however, seem to be a lady in distress. I moved front, cuffed the fellow up a bit, and tossed him out of the tent on his ear. Apparently he was there without any buddies because all the other sailors in the tent were on *my* side. The girls' screams must have reached the ears of the one policeman on the lot because he came galloping into the tent. The two girls explained what had happened. He thanked me, shook my hand, and hustled the sailor off.

Arabella was bubbling with gratitude. "Ain't I seen ya somewheres before?" she asked. I told her yes, that she used to wait on me and a friend at the American Garden. "Oh sure!" she said. "I remember."

She didn't, of course, but it was nice to hear her say so. I asked if I could buy her some beers after the last show. (I assumed there was a bar *somewhere* in the area.) "Sure," she said. "Come around about one o'clock."

I showed up at one, but it didn't work out. There were two sailors there with a rented car, and the two girls were going with them to a spot called the Coconut Paradise, a few miles out of town on the road to Jacksonville. Arabella said it was open all night and asked me if I'd like to come along.

I looked first at one sailor then the other. Neither of them said anything. "Thanks, but no," I said. "I have to get back to my ship."

Arabella gave me a hug and a slobbery kiss on the mouth. She smelled of fresh powder and stale perspiration. "Some other time," she said. I said, "Roger."

I walked back to Green Cove and had a lousy cup of coffee in a fly-infested restaurant. Then I caught the motorboat service back to the nest where the once-mighty M is anchored. While I was getting undressed, the machinist's mate who sleeps in the sack under me asked me if I'd made out. "No," I told him, "I missed out bigger than shit."

Dear Homer:

Tomorrow I leave the *USS Montgomery*. I'm astonished at how sentimental I feel. I suppose it's natural to get attached to any spot where you've lived for several years, especially if it's isolated from the rest of the world. There isn't a square foot of the old girl, outside the engine compartments, that I'm not acquainted with. I can move about her in total darkness, knowing just where to put my hand on every ladder and hatch and stanchion.

She lookes like a ghost ship. The white plastic stuff is draped like shrouds over all the dead gun stations. (I know some sects believe that dogs and cats go to heaven, but has anyone ever argued that a ship might have an immortal "soul"?) The depth charge racks are empty. The decks are covered with gray paint. Most of the compartments have been dehydrated and sealed shut. I climbed up to the pilot house this morning for a last look. The helm was disconnected, and I spun it like a carnival wheel. Only about a dozen of us are still in the crew. We've been sleeping next door on the *Pillsbury*. The little waves in the river rock the ships just enough to let you know they're still floating.

It wasn't a bad life. I worked hard, the chow was terrible, and of course there was always the chance I might get killed. But I slept well at night. And there were girls in the ports and good guys on board to chew the rag with.

To tell you the truth, Homer, I'm frightened by the thought that maybe I enjoyed Navy life too much. There's a peculiar sense of freedom that comes with lack of freedom. No decisions. You just obey orders. You don't even have to pick out the color of the socks you want to put on in the morning. I'm actually feeling apprehensive about going back to Chicago to take up where I left off. There are so many big decisions to make! So many things I have to get straight in my mind. . . .

Dear Homer:

. . . I think the greatest lesson I've learned is that most men are *good*. Oh, I know there's plenty of cruelty and self-seeking in all of us, and if someone wants to call that "original sin" I suppose there's no harm in it. I'm convinced, though, that goodness is the stronger impulse. I think most people love more than they hate.

At least happy people do. Maybe you're right about "sin" being no more than a mental illness that results from bad conditioning. I know this is what you've always tried to tell me. Or is there a deeper component that lies in the mystery of our "will"? I wish I knew the answer!

I do know that I still believe in God. I have no sense of estrangement. I can't believe that my loss of faith in orthodox Christianity is *against* God's will. And yet I still don't know exactly what to do with Christ. I can't quite bring myself to believe that he was just another man, like you and me. It's true that I no longer believe he was God on earth (you've helped convince me of *that!*), but I still can't stop ending my prayers with "in Jesus' name." In my mind I know it would make more sense to end them with something like "in the name of Thy disciples." This would take in all the great prophets of non-Christian faiths. But in my heart I haven't been able to give up the phrase I'm so accustomed to.

That Christ was wrong on many counts—his views on hell and Satan, for example—I have no doubt. Yet in so many ways he still seems to me a towering personality. I have lots of thinking to do about him. Right now he's a kind of luminous blur on the pages of history. I can't get his outlines clear. I can't make out the essence of his personality.

I must read Schweitzer's *Quest of the Historical Jesus.* I should have read it years ago. . . .

Dear Homer:
I have a few hours to kill here at the Jacksonville Separation Center before I catch a bus. I'm still wearing my Navy blues, but there's a ruptured duck on the jacket. I'm a civilian again!

The separation center did everything to leave us with a favorable final impression of the Navy. The chow was good. The bunks were large and clean and separated from each other by several feet. The officers spoke to us politely!

They showed us a short movie film starring, of all people, Robert Benchley. He was wearing a sailor suit and going through the discharge procedure. In one scene he'd been standing in line for a long time when an officer came over, expressed rage at the fact that the sailors were being forced to stand, and ordered a lieutenant to bring the men some chairs "on the double!" Benchley fainted.

It isn't *quite* that way, but the center's doing its best. There was a sort of ceremonial "graduation" this morning. About two hundred of us filed past a bored lieutenant-commander who gave each of us a rolled-up certificate and a limp handshake. I said "Thank you, sir," and thought to myself that that's the last time I'll ever say "sir" to anybody.

Outside, in the bright Florida sunshine, I unrolled the fake parchment. It's a message from President Truman printed in fancy letters and suitable for framing. It extends to me the "heartfelt thanks of a grateful nation." Because of my "fortitude, resourcefulness, and calm judgment," it says, so help me, the nation is looking to me "for leadership and example."

I feel like I felt ten years ago when I graduated from high school, only the sensation of release is a thousand times greater. It's more like what I imagine an amnesia victim must feel when he begins to remember a former life. Already my four years in the Navy are starting to fade out of my memory. My mind is crowding with visions of Chicago, of the university, of Sand Springs and Tulsa, of my mother and sister and stepfather, of you and Edna.

I walked to the barracks to get my traveling bag and take a cold shower. I got undressed, flung a towel over my shoulder, and walked to the head. A large placard on the door said, "Secured until after inspection." Inspection? No one had told *me* about any inspection. With huge delight I proceeded to go in and take a shower anyway. While I soaped myself I hoped an inspection party, headed by an admiral, would invade the head before I finished. What could the Navy do to me?

Someone had scratched on the shower's tiling, "Kilroy was here." It must be a joke. I've seen the phrase all over the place.

Last night's paper said that Professor Anton J. Carlson, of the University of Chicago, had informed the press that atom bombs could never destroy the entire human race. They might wipe out civilization, he admits, but some men and women would survive in little pockets here and there. They would manage to keep the species going. I'm sure the members of Comte's temple in Liverpool will be cheered to hear this. It would be rather embarrassing, would it not, trying to worship humanity if you believed that humanity was about to become as extinct as the dinosaurs?

I'll write to you from Sand Springs as soon as I know when I'll be in Chicago. I can hardly wait to see you and Edna again.

As ever,

Peter

Part III

AFTER THE WAR

It is impossible to calculate the moral mischief, if I may so express it, that mental lying has produced in society. When a man has so far corrupted and prostituted the chastity of his mind, as to subscribe his professional belief to things he does not believe, he has prepared himself for the commission of every other crime.

—THOMAS PAINE

19

Electronic Machine

Peter stayed with his family in Sand Springs for almost a month. A long letter from him complained of how hard it was to discuss religion with his parents and his sister. (Gabrielle had finished high school and was working as a receptionist for one of the large oil companies in Tulsa, but she still lived at home.) It was especially difficult talking to his mother. "I try not to be a hypocrite," he wrote. "It's impossible. I don't like to upset her. So when she starts throwing Biblical verses at me, I just nod as if I'm agreeing. I feel like a Pharisee. . . ."

Peter returned to Chicago in late March, 1946, in time to enroll for the divinity school's spring quarter. He came by bus, phoning me from a south side terminal when he arrived. Forty minutes later, through a front window on the second floor of my house, I saw him striding rapidly along Harper Avenue. He was in civilian clothes, carrying a blue cloth traveling bag and sporting a mammoth walrus moustache. I bounded down the stairs to greet him.

"I kept it just to show you and Edna," he said at the front door as he twirled the ends of the black underbrush with an exaggerated flourish. "I'll shave it off tomorrow. I promise."

He couldn't have looked better. Tanned face, crew-cut hair, blue eyes glinting with energy and good humor. The creases that formed at the corners of his eyes when he smiled were deeper. The slight twist of his nose was scarcely noticeable. He was wearing a light gray suit which I guessed to be new, though it was baggy at the knees and rumpled from the bus ride. As always, his shoes were down at the heels and in need of polish.

When Edna entered the room—she had been out buying groceries—she exploded with a mock scream at the sight of Peter's moustache. They embraced warmly, then we all celebrated with a round of drinks. Peter stayed for dinner, of course, and we were up until early morning talking about a thousand things that somehow had eluded our correspondence.

He was eager to get back to his studies. "I want to reread Barth," he said, "and to read Kierkegaard and Tillich and Niebuhr. Especially Niebuhr." He leaned back, hands clasped behind his head. "I've got to decide what to do with Reinhold Niebuhr."

"And if you have to discard Reinie?"

He ran a hand through his short hair and smiled without replying.

Although Peter carried a full schedule of courses during the spring quarter, they were not difficult subjects, and his major interests lay, as usual, in outside reading. He plunged at once into Barth, pushing aside peripheral doctrines and going straight to what he considered the most significant, albeit most obscure, aspect of Barthianism: its Christology. And the more he read, the more puzzled he became.

"If I could only be sure of what Barth means by nonhistorical," he said one evening. "Does he mean an event that takes place *only* in the wholly-other realm?"

"I don't quite follow," I said.

"Well, take the Resurrection of Jesus. Barth calls it nonhistorical. It's nonhistorical because Jesus is part of the Godhead and God's in eternity, not time. I can understand all that. What I can't get clear is whether Barth thinks this transcendent event also took place in *our* history. Does he think the tomb actually became empty?"

Unfortunately, Professor von Cloven, our local authority on Barth, was in Basel that spring, visiting Barth himself, so we could not turn to him for aid. And I was no help because I had never been interested enough in Barth to concern myself with these fine distinctions. I knew of course that the question Peter raised had been the subject of countless treatises by Christian thinkers of the past. It is impossible to invent a new approach to any problem about the supposed relationship of Jesus the man to the eternal Christ of the Trinity. Christologies so bizarre that you would think only a lunatic could hold them have been at the heart of now-forgotten heresies that once held the allegiance of hundreds of thousands. The question at hand, however, was a simple one. What does Barth believe? Did the man Jesus, in Barth's Christology, rise bodily from the dead or did his corpse remain permanently on earth? It seemed to Peter, as it did to me, that here was a clear-cut either/or, a choice of only one of two alternatives.

We found the strongest evidence for Barth's orthodoxy in his *Credo*, a series of lectures on the Apostles' Creed. In discussing the phrase "under Pontius Pilate" Barth makes very plain his belief that these words are in the creed precisely to "date" the narrative. It tells us that "at such and such a point of *historical time* [the italics are his] this happened."

"If the Word became flesh," Barth continues, "then it became temporal, and the reality of the revelation in Jesus Christ was what we call the lifetime of a man. It was not only that, but it was also that. It is an eternal but no timeless reality; it is at once an eternal and a temporal reality. It is not a timeless essence of all or of some times. It is not to be discovered by laboriously extracting such a thing as a timeless spirit or a timeless substance out of all times or out of definite times, even that of the years 1 to 30. It will never be understood by anyone who is irritated by its concretion, who would like to free it of the temporal that clings to it, who fancied that he could get past its temporal concretion to its ideal substance. It is essentially concrete and therefore temporal and therefore capable of temporal definition, in the same way as, say, the rule of Pericles in Athens. The man who is hankering after the so-called 'eternal verities' had best, if he is determined not to be converted, leave his faith uncontaminated with Christian faith. Revelation is *hic et nunc*, once and for all unique, or it is not the revelation to which Holy Scripture bears witness."

In his comments on the Resurrection passages of the Apostles' Creed, Barth becomes more explicit. "We have here to do with an occurrence which. . . takes place also in space and time. . . in the continuum of the history of our world." Again: ". . . there cannot be any talk of striking out the empty grave." He goes on to say that he is fully aware of the "remarkable disorder" in the four Gospel accounts. It is as though the writers fell into a kind of "stammering," as if "from the effects of an earthquake." After all the contradictions have been reckoned with, he argues, there remains the inescapable fact of a sudden, unanimous belief of the disciples in the miracle of a corporeal resurrection. This miracle "cannot be repudiated. . . but on the contrary can only be thankfully affirmed."

In his earlier commentary on Romans, Barth had been equally emphatic. Although he calls the Resurrection the one great "non-historical" event of history, he makes clear that he does not mean that the event was not observable by human beings. One must reject, he declares, such explanations as (1) Jesus was not really dead, (2) Deception by the disciples who may have stolen the body, (3) Deception by Jesus himself, (4) Visions, subjective or objective, (5) All other "spiritualistic or anthroposophical theories." These false explanations all have in common, he writes, an unwillingness to recognize that Jesus was God himself who had entered history to triumph over history and, in so doing, signify our triumph, through Him, over death.

In Barth's *Credo* even the Virgin Birth is defended as historical. The Incarnation, he argues along ancient lines, could not be accomplished without a divine creation inside Mary's womb. Only in this way could God enter history without becoming part of history's causal nexus. "There is nothing said about an intermixing of God and man, or a change of God into a man, or of a man into God, but simply this—that without ceasing to be God, God becomes and is at the same time man."

All this testified, it seemed to Peter and me, to a Christology indistinguishable from that of the Pope or Billy Graham. Alas, it is not so simple! In a later work, *The Resurrection of the Dead* (a commentary on First Corinthians), Barth again considers the empty grave. Now his words take on a curious ambiguity. He tries to dismiss it as a question of no great importance.

"The tomb may prove to be a definitely closed *or* open tomb; it is really a matter of indifference. What avails the tomb, proved to be this or that, at Jerusalem in the year A.D. 30?" The grave of Jesus, he continues, is like a valley between two huge mountains. One mountain is "Christ died for our sins," the other, "He rose again." Beside those two facts, the question about the tomb is trivial. "Time and place are a matter of perfect indifference." Was the body stolen? Could it be that Jesus was not really dead? Let us not wrangle, said Barth, over such foolish problems. To declare the tomb empty is to enter the Scylla of a "gross mythology." To deny that the tomb was empty is to enter the Charybdis of a "refined spiritism."

It was passages such as these which led von Cloven, in his book on Barth, to find in Barth's later Christology a modern variant of the ancient Nestorian heresy. This school, founded by a fifth-century Syrian ecclesiastic named Nestorius, split Jesus Christ into two personalities. In old Judea a man of flesh and bone was for a time possessed by the eternal Logos. When did this union take place? Perhaps at the time of Jesus' conception, perhaps at the time of his birth, perhaps when he was baptized by John. The cry on the cross, "My God, my God, why hast thou forsaken me?" was the cry of Jesus, uttered in dreadful agony after Christ had abandoned him. Jesus died, Christ lived on. The present situation in Heaven, as one of Peter's Navy letters had suggested, is none too clear. Does the soul of Jesus live apart from the Christ? Or are the two reunited for eternity?*

---

*I have tried (not hard enough?) to avoid burdening my narrative with excessive erudition. But I would not want any reader to suppose I am not aware that all these complicated conundrums about the double nature of Jesus Christ were thoroughly explored, and every conceivable position taken, by Christian writers of the first few centuries. The first great heresy of Christology, Docetism, was one of the most delightful. Essentially it is the view that Christ never had a corporeal body at all. What his

Peter and I finally concluded that von Cloven had been totally wrong in trying to pin a Nestorian label on Barth. In the latest of Barth's pronouncements that we could find on such matters, in the early volumes of his *Dogmatics*, there seemed to us a strong rejection of anything resembling the views of later Nestorians (Nestorius himself was not a Nestorian), as well as nothing to support the view that Barth did not believe in the empty tomb.

In Volume I, for example, Barth distinguishes between what he calls myth and legend. A myth has no historical basis even though it may symbolize a spiritual truth. A legend springs from an actual occurrence, although details about it may be distorted. The Resurrection of Jesus is a legend, not a myth. To interpret it as myth, writes Barth, is to introduce an "intolerable distinction" between history and eternity, to indulge in the "lowest depth of modern misunderstanding of the Bible." Exactly what took place on that Easter morning is a historical question we cannot answer. Moreover, we do not *need* to answer it. By faith we know that Jesus rose again. Nowhere did Barth say that the tomb was not empty. All he said was: Let's not talk about it.

Thus did Barth, if Peter and I read him right, perform a clever sidestep to avoid facing squarely all those irritating historical questions that refuse to go away. It is a step that all the modern German theologians have mastered, and none so well as Bultmann. In his book, *Jesus*, we are told that about the historical Jesus he can tell us nothing. When Bultmann and his acolytes finished their demythologizing, Jesus of Nazareth, the man of flesh and bone, disappeared completely from the Biblical scene.

"The skeleton of Jesus," Peter said one day after a shout of exasperation (we had been wrestling for an hour with an opaque passage in Barth's *Dogmatics*), "is the skeleton in the closet of Protestantism. *Did or did it not remain on earth?*" He shook his head. It seemed incredible to him that a great theologian could shrug his shoulders and pretend that the question was unimportant.

Although it was Barth's cowardly evasion of this question that first irritated Peter, there were other aspects of Barth's theology that began

---

contemporaries saw and heard as Jesus was a phantom, and therefore God's birth, sufferings and death were all illusory. (The doctrine of Mary's perpetual virginity followed easily, for the phantom had no difficulty gliding through her unbroken maidenhead.)

The Docetic view is supported by a startling scene in the Acts of John in which Christ appears to John on the Mount of Olives while across the valley his still-living body is being nailed to the Cross. There are so many fascinating anecdotes like this in the New Testament Apocrypha (especially the stories about the infant Jesus) that one would suppose a paperback edition of these manuscripts would be available. But today's Christians seem to have little curiosity about the early sources of their faith.—H. W.

to annoy him as much as they had once inspired him. The *Dogmatics* became for Peter, as it had always been for me, a narrow, quarrelsome, provincial, egocentric, unwholesome, unconsciously comic, and altogether unlovely work.

Peter had been reading William James, and he was much taken by James's attacks on determinism and his defense of free will as a creative act that injects unpredictable (even for God) novelty into history. Barth, on the contrary, was forever proclaiming the Calvinistic notion that God, outside of time, sees all of human history. There was in Barth a deep strain of fatalism almost as strong as the fatalism (quite plausible, it seems to me, if one posits an omniscient deity) of America's Two-Seed-in-the-Spirit Predestination Baptists. (Do they still have churches in Kentucky and Tennessee?) In an earlier chapter I spoke of Barth's conviction that God calls us, then God within us answers. At one time Peter had been uplifted by this view. Now he found it exasperating. God knocks on your door. Do *you* get up and let him in? No, Barth seemed to say. While God outside is knocking, God inside unbolts the door and lets himself in.

Most of all, I think, Peter became annoyed by Barth's compulsion to call "demonic" all religions outside the Christian revelation. "What is the likelihood that Christianity, so interpreted, will be heard gladly or with conviction by the people of other faiths?" asks Brand Blanchard in his hatchet job on Barth. ["Critical Reflections on Karl Barth," in *Faith and the Philosophers*, edited by John Hick, St. Martin's Press, 1964.] "Surely not very great. They will suspect, and with some reason, a hidden link to that Western arrogance of which they carry long memories. They are invited to accept, without argument and in scorn of argument, a deity who has focused his favors on a fraction of the race—and not their fraction. They do not see why revelation should come through one scripture only, or one life only, or why the miracles of one faith should be true miracles and those of all others fraudulent, even when equally well attested, or why religious experiences that seem qualitatively very much alike should be revelatory in Basel and illusory in Bombay."

After abandoning Barth—he was never able to read him again—Peter turned his attention for the first time to Sören Kierkegaard, the brilliant, tormented Dane who in a way started both the Neo-Reformation trend in Protestant theology and the existential movement in philosophy. It was "refreshing," Peter said one day, to find that Kierkegaard made no attempt to hide his acceptance of the Virgin Birth and the bodily Resurrection behind muddy ambiguities.

I did not find it refreshing. Nor did I try to reread Kierkegaard during the summer that Peter studied him. The Dane's neurotic temperament and convoluted writing style have always repelled me. Nevertheless I tried to listen sympathetically whenever Peter talked about this or that aspect of Kierkegaard's Christology.

Peter was intrigued by Kierkegaard's belief that religious faith is a pure leap of will, uncontaminated by reason or empirical knowledge. It is easy to see how this could apply to what Kierkegaard called the "second-hand" disciples who lived after the time of Jesus. Did it apply also to those "first-hand" disciples who knew the Master? Yes, said Kierkegaard, it did. Even to those who knew Jesus best, it was faith and faith alone that gave them eyes to see his divinity.

To support this astonishing claim Kierkegaard developed his famous concept of the "Incognito." God, disguised as Jesus, walked the earth in a "strict incognito such as only an almighty being can assume, an incognito impenetrable to the most intimate observation." Most contemporaries of Jesus saw him as an ordinary man. "Is not this the carpenter's son?" The few who accepted his divinity did so by an act of will no different from the decisions of believers of today. Every man who has lived since the time of Jesus is in this sense a "contemporary." It would not be fair of God if those who saw and heard Jesus found it easier to believe than those who through no fault of their own had the ill luck to be born later.

Kierkegaard puts it simply. It is "more worthy of God to make his covenant with men equally difficult for every human being in every time and place." There is no way today to "prove" that Jesus was God, or even to establish the probability that he was. Nor was there a way at the time when Jesus lived. It was and is as hopeless to prove that Jesus was divine as to prove that a footprint on the sand was left by an angel masquerading as a man.

Peter quickly realized the monumental difficulties in trying to maintain this doctrine alongside a belief in the miracles. "It's a poor incognito," he said one hot afternoon when we were drinking beer in a dark, back booth of a deserted tavern on Fifty-fifth Street, "to go about turning water into wine, walking on the sea, and snatching dead men from the grave!"

Kierkegaard did not evade this objection. Unless Christ's contemporaries made a leap of faith, he argued, the miracles would seem to them no more than inexplicable illusions performed by an itinerant magician. Perhaps they were conjuring tricks. Maybe they were the work of demons. Kierkegaard says somewhere that if a person had followed Jesus for years, watching his every move, and with a hundred spies assisting him, they would see nothing, *not a thing*, that would penetrate God's great disguise.

"When I was in high school," Peter said, as we sat in that dank, shadowy bar, "I read a science-fiction story about an electronic machine. It could reconstruct scenes from the past. It would analyze records left by light on the atoms in old rocks, then play the records like a phonograph. Only instead of sound it threw images on a screen and you could see a movie of events that happened thousands of years ago.° Suppose we had a machine like that. Suppose it could show us scenes in sound and color. Can you imagine anybody today seeing Lazarus walk out of the grave or Jesus rising from the dead and still think that Jesus was an ordinary mortal?"

I signaled to the bartender for two more beers. And it's just as hard, I said, to suppose that any Christian today could see such a movie, if it showed a demythologized, Bultmannized Jesus, and still think the man was divine. Consider what such a picture might reveal. First we see Mary, a virgin in her teens, seduced by a stranger, perhaps a Roman soldier. We hear angry quarrels between Mary and Joseph. We watch young Jesus growing up as an ordinary boy while his mother has other children. We see him commit the usual petty sins of childhood. When he becomes a young man we observe him eat, hear him belch and break wind, and see him relieve his bladder and his bowels. We learn the secrets of his sex life. We see no miracles performed by him except the kind of faith healing that is the stock in trade of today's Pentecostal windbags. After his death we see what happened to his body and hear how all the false rumors of his Resurrection start and grow. Do you think, I asked, that anyone watching such a movie could muster up enough faith to penetrate God's incognito?

Peter agreed. It wouldn't be easy.

But, I continued, what a marvelous thing it would be if we had such a machine and could dispense once and for all with the blasphemous fable of the Incarnation.

"Blasphemous?" said Peter.

Yes, blasphemous, I said. God assumes the form of a man to get himself murdered as a blood sacrifice to himself, to persuade himself that he ought to forgive his own creation, humanity, for the disobedience of

---

°Peter was never able to recall the author or title of this story. A friend who is an expert on early science fiction, tells me that it must have been Eric Temple Bell's novel, *Before the Dawn*. It was written under the pseudonym of John Taine and published by Williams and Wilkins in 1934 when Peter was fifteen. Peter undoubtedly read an earlier serialization in a science-fiction magazine.—H. W.

Adam and Eve. What kind of God is that? Did you ever think of all the
good people in the world that this monstrous fable insults? It insults
women by having God become a man. How long do you think our
emancipated modern ladies are going to buy *that*? It insults the black
and brown and yellow races by having God become a white man. Do
you think the great emerging cultures of Africa and China and India,
not to mention our late enemy, Japan, are going to buy *that*? How long
will American Negroes buy it? It insults the Gentiles by making God
a Jew. It insults the Jews by telling them that they turned their backs
on their own Messiah. It insults persons with normal sex lives by de-
picting Jesus as so lacking in sexual appetite that it did not constitute,
as it did for so many saints, even a temptation. Come to think of it, I
said, it even insults the old by having Jesus die young. The orthodox
are forever telling us about how God became a man so he could
experience first hand all the sufferings of humanity. What about the
sufferings of the aged?

Peter was staring at me with a strange smile.

Let's go a step further with your thought experiment, I said, leaning
back to hook my thumbs in the pockets of my mustard-colored vest.
That electronic device isn't much different, except in degree, from
historical criticism. To be sure, New Testament exegesis is vague and
fragmentary. We'll never learn what really happened in old Judea.
Barth is certainly right about that. But at least we can analyze the few
relevant documents in the same way that we analyze other documents.
We can explore their implications. For example, if the Virgin Birth
occurred as Matthew and Luke say it did, we can ask why Jesus never
mentioned it, and why Mark and John don't mention it, and why
Saint Paul says not one word about it. It would have fitted so beautifully
into Paul's mythology of the atonement. The only explanation, surely,
is that Paul never heard of it. And we can ask why Joseph and Mary,
if *they* had ever heard of it, would be so amazed [Luke 2:48] when
they found their precocious twelve-year-old talking with learned doctors
at the temple in Jerusalem. How could they have forgotten so soon
all those wild things that Gabriel told Mary? We don't have an electronic
machine, but we do have ways of reaching probable conclusions.

"Yes, of course," Peter said quickly and much to my relief. (I had
taken a long chance that nothing I said would offend him.) "And those
probable conclusions are bound to influence what one believes." He
scowled into the glass of beer he was holding. "I suppose the only way
to have a really pure leap of faith, the kind of leap that Kierkegaard
wanted it to be, is to forget about the miracles."

He drained his glass and set it on the table with a bang like a pistol
shot. "Miracles *contaminate* faith," he said.

20

The Molecules of Jesus

During the summer of 1946, Peter devoted most of his extracurricular reading to Paul Tillich and Reinhold Niebuhr. He found Tillich's Christology even more mystifying than Barth's, though it was at once apparent that Tillich was much closer to Bultmann than Barth. Indeed, he was light years away from Barth. "Every literally understood myth is absurd," Tillich declared, "and therefore I stand completely on the side of the famous demythologizing program of my colleague and friend, Rudolf Bultmann." Although Tillich considered myth essential to the language of faith (more so, perhaps, than Bultmann), he went even further than Bultmann in regarding the Nazarene as little more than an artifact, almost irrelevant to the Christ of faith.

It is what Tillich liked to call the New Testament "picture" of Jesus, elaborately embroidered with myths and symbols, that was and is the keystone of Christianity. No harm is done if scholars do what they can to reconstruct the man of flesh and bone, but the task is so hopeless that such efforts can add nothing significant to the vitality of the church. It is the New Testament's picture, and it alone, that is essential for Christian faith. If historians some day decide it is improbable that a historical Jesus even existed, Tillich was once able to say, it would not in the least undermine the certainty of Christian faith!

What kind of historical event, if any, did Tillich believe was the source of the Bible's four accounts of the Resurrection? Peter was unable to find out, although he guessed that Tillich shared the liberal theologian's disbelief in the empty tomb. It was not until ten years later that Tillich published the second volume of his *Systematic Theology*, which contains the fullest description of his flabby Christology. Having recently checked its section on the Resurrection (pages 153–165), I can now report that Peter's intuition was correct.

Trying to summarize Tillich is always risky, and unfortunately he is no longer with us to explain how he has been maligned. Nevertheless, I think it worthwhile to give here the best account I can of Tillich's attitude toward the Resurrection. It is a first-rate example of the kind of theological obfuscation that I think had such a strong influence on Peter's catastrophic Easter sermon.

Tillich admits quite candidly that God may have revealed himself in other ways on other planets where there may be intelligent life. Even on this earth, in future "historical continuums," there may be new revelations. Mankind may be radically transformed by evolution or genetics. It may cease to exist, and some other species may acquire intelligence and religious awareness. But in our present historical continuum God has disclosed himself as Christ. Christ is, therefore, a unique religious figure, not to be transcended by any other figure in our history.

What Tillich calls the New Being, or "God-for-us," was united with the man Jesus in a way that does not apply to any other man. Nevertheless Tillich rejects all the miraculous elements in the Bible's account of Jesus' life. Kierkegaard's notion, that faith is at all times equally difficult, is made stronger than Kierkegaard would have dared make it. Kierkegaard could not doubt the miracles. He could only argue, unconvincingly, that witnesses had no way of knowing that the miracles were authentic. For Tillich, as for Bultmann, the miracles are no embarrassment. There *were* no miracles.

The Crucifixion, Tillich writes, was indeed an event that could have been photographed. But not the Resurrection. It is not a legend, as Barth maintained, but a divine symbol which became attached to the myth of the open tomb. A mature Christology must reject the doctrine of physical revivification. If one tries to defend it, "the absurd question arises as to what happened to the molecules which comprise the corpse of Jesus of Nazareth. Then absurdity becomes compounded into blasphemy." Also to be rejected is the notion that the soul of Jesus came to his disciples in visions or displayed itself to them like the apparitions of a seance. This, too, is childish superstition.

A third approach, a subtle variation of the inner vision theory, is currently a favorite among liberal clerics. God acted on the minds of the disciples in such a way that they became aware of the continued existence, in Heaven, of their Lord and Master.

This, also, is rejected! Eternal life for Tillich, whatever it may be like (do not ask *me*), is not a continuation of the soul, with or without a body, in some higher continuum of space and time. (Tillich does not believe in personal immortality.) To think of the Resurrection of Christ as meaning that Jesus of Nazareth, the carpenter's son, simply moved on to some higher plane of existence, preserving his earthly memory and personality, is still too primitive a view to merit Professor Tillich's respect.

It is hard to imagine that Tillich has any alternative left except to drop the Resurrection doctrine altogether. That is to underestimate his metaphysical adroitness. He reaches into the folds of his Hegelian sleeve to produce a fourth approach which he calls the "restitution theory." Although it sounds extremely profound, it turns out to be little more than this: The disciples of Jesus became convinced, through faith, that the Master had not totally vanished, that he remained for all eternity united to God. In Tillich's words, the Resurrection was the "ecstatic confirmation of the indestructible unity of the New Being and its bearer, Jesus of Nazareth. In eternity they belong together." Again: ". . . the Resurrection is the restitution of Jesus as the Christ, a restitution which is rooted in the personal unity between Jesus and God and in the impact of this unity on the minds of the apostles." Can you imagine Billy Graham or Norman Vincent Peale trying to explain *that* to their listeners?

It has often been pointed out that Tillich held what is called an "adoptianist" Christology. There is nothing new about this view of the Incarnation. It is close to Nestorianism, and the Christian Fathers debated every conceivable angle on it with idiotic frenzy. Adoptianism holds that Jesus was not a pre-existing part of the Trinity who took on human flesh (a view which Tillich scornfully calls "mythological metamorphosis"), but rather a man who was specially chosen by God to be his adopted son. "Jesus was grasped by the Spirit at the moment of his baptism," Tillich writes (*Systematic Theology*, Vol. 3, page 144). "This event confirmed him as the elected 'Son of God.'"

Once the act of adoption had occurred, however, a new and eternal unity was created. For Tillich, the awareness of the disciples of this timeless unity is the reality, and the only reality, behind the Resurrection myth. True, the disciples may well have falsely imagined that they had seen a living Jesus in the flesh, but this was not the heart of their experience. Their true experience of the Resurrection was essentially no different from the experience of Saint Paul on the road to Damascus or, for that matter, from the experience of every man and woman of Christian faith since. It was, in Tillich's words once more, the ecstatic conviction "that the death of Jesus of Nazareth was not able to separate the New Being from the picture of its bearer."

By "picture of its bearer" I believe that Tillich meant the historical Jesus, but I am not sure. It is characteristic of his infuriating vagueness that he would substitute here the word "picture" for Jesus. It is possible, I suppose, to interpret his sentence to mean that God is united for all eternity with nothing more than the New Testament's *picture* of Jesus. Since that picture is, for Tillich, largely mythological, his sentence would tell us that, throughout eternity, this historically inaccurate picture of a man is attached to God. And because God, for Tillich, is timeless Being-itself, or that which eternally is, his sentence could reduce itself to the mighty assertion that the New Testament's picture of Jesus will forever be the New Testament's picture of Jesus. For all eternity it will be the picture by which Being revealed itself to us in our present historical continuum. Let us hope that Tillich meant more than that.

Regardless of how we interpret Tillich's restitution theory, is it not apparent that he has stripped from the Resurrection everything that the Gospel writers and Saint Paul believed essential? "If Christ be not risen," said Paul, "then is our preaching vain, and your faith also is vain." Can anyone except a German metaphysician doubt for a moment, reading that remark in context, that Paul meant a miraculous reappearance on earth of the corporeal Christ?

A theory that cannot be refuted is, as Karl Popper has taught us, without significant content. Tillich's view of the Resurrection is such an empty theory. By divorcing it completely from anything that could have been caught by a camera, or from any statement that a witness could have made about what he fancied he saw, even from any statement about what he fancied he believed, Tillich has rendered his restitution theory irrefutable in principle. Indeed, his entire Christology is in this sense vacuous. How could any part of it be challenged?

The New Being, Tillich tells us, adopted Jesus at the time of his baptism. Suppose an electronic machine's motion picture of the life of Jesus, or (more realistically) historical criticism, found that Jesus was never baptized by John. Would not this count against Tillich's adoptianism? Not in the least. A Tillichian would remind us that it is the Biblical "picture" of Jesus that tells us of his baptism, and this picture, with this particular myth, is all that matters. It is easy to forget that when Tillich writes about Jesus he is writing only about the New Testament picture, not about the man himself of whom we know almost nothing. Thus have Tillich and his fellow-travelers invented a Christology safe from all conceivable attack; but for this safety they have paid a terrible price. It is a Christology so thin and bloodless that no ordinary man, woman or child can find it interesting.

John Updike, whom I mentioned in Chapter 10 as a one-time Barthian, has written a splendid poem entitled "Seven Stanzas at Easter."

I do not know if Updike still believes in the empty tomb. I do know that in this poem he has said, it seems to me, the final word on Tillich's misty Christology. It is a ringing either/or that would have delighted the hearts of Paul and Kierkegaard. With the permission of Updike and his publisher, here is the poem in its entirety:

Make no mistake: if He rose at all
it was as His body;
if the cells' dissolution did not reverse, the molecules
*   reknit, the amino acids rekindle,*
the Church will fall.

It was not as the flowers,
each soft Spring recurrent;
it was not as His Spirit in the mouths and fuddled
*   eyes of the eleven apostles;*
it was as His flesh: ours.

The same hinged thumbs and toes,
the same valved heart
that—pierced—died, withered, paused, and then
*   regathered out of enduring Might*
new strength to enclose.

Let us not mock God with metaphor,
analogy, sidestepping, transcendence;
making of the event a parable, a sign painted in the
*   faded credulity of earlier ages:*
let us walk through the door.

The stone is rolled back, not papier-mâché,
not a stone in a story,
but the vast rock of materiality that in the slow
*   grinding of time will eclipse for each of us*
the wide light of day.

And if we will have an angel at the tomb,
make it a real angel,
weighty with Max Planck's quanta, vivid with hair,
*   opaque in the dawn light, robed in real linen*
spun on a definite loom.

Let us not seek to make it less monstrous,
for our own convenience, our own sense of beauty,
lest, awakened in one unthinkable hour, we are
  embarrassed by the miracle,
and crushed by remonstrance.

After Tillich, Peter turned to all the books by Reinhold Niebuhr that he could obtain. He had read one or two before. Now he read them again, and others, with special attention to Niebuhr's Christology. I vividly recall a late summer afternoon, toward the end of August I believe, when Peter strode into my living room, a thick volume in his hand and an expression of intense vexation on his face. The book was the single-volume Scribner's edition of Niebuhr's two greatest works: *Human Nature* and *Human Destiny*.

He tapped a finger on the book's brown cloth cover and said angrily: "Can you imagine this? There are six hundred pages here. It's a full statement of the theology of America's most famous Protestant thinker. How many references do you suppose there are to the Resurrection of Christ?"

I spread my hands. "How many?"

Peter sank into the sofa, lit a cigarette, then counterfeited inhaling by taking a deep breath through his nose and letting the smoke escape through his nostrils. "Not one! Not a single one! Here, let me show you."

He picked up the book again and opened it to the index. Under the heading, "Christ—divinity of," he pointed out, were many subheads. None concerned the Resurrection. He thumbed back a few pages. "And here," he said, "is an index of all the scriptural passages quoted or cited in the book. Not a single passage from Matthew twenty-eight, Mark sixteen, Luke twenty-four, or John twenty, the four Resurrection chapters!"

"Don't shout," I said, "You'll wake up Edna. How the devil can you remember the numbers of those chapters?"

He looked blank for an instant before he grinned. "And first Corinthians fifteen," he said, his voice lower. "Niebuhr does have a few quotes from *that* chapter, but they're not about the Resurrection."

"And so?"

"And so," Peter replied, tossing the book back on the coffee table where it landed with a smack, "it means that Reinie just won't tell us what he thinks. I've wasted two weeks trying to find out. I even asked a student who did work under him at Union. *He* didn't know either. Can you beat that? How can a man write six-hundred pages about Christian theology and not say what he believes about the biggest miracle in the Bible?"

"Does he say anything about the Virgin Birth?"

Peter nodded. "He worked up enough courage to say he rejects it. There's one reference."

"On the basis of that, can't you guess what his attitude would be on the Resurrection?"

Peter shook his head violently. "He talks most of the time as if he agrees with Tillich. But it's hard to be sure. He heaps scorn on the liberal view that Jesus was a 'very, very, very good man.' On the other hand he says that the traditional view of Christ as truly God and truly man, in one person, is 'logical nonsense.'"

I found Peter's perplexity amusing. Here he was in the twentieth-century, at a great secular university, and fretting over trivia about as relevant to modern life as the mythology of ancient Egypt. Outside of our seminaries, what Protestant cares a rap about Niebuhr's Christology? Or anybody's Christology?

"I think I recall marking a passage in one of Niebuhr's earlier books," I said. "It's a book I don't think you've seen. The passage may be relevant."

I got up and found my copy of *An Interpretation of Christian Ethics*. The underlined passage was on page 120. I read it aloud:

> *The relation of the Christ of the Christian faith to the Jesus of history cannot be discussed within the confines of this treatise in terms adequate enough to escape misunderstanding. Perhaps it is sufficient to say that the Jesus of history actually created the Christ of faith in the life of the early church, and that his historic life is related to the transcendent Christ as a final and ultimate symbol of a relation which prophetic religion sees between all life and history and the transcendent.*

Peter wagged his head in disbelief. "Are you sure you're not reading Tillich? It would be so easy for Niebuhr to say it clearly if he wanted to.* Jesus *created* the Christ of faith!"

---

* I cannot pretend to have read everything Niebuhr has written, but his least equivocal statement on the Resurrection that I have since been able to locate is in his reply to critics, on page 438 of *Reinhold Niebuhr: His Religious, Social, and Political Thought*, edited by Charles W. Kegley and Robert W. Bretall (Macmillan, 1956). Modern scholarship tells us, Niebuhr writes, "that the story of the empty tomb was an after-thought and that the really attested historical fact was the experience of the risen

A strange sound came from Peter's mouth. It was part guffaw and part snort. He walked to a front window, looked out on the street, and muttered something under his breath. I cannot swear to it, but it sounded like "Bultmann shit."

He stood there a while. And then he heaved a gigantic sigh. It was the sigh of a man who is taking one last look at the homestead where he spent his childhood; who is leaving it, never to return.

Christ among his various disciples. I accept that fact together with the certainty that the Church was founded upon the assurance that Christ was indeed risen."

From that statement I can only conclude that Niebuhr, like his friend Tillich, rejects the bodily Resurrection. Whether he believes that the disciples' "experience of the risen Christ" was a ghostly visitation by the man who had just died or merely an ecstatic inner feeling that Jesus and God were eternally united, as Tillich argued, is something I have not yet been able to discover.—H. W.

21

Martha

Imagine yourself in a room with walls that are papered bright green. You walk to an adjoining room where the walls are also green, but the shade is imperceptibly bluer. You enter a third room, bluer than the second. Again the difference is too small to be noticeable. After passing through fifty rooms, each slightly bluer than the last, someone hands you a sample of the wallpaper in the room where you started. You are astonished by how green it is. Suddenly you realize that the room you are now in is not green at all. It is blue.

Something like this happened to Peter as he moved through the intellectual corridors of Gray City. The war had temporarily interrupted his progress from room to room, but now, as he struggled with the complicated Christologies of Barth, Tillich and Niebuhr, he began to move again. He realized, of course, that his attitude toward the divinity of Jesus had been changing over the years, but it was not until one afternoon, in the early fall of 1946, that a small episode suddenly brought home to him the full magnitude of the change.

He had attended a Sunday morning service at the University of Chicago's Rockefeller Chapel to hear a guest sermon by the Reverend Norman Wesley Middleton. Dr. Middleton was the pastor of Calvary Methodist Church in Winnetka, one of the largest and wealthiest churches in the Chicago suburban area. He and I were old friends of a sort, in spite of the fact that he looked upon me as an underfed political radical, and I regarded him as an overstuffed right-wing conservative: an amiable imposter who combined a simple-minded Pollyanna piety with Machiavellian money-grubbing. While the Protestant journals were printing articles about existential anguish, the torture of doubt, and the possibility of a worldwide atomic holocaust, the rotund, cherry-faced Dr. Middleton was preaching on such stirring topics as:

Really—Life Can Be Wonderful!
Why Worry When You Can Pray?
How to Live with a Lift.
When Things Go Wrong, Make Them Right.
No Matter What, Life Can Be Terrific!
Life Really Can Be Wonderful.
It Pays to Cultivate Hope.
Sure Life Has Meaning—Even Today.
Think Big, Pray Big, Believe Big.
Life Has *Great* Possibilities.
Life Can Be Really Wonderful.
There Are Good Days Ahead.
Don't Be Tense—You *Can* Relax.
Life Can Be Wonderful—Really!

The title of Middleton's sermon, at the chapel service Peter attended, was "Three Steps for Improving Your Personality." Note the brilliant use of that word "personality." It is one of Middleton's favorites. He did not speak on how to improve your "soul." That would have sounded too much like the language of Jesus, who warned against losing it. Too many people would have been frightened away from the service. Nor did he speak on how to improve your "character." That would have suggested a series of moral admonitions that would make his listeners uncomfortable by reminding them of their weaknesses. "Personality" is just right. It implies that the good doctor is going to disclose three valuable secrets on how to make oneself more attractive and popular, better able to win friends and influence people. Peter had listened to the sermon with alternating fits of boredom and amusement. He was amazed, however, to observe that attendance at the chapel was unusually large. And the congregation actually sat still and listened!

The divinity students of the four federated theological schools had been invited to tea at four o'clock that afternoon, in the Commons Room of the Chicago Theological Seminary, to meet Middleton. After the chapel service Peter took a walk west along the Midway to Cottage Grove Avenue where he stopped to look, as he had often done before, at Lorado Taft's masterpiece: that massive concrete fountain with its

hundred figures of humanity moving like a tidal wave past the immov-
able grim statue of Time. He read again, on the monument's plaque,
those lines by Austin Dobson which had inspired the artist:

> Time goes, you say? Ah no!
> Alas, Time stays; we go.

Peter was then twenty-seven. It was time, he thought, for him to get
to work on God's business. It was time to marry, to have children. He
thought of Taft's other famous statue, the Great Spirit, a reproduction
of which stood in the hallway of the Oklahoma high school he had
attended. The almost naked Indian, astride his horse, arms extended,
face upturned, is praying to his god. But is it the God of the Bible to
whom he prays or, as Barth firmly believed, just another idol? Is the
mythology of Christianity, Peter asked himself, really superior to the
mythology of those Indian tribes?

He walked back to the campus where he ate lunch in the coffee shop
that opens on the corridor of Mandel Hall. He still had an hour or two
of time to kill before the tea. Kill time? Who can kill time? Can God
kill time, or is God, too, growing and changing in time as William
James had suggested? He read some copies of *Time* in the lounge of the
Reynolds Club, then sauntered outside into the small court that sur-
rounds the water fountain behind Mandel Hall.

It was a cool September afternoon, but the sun had emerged from
behind a clump of clouds, and the sunlight was so warm that he did not
bother to put on the Navy pea-jacket he was carrying. Dead leaves
tossed about in fitful flurries. Above and behind him the bells in Mitchell
Tower began to clang a hymn. It was William Cowper's well-known
spiritual which begins:

> There is a fountain filled with blood
> Drawn from Immanuel's veins,
>   And sinners plunged
>   Beneath that flood
> Lose all their guilty stains.

Years had gone by since he had heard or sung that hymn. The old
familiar melody brought tears to his eyes. A thousand memories jostled
inside his skull: memories of Sundays in Moody Memorial Church,
gatherings of the Chicago Christian Fellowship in little upper rooms,
and on down the gray corridors of backward time, memories of revival

meetings in sawdusty Oklahoma tents where he had bellowed that hymn, his heart overflowing with praise for the infinite love that enabled God to sacrifice his only begotten (not adopted!) Son for the sins of Adam's progeny.

Peter walked to the fountain and plunged his hand beneath the cold water in the circular stone basin. As the tower bells continued to play, he sang the hymn's second and third stanzas to himself. Then abruptly, with a shock of recognition that sent a convulsion down his spine, he realized that the words had become offensive to him. He had written to me about a similar experience on his ship, when he discovered that a Fanny Crosby hymn seemed meaningless, but his emotion now was more disturbing. It was not that he felt indifferent to Clough's imagery. He felt *repelled* by it.

It was the redness of the blood, stark against the university's gray background, that repelled him. It brought to mind the myriads of blood sacrifices that were part of all those pagan cults he had studied in Haydon's course on comparative religion. At one time he had actually believed that those gory ceremonies were foreshadowings of Calvary, faint glimpses God had permitted to pre-Christian cultures of the great Sacrifice-to-come. Now his opinion had swung to the opposite side. The Cross was only the latest, perhaps greatest, expression of the same primeval, unconscious yearnings that had prompted the earlier sacrificial rituals. No longer did the blood of Christ, as Christopher Marlowe so dramatically phrased it, stream in the firmament. The symbol of being washed in the blood of the Lamb was too grotesque to be true or beautiful. Were there not even undertones of vampirism and cannibalism in the communion service?

Water was still clinging to his hand, and a spray of droplets, blown by the wind, cooled his hot forehead. He thought of Moody's sermon on the blood, the sermon that had so deeply stirred him as a boy. Take the scarlet thread out of the Bible, Moody said, and the book would not be worth carrying home. The scarlet thread was there. There was no way to take it out of the Bible. Was the book worth carrying home?

"The blood of Jesus Christ," Peter said to himself, "cleanseth us from all sin. First John, chapter one, verse seven."

He shook the drops from his hand. They were drops of water. His hand trembled. While he stood there, with the blood-stained leaves drifting around him, he prayed a double prayer. He asked God for forgiveness if he had, through carelessness or pride, abandoned the true way. And he prayed for courage to go forward, in God's will, in whatever direction God wanted him to go.

"I felt absolutely no remorse," he said, trying years later to recall the incident, "but I did have a bewildering sensation of having lost my way. It was like finding myself in a rowboat in the middle of the gray Atlantic. No charts, no compass, and a cloudy sky overhead. What should I do? In what direction should I row? Since I was a boy I'd taken for granted I'd someday be a minister. Now I began to wonder. . . ."

I was chatting with Dr. Middleton, at the tea in the Commons Room, when I saw Peter enter a side door and drape his mud-stained pea-jacket over the back of a chair. I nodded to him across the room, and when he came over I introduced him to Middleton and to the pastor's daughter, Martha. Martha, just turned twenty-one, had recently taken up residence in the University of Chicago area. She had graduated the previous spring at Northwestern University in Evanston, only a few miles south of where the Middletons lived. Her major college interests had been music and French. Although she was now studying advanced piano at the Chicago School of Music, in downtown Chicago, she was living at International House, on the Midway, at the eastern fringe of Gray City.

I had observed a tense, distracted expression on Peter's face when he entered the room. As he shook Middleton's chubby paw he complimented him warmly on his morning sermon. There was a slight, uncharacteristic half-smile on Peter's face while he made these remarks, a sort of frozen grimace I had never seen before. He seemed to unwind a trifle when he began to talk with Martha. Her father was captured by two divinity students—they wanted to ask him about the role of psychology in the handling of large suburban congregations—and I myself moved away, leaving Peter and Martha to themselves.

Martha, I noticed when I stole some side glances, had a lovely profile. Her forehead was high and beautifully rounded, and she had well-proportioned features which from the side or even three-quarter view gave the impression of a narrow, aristocratic face. When you saw her face from the front, however, you were surprised by the width of the oval and the space between her eyes. The eyes were pale gray, clear and luminous. Her hair: light brown, almost blond. She was wearing an expensive tailored dress, its colors white and gold, and its modest lines giving discreet hints of an excellent figure.

While I conversed with one of my duller colleagues, I tried to keep my left ear cocked for the conversation between Peter and Martha that was taking place a few feet to my left. The general hubbub made it impossible to hear what they were saying. Out of the corners of my eyes I could see Martha smiling animatedly while Peter talked. When she left with her father, I heard her tell Peter that if he were ever in International House to try her on the house phone. She would, she said, enjoy continuing their "fascinating discussion."

Peter let only a few days go by until he followed up on this suggestion. A few weeks later he was seeing Martha often. Before the end of the fall quarter he had accepted several dinner invitations (including Thanksgiving) to the Middleton home in Winnetka.

There were, of course, numerous evenings when he brought Martha Middleton to my house. Edna and I liked her well enough, though we were amused by her impulse to agree too quickly with anything anyone said. It was not so much conscious deception on her part as simply an effort to be charming and agreeable. Her father had a similar personality. Indeed, he was a paradigm of the type of person praised in Dale Carnegie's then-popular books. He was a fat, jolly-good fellow, seemingly incapable of clashing with anybody. It was, I suppose, one of the secrets of his remarkable success. He was the best known, most popular minister in Chicago's entire northern suburban and exurban areas.

And Martha was a young, female version of the "Dale Carnegie man." She read *Reader's Digest* and the *New Yorker* (especially the *New Yorker* ads). She absorbed all the best-selling books, attended the better movies, visited the fashionable art galleries. She was quick to pick up phrases and ideas from a conversation and give the impression of greater familiarity with a topic than she actually had. She seldom talked about herself. It was always *you* that she was interested in. When you conversed with her, you felt as if you were being interviewed. Edna and I could not guess what her actual views were on any important controversial topic. She was sweet, kind, modest, considerate, with a built-in antipathy toward any sort of argument that threatened to become inflammatory.

"The United States is certainly in no moral position to play the role of world leader in outlawing the atom bomb," Peter pontificated one evening when he and Martha, and Edna and I, were chatting in our living room. "You can't blame Russia for distrusting us. They haven't forgotten that after the first World War we sent troops into Russia to help the British try to put down the Bolshevik Revolution. The way I see it, our big job now is to convince Stalin that the United States really wants world peace."

"That's what I think, too," said Martha. "If we can only make Stalin believe that, maybe he'll cooperate with the United Nations. Maybe Russia and the United States can learn how to get along with each other."

"Maybe," I said. "But I'm not quite so optimistic. Stalin still thinks that every nation outside the Soviet orbit is on a downhill path and that Communism, directed by the Kremlin, is destined to spread over the entire globe. How can we be sure that Russia, after she builds her own arsenal of atomic weapons, won't use them, or threaten to use them, to extend Red control over new territories?"

Martha tilted her pretty head to one side and frowned. "Yes," she said, "I hadn't thought of that."

Peter looked dumbfounded. I had been having strong doubts about Russia since the war. This was the first time I had openly expressed them in Peter's presence.

"But, Homer," he said, "surely you don't think that Stalin wants to grab any more territory, do you? He has too many internal problems to worry about. I can't believe Russia would ever use the bomb except to defend herself against an attack."

"I don't think so either," said Martha.

"Well," I said, "the Chinese civil war is still going on, and it looks as if it won't be long until all of China is Communist."

"That's true," Martha said.

Peter was trying to control his excitement. "But *Russia* isn't fighting China! The war in China is being fought by Chinese farmers against the wealthy landowners and a corrupt Chinese government."

Martha nodded and then looked toward me.

"The Chinese Reds are part of the International Communist movement," I said. "You can be sure they're getting directives, as well as military help, from Moscow."

Martha looked at Peter.

"I'm *not* sure," he said angrily, his color rising. "The Chinese reformers are just poor peasants who found some leaders able to organize them well enough to start a successful rebellion. Naturally the Russians are sympathetic. Maybe they're helping with ammunition and food supplies and military advice and so on. That's not the same, though, as invading a country where they're not wanted."

My wife, sitting in a far corner of the room, had been preoccupied with her knitting. I noticed that the needles had stopped wigwagging. Her large brown eyes, peering over the half-glasses she wore when she knitted, were studying Martha's face.

Martha put down the drink she had been sipping and walked to the piano. "Oh, let's not argue about politics. Let me play something I've been working on."

She had, of course, wanted desperately to agree with both Peter and me. When she saw that we were taking contrary positions she couldn't bear to let the debate go on. I don't think Peter was aware then of her strong aversion to controversy. If he was, he did not consider it important.

Seated at the piano, her face illuminated by the yellow light from a floor lamp, Martha was a vision of youth and beauty. Her dress, cut low in front (but not too low), was of dark maroon velvet, a dress that Edna told me must have cost her father a pretty penny. She played a concerto—I cannot now recall the composer whose name she mentioned —and she played it extremely well. I could see that the music meant a great deal to her, more than to any of the rest of us, especially Peter who was inclined toward tone deafness and had little interest in classical music. He listened, however, with rapt attention.

Middleton and I were at that time on the board of governors of the Chicago Brotherhood of Jews and Christians. One afternoon in early December, after a board meeting in the organization's Loop head-quarters, I was not surprised when Middleton asked me what I thought about Peter's future. Peter expected to obtain his doctor of divinity degree in June. Did I consider him mature enough, experienced enough, Middleton wanted to know, to serve in his Winnetka church as one of his three assistant ministers?

"I'm sure he is," I said.

"Do you know anything about his family background?"

I gave a slightly dishonest answer. "Not much. His father had something to.do with the oil business in Oklahoma. He's no longer living. His mother remarried."

"Yes, so he told me," said Middleton. "Have you met his mother or stepfather?"

I told Middleton I had.

"What sort of people are they?"

"They're good Christian souls. They're both very active in their local church."

"Peter gave me the impression that it's a Pentecostal church. Is that true?"

"Well, yes," I replied. "But Peter has broken away from all that. His views are broader now."

"Hmmm," said Middleton. "It's odd that Peter didn't have a com-mission in the Navy. Do you know why?"

"I don't think he wanted one."

"Hmmm."

"Peter and Martha seem to be getting pretty serious about each other," I said.

Middleton took off his rimless spectacles. Were they window glass, I wondered, like the Nazi submarine captain's monocle Peter had written about? Did he wear them only to look more dignified? Slowly, with a spotless white silk handkerchief, he wiped the perspiration from the wire ear hooks. "They do indeed."

He smiled when he said it. But it seemed to me that the Reverend Norman Wesley Middleton, though smiling, was not happy at all about the prospect of acquiring Peter either as an assistant or a son-in-law.

22

Between the Horns

Demythologizing the life of Jesus eliminates many problems for the modern Christian. At the same time it creates agonizing new ones. If the Gospels can be trusted—and what else is there to trust?—it is hard to deny that Jesus believed himself to be the Messiah promised to the Jews and that within the lifetime of his disciples he would return to earth in power and in glory. If Jesus is to remain the church's central figure, superior to all other religious leaders, a liberal Protestant must somehow explain the Master's errors. Peter had Bultmannized his Christ. He had accepted a human Jesus. Throughout the winter of 1946-47, as his relationship with Martha grew more "meaningful," his hidden thoughts became preoccupied with a new and curious question: What justification did he have for considering his faith "Christ-centered"?

"You know, Homer," he said one day, "a difference in degree can make a great difference in quality. When the sun goes down, light fades from the sky by slow degrees. It doesn't mean there isn't any difference between night and day. *Of course* Jesus was a man. But his religious insights were so much deeper than anyone else's that they give his teaching a special authority."

"Such as his teaching about hell?"

Peter didn't answer.

"You've got to be careful you don't apply a double standard. It's hardly cricket to pick out just the wise remarks of Jesus in the Bible, then compare them with the foolish remarks of Mohammed in the Koran."

Peter did not think he was doing that. Nevertheless, the gnawing questions about the mistakes of Jesus refused to go away. Let us put the problem starkly. If Jesus was not an incarnation of one-third of the Trinity, what attitude should a Christian take toward Jesus' claim that he was God?

One of the most crushing ploys of the orthodox has been to confront a sceptic with the following dilemma: Christ was God or he was mad. It is an either/or that goes back to the time when Jesus was alive. In the tenth chapter of John, Jesus told his listeners that he, the man of flesh and bone who stood before them, had the power to give his life and to take it back again. I quote from the translation by Gray City's own Edgar Johnson Goodspeed:

> *These words caused a fresh division of opinion among the Jews. Many of them said,*
> *"He is possessed and mad! Why do you listen to him?"*
> *Others said,*
> *"These are not the words of a man who is possessed. Can a madman make blind men see?"*

For the orthodox Christian there is no dilemma. He believes that Jesus, being God, *did* have the power to make blind men see, to give his life and take it back again. For modern liberals, who cannot believe these things, the either/or returns with all its original terrifying force. I continue with the passage:

> *That was the time of the Rededication Festival at Jerusalem. It was winter time and Jesus was walking up and down inside the Temple, in Solomon's Colonnade. So the Jews gathered around him and said to him,*
> *"How much longer are you going to keep us in suspense? If you are really the Christ, tell us so frankly!"*
> *Jesus answered,*
> *"I have told you so, and you will not believe it. . . . The Father and I are one."*
> *The Jews again picked up stones to stone him with. Jesus answered,*
> *"I have let you see many good things from the Father; which of them do you mean to stone me for?"*
> *The Jews answered,*
> *"We are not stoning you for doing anything good, but for your impious talk, and because you, a mere man, make yourself out to be God."*

Jesus answered,

"*Is it not declared in your Law, 'I said, "You are gods" '? If those to whom God's message was addressed were called gods—and the Scripture cannot be set aside—do you mean to say to me whom the Father has consecrated and made his messenger to the world, 'You are blasphemous,' because I said, 'I am God's Son'?*"

That final rebuttal by Jesus, of which I have quoted only the first half, has always struck me as an evasive quibble. He had been asked to speak frankly. Surely he realized that the sense in which the Jewish scripture spoke of all men as gods was infinitely removed from the sense in which he had spoken of himself as God. At any rate, this ancient either/or, this choice between divinity and psychosis, still haunts the Protestant mind. Is it a valid dilemma? Apologists for orthodoxy have not hesitated to exploit it to the full, and one could fill a book with instances from the rhetoric of the Church Fathers to the orations of Bishop Fulton Sheen and the Reverend Billy Graham.

Dr. J. Gresham Machen, whom I quoted in a previous chapter as the last of the scholarly fundamentalists, expressed the dilemma this way in his book, *Christianity and Liberalism:*

> *The real trouble is that the lofty claim of Jesus, if, as modern liberalism is constrained to believe, the claim was unjustified, places a moral stain upon Jesus' character. What shall be thought of a human being who lapsed so far from the path of humility and sanity as to believe that the eternal destinies of the world were committed into His hands? The truth is that if Jesus be merely an example, He is not a worthy example; for He claimed to be far more.*

Clive Staples Lewis, the widely-admired British apologist for the Church of England, uses even stronger language in *The Case for Christianity:*

> *I'm trying here to prevent anyone from saying the really silly thing that people often say about Him: "I'm ready to accept Jesus as a great moral teacher, but I don't accept His claim to be God." That's the one thing we musn't say. A man who was merely a man and said the sort of things Jesus said wouldn't be a great moral teacher. He'd either be a lunatic—on a level with the man who says he's a poached egg—or else he'd be the Devil of Hell. You must make your choice. Either this man*

was, and is, the Son of God: or else a madman or something worse. You can shut Him up for a fool, you can spit at Him and kill Him as a demon; or you can fall at His feet and call Him Lord and God. But don't let us come with any patronising nonsense about His being a great human teacher. He hasn't left that open to us. He didn't intend to.

Gilbert Chesterton, in his *Everlasting Man,* a book that once almost persuaded Peter to become a Roman Catholic, says it this way:

No modern critic in his five wits thinks that the preacher of the Sermon on the Mount was a horrible half-witted imbecile that might be scrawling stars on the walls of a cell. No atheist or blasphemer believes that the author of the Parable of the Prodigal Son was a monster with one mad idea like a cyclops with one eye. Upon any possible historical criticism, he must be put higher in the scale of human beings than that. Yet by all analogy we have really to put him there or else in the highest place of all. . . .

. . . Stark staring incredulity is a far more loyal tribute to that truth than a modernist metaphysic that would make it out merely a matter of degree. It were better to rend our robes with a great cry against blasphemy, like Caiaphas in the judgment, or to lay hold of the man as a maniac possessed of devils like the kinsmen and the crowd, rather than to stand stupidly debating fine shades of pantheism in the presence of so catastrophic a claim. There is more of the wisdom that is one with surprise in any simple person, full of the sensitiveness of simplicity, who should expect the grass to wither and the birds to drop dead out of the air, when a strolling carpenter's apprentice said calmly and almost carelessly, like one looking over his shoulder: "Before Abraham was, I am."

Was Jesus paranoid? Did he have, to put it with painful humor, a Messiah complex? In England and America, very little has been done by professional psychiatrists to explore these shocking possibilities. There is one crude 1912 attempt by an American psychiatrist, William Hirsch, in *Religion and Civilization: Conclusions of a Psychiatrist.* Peter read it and was unimpressed. He turned to the larger European literature on the problem, in particular to books by the German writer George de Loosten and the Danish writer Emil Rasmussen, but mainly to the four-volume French work by Charles Binet-Sanglé, *The Insanity of Jesus.*

It would be unpleasant and beside the point if I reported here in any detail the many discussions Peter and I had, in the early months of 1947, about this literature—especially the questions it raises concerning relations between Jesus and his parents and siblings, and about his possible latent homosexuality. Remember John, the disciple "whom Jesus loved," whose head rested on Jesus' bosom at the Last Supper (John 13:23) and to whom he entrusted the care of his mother (John 19:26-27)? I shall say no more than that Peter eventually rejected the dilemma by going between its horns to a third alternative, an alternative he found best expressed by Albert Schweitzer in his 1913 doctoral dissertation, *The Psychiatric Study of Jesus*.

Although Schweitzer's little book has been available in English since 1948, when Beacon Press issued a translation, it is hard to find a liberal Protestant who has read it; or indeed, to find one who has even heard of it. Yet I can think of no more important book for him to read. Schweitzer begins by accepting the fact that Jesus did believe himself to be, in truth, the Messiah, and that he would return to earth before his generation had passed away. He was mistaken, Schweitzer admits, on both counts. He may even have been subject to hallucinations that strengthened such beliefs.

Nevertheless, Schweitzer argues, the charges of paranoia are unjustified. Most of the extreme claims to divinity attributed to Jesus are in the Gospel of John, long recognized by New Testament scholars as the least trustworthy of the four accounts. The picture of Jesus in the other Gospels is that of a more humble man who made less outrageous claims. Moreover, Schweitzer continues, we must not make the easy mistake of removing Jesus from his cultural milieu, of judging him by today's cultural norms. In Jesus' time the expectation of a Messiah was so strong in the Jewish community that it is not difficult to comprehend how a wise and good man of lowly birth and descended from David (two criteria by which the Messiah was to be identified), who found himself drawing enormous crowds by his preaching and seemingly miraculous healing, would come to regard himself as the Messiah without being driven to that belief by neurotic compulsions.

In an age when everyone believed in the divine right of kings (I now bolster Schweitzer's arguments with some analogies of my own), a king need not have been paranoid to believe that he possessed divine right. Today, when traditional Catholics still believe in the infallibility of the Pope (when he speaks *ex cathedra*), a Pope need not be paranoid to believe that (when he speaks *ex cathedra*) he speaks with the true voice of God. Reflect on the culture of old Judea, Schweitzer asks his reader, with its pervasive Messianic expectation, and you can understand how a sane man could have believed himself to be the chosen Son of God. Jesus was mistaken. He was not mad.

Peter was filled with admiration for Schweitzer in facing this problem

so courageously. He called my attention to the following truly remarkable passage in Schweitzer's book:

> Should it really turn out that Jesus' object world must be considered
> by the doctor as in some degree the world of a sick man, still this
> conclusion, regardless of the consequences that follow from it and the
> shock to many that would result from it must not remain unuttered,
> since reverence for truth must be exalted above everything else. With
> this conviction I began the work, suppressing the unpleasant feeling
> of having to subject a great personality to psychiatric examination, and
> pondering the truth that what is great and profound in the ethical
> teachings of Jesus would retain its significance even if the conceptions
> in his world outlook and some of his actions had to be called more or
> less diseased.

I did not argue with Peter about the soundness of Schweitzer's thesis,
even though I felt that the good doctor had not approached his topic
as objectively as he had imagined. It was his earlier masterpiece, *The
Quest of the Historical Jesus*, which more than any other book demol-
ished the liberal's picture of Jesus as a sweet-faced, gentle man who
went about patting children on the head, urging everyone to love his
enemies and to work for a Kingdom of Righteousness that would
gradually dawn on the earth in response to the efforts of ministers,
missionaries, YMCA secretaries and other Christian do-gooders. It was
the shattering of this imaginary portrait, and the restoration of a
historical Jesus who really believed his own earth-shaking claims, that
made possible the revival of the view that he may have been maladjusted. Surely this must have weighed heavily on Schweitzer's conscience. He himself, in the preface to his psychiatric study, speaks of
being "compelled" to undertake it because of misconceptions aroused
by his *Quest*. I have often fancied that his later break with his culture,
to live a life of privation in Africa, was prompted in part by deep guilt
feelings over the waves his *Quest* had set in motion.

Peter, too, it seemed to me, was not entirely happy with Schweitzer's
way of going between the horns of that awful either/or. But it was the
best solution he could find and, for a time at least, he made the most
of it. "I can't believe," he said one day, echoing Schweitzer's sentiments,
"that God would wish that such studies of Christ *not* be made. All truth
is God's truth." But his voice was toneless and his eyes sad.

Although Peter had been a minister of the Pentecostal Holiness
Church since he was sixteen, he planned to be ordained again, in a less
comic ceremony, as soon as he obtained his doctor of divinity degree

in June, 1947. Originally his plans were to enter the Baptist ministry. But Martha's father offered him a job as an assistant minister of Calvary Methodist Church and suggested that he switch to Methodism. Peter had no objection. In late March, however, as the day of his ordination grew nearer, Edna and I began to notice small signs of growing inner unrest. At first we dismissed them as symptoms of too much work combined with too little sleep. He was seeing Martha almost every evening, sometimes returning to his dormitory as late as two in the morning, then getting up after a few hours of sleep to attend early morning classes. And there was the problem of his doctor's thesis. He had postponed the decision on what to write about until as late as the first of the year. Even after he had accepted my suggestion that he write on the Christology of Schweitzer, he did not start the actual writing until late February. But there was something else, something more fundamental, that was troubling him. He was losing his enthusiasm for the ministry.

It is my impression that Peter did not discuss these doubts with Martha at any time. Indeed, he did not even discuss them with me until one evening in April. Edna had retired early, and he and I were alone in my sitting room.

"It's not that I have any doubts about God," he said, scowling at the rain that was pounding the front windows. "It's just that I can't see myself standing up in front of a congregation and . . . ." His voice trailed off. There was a slight nervous twitch of his head.

He had, he told me, been reading Kierkegaard's notes for a novel: notes that had first been published in a Danish magazine under the title, *First God's Kingdom*. The novel (which Kierkegaard never wrote) was to be about a theological student whose name, by a coincidence I noted in my first chapter, was Ludwig From. Ludwig was tormented by the thought that his plans to become a preacher were not honest. Was he entering the ministry because he wanted, above all else, to labor for the Kingdom of God? Or was he entering it because he enjoyed speaking to an audience, because he knew of no other way to earn a living, because he wanted a comfortable income as the pastor of a middle-class church?

"I feel the way young Barth must have felt," Peter said. "The good people of my flock will be sitting there, looking up, expecting me—expecting *me*!—to talk to them about God, to tell them what they should believe and what they ought to do. How can *I* do that when I don't know myself what to believe or do?"

"Look, my dear boy," I said. "Don't think for a minute that your fears are unusual. Thousands of students who graduate from seminaries and become pastors have exactly the same fears. Like you, they have to decide between staying in the on-going tradition of Protestantism, taking part in shaping it, moving it in the right direction, or leaving the tradition altogether. If you leave it, where can you go? Abandon theism and you can always become a Unitarian and work inside the Unitarian tradition if you like. But you haven't abandoned theism. You believe in God. You believe in life after death. You believe in the superiority of the Protestant tradition over all others. I respect those beliefs. But you can't be of any service to that tradition unless you stay within it."

Peter looked confused. "I can't figure you out, Homer. I always thought you wanted Protestant theism to wither away."

"Ultimately, yes. But that could be centuries in the future. Cultures change slowly. Religious traditions never explode like pricked balloons. They grow. They evolve. Christianity is the only viable religious faith the Western world has. Protestants and Catholics are not going to stop attending church. Their habits are too deeply ingrained. And as long as they go, somebody has to preach to them. Better it be someone like you than a throwback to the past like Billy Graham. As one of my old professors liked to put it—I know you've heard me say this before—you have to choose between being a truthful traitor or a loyal liar. I myself decided to be a truthful traitor. If you feel you can't be a loyal liar, that you have to talk straight and honest to your congregation, then I agree. It's better to become a Unitarian minister or no minister at all. But why be a traitor to your tradition? You have a chance to take part in a monumental work—purging the church of superstition. Remember Robert Ingersoll's switch on those lines of Pope? 'An honest God is the noblest work of man.' You can help the church come to grips with the great secular tasks of abolishing war and poverty and racial hatreds. You can help make the church a great force for good. You've been trained to be a minister. You're a marvelous public speaker. Everybody likes you. No one would make a more dedicated pastor. Don't throw away the chance. Stick with it. In the deepest sense you'll never have to compromise."

Peter was smiling a crooked smile when I finished this long-winded piece of advice. "A truthful traitor or a loyal liar," he muttered. "What a choice!"

I noticed it again. That involuntary head-shake. It was as though an invisible hand had seized his head and jerked it suddenly to one side. I doubt if he was aware of it. He rubbed his fingers up and down one cheek. We sat and listened to the rain.

Then he picked up his glass—it had held a mixture of scotch and water—rattled the ice and carried it to the kitchen for a refill.

23

Disenchantment and Diamonds

Although Peter managed to complete several months of research on Schweitzer's Christology, he started much too late on the actual writing of his doctoral thesis. When it was apparent that he could not finish it in time to receive a degree in June, 1947, I suspect he was immensely relieved. The delay gave him an excellent excuse for postponing his ordination—the day on which he would ratify his choice between truthful treason and the loyal lie. The G.I. Bill made it easy for him to pay for continued studies, so he decided on one more year of graduate work. It would provide plenty of time to complete his thesis, and more time to consider carefully, without pressure, exactly what he intended to do after he left Gray City. It also meshed smoothly with Martha's desire to complete another year at the Chicago School of Music. Neither they nor Martha's parents could see anything to gain by rushing their engagement. All things considered, Edna and I agreed that Peter had made a prudent decision.

Since the end of the war, Peter had been too preoccupied with shaping his Christology to give much thought to politics, and Martha's entrance into his life had made it even more difficult for him to become involved in activities unrelated to his studies. Besides, it was a time of political lassitude on the nation's campuses. The molders of liberal and radical opinion, staggered by the implications of the atomic bomb and disenchanted by increasing evidence of Stalin's paranoia, were keeping relatively quiet while they tried to think their way to new positions. Officials of the American Veterans' Committee and the National Council of American-Soviet Friendship had sought Peter's assistance, but he had reluctantly backed away and restricted his activities to only one organization, a state group called the Independent Voters of Illinois.

The decision to continue graduate work another year had a remarkable effect on Peter. He became more relaxed. That strange nervous tic of his head disappeared. Indeed, I had never seen him happier. Now that he had resigned himself to accepting Jesus as no more than a great moral and religious teacher, the last vestiges of conservative Christian doctrine dropped out of his mind. And with more free time at his disposal, he slowly began to take a renewed interest in political affairs.

In England, the Labor Government had nationalized the coal mines and soon would be taking over British railways. Congress had appropriated four hundred million dollars to oppose Communism in Greece and Turkey. The Marshall Plan was getting underway to halt the march of Communism in Europe. Thomas E. Dewey was girding himself for a triumphant march into the White House in 1948, over the prostrate body of Harry Truman. In Illinois, Adlai Stevenson was emerging as the Democratic candidate for governor. Gray City's own Paul Douglas, now a Marine Corps hero with a Purple Heart, would soon be running for a seat in the U.S. Senate. There was no hope, of course, for any change in Chicago's eternal Democratic machine.

Early in 1947 the IVI (Independent Voters of Illinois) began to show signs of a classic left-right split: the Commies and their followers versus the non-Communist liberals. In the American Communist Party, Browderism had been replaced by Fosterism, and the Party stalwarts were in no mood for concessions. Simultaneously, American liberals, to their great astonishment, were discovering that things were not what they thought they were in Russia. Information about the labor camps and Stalin's purges had swelled to such proportions that one no longer could dismiss it all as fables concocted by White Russians, Trotskyists, and William Randolph Hearst. Liberals were being goosed by Arthur Koestler's *Yogi and the Commissar* and *Darkness at Noon*, and chuckling over the symbolism in George Orwell's *Animal Farm*. They were starting to ask themselves Orwellian questions that they should have asked before the war:

How is it that we civil libertarians, horrified by capital punishment at home, were able to justify as "historical necessity" the endless state executions in Russia?

How is it that we, so quick to publicize the suffering of starving masses in Africa and India and China, refused to believe that there were famines in the Ukraine?

And what in the name of holy pragmatism possessed us when we accused men of the caliber of John Dewey and Edmund Wilson and

Norman Thomas of being "fascists" every time they uttered a remark faintly critical of the Soviet Union?

The Stalinoids were a breed more stubborn and thick-headed than the Stalinists. Before the war, the American Communist Party had lost every intellectual and cultural commissar it had except Howard Fast, who hung on desperately until he finally discovered, in the mid-fifties, that Stalin didn't like Jews. With sorrow I report (for the indictment applies also to me) that it was not until the late forties that the full impact of the collapse of Bolshevism as a viable political philosophy hit the fellow-travellers of Gray City.

As soon as Peter began regularly attending meetings of the IVI he found himself squeezed between the two ferociously battling factions. At first he tried to take a mediating position, arguing that both sides should damp down their differences for the sake of unity, although his sympathies clearly leaned toward the Communist side of the conflict. He had persuaded Martha to join IVI, but doorbell ringing and envelope licking were distasteful to her, and she did little more than accompany Peter to a few local meetings and one city-wide rally.

For many months Peter had been aware of my growing disenchantment with the Soviet mystique. (No one can say that I was a "premature" anti-Communist!) Still, it must have been a blow to him when he discovered one afternoon, at an IVI meeting in the basement of my church, that I had been secretly participating in anti-Communist caucuses within the organization.

Our first discussion in depth about these matters took place in my house one frosty October evening in 1947. For several hours I did my best to convince Peter that there was a large and rapidly growing literature critical of the Soviets, written not by conservatives or reactionaries but by intelligent, well-informed liberals and socialists. I had expected Peter to react with anger. To my delight his attitude was one of intense eagerness to read the books I recommended.

Was it that his disenchantment with conservative Protestant theology had given him a healthy mistrust of all dogma? It was partly that. But even in the days of his most ardent fellow-traveling he had preserved in the back of his head a deep suspicion of Communist philosophy. Its inverted Hegelian metaphysics had always struck both of us as balderdash. Even on political and economic questions, I suspect that he had always harbored more misgivings than he had been willing to admit. Neither of us, I hope it is fair to say, fellow-traveled blindly. In the days of popular-front enthusiasm, we had looked upon the Party as the most energetic and best organized opposition to fascism. We had gone along with the comrades because no other radical group in the United States at the time seemed to be getting any work done. The democratic socialists were weak and splintered. The Trotskyists and the De Leonists were miniscule. The old anarchist movement was dead. The labor movement was strong and growing, but its members seldom looked beyond union goals of higher pay and better working conditions. As fascism threatened to take over the world, where else could we look except to Russia?

But now the climate of political opinion on the campuses of America was rapidly changing. The *New Republic* began to intimate that Stalin was not quite the hero depicted by our wartime propaganda. ("Listening to Stalin's quiet words," Elliott Roosevelt had written, recalling his father's meeting with Stalin at Teheran, "watching his quick, flashing smile, I sensed the determination that is in his name: Steel.") Liberals were discovering that the *Nation* could not be trusted, and that its archenemy, the *New Leader,* was not the reactionary, red-baiting sheet they had so often been told it was, but a democratic socialist magazine printing articles they should have been reading all along.

I have already mentioned the influence of Koestler and Orwell. Other persuasive voices soon were telling the same eye-opening stories. (I started to list here the writers and intellectuals around the world who deserted Party ranks, most of them before the war, but when the list reached fifty names I decided not to mention any.) Leo Cherne, Sidney Hook, and young Arthur Schlesinger, Jr., were launching broadsides against the comrades in *Life, Look* and other mass circulation magazines. Max Lerner, that perfect model of the "other directed" liberal (to apply David Riesman's almost forgotten phrase), caught the trend on his finely-tuned radar scope. If you were a constant reader of Lerner's *New York Post* column during the forties, you would not have been aware of any day on which Lerner made a dramatic switch. Like those blue-green rooms I described at the beginning of Chapter 21, Lerner's column evolved slowly, by imperceptible mutations, along a continuum of increasing de-Stalinization. Reinhold Niebuhr, whose influence on both students and faculty of the federated seminaries of Gray City continued to be enormous, emerged as an outspoken anti-Communist. Among the great Continental theologians of neo-orthodoxy, Emil Brunner became the most vocal opponent of the Soviet system.

Only Karl Barth and a few of his friends seemed unconcerned about Russia. The cold war between the Soviet Union and the United States, said Barth, was an "unholy battle" between two "quarreling giants." The church, he declared, should sit this one out. "As Christians it is not our concern at all. It is not a genuine, not a necessary, not an interesting conflict."

Why, then (asked his critics), had he shouted such an unqualified "No!" to Nazi totalitarianism? Because, Barth replied, Nazism was altogether different. Its ideology, unlike that of Communism, was "quite simply a mixture of madness and crime in which there was no trace of reason." It is absurd, he went on, to regard Communism and Nazism as twin evils, "to mention a man of the stature of Joseph Stalin in the same breath as such charlatans as Hitler. . . ." Behind the admittedly bloody hands of Communism are at least the ideals of justice. Most of all, insisted Barth, Communism has never been guilty, as was Nazism, of pretending to be a Christian movement. "There is nothing of the false prophet about it. It is not anti-Christian. It is coldly non-Christian. It does not seem to have encountered the Gospel as yet. [!—H. W.] It is brutally, but at least honestly, godless."

For Barth, the West was just as godless. Worse still, it pretended to be otherwise. The Protestant church, said Barth, is not called upon to choose between American and Russian materialism. It must go its third way, down a path between the snarling monsters. Christians must wait and suffer like the Christians of ancient Rome. Barth wrote a long letter to the Hungarian Reformed Church recommending passive cooperation with, not opposition to, its Communist government.

Peter, I was happy to observe, no longer cared what Barth believed about anything. If Barth's neutrality influenced him at all, it was an added reason to side with Barth's old enemy, Brunner. When Peter read the books by Koestler that I had recommended, the effect on him was instantaneous and electric. It was like a conversion in reverse. With a sudden shock he realized that his pre-war Soviet sympathies had been as ill-informed and naive as his earlier enthusiasm for fundamentalism. Peter seldom did things halfway. He subscribed at once to the *New Leader* and to Dwight Macdonald's marvelous little magazine, *Politics*. He read a newly revised edition of David Dallin's upsetting book, *The Real Soviet Russia*. He read Dallin's even more explosive 1947 treatise, *Forced Labor in the Soviet Union*. (Years later it was amusing to watch the last remaining die-hard Stalinoids in Gray City finally accept the full horror of Stalin's purges, but not until Khrushchev had made his famous speech revealing Stalin to be even more insane than Dallin had imagined.) He read Franz Borkenau's *World Communism*, Arthur Rosenberg's *A History of Bolshevism*, Boris Souvarine's *Stalin*, David Shub's *Lenin*.

We had countless discussions about this literature, and the more we talked the greater our disenchantment grew. By the end of 1947 Peter and I were in substantial agreement. The Russian experiment had failed.

Marx's great utopian vision of a classless society was more remote than ever from the Russian scene. The Soviet Union, to put it plainly, was just another police state. It differed from Hitler's Germany and Franco's Spain only in the mythology by which its crimes were rationalized. The redness of the Russian flag became for Peter, like the redness of the blood of Christ, a symbol of futile sacrifice.

"What amazes me," Peter said on one occasion, "is how clearly certain writers saw the truth from the very beginning, only we wouldn't listen. Rosa Luxemburg, for instance. And Karl Kautsky. And Bertrand Russell."

"Don't forget Wells," I said.

I dug out of my files a tattered Communist Party pamphlet that had reprinted H. G. Wells's 1934 interview with Stalin, and we read it again, along with Granville Hicks's simple-minded introduction (written, of course, before Hicks broke with the Party). When the pamphlet first appeared, both Peter and I had marveled at Wells's stupidity. Did he not represent the petty bourgeois mentality, unconsciously revealing (as Hicks put it) "the hopeless confusion and intellectual emptiness of liberalism"? Now as we reread the dialog, how tired and dogmatic Big Brother sounded, spouting his patronizing, old-fashioned Marxist bromides! How polite, sensible, and restrained Wells had been!

I must add that neither Peter's disenchantment nor mine was accompanied by that emotional wrench which turned so many Party members from the breasts of Mother Russia to the breasts of Mother Rome, or (as in the case of Whittaker Chambers and others) to Protestant or Jewish traditionalism.° We had not taken Communism all that seriously. We were never Party members. For neither of us had Bolshevism been, in Tillich's phrase, our ultimate concern. Peter was a theist when he played his Soviet language game, and he continued to be one now. In my case, the Soviet experiment had been no more than a small aspect of a long-range humanist trend, of what Wells was fond of calling the "Open Conspiracy." To be sure, the failure of the Russian experiment now seems to me a tragedy of classic proportion—indeed, *the* political tragedy of our century. But recognizing that tragedy did not crumble the foundations of my humanist faith.

°An example of a sharp turn from Communism to Protestantism, to this day almost unknown in literary circles, is the strange case of Joy Davidman. The daughter of New York Jewish parents, Joy joined the Communist Party after graduating at Hunter College, became a movie critic for *New Masses*, and the wife of William Lindsay Gresham (author of what Peter tells me is the best novel ever written about carnival life, *Nightmare Alley*). After "growing up and walking out" of the Party (as Joy once expressed it) she wrote a series of articles for the *New York Post* under the heading "I Was a Communist," became a Presbyterian convert, divorced her husband, took her

Nor did our disenchantment change our loyalties to freedom and justice. We simply realized, as we had not before, that freedom and justice had been betrayed by the Soviet Revolution. In trying to understand the causes of the Russian failure, we rediscovered ancient and forgotten truths about the democratic process: the indispensable role of liberty in thought, religion, speech, journalism, science, and the arts; the indispensable role of conflicting parties and genuine elections.

Peter soon was on my side of the growing left-right split within the Independent Voters of Illinois. The rift was impossible to heal. By the end of the year the Commies and their friends had pulled out of IVI to enter the newly-born Progressive Party, painstakingly set up by the comrades to promote the presidental candidacy of poor, befuddled Henry Wallace—a candidacy that would soon come within a hair of throwing the 1948 election to Thomas Dewey. The remaining members of IVI voted to affiliate with another newly-formed group, the anti-Communist Americans for Democratic Action.

Martha, of course, went along with us. At the start of 1947 she had seemed to share Peter's sympathies for the Communist faction in IVI. At the end of the year, after Peter had made his flip-flop, she quickly caught the essence of his new approach and memorized the appropriate phrases. She had not minded when he was pro-Stalin. She thought it fine when he became anti-Stalin. As for her religious views, Edna and I (perhaps Peter also, though I did not ask him) realized that they, too, were bland and amorphous. We never heard her volunteer an opinion on any religious question. As the daughter of a liberal minister, attending Sunday services had, of course, become an established pattern of her life. But we had the impression that she seldom listened to what her father said in the pulpit. When she and Peter visited us, and the conversation turned to theological or political topics, Peter and I would talk to each other while Edna and Martha conversed about other things.

One freezing evening in December, when Peter and Martha dropped by to exchange Christmas packages with us, my wife instantly perceived

---

two sons to England, and in 1956 married that distinguished, aging (he was 58) bachelor and Anglican replica of Chesterton, C. S. Lewis, from whom I quoted in the previous chapter.

Joy had earlier been smitten by Lewis' book, *Miracles*; indeed, her purpose in going to England had been to meet and marry Lewis, with whom she had corresponded but who was not yet aware of her intentions. The title of Lewis' next book, *Surprised by Joy*, was a play on words that could be appreciated only by those who knew what had happened to him. Gresham (whom I once had the pleasure of meeting in New York) maintained that the book's title was a thumping understatement. It should have been, he said, *Overwhelmed by Joy*. All three participants in this improbable triangle are now dead.—H. W.

that Martha was in a state of suppressed elation. As soon as she removed her white gloves we caught sight of the glittering diamond on her left third finger. I shook Peter's hand, gave Martha a peck on her rosy cheek, and hastened to the kitchen to celebrate the occasion with a round of old-fashioneds.

Peter seemed strangely embarrassed by our enthusiasm, even a trifle sullen. Martha was radiant. She was wearing a sapphire blue dress, expensive and very chic. A wedding date had been set for the Sunday following Easter, and old plans were back for Peter to join Middleton's staff as soon as he received his doctorate and had been ordained.

Peter followed me into the kitchen for a second round of drinks. "I plan, my dear Homer, to be the biggest liar in Winnetka," he said, keeping down his voice so that Martha and Edna in the living room would not hear. He grinned, then abruptly frowned and handed me his empty glass. His head twitched.

"We had an argument about the ring," he said. "It's the first serious argument we've had."

"Yes?" I asked, not looking up. I was busy mixing sugar and bitters in the bottoms of four old-fashioned glasses.

"I wanted to get a small, inexpensive ring," Peter continued. "But Martha convinced me that if I did it would embarrass her and her family. Of course I agreed to get the kind she wanted. I'd saved enough from the Navy to pay for half of it. Her father kicked in the other half. Then we got into one of those crazy arguments about whether diamonds are *really* beautiful or whether people just think they are."

I plopped a cherry into each glass and nodded. It was I who had introduced Peter, before the war, to Thorstein Veblen's *Theory of the Leisure Class.*° It had become one of his favorite books. For Peter, Veblen's theme was supported by much more than socialist economic theory. It was supported by the Gospels. Has anyone in the history of the world ever expressed greater contempt for what Veblen called "conspicuous waste" than did Jesus Christ?

°When I was a young divinity student at Meadville Seminary, Veblen was still teaching economics at the University of Chicago, and I had the pleasure of attending his lectures on the theory of the leisure class. At the end of the course a group of us presented him with a gold watch chain to replace a large safety pin he always used for fastening his watch to a vest pocket. Veblen was furious. Did we not realize that his safety pin, which cost less than a penny, did the job just as well, was just as beautiful, as our expensive gold chain? He lowered by one notch the grade of each of us on the grounds that our gift proved we had failed to comprehend the main point of his course. How amused he would have been to know that solid-gold safety pins are now sold as clothing accessories for ladies, and as collar and tie clasps for men!—H. W.

"Have you noticed," Peter asked, "how impossible it is, how *completely* impossible, for almost anyone in America, especially any female, to agree with Veblen? It seems so obvious to me that nobody in his right mind would think a diamond was prettier than, say, a piece of cut glass if the prices got transposed. But Martha can't see it. She thinks there's something about a diamond, something in the *stone itself*, that has a quality like great music!" He wagged his head. "I reminded her that Jesus once told a rich man to sell all his possessions and give the money to the poor. Do you know what she said?"

I chuckled, finished pouring the Bourbon, and said, "Tell me, Pete."

"She said, 'Don't be silly. That doesn't have anything to do with it.'"

I stirred the four old-fashioneds and transferred them to a small wooden tray. Then I clapped Peter on his shoulder. "She's right. Jesus has *nothing* to do with it. Forget about the lilies of the field that toil not and yet are clothed like Solomon in all his glory. Forget about the camel and the needle's eye. That was long ago. It was in a different time and a different place. Martha's behaving like any ordinary American girl. What else did you expect? Status symbols are a part of American life you'll have to live with, especially if you live in Winnetka. You'll *have* to compromise. There's *no* way out. Wait until you and Martha are married and start discussing the relative merits of stainless steel and sterling silver, fur coats, and the importance of owning a really fine set of china."

Peter shuddered. His head jerked to one side. We returned to the living room and I handed out the drinks. Martha was sitting at one end of the sofa, near our small, synthetic Christmas tree. She flashed Peter a dazzling smile.

Peter raised his glass toward the tree's glittering star of Bethlehem. He started to say something, but he thought better of it and lowered his arm. Then he bent over and kissed Martha gently on her forehead.

24

The Unknown Tongue

Peter visited us infrequently during the winter of 1947–48. He had finished writing his thesis the previous fall, but now he was busy revising, polishing, and retyping it. Almost every weekday at six o'clock he would meet Martha for dinner at International House, and Sundays were usually spent with her family in Winnetka. Not the least of his burdens, I imagine, was having to attend Calvary Methodist Church on Sunday mornings to hear the Reverend Middleton huff and puff and blow one of his inspirational addresses. Peter was not in any of my classes for the winter quarter, though our paths occasionally crossed on the snowy campus or in the drab corridors of Swift Hall. He seemed always on the run. We would pause to exchange a few pleasantries, then he would scowl, consult his wrist watch, and off he would go.

Each time I saw him he seemed better dressed than before. Martha had not been able to persuade him to buy a hat, but there was a steady succession of new suits, new shirts, new shoes, and new neckties. His old Navy pea-jacket had been the first to go. Martha had informed him on their second date, more than a year previous, that it smelled strongly of diesel oil. Peter had been reluctant to part with the jacket, but Martha settled the matter by simply carrying it to the basement of International House and stuffing it into the incinerator. He shaved every morning. He went to a first-class barber.

One slushy afternoon in February, when Peter was my luncheon guest at the Quadrangle Club, I mentioned that he looked a trifle haggard. Yes, he said, for the first time in his life he was finding it difficult to sleep at night. I persuaded him to see my doctor for a physical checkup. The doctor assured me the next day that Peter was in robust health. He attributed the insomnia to three impending events: marriage, examinations, and ordination. How can you expect the boy, the doctor asked me, *not* to be worried? He gave Peter prescriptions for a month's supply of a mild tranquilizer and about a dozen sleeping pills.

Peter did not fill either prescription. He was, however, concerned enough about his sleeping problem to rent a locker in the University of Chicago's Bartlett Gymnasium. Every other day he went there for an hour or two to pound a punching bag, swing on the parallel bars, and take a quick swim in the pool.

Toward the end of February, Peter's mother had a mild heart attack. It was not believed serious enough to warrant a trip to Oklahoma, but early in March she had a second, more severe attack, and Peter's stepfather wired for him to come. I did not hear from Peter until the following week when he telephoned from the Chicago Municipal Airport on his return. Could he, he asked, come directly to my house?

I told him he could, and inquired about his mother, but he hung up without replying. When he arrived, we guessed the worst. "Dear Peter," Edna said as she embraced him.

"I think you could use a strong drink," I said.

He shook his head violently. "No, no, Homer. That's exactly what I don't need."

We moved from the vestibule to the living room where Peter sat on the sofa without removing his overcoat. He looked like a man recovering from a long illness. He had lost weight. His face was thinner. He needed a shave. His hair was uncombed. Every few minutes his eyebrows would come together in a momentary scowl, at times accompanied by that involuntary tic of his head.

"Would you like some coffee?" Edna asked.

"That would be great."

As soon as Edna left the room, he turned and glared at me with an expression that struck me as more hostile than friendly. "Homer, I've been practicing the great twentieth-century Protestant art of loyal lying."

His head jerked to one side. He ran a hand over one eye and down his cheek. There was a long, painful silence. When I realized that he did not intend to speak again, I asked:

"Does Martha know you're back?"

He shook his head.

"Why don't you stay here tonight? You can sleep as late as you please and phone Martha tomorrow after you get rested up."

"Thanks, Homer. I'd like to do that."

"And take off your overcoat."

He stood up, surprised to find that he still had it on. I took the coat from him and hung it in the hallway closet. Edna returned with a cup of steaming coffee and some sweet rolls. We made a few attempts at conversation, but Peter either did not reply or he responded with monosyllables that led nowhere. Then suddenly he began to talk. The emotions he had been holding back poured out of him in an uncontrollable torrent.

It was not grief at all that had shaken him, for his mother had experienced a miraculous recovery. Indeed, when Peter left she was back at home in excellent spirits, doing all her usual chores and teaching Sunday School at Holiness Tabernacle. For that, of course, he was happy and grateful. It was something else that troubled him, something strange that had happened to him at his mother's bedside.

Peter, you must understand, had never let his mother know the full extent to which he had outgrown his Pentecostal faith. To be sure, she suspected that changes had taken place. But had Peter lost his soul? Fundamentalists today, like Protestants of old, still divide over the terrifying question of whether a person once converted can "backslide" to the point at which eternal salvation is in jeopardy. Some argue that a convert remains forever a child of God regardless of how far he slides backward into sin and disbelief. Others argue just as earnestly that it is possible for a "twice born" soul to fall from grace, to lose his second birth, to rejoin the ranks of the damned. It is not so much a division along denominational lines as it is a division among individual fundamentalist ministers and churchgoers. Peter's mother was one of those who took the grimmer second view.

He was sitting by her bedside early one afternoon, he told us, holding her thin hand while she prayed aloud, asking God to keep her son always in the shadow of the Cross. They were in a small double room of a Catholic hospital in Sand Springs. A portly lady in the other bed was snoring noisily under heavy sedation. Peter's stepfather was at work, and his sister Gabrielle, who had been there all morning, was not yet back from lunch. Peter kept his head lowered while his mother pleaded with him to promise that he would never, under any circumstances, let anything turn him aside from his divine calling, from the exercise of his great gift of evangelism.

"It was the most awful moment of my life," Peter said. "I *had* to promise. What else could I do? The doctor told me there was a good chance she'd pull through. I didn't want to upset her. Even if there hadn't been a chance, how could I. . . ." He couldn't finish. His desperate blue eyes moved from mine to Edna's, then back to mine again.

"She asked me to pray," he continued. "I closed my eyes. I asked the Lord to give my mother strength, to help her back to health. She put her hand on my arm and interrupted me. I had misunderstood. She didn't want me to pray for *her* at all. She wanted me to pray for *myself*. She wanted me to ask God for a new baptism of fire, for the old-time power, for the Pentecostal power."

"Of course you did," Edna said.

"Yes, Edna, I did!" he exclaimed. "I said everything she wanted to hear. I asked God to forgive me for my sins. I asked him to forgive me for my doubts. I prayed for strength to withstand the wiles of Satan."

Peter stood up. The saucer and the empty cup he had been balancing on his knee clattered to the carpet. The cup broke in half.

"And all the time I prayed, my mother was lying there, looking at the ceiling and shouting 'Thank you, Jesus!' The lady in the other bed kept snoring. I kept on praying. I knew that everything I said was a lie. It was a mockery of my mother's faith. But I couldn't help it. The words seemed to be coming from above. I felt as if my lips were instruments through which God himself was speaking."

Peter had been striding back and forth across the room. He stopped and turned to face us. "Homer, Edna—I believed! All the lies I'd been speaking—they seemed as if they weren't lies at all. I really wanted God's forgiveness. I really wanted to get back on the one true way. God was listening. He was filling me with a new faith. *I believed!* I felt the way I did as a boy when I was converted in Holiness Tabernacle. I felt the way I used to feel when I preached at revival meetings. *I could feel the power coming!* Everything I'd thought and done since I came to Chicago rose up in front of me like a horrible nightmare. It had all been a snare of Satan. His trap had caught me for a while. Now I was free again! I waved my arms. I shouted thanks to Jesus. I praised God for the precious blood that still flows from Calvary, the blood that had washed me whiter than snow. I rededicated my life to Christ. I begged for a new baptism . . . "

Peter was breathing hard. His forehead dripped with perspiration.

"And then it happened! Remember, Homer, the second chapter, second verse of Acts? I heard the sound of Pentecost! It was like a mighty rushing wind. I could feel the heat from the tongue of fire on my head. I could see the room light up. I began to babble. I began to speak in the Unknown Tongue!"

Edna and I looked at one another. A pink flush colored her dark cheek bones.

"I've read your paper on glossolalia, Homer. And of course I heard it hundreds of times when I was a boy. But it had never happened to *me*. I couldn't control it. I couldn't stop it. They were crazy words, meaningless words. They were Jabberwocky words. They went on and on and on and on . . ."

Peter sat on the sofa and buried his face in his hands. "Oh God," he said, "let this cup pass from me."

Edna picked up the two jagged pieces of china from the carpet. She put them on the saucer and carried them to the kitchen.

Peter looked up. "When I finished jabbering, I saw a nurse and two nuns standing in the doorway. They looked frightened. The lady in the other bed was still snoring. My mother had fallen asleep. She was breathing quietly. Her face looked calm and peaceful."

When Edna returned to the living room, Peter was slumped silently on the sofa, staring straight ahead with wild, despondent eyes. She sat next to him and took one of his hands in hers.

"Why don't you go to bed now," she said gently. "You need a good night's rest."

"Edna's right," I said. "We can talk about it tomorrow."

He stayed the night in our guest room, sleeping like a baby. Edna did not wake him until two-thirty in the afternoon. A bath and shave improved his appearance considerably, although there still were purplish patches beneath his eyes. The twitching of his head had stopped. Edna prepared a substantial meal for him, and we were pleased to see that his appetite was good.

"Do you want to call Martha now?" I asked when he finished eating.

"No, not yet. I'll phone her from the dormitory."

Although I spoke to Peter on the telephone the next day, we did not see him again until he and Martha visited us the following week. Peter had gained back most of the pounds he'd lost and was beginning to look more like himself. He had told his mother nothing about Martha. Nor did he ever tell Martha what had happened to him during that visit home.

25

First Draft

Monday, March 22, was a typical early spring day in Chicago—overcast sky, windy, cold, with a depressing drizzle in the air. Some bush-league theologian had delivered a morning lecture in the divinity school's Joseph Bond Chapel, and I happened to be walking past the entrance just as clumps of students were coming out. Peter stopped to inspect the gray sky while he buttoned up a light brown topcoat that I hadn't seen before. And he was wearing a hat!

"Hello, Peter," I said.

"Hello, Homer."

"You look good in a hat."

"You think so? I hate the damn thing. Martha insisted I get it. The topcoat, too. They're gifts, actually. Martha dragged me into Marshall Field's men's store last Saturday and picked out both of them. The Middletons have a charge account there."

He turned up the collar of his topcoat, then took a pair of brown suede gloves out of the pockets. Peter seldom wore gloves, even on the coldest days, and when he did they were black woolen gloves left over from his naval service.

He cackled with laughter at the astonishment on my face, then abruptly his expression went blank. "Let's sit down for a few minutes, Homer. Are you in a hurry?"

I was in no hurry. We walked to the "C-bench," a large stone bench, curved like the letter C, in front of Cobb Hall. I opened the umbrella I was carrying and held it over our heads while we sat, and Peter brought me up to date on his wedding plans. He had wanted a simple ceremony in the small Rose Chapel, in the basement of Calvary Methodist Church, with only the immediate family and a few friends present. Martha and her mother refused to consider it. The ceremony was to be in the church proper, with an orchestra and a 20-voice choir. One of Middleton's assistant pastors would officiate while Middleton gave away the bride. It had slowly proliferated into an intricate social affair to which half the church members had been invited. Three bridal showers were being planned.

"It usually works out that way," I said. "Don't hold it against Martha. Getting married is the first big social event in a girl's life. You can't blame her for wanting to make the most of it. Besides, the Middletons can afford it."

"That's not the point. It's what *we* could do with the money."

"You can't mean that seriously. You'll have a good starting salary. And surely Martha has money of her own. Middleton once told me he'd established a sizeable trust for her."

It was not a very diplomatic remark. Peter's long glassy blue stare was followed by a sudden grin. "We've decided on my best man."

"Who?"

"You," he said, jabbing me in the chest with his thumb. It was a hard jab that actually hurt.

"That's ridiculous. I'm much too old."

"Nonsense! And who says there's any age limit for the best man? I've already discussed it with Martha and her mother and father. They're delighted."

"All right, if you insist."

I wondered who was lying; Peter in telling me that Middleton was delighted or Middleton in saying that he was? All the same, it would be amusing to participate.

When I write that it would be "amusing," I don't wish to suggest that I took the wedding lightly. The reader surely knows by now that I was far from happy about Peter's marriage. Neither Edna nor I had been able to share his enthusiasm for Martha, but we were wise enough to realize that it would be futile to interfere. Besides, older people are often blind to certain virtues of the young. We had not at first been pleased with our daughter's choice of a husband; but she had married him anyway, and it had been a good and stable marriage. Over the years we had discovered many admirable qualities in our son-in-law. Perhaps Martha would make just the sort of wife that Peter needed. Perhaps serving as an assistant pastor of a church so typical of wealthy suburban churches as Calvary Methodist was just the sort of training that he needed. For a while I had secretly hoped that Peter would move close enough to my humanist philosophy to join my own staff at Midway Community

Church. I had even considered the possibility that he might become its pastor when I retired. But his falling in love with Martha had changed all that.

"Now," I said, as we sat there under my umbrella, my chest still throbbing, "*I* have a favor to ask of *you*."

Peter shot me a suspicious side glance.

"Easter comes early this year," I continued. "In fact it's March 28, and that's next Sunday. I'd like you to preach my second Easter sermon."

"But I'm not even ordained."

"You're still a Pentecostal minister," I said unkindly, as Peter winced, "but what difference does it make? I'm always having guest speakers who aren't official men of the cloth. You know that."

"Isn't your bulletin already printed?"

"Yes. And I know that members of a church always expect to hear their own pastor orate on Easter. But last year we had to turn away several hundred people, so this year we're having two services—one at eight-thirty and one at eleven. I'm still recovering from a cold and a severe attack of laryngitis. Haven't you noticed how hoarse I sound? I can get through the early sermon all right, but I doubt if my voice will hold out for the later one. I'm really in a bind. If you can help me out, I'll be eternally grateful."

The little drops continued to tap the top of my umbrella while we sat and brooded. I did not tell Peter that I had another reason. I wanted him to have the experience of preaching in my church; to get the feel of my congregation before he disappeared into the suburbs like most of my former students; before he collapsed into the comfortable arms of Martha and Middleton Methodism.

"It's awfully short notice," Peter said finally. "How can I get a sermon ready in less than a week?"

"Well, when you get a church of your own you'll be doing it every week."

Peter still protested. Was not Easter, above all other Sundays, the occasion to speak of eternal life? And were not all the members of my congregation humanists who did not believe in life after death?

Not true, I said. Most of them are humanists, but some of them believe in both God and immortality. It's a matter of degree. Middleton's congregation, I explained, is a different mix. His majority is conservative, his minority progressive. In both cases the minister has the same difficult job. He must hold together a divided congregation. On Easter Sunday in particular he must be careful not to offend either side. Give the impression of taking the Easter myth too literally, I said, and you alienate your liberals. Fail to treat it with sufficent reverence, and you antagonize your conservatives. Some of my leading financial contributors, I reminded Peter, were conservatives. That's why, I confessed, I always looked forward to Easter tightrope-walking with such trepidation. The Easter sermon calls for enormous diplomatic skill. You might as well begin now, I said, to practice some of the basic tricks of your trade.

Peter listened with a frozen half-smile. "But you don't have communion service. Middleton does. You don't make your people stand up and recite the Apostles' Creed. Middleton does."

"True, true. But let's not jump on the old boy for that. Did I ever tell you the story about Benjamin Jowett, the Greek scholar at Oxford? You know, the man who translated Plato?"

Peter shook his head.

"Well, Jowett would recite the Apostles' Creed in chapel by saying 'I' in a loud voice, then he'd whisper 'used to' to himself, followed by 'believe' in a loud voice."

Peter didn't laugh.

"The point is," I went on, "that it's not easy to stop churchgoers from reciting creeds. It's not easy to stop them from doing *anything* in church that they're accustomed to. They want to sing the same old hymns and go through the same old rituals they remember from their childhood, even if they don't believe the doctrines any more. A liberal pastor has to keep all the outer trappings of his denomination while he slowly teaches his congregation new meanings for the old symbols. It may seem like hypocrisy, but in a more basic sense it isn't. Middleton's just fulfilling, in his own way, his task as the loyal liar. If he didn't, Calvary Methodist Church would split apart at the seams."

"Maybe it should," muttered Peter. "Neither cold nor hot. . . ."

"You don't have to finish," I said, "I know the passage well. The Laodicean church was neither hot nor cold. And because it was lukewarm, the Christ of the Apocalypse said he'd spew the church's angel out of his mouth. But nothing's easier than being hot when you have a revealed dogma to preach. Nothing's easier than being cold when you despise a dogma so much that you want to obliterate all its myths. Only the fanatic blows hot or cold. The church today *has* to be doctrinely tepid. It's the only way it can survive. It doesn't have to be tepid about other things. Racial justice, for instance, or economic justice, or. . . . "

"But Middleton is tepid about those things, too. There's not a single black family that goes to his church. Can you imagine Middleton ever preaching a fiery sermon on civil rights?"

"Perhaps," I said smiling, "*you* can change that."

"Perhaps," replied Peter, not smiling.

A cold wind slashed across the campus. We tightened the scarves around our necks and remained there for several minutes without speaking, watching the undergraduates go by in both directions. A girl with a raincoat over her sweatshirt sat down on the C-bench opposite us and unwrapped a sandwich. Two alert pigeons, anticipating crumbs, swooped down from the gables of Cobb Hall and strutted in front of her.

Peter suddenly laughed and slapped his thigh. The girl looked up, startled. The pigeons flapped away.

"Of course, Homer, you're absolutely right."

"Then you'll do my Easter sermon?"

"By God, I'll do it!"

We stood up and shook hands. It was like closing a business deal. You preach my sermon; I'll be your best man. Peter declined my invitation to lunch. Too busy, he explained, retyping his thesis. And now he had a sermon to prepare. I walked him under my umbrella to the coffee shop in Mandel Hall, where he could grab a quick bite, then I crossed University Avenue to enter the Quadrangle Club.

On Thursday morning I phoned Peter to make sure he hadn't forgotten his promise. No, he hadn't forgotten. As a matter of fact, he told me, he had already typed out a rough draft of what he planned to say. Yes, he'd be happy to let me look it over. Could he drop over, he asked, about 4:30 that afternoon?

Peter arrived with the manuscript of his sermon rolled into a cylinder and projecting from a pocket of his topcoat. He was dressed elegantly in gray wool slacks and a dark maroon cashmere sweater. I sent him to the kitchen, where Edna was preparing cocktails, while I sat down with the manuscript.

When I read what he had written, I was enormously relieved. He had called his sermon "The Secret of Easter." The Resurrection of Christ had not been stressed as a symbol of personal immortality, nor had he explicitly denied the survival of the soul after death. It was, in short, a fine specimen of a theologically tepid sermon, yet filled with colorful imagery and arresting metaphors. He had typed it out in full, on Manila paper, complete with instructions on when to pause for dramatic effect or for a sip of water. I'd heard Peter speak before from a written text, so I knew he could do it superbly, in a way that did not seem as if he were reading or even following a prepared outline. At one or two spots I could have suggested changes, but on the whole I was so pleased that I did not make a single criticism.

"Congratulations, Pete," I said, rolling up the yellow pages and slipping the rubber band around them. "You've done a truly magnificent job."

"Of saying nothing?"

"On the contrary. It's a splendid affirmation of life and hope. My people will love it. Have you finished your old-fashioned?"

Peter stared at his drink for a moment, then suddenly he began to sing. It was the last verse of a hymn that I remembered hearing Homer Rodeheaver, Billy Sunday's music man, sing at one of Billy's revival meetings in Soldier Field more than twenty years ago:

> *If the Lord never changes, as the fashions of men,*
> *If He's always the same, why, He is old-fashioned, then!*
> *As an old-fashioned sinner saved thro' old-time grace,*
> *Oh, I'm sure He will take me to an old-fashioned place.*

Edna, hearing the singing, came into the living room carrying her cocktail, and listened with amusement while Peter went on to the chorus:

> *'Twas an old-fashioned meeting, in an old-fashioned place,*
> *Where some old-fashioned people had some old-fashioned grace:*
> *As an old-fashioned sinner I began to pray,*
> *And God heard me, and saved me in the old-fashioned way.*

Then he lifted high the drink in his hand, like a priest elevating the chalice. "To you and me," he said. "To the loyal liars!"

26
Come and See

On Saturday, March 27, 1948—the day before Easter—Peter and Martha, and Dr. and Mrs. Middleton, were dinner guests at the home of James Abernathy of Winnetka. Abernathy, who owned a large advertising agency in Chicago, was a trustee of both Northwestern University and Calvary Methodist Church. He was Calvary's firmest financial pillar. It was he who had supplied the initial capital for establishing Wesley Memorial Clinic, the first church-operated psychiatric clinic in the United States. (It preceded by several years the better publicized Religio-Psychiatric Clinic organized by Smiley Blanton in New York City for Norman Vincent Peale's Marble Collegiate Church.)

On the rare occasions when I had spoken to Abernathy he impressed me as an intelligent, well-informed gentleman with a conservative political bias. His wife, I'd been told, was a devout Methodist. Did that explain why Middleton's church had snared such a large share of Abernathy loot? Although Abernathy had been guarded and uncommunicative whenever our conversation touched on religion, I had a strong impression that his private views were not much different from mine, that his church interests were probably little more than deference to his wife's piety and a way of cutting income taxes.

Peter had wanted to decline the dinner invitation so he could spend the evening putting finishing touches on his Easter sermon, but Martha insisted on their going. Her father, I suspect, had impressed upon her the importance of having Peter establish cordial relations with the Abernathys. Saturday afternoon, before the two of them left for Winnetka, they came by to see us briefly.

Edna and I wondered why they bothered to come at all, but when I opened the front door we both suddenly understood. Martha wanted us to see their new car (a premature wedding gift from her father) which was parked in front of our house, and to see the two of them in their Easter upholstery. Martha (we soon learned) had been the driver. Peter had driven his family's model-A Ford when he was in high school, but he had not driven a car since. Traffic conditions and cars had changed so much since then that he was understandably reluctant to take the wheel, especially to risk the fast-moving lanes of Lake Shore Drive. Martha had already arranged for him to take driving lessons from a school in Winnetka.

I must admit that Peter, though still a bit under his usual weight, had never looked handsomer. A richly-patterned silk tie was clipped to his white shirt front with a large gold pin. His hair had been expertly cut. His ears and nose (in both of which he tended to be hirsute), even his eyebrows, were neatly trimmed. Martha was wearing a stunning pale green dress. Her accessories were conspicuously elegant: a necklace of matched pearls, pearl earrings, a gold bracelet, and a gold lapel pin set with emeralds and diamonds. She was happy and smiling, though I fancied I could detect traces of apprehension in her many glances toward Peter.

Peter was in a dour mood. He spoke little, and when he did his voice was toneless and unpleasant. He grinned frequently. Several times he broke into that odd, raucous laugh I had heard before, a laugh that seemed out of all proportion to whatever remark or incident triggered it.

Martha excused herself to tidy up in the bathroom at the top of the stairs. As soon as she was out of sight, Peter whirled toward me.

"Remember that episode in Mark when the two Marys—Mary Magdalene and Mary the mother of James and Salome—came to visit the tomb at sunrise?"

I nodded.

"They had sweet spices," Peter continued. "They planned to anoint the body of their Master. They wondered who would roll away the stone."

"I remember."

Edna came over and stood beside me.

"And remember how they found the sepulchre open and an angel inside? The angel told them Christ had risen. Do you remember what the angel said next?"

Peter had turned toward Edna when he asked this question. She looked mystified and glanced at me. "Sorry," I said. "I don't recall, either."

"It's in Mark sixteen, verse seven. The angel said, 'But go your way, tell his disciples and Peter that he goeth before you into Galilee. . . .'"

"Yes, yes," I said impatiently. "I recall the passage now. The angel didn't include Simon Peter among the disciples because Peter had denied being a disciple. Why do you mention it?"

"Because, Homer, last night I had a dream. It was a dreadful dream. I dreamed I was *there*. I dreamed that *I* was Simon Peter."

I could hear the toilet flushing in our upstairs bathroom while Peter gazed off into space, through the walls, and into ancient Judea. "At first I didn't realize who I was. It was early, very early in the morning. I was playing golf at the Winnetka Country Club. Have you ever been there?"

"I think Middleton and I played a round together there once."

"Well, it's a great golf course, I suppose. Martha took me to the club a few weeks ago and showed me the grounds. This spring she wants to teach me how to play. You know, Homer, I've never played a real game of golf in my life—just miniature golf back in Oklahoma when I was in high school. But last night I dreamed I was on that course. I was standing on one of its greens. The sun was coming up. The grass was wet with dew. Hundreds of people watched while I tried to putt a ball into the hole. It kept missing. Each time I hit it, the stupid ball would graze the cup and roll a few feet beyond. Then a girl came running toward me."

Peter burst into a strident laugh. "Can you guess who it was?"

"I haven't the slightest idea."

"It was Angelina. She was dressed all in white. Her face wasn't clear at first, but I recognized the hair. It streamed out behind her as she ran—like a bright red flame. She stopped in front of me. 'Come and see!' she cried. 'The Lord is risen! Come and see!'"

Peter made beckoning motions with his hand while Edna slipped her arm through mine. "And then?" I asked.

"And then," said Peter, "I realized that I was naked! I had *nothing* on. I was just standing there, nude, in front of Angelina and all those people. I had a golf club in one hand. Suddenly I understood. I was Peter the Apostle! I remembered everything. I remembered saying three times that I didn't know the Lord. I remembered the cock crowing. I remembered weeping. I broke the golf club over my knee, flung the pieces on the grass, and ran to the sepulchre. The big stone had been rolled to one side. John was standing at the entrance. He was afraid to go in. I plunged through the opening."

Peter took a handkerchief from a rear pocket and blotted his forehead with a shaking hand. "There was no angel inside. There was only a corpse. It lay there, stretched out on a slab of marble. Its eyes were closed. The face was gray. It was wrapped in bloody winding sheets. The crowd had followed me. I could sense them, thousands of them, standing outside the tomb. They were waiting for me to come out, to come out and tell them what I'd seen."

Peter stuffed the handkerchief back into his pocket.

"I walked outside. I lifted up my arms like this." He raised his hands high in the air, palms toward us. "'Go home, good people,' I said. 'Go home! The news is false. The Lord is dead.'"

We could hear Martha's rapid footsteps on the stairway carpet. "Pete, my sweet," she sang out. "We have to hurry or we'll be late."

Peter lowered his voice. "That's all. I woke up."

I stepped into the hallway to help Martha on with her light green wool spring coat.

"You should be doing this, dear," she said over her shoulder to Peter.

"I'm sorry, sweetheart. Homer moves faster than I do."

"I've had more practice," I said.

"You'll be hearing Peter preach tomorrow, won't you?" my wife asked Martha. "Shall we meet and sit together?"

Martha looked crestfallen and shook her head. No, she would love to be there but she just couldn't. Her father, she explained, expected every-one in his family to be in *his* church on Easter. Besides, there was so much to be done in Winnetka, so many preparations to make for the wedding. She was sure that Peter would give a super-marvelous ser-mon. She was *so* sorry she had to miss it. She had wanted for a long time to attend services at my church, but it would have to be some other Sunday. Peter, smiling faintly, didn't seem to mind.

"I'll be expecting you no later than ten-thirty," I said to him at the door. "Use the back entrance and come directly to my study. The service starts promptly, you know, at eleven."

"Don't worry, Homer. I'll be there."

Edna drew back the curtain, and through a front window we watched them leave. Martha stood by the car's door on the driver's side until Peter remembered to walk around and open it. He helped her in, closed the door, then completed his circuit around the car and climbed into the front seat beside her. It was an enormous cream-colored Oldsmobile, plastered with chrome and backed by tail fins that looked like rocket engines.

We stood by the window until the mammoth car silently glided away. There was a wistful look in Edna's eyes as she let the curtain fall. She took my hand.

"What a crazy dream," I said. "Did you notice all those sexual sym-bols? I'm worried about Peter. Do you think they'll make a go of it?"

"No," Edna said.

27

Knockout

Reports of what took place at the Abernathy home on the night of Holy Saturday did not reach me until several days after Easter. I will try to reconstruct the scene and dialog as accurately as I can, drawing on information obtained from Middleton, Abernathy, Martha, and (much later) from Peter himself.

The Abernathys lived in an enormous English Tudor house in Winnetka, on a large estate that bordered Lake Michigan. When Peter and Martha arrived, her parents were already there.

"Sorry we're a bit late," Peter said to Abernathy in the foyer. "The cars on Sheridan Avenue were bumper to bumper."

"You're not late," said Abernathy, a tall, gray-haired man with black, heavy-rimmed glasses. "The Middletons came early. But you'll have to catch up with us. We're ready for our second round of martinis. Martha! You look ravishing!" They embraced.

"Isn't it furnished beautifully?" Martha whispered to Peter as they followed Abernathy into a huge living room.

Peter didn't reply. He could feel his shoes sink into the thick wall-to-wall carpeting as he crossed the room to take the hand of Dr. Middleton's wife, Eleanor, a stately blond woman with clear gray eyes like her daughter's. Middleton, standing nearby, shifted his cocktail glass to his left hand so that he and Peter could execute a quick handshake.

"Good to see you, my boy."

"My wife, Clarissa," Abernathy said to Peter as he gestured toward a thin, sad-faced lady seated at one end of a sofa.

Mrs. Abernathy extended her hand as Peter approached. "How nice to meet you at last," she said in a soft southern drawl. "I've heard so much about you."

"Don't believe a word of it," said Peter.

A small, pretty Negro maid entered the room with a tray of martinis. Martha and Peter each took a glass. Martha clinked the rim of Peter's glass with the rim of her own.

"To Holy Saturday," Peter said in a loud voice.

A noticeable silence settled over the room. Martha, visibly annoyed, sipped her drink circumspectly. Peter drank most of his as if it were water.

"Clarissa, I just *love* your new drapes," said Martha, turning toward the windows.

"Thank you, dear," said Mrs. Abernathy. "But don't get too close to them. They smell something *awful*. I had them sprayed last week. We've had so much trouble with moths this winter. They simply *ruined* the drapes I had there before."

"I remember them," said Martha. "They were such a lovely shade of lavender. What a pity. Couldn't they be mended?"

"Oh, I suppose they could. But we decided to pass them on to the Salvation Army."

Peter, bored by this conversation, sauntered over to the grand piano to have a look at an immense leather-bound Bible resting on top of it. When he touched one of the big copper clasps that locked the covers, a spark leaped between the clasp and his fingers. He jerked back his hand. Everyone laughed.

"It's the static in the rug," said Abernathy. "I'm surprised there's so much electricity in the air tonight. It's strongest in the winter, especially on cold dry evenings."

"When I was a little girl," Martha said, "I used to take off my shoes and shuffle my feet on this rug. It would make my hair stand up on my head."

"You looked so comical," said Martha's mother.

"I wonder if it would still do that," Martha said.

Peter, holding an empty glass, abruptly left the room. When he returned, glass filled, Martha had removed her shoes and was walking across the rug, sliding her stockinged feet. A small clump of hair on the top of her head pointed heavenward like the rope in the Hindu rope trick. There was much laughter. Abernathy clapped his hands.

Peter lifted his martini upward. "To the power," he said. "To the great power of God's electricity."

The maid appeared at the hallway entrance to announce dinner. She looked nonplussed and embarrassed when Peter winked at her over the top of his glass.

The dining room had been darkened and the long table illuminated by sprays of white candles at opposite ends of the table. The fine Wedgewood china and the polished sterling silverware gleamed in the flickering candlelight. Mrs. Abernathy directed everyone to his assigned chair.

"Please hold the chair for me," Martha whispered to Peter, who seemed totally preoccupied with finishing his drink.

"Would you ask the blessing, Peter?" Mrs. Abernathy said when they were all seated.

"Yes, certainly."

Martha shot Peter an apprehensive glance as their heads lowered. A long moment of awkward silence followed before he drained his glass and cleared his throat.

"Our Father in Heaven," he intoned, his voice a bit unsteady, "we thank Thee that in a world where millions suffer from hunger and malnutrition, we in America are blessed with a conspicuous abundance of food and drink. We thank Thee that in a world where millions suffer from a lack of adequate clothing and shelter, we in America are blessed with fine clothes and beautiful homes. We pray that Thou wilt fill us with love for our less fortunate brothers and sisters. We pray that Thou wilt help us to use our great riches with humility and responsibility; that Thou wilt teach us how to distinguish the eternal values from the honorific emblems of vanity and pride. . ."

At this point, Martha told me later, she raised her eyes to glance at her father. He had lifted his head and was gazing at Peter with open-mouthed incredulity.

"Help us, O God," Peter continued, eyes closed, his voice steadier now and louder than it should have been. "Help us to remember the words of Thy Son when he said, 'Lay not up for yourselves treasures upon earth, where moth and rust doth corrupt, and where thieves break through and steal. But lay up for yourselves treasures in heaven, where neither moth nor rust doth corrupt, and where thieves do not break through nor steal. For where your treasure is, there will your heart be also.' In Veblen's name we ask it. Amen."

The long period of strained silence that followed this prayer was finally broken by Dr. Middleton. "What's the trouble, Jim, with Northwestern's basketball team this year?"

The conversation dribbled from basketball to football, and from football to the University of Chicago's nonexistent football team.

"The main trouble with Chicago," said Abernathy, "is Hutchins. Did you see that piece about him in the *Chicago Tribune* last month?

A reporter asked him if he approved of a college program of physical education for all students. Do you know what he said? He said that, as far as he was concerned, whenever he had the impulse to exercise he'd lie down until it passed away."

Everybody chuckled except Peter. Hutchins, Peter explained, was only being funny. He was repeating a quip originally made by Robert Benchley. The University of Chicago was not against physical fitness. Hutchins just wanted to change the emphasis, said Peter, from competitive sports between colleges to sports within the college.

Martha, anticipating an argument, broke in to compliment Mrs. Abernathy on her tablecloth and the silver candelabras. "How often do you polish them?"

For the next twenty minutes the conversation revolved around sterling silver and the best methods of keeping it free of tarnish. Peter ate in silence, scowling at his plate. Over Martha's protests he asked for a third martini instead of coffee with his dessert.

In the living room, after dinner, the three ladies drifted to one end of the room, the three men to the other. Middleton and Peter accepted one of Abernathy's cigars.

"I understand, Peter," said Middleton, after a few puffs, "that you're preaching an Easter sermon tomorrow at Wilson's Community Church."

Middleton was a large man, about as tall as I but with considerably more girth. His weight must then have been about 250 pounds. His face, though round and pink-cheeked, was by no means flabby. Indeed, many women thought him extremely good-looking. He had bushy gray eyebrows and dark hair graying at the temples. His small crafty eyes, behind his rimless glasses, were almost as blue as Peter's. When he spoke, his voice was deep and resonant, with that exaggerated accuracy of pronunciation so characteristic of men of the cloth.

Peter took the cigar out of his mouth and nodded toward Middleton. "Glad you brought that up, Norman. I wanted to speak to you about it. I do have a problem."

"I'll be happy to help in any way I can."

"I'm puzzled," said Peter, "about how to handle Christ's bodily Resurrection. Do you think I should say something about it?"

Middleton's chair creaked as he shifted his weight. "It would be wise, I imagine, to avoid anything doctrinaire. There are, you know, so many different points of view. It would be best, I think, to concentrate on the spiritual meaning of the Resurrection, on the Lord's triumph over death, on. . ."

"But," interrupted Peter, "it doesn't seem right to avoid the corporeal Resurrection entirely. After all, isn't that what Easter's supposed to commemorate?"

"Yes, certainly. But the spiritual meaning of the event is what should be emphasized, don't you think?"

It was at this moment, Peter told me, that he became aware that the ladies seated in back of him, at the other end of the room, had stopped talking. They were listening.

Peter leaned back against the soft purple cushions of the sofa, puffing his cigar and smiling as if enjoying a private joke. "If the physical event didn't take place, Norman, how can it have much spiritual meaning?"

"Oh, I didn't say the event didn't take place," Middleton hastened to say, with a glance at Mrs. Abernathy. "I only meant that the spiritual message of Easter is more important than any narrow historical interpretation about which we can never be certain."

"True, Peter agreed. "Still, I'm curious to know what you think actually happened. Did the body of Jesus really rise from the dead?"

Dr. Middleton glanced across the room at his wife, then at Mrs. Abernathy. He turned and looked at Mr. Abernathy. No one said a word. Middleton leaned forward to carve his cigar's ash into the ashtray on a small table near him. "I don't think this is the time or the place, Peter, to discuss such questions."

"Why not?" said Peter. He glanced around the room for support but found everyone, including Martha, staring at him blankly. He gave an explosive little laugh. "You must have *some* opinion, Norman, about what happened."

"Please, Peter," Martha called out from the other end of the room. "Do let's talk about something else."

Abernathy had been following the dialog with amused interest. "I'd like to hear what Norman has to say."

The Reverend Norman Wesley Middleton narrowed his eyes while he took several contemplative puffs on his cigar. "Of course, Jim, I do have an opinion. But the question isn't a simple one. It would take a long time to make my position clear. I don't think I could do it now without being misunderstood."

"But the question *is* simple," Peter persisted. "There's nothing complicated about it. Either Jesus rose bodily from the dead or he didn't. Do you think he actually appeared, in the flesh, to Simon Peter and Thomas and all the others?"

"The spirit of Christ could not be confined to the tomb," said Middleton, "because it was God's own eternal spirit. Jesus manifested himself to the hearts of his disciples. That same spirit of Christ lives today in the heart of every Christian."

Peter slowly put his cigar down on the blue glass ashtray that was anchored with two weighted cloth belts to the curved arm of the couch. "My dear future father-in-law, you know very well that that's not the point. Do you think the disciples saw Jesus in the flesh? Do you believe that the risen Jesus actually ate a piece of broiled fish and some honeycomb? Did he really say, 'Behold my hands and my feet, that it is I myself: handle me, and see; for a spirit hath not flesh and bones, as ye see me have.'? That's the last chapter of Luke, verse thirty-nine."

Middleton smiled and looked around the room. "Let's not monopolize the conversation, Peter. We can discuss these things some other time."

"I find it intensely interesting, Norman," said Abernathy. "I've always wondered myself exactly what your views were on the Resurrection. Frankly, I'd like to know."

These remarks produced a painful silence. Peter twiddled his thumbs and grinned. Mrs. Abernathy glanced nervously back and forth from her husband to the minister. It had probably never occurred to her before that Middleton had the slightest doubts about the empty tomb. Mrs. Middleton's face was expressionless.

Martha was on the verge of tears. She came over to where Peter was sitting and put her hand on his arm. "Please, Peter. Not now. You've had too much to drink. If you argue any more you'll just get worked up about it. You mustn't. We have to leave soon. You have a sermon to preach tomorrow, remember?"

"There's no need for Peter or anyone else to get worked up, Martha," said Abernathy coldly. "We'll drop the topic in a moment." He turned to Middleton. "How would you answer Peter's last question?"

Middleton dabbed his forehead with his handkerchief. "We all know that the New Testament isn't a completely accurate history. That is, it's not accurate in every detail. On the other hand we know we can trust its main outlines and the great spiritual truths it contains. One of those great truths is the truth of the Resurrection."

Peter started to say something but Abernathy spoke first. "I don't think that's responsive, Norman. Peter wanted to know if you thought the risen Jesus had flesh and bones. Surely that's a simple question. Do you?"

"In a spiritual sense, yes."

"What in thunder does that mean?" Abernathy asked.

"It means that the eternal Christ, whom they knew as a living man, was revealed to their hearts."

Peter uncorked a loud guffaw. "We're going around in circles. That's what you said before. Do you mean that the disciples had a vision of Jesus while the body was somewhere else? Did they see him with their *eyes*. Was there an image of Jesus on their retinas?"

Please, Peter," Martha pleaded again, her face pale. "Please keep your voice down."

Middleton stood up and walked heavily to the fireplace. Behind him on either side, two huge oil portraits of sombre-faced Abernathy ancestors glared into the room from their enormous gold frames. Middleton, hands clasped behind his back, stole a glance at Mrs. Abernathy. She was sitting stiffly and listening with an expression of intense bewilderment.

"I can't see that it matters," Middleton said, mopping his forehead. "The disciples were certainly convinced that they saw Jesus with their eyes. But these are secondary questions. The important thing, the primary thing, is the eternal reality behind the temporal symbol. As my friend Norman Vincent Peale likes to say. . ."

"Who cares what Peale likes to say," Peter broke in as he suddenly stood up and walked to the piano. "Let's see what the Bible likes to say." Sparks crackled when he flipped open the copper clasps. He picked up the mammoth volume, turned the pages rapidly until he found Chapter 20 of the Gospel of Saint John. Slowly, speaking in a cruel parody of Middleton's sermonizing style, he read aloud:

> The first day of the week cometh Mary Magdalene early, when it was yet dark, unto the sepulchre, and seeth the stone taken away from the sepulchre.
>
> Then she runneth, and cometh to Simon Peter, and to the other disciple, whom Jesus loved, and saith unto them, They have taken away the Lord out of the sepulchre, and we know not where they have laid him.
>
> Peter therefore went forth, and that other disciple, and came to the sepulchre.
>
> So they ran both together: and the other disciple did outrun Peter, and came first to the sepulchre.
>
> And he, stooping down, and looking in, saw the linen clothes lying; yet went he not in.
>
> Then cometh Simon Peter following him, and went into the sepulchre, and seeth the linen clothes lie.
>
> And the napkin, that was about his head, not lying with the linen clothes, but wrapped together in a place by itself.
>
> Then went in also that other disciple, which came first to the sepulchre, and he saw, and believed.
>
> For as yet they knew not the scripture, that he must rise again from the dead.

Peter slammed the big Bible shut, then heaved it back on the piano. The strings gave forth a discordant twang.

He turned to face Middleton. "Let's put it this way, Norman. The Bible says that the body of Jesus vanished. Where did it go? Did Jesus recover and escape, the way Lawrence and Harris and Moore tell it in their fictional accounts?° But if Jesus didn't really die, then the Resurrection is just a fable based on a hoax. So let's assume there actually was a corpse. What happened to it? There are only two possibilities. Either it was revivified, the way the Gospels tell it, or it wasn't. If it wasn't, it stayed on earth. There isn't any third possibility. What happened to the body? Did it come alive or didn't it?"

Peter had been pronouncing his words carefully, relentlessly, with great distinctness. Abernathy was smiling. Mrs. Abernathy continued to look unhappy and confused. Mrs. Middleton's face remained undecipherable. Tears were sliding down Martha's cheeks.

Middleton stood silent as a statue. He seemed to be smiling, but somehow his expression was as vacuous as his wife's.

"Are you willing to give us your opinion on that, Norman?" Abernathy asked.

°Peter refers here to D. H. Lawrence's novella, *The Man Who Died*, Frank Harris' short story, "The Miracle of the Stigmata," and George Moore's novel, *The Brook Kerith*.

Lawrence's account, the most blasphemous of the three, depicts Jesus as a sexually inhibited man whose desires were sublimated by his Messiah complex. Disillusioned by his near death on the Cross, he experiences his true Resurrection ("I am risen!") when he has his first sexual encounter in Egypt with a priestess at a Temple of Isis, who believes him to be an incarnation of Osiris. For a sympathetic analysis of the novella by Tom F. Driver, a professor at Union Theological Seminary, see his article, "Sexuality and Jesus," reprinted in *New Theology No. 3*, a 1966 Macmillan paperback edited by my good friends Martin E. Marty and Dean G. Peerman.

Harris' ironic story, surely the best thing he ever wrote, is in his book *Unpath'd Waters*. Jesus recovers, changes his name to Joshua, and becomes a gentle, self-effacing carpenter in Caesarea. He never tells his wife, Judith, who he really is, even after she is converted to Christianity by Paul's preaching on the Resurrection. Joshua fails to convince her that Paul is distorting the teachings of Jesus, whom he says he heard preach in Jerusalem. Judith leaves him. When Joshua dies, the scars of his old wounds are found on his body. Paul proclaims it a miracle. Because Joshua was the last unconverted Jew in Caesarea, God placed the Stigmata upon him as a sign to the world. Mass conversions result.

Moore's marvelous novel, published in 1916, tells how Jesus is helped back to health by Joseph of Arimathea, the rich man who arranged for his burial. The two join an Essene sect which has settled near the Brook Kerith, a sect of which Jesus had earlier been a member. For the next thirty years Jesus tends sheep there. Horrified by Paul's proclamations of the Resurrection, he plans to go to Jerusalem to set the story straight. He tries to convince Paul who he is, but Paul considers him an insane imposter, and Jesus realizes that no one in Jerusalem will believe him. He goes instead to India. These are only the highlights of a rich tapestry of characters and events, narrated by a master story-teller.—H. W.

"I don't like the way the question is phrased. The important. . ."

"The important thing," Peter shouted angrily, "is whether you are going to answer the question."

"It doesn't deserve an answer."

"I think it does," Abernathy said quietly.

Peter moved closer to Middleton so he could shake a finger in front of the minister's face. "Don't you have an opinion about what happened to the corpse of Jesus? Don't you have a *suspicion.* about what happened?"

Martha ran over and tugged on Peter's jacket. "Peter! Please! Come and sit down."

He pushed her ungently aside. Once more his index finger pointed like a dagger toward Middleton's nose. In an icy voice he said. "In the name of the Father, the Son, and the Holy Ghost, tell us what you believe."

Middleton remained immobile, hands behind his back. "I prefer not to discuss it."

None of them saw the blow start. It was a quick, short jab that clipped one side of the Reverend Middleton's broad mouth. The minister dropped to the floor with a crash that shook the house. Martha screamed.

Peter stood there moronically, his eyes glazed, his knuckles bleeding, while Abernathy knelt on the floor to loosen Middleton's tie and unbutton his collar. Mrs. Abernathy, with exclamations of "Oh, dear!" and "How dreadful!", left to get a towel and wet washcloth. No one could remember afterward what Mrs. Middleton's reaction had been. She hovered in the background, saying nothing, doing nothing, letting the Abernathys take over.

"You fool! You idiot!" Martha screamed at Peter. "Why did you do it?" She pounded her fists against his chest. "Why? Why?"

He seemed scarcely to notice.

Abernathy, still on his knees, removed Middleton's spectacles. He took the washcloth from Clarissa and wiped some blood from the minister's lower lip.

"He'll be all right, Eleanor," Abernathy said to Mrs. Middleton. "I think he's coming to."

Peter glowered at Martha. Martha glowered back. He wheeled on his feet and walked unsteadily out of the room. In the hallway closet he found his topcoat and slowly put it on. He did not take his hat. The little maid was standing in a doorway to the kitchen, watching with wide, frightened eyes. Peter threw her a kiss. Then he opened the front door and stepped out into the cool night.

He headed east, cutting through the Abernathy estate until he reached the shore of Lake Michigan. For an hour or more he sat there, on a large slab of granite, feeling miserable and empty, listening to the melancholy sounds of the water as it sloshed around the rock. A cold March wind numbed his face, whipped through his hair.

He wept and prayed.

Peter never told me what he prayed. Was it for forgiveness? For Martha? For Middleton? Was it for help for himself in the uncertain years ahead?

He walked south along the lake, then turned west and followed a winding dirt road until he came to a main traffic artery. A cab took him to Winnetka's North Shore Station. He was beginning to feel nauseated. In the station's tiny, foul-smelling men's room he urinated and vomited into the toilet bowl.

After rinsing his mouth at a grimy wash basin he studied his reflection in the cracked, filthy mirror above the sink. A white face, with insane eyes, stared back at him. He slammed his fist into the mirror, shattering the glass. His knuckles began to bleed again. He blotted them with toilet paper and wrapped his handkerchief around the hand.

At the deserted station's food counter—he was the only customer—he drank half a cup of stale black coffee.

At one-thirty he boarded a train that carried him back to Chicago's Loop. It was nearly four in the morning when he finally reached his dormitory.

He made no attempt to sleep. After working for a while on his sermon, he showered, shaved, stuck adhesive plasters on three knuckles, then went out for breakfast at an all-night cafeteria on Fifty-fifth Street near the Illinois Central Station. Through the plate glass windows he watched the street slowly brighten in the rays of a rising sun.

Easter Sunday was going to be a beautiful day.

28

The Secret of Easter

When the wall clock of my church study showed 10:45 and Peter had not yet arrived, I was gripped by a strong sense of foreboding. Extrasensory precognition? Or was I merely thinking of the high premium he placed on punctuality and recalling the many signs of his mounting nervous tension? Another five minutes slipped uncomfortably by before I heard his hurried footsteps in the hall outside my open door.

"Sorry, Homer," he said, a trifle out of breath. "I've been walking through Jackson Park. It took longer to get back than I thought. How did the early service go?"

He was immaculately dressed in an Oxford-gray summer suit, dark maroon necktie, white shirt, white handkerchief in his breast pocket, and a white rosebud in his lapel. But he looked tired and agitated. The whites of his eyes were streaked with red.

"We had about five hundred people," I said, my voice a trifle husky. "Are you sure you feel all right?"

He saw me staring at the three adhesive plasters on the knuckles of his right hand. "I scraped them last night," he said, covering the knuckles with his other hand. "It's a long story. I'll tell you about it after the service." His head twitched slightly.

"What's the matter with your eyes?"

"I didn't get much sleep last night. I'll be okay."

"I doubt if it will be noticeable beyond the first few rows."

We went quickly over the church bulletin. I indicated the spot in the preliminary ceremonies at which I wanted him to give a prayer. "You haven't made any changes in your sermon, have you?"

"No, my dear Homer. It's the same stirring, beautiful, profound sermon. Don't worry about it."

The bells in our tower carillon began to play a hymn. I led Peter down the hall and through a small door that opened into the rear of the chancel. We mounted a short flight of stairs to the rostrum. After Peter deposited the typescript of his sermon on the pulpit desk, we took our seats in the two ornate highbacked chairs behind the pulpit.

Peter's slight nervousness had miraculously vanished. Like an old pro, he smiled and nodded to Edna, who was sitting about five rows from the front, then he crossed his legs in a relaxed manner and let his gaze wander over the congregation. Our organist, Beulah Schwatzer, seated below us and to our left, was in the midst of a lively toccata. She looked up at us with a beatific smile.

As always on Easter Sunday, Midway Community Church overflowed with happy Hyde Park worshippers. More than a hundred people were standing in back, and others were sitting on steps in the balcony aisles. The scene had a typical Easter look. Wide-brimmed straw bonnets (the fashion that spring) formed a random mosaic of pastel colors. The morning's slight chill had provided the ladies with a splendid excuse to wear their fur stoles. Mrs. M., our wealthiest widow, was attracting considerable attention with a stole which I guessed to be platinum fox. It wouldn't have seemed like Easter without Mrs. M. We saw her only once a year, always with a new fur piece.

The air swirled with fragrance. It wafted from the lilies that covered the altar, from the roses and gardenias pinned on the ladies, and from their perfumed ear lobes. The altar lilies this year were the gift of Mrs. M. She had asked me to state in our printed bulletin that she had given them "for the glory of God and in the memory of her beloved husband." Mr. M. had accumulated his millions by charging high rents for his crumbling, rat-infested apartments in the Black Belt section of our fair city.

The service opened with everyone standing and struggling to sing all five stanzas of a hymn. The tune was so dreary, the lyrics so banal, that I could not imagine why my choir director (a professor in the University of Chicago's music department) had chosen it. It would have been better, I thought as I closed the hymnal, if at least two stanzas had been omitted. Only our choir could be heard during the singing of the final stanza. But Peter's sermon was to be shorter than mine usually were, and my choir director may have decided that he needed to fill in the time.

I made some announcements, apologized for my laryngitis, and explained who Peter was and why he was there. Harriet Allen, a black girl active in our young people's work, opened the Bible on the lectern to read the first fourteen verses of the fifteenth chapter of Paul's First

Epistle to the Corinthians. Peter had requested this Scripture reading because it contained, in verse 14, the heart of his sermon: "And if Christ be not risen, then is our preaching vain, and your faith is also vain." Miss Allen read the verses slowly and with great effectiveness.

It was now time for Peter to stand and pray. His prayer, delivered at the lectern, was brief and tactful. It expressed thanks for the coming spring and pleaded for a heart receptive to the life-affirming, joy-abounding message of Easter.

After the offering, our 50-voice choir, on their feet in the loft above and behind us, sang the "Hallelujah Chorus" from Handel's *Messiah*. Personally, I have always found this chorus boring. I much prefer Brahms' "Mary Magdalene" or Weelkes' "Hosanna to the Son of David," but it had been several years since the choir had sung Handel's chorus, and my director had insisted on it. The rendition was impressive; he had trained his voices well.

Peter remained in his chair for a full half-minute after the last notes of the chorus had died away—shrewd timing, I said to myself—before he arose and walked slowly to the pulpit. He rearranged his papers, took a sip of water from the glass on the side, then looked up and began to speak. The late morning sunlight, filtering down through the many-colored glass on our east wall, stained one side of his young, earnest face.

"If Christ be not risen, then is our preaching vain," Peter began in low, modulated tones. "Those are the words of Saint Paul, a man whom tradition pictures as an ugly, baldheaded little hunchback, but from whose large soul and mind came the first great construction of Christian doctrine. Scholars like to call it 'Pauline theology.' But so fundamental were Paul's views, so clarifying, that they became a major part of that collection of remarkable documents we know today as the New Testament. The scaffolding Paul built became the framework of all the theologies of all the branches and sects of Christendom. Roman Catholic, Greek Orthodox, Protestant—these traditions differed and still differ in many significant ways, yet all of them find in the writings of Saint Paul the central fibers of their faith. *Every* Christian theology is a 'Pauline' theology."

I settled back in my chair with a sigh of relief, stifling an impulse to open my jacket and rest my thumbs in the lower pockets of my white damask vest. Peter was speaking well, and with great self-assurance. My congregation was listening with uncharacteristic attention.

"If Christ be not risen," Peter repeated, "then is our preaching vain. What did Paul mean by those startling words? Why is it that for almost two thousand years Christendom has found in the Easter story the very heart and soul of Christian faith? Why is it that today, in our most advanced, our most enlightened churches—churches which have made the greatest progress in rising above the narrow supernaturalism of earlier ages of faith—why is it that even in *these* churches, in churches such as *this*, it is on Easter Sunday that attendance is always greater than at any other time of the year?"

With a sweeping motion of his knuckle-bandaged hand, Peter indicated all those who were standing in the vestibule and sitting in the balcony aisles.

"What is the great secret of Easter? The answer is not hard to give. The secret of Easter is the Christian assurance of the triumph of life over death. It is the light that blazes forth from Christ's empty sepulchre, the light that dispels the darkness of fear. It is the trumpet blast that announces the ultimate victory—the victory of God over Satan, of good over evil, of eternity over the short days of our years. It tells us in ringing tones that goodness is immortal. 'There shall never,' as the poet Robert Browning once wrote, 'There shall never be one lost good.' Evil and death have been defeated. The things that belong to God will endure forever!"

Peter hesitated for a moment, then dropped his voice to a more conversational tone.

"A Mohammedan once said to a Christian missionary that the Moslem religion possessed positive proof that its prophet, Mohammed, had really lived. The proof was in the prophet's tomb, a tomb that still exists, I'm told, beneath a great mosque in Medina. A Christian, the Mohammedan added, cannnot even prove that his prophet, Jesus Christ, actually existed. 'Where,' he asked the missionary, 'is the tomb of Jesus?' The missionary answered, 'Yes, it is true we have no tomb. It is because we have no corpse.' *That,* my friends, is the glorious secret of Easter. And the secret of Easter is the secret of our faith. *We have no corpse!*"

Peter shifted a page of his manuscript from top to bottom, took a swallow of water, and continued. "Martin Luther was once in a state of profound spiritual depression. A friend, glancing through the doorway of Luther's study, saw him write with his finger in the dust that had collected on a table top." Peter paused to write in the air, on an imaginary table, with an extended forefinger. "And what did Luther write? He wrote, '*Vivit, vivit*'—'He lives, he lives!' The Christian faith has no corpse. It has a conqueror! It has a living Lord and Master who, as he himself told us, is with us always, even unto the end of the world."

Peter grasped each side of the pulpit and bent slightly forward as though studying the upturned faces of his listeners in the first few rows.

"If Christ be not risen, then is our preaching vain. Perhaps some of you here this morning are doubting Thomases. A dead body, you say, cannot live again. Once the heart, that marvelously intricate little mechanism, has ceased to pulsate, and the cells of the brain no longer receive an adequate supply of oxygen, the inevitable, the irreversible process of decay and corruption begins. Granted! But are you not imposing a narrow, trivial, altogether unworthy interpretation on the great Easter story?"

He turned his head to give me a quick glance. His face was solemn but his blue eyes seemed to be bright with a curious kind of mirth. "As long as we argue, as long as we quibble, about the physical, corporeal Resurrection of the body of our Lord, we are only tilting, like Don Quixote, at a harmless windmill. Is not the real giant, the giant secret of Easter, something greater than that? Is it not the victory of Christ's spirit? As Harry Emerson Fosdick once beautifully expressed it: '. . . the nails that pierced his hands and feet did not pierce his truth. The spear thrust into his side could not reach his faith. The final paroxysm of his body did not shake his soul.' And if you doubt the truth of this, my friends, you have only to consider the history of the Western world. The proofs are in the stones and mortar of countless churches and cathedrals. The proofs are in the consecrated lives of millions and millions of Christ's followers."

From where I sat, the back of Peter's head was toward me most of the time, but occasionally, when he gestured and looked to one side, I could see his profile.

Was that a faint smile at the corner of his mouth?

"The death of Jesus," he went on, his voice ringing out in clear tones that held his audience spellbound, "was a death of ignominy and disgrace. He was executed like a common criminal, between two miserable thieves. His most loyal followers had deserted him. Even Simon Peter was ashamed to admit he knew the Master. Christ's mission had been to establish on earth a kingdom of righteousness. The mission obviously had failed. It may be that even Jesus himself was overwhelmed by a tragic sense of personal defeat when he cried out on the Cross, in existential agony, 'My God, my God, why hast Thou forsaken me?'

"But so great was the soul of Christ, so filled with the love of God and man, that the grave could not hold it. It burst the iron chains of death. It entered into the hearts and minds of his disciples, giving them hope and courage and a new dedication to their task of establishing God's church, of carrying the good news of the Gospel around the world. 'Christ liveth in me,' said Saint Paul, though he had never seen the Lord in the flesh. And in his letter to the Philippians he wrote, 'Let this mind be in you, which was also in Christ Jesus.' "

Peter shot me another blue-pink glance. My heart sank. His face was wearing that same frozen, mask-like smile I had observed a year ago when he was in such an agitated state about the prospect of his ordination. A terrible thought struck me like a lightning bolt. When I read the first draft of Peter's sermon it had impressed me as a sincere attempt to build a theologically inoffensive message of inspiration around the Easter fable. Could it be that Peter never intended it to be that at all? Had I read it too hastily? Was it possible that Peter, deliberately and cynically, had composed a malicious parody?

"We do not have to interpret those words of Paul," he continued, "in any crude mystical way. The mind or spirit of Christ Jesus is in the heart of every man and woman who knows how to love—to love God, to love others, to love truth, to love justice. It is the vital, dynamic, creative spirit that refuses to submit to the world's imperfections, the spirit that strives tirelessly and unselfishly to build the Kingdom of God on earth, a Kingdom in which every individual, however humble, whatever his station in life, whatever the color of his skin, may find the fullest expression of his God-given personality. 'Heaven and earth shall pass away,' said Jesus, 'but my words shall not pass away.' They will not pass away because they are words that express a divine love which alone can triumph over evil and death. And because love is eternal, so also is the spirit of Christ eternal.

"Today, the spirit of Jesus is stronger than ever before. He is more alive at this moment, on this Easter Sunday, than when his feet trod the soil of ancient Judea. He is more alive because his message of universal love has now spread to the uttermost corners of the earth. Wherever scientists are gathered together, seeking a cure for some dread disease, there is the spirit of Christ. Wherever teachers are carrying the torch of knowledge to undeveloped cultures, or passing back the torch to oncoming generations, there is the victory of the Son of God.

"He walks beside the enlightened political leader for whom the welfare of his people, not personal political power, is his ultimate concern. He stands beside the loving mother who devotes her life to the welfare of her children. He guides the fingers of every artist and poet and musician who brings new beauty into the world. At times we may not be aware of his presence, just as those two saddened disciples on the road to Emmaus failed to recognize the risen Lord when he walked beside them. He is here just the same. He is in the midst of every organization, every institution, every university, every group that has for its goal the Christian ideal of the Brotherhood of Man. And when we let him enter into our own hearts and minds, when we let him live within us, we, too, participate in his immortality. The love we express by our actions will never die. 'There shall never be one lost good.' Every deed of love enters the stream of human history as an everlasting contribution to the coming Kingdom of Righteousness."

I was no longer listening to Peter's hackneyed phrases. I was trying to observe his face. Each time he turned his head I could glimpse that frozen smile. Was I exaggerating it in my mind? Was it noticeable to the congregation? There seemed to be an increasing restlessness in their movements. They looked at one another more often than they should. They whispered to one another. And Edna? There was no doubting the apprehension in her eyes.

"Today," Peter said, "when scientists have at last discovered how to split the atom, when they have given humanity the power to destroy itself utterly, we find ourselves surrounded by prophets of gloom and doom. It has become unfashionable to talk of progress. H. G. Wells, shortly before his death, wrote that a 'frightful queerness' had descended upon the world. Can it be that humanity, as Wells argued in his last book, has finally reached the end of its tether? Can it be that before us stretch the cruel, senseless centuries of slow recovery—perhaps of *no* recovery—from a worldwide atomic holocaust? Will the species *Homo sapiens* become as extinct as the dinosaurs? Is it possible that Christ is really dead, and that our faith is vain?

"Today the prophets of gloom and doom are to be found even within the ranks of Christendom. Has not Karl Barth, the greatest of this century's theologians, warned us of the black storm clouds ahead? Has not Arnold Toynbee, that devout Anglican historian, prophesied the fall of Western civilization in words almost as ominous as those of his predecessor in pessimism, Oswald Spengler? From every side, Christian and non-Christian alike, apocalyptic voices are warning us of the wrath to come."

The smile had vanished now from Peter's face. His lips were compressed. "It is when we forget the invincible hope of Easter," he said grimly, "that we find ourselves swayed by these persuasive voices of defeat. I've been told that radioactive dust from Hiroshima and Nagasaki still floats in the earth's upper atmosphere. Certain it is that this dust hangs like an eternal pall over our heads and hearts. Is there a thinking man or woman today who has not become—I believe the proper scientific term is 'contaminated'—contaminated with a bleak sense of hopelessness, of futility? Christ is indeed dead, we say to ourselves, if only unconsciously. Christ is dead. Perhaps God, too, as Nietzsche informed us, is dead. There *is* no hope. Our preaching and our faith are vain."

Peter ended on a weary note. He adjusted his papers. He took a sip of water. The congregation now appeared to be mesmerized, as silent as a tomb. He looked up and resumed:

"No poet ever plumbed more deeply the depths of existential despair than the British poet James Thomson. His *City of Dreadful Night,* wrung from his tormented soul by years of poverty, drugs, ill-health, and lack of religious faith, is seldom read today, nevertheless it expresses in unforgettable language the contemporary mood. Let me read to you a single stanza from this long and bitter chant of nihilism."

Peter lifted a sheet of paper from the pulpit desk and read in a desolate voice:

> *The sense that every struggle brings defeat*
> > *Because Fate holds no prize to crown success;*
> *That all the oracles are dumb or cheat*
> > *Because they have no secret to express;*
> *That none can pierce the vast black veil uncertain*
> *Because there is no light beyond the curtain;*
> > *That all is vanity and nothingness.*

He let his bandaged hand, which had been holding the sheet, fall listlessly back on the desk. "Yet it is precisely in the darkest midnight hour," he said, his voice gaining slowly in intensity, "when all hope is gone, when our hearts are heaviest with resignation and defeat, that we hear the triumphant trumpet tone of Easter. *Vivit, vivit!* He lives, he lives! No matter how dark the days ahead may seem, we know by faith that the spirit of Christ will never die!"

Peter stopped shouting. He glanced down at his typescript and seemed to be reading ahead without speaking.

He began to chuckle.

There was no mistake about it. From where I sat behind him, shuddering, I could hear the sound distinctly. It was a series of low, mirthless chuckles, accompanied by a convulsive quivering of his shoulders and that quick jerk of his head to one side. I glanced at the congregation. They were watching Peter with frightened fascination. A murmuring, like a swarm of bees, grew louder.

Peter regained his composure. He stopped smiling. His hands gripped the pulpit's sides. The knuckles of his left hand were white. On his other hand I could see the three oval spots of adhesive. They were crimson spots. A large drop of blood formed on the lowest knuckle, detached itself, and fell to the carpet.

He began to speak again:

"The world has been black before. But always before, after the long and dreadful night, has come the white radiance of a new Easter morning. After every winter has come the spring. The terrifying forces of the atom may indeed bring temporary chaos, yet they are the same forces that also can give to the human race a great new source of energy, boundless energy, energy that can usher in an undreamed-of world of leisure, peace, and abundance. Are not the forces of the atom as much a part of God's universe as the forces of fire and steam and electricity? We cannot, we must not, let the voices of despair drown out the Easter voice of hope. The red lights of history can yet turn to green. We must tune our ears and hearts to the 'Yea!' that sounds above the 'Nay!' Christ is *not* dead! Our preaching is *not* vain!"

Peter looked up from his typescript and laughed.

It was an ear-splitting, uncontrolled flood of maniacal laughter. Several women screamed. I sat paralyzed in my chair while Peter removed his jacket. He turned, glared at me with bloodshot eyes, and flung the coat in my lap. It was an old platform trick that he had often used when, as a boy evangelist, he reached a climax of revival oratory. The armpits of his shirt were dark crescents of perspiration. His hands fumbled with the knot of his necktie.

"And with the Easter trumpet sounding above us and ringing in our ears," he cried, pulling the tie out of his collar with a mighty yank, "we can turn from the black despair of James Thomson to the bright hope of another Thompson. . ."

I put Peter's jacket on the empty chair next to me, stood up, and went over to take his arm. He wrenched the arm free, then gave a vigorous shove on my chest. I executed a magnificent pratfall. Half the congregation rose to its feet. More women screamed. One sweet old lady in the balcony, I learned afterward, fainted dead away. From my supine position on the platform I could see Edna trying to work her way to the nearest aisle. About a dozen men were in the aisles and running forward.

Peter hurled his tie to the floor. He ripped open his shirt, sending buttons flying. "Unlike James Thomson, his contemporary," he shouted, "Francis Thompson was a poet of Christian faith. . . ."

He removed his shirt and threw it violently into the face of a man who had mounted the stairs and was coming toward him. "The words of Francis Thompson express far better than any poor words of mine," Peter yelled, "the glorious, the eternal secret of Easter!"

Three husky men were on the platform. I rolled over, got to my hands and knees, and crawled quickly out of their way.

One of them approached the pulpit, but a blow from Peter's left fist caught his cheekbone and he sank to the floor with a groan, burying his face among the lilies. Other men were coming down the aisles. While the two men on the dais circled cautiously around Peter, he bellowed forth a poem, shouting at the top of his lungs so he could be heard above the uproar.

He had intended, I knew from having read the first draft of his manuscript, to end his sermon by reading Francis Thompson's beautiful lyric, "The Kingdom of God," with its graceful closing lines:

> Yea, in the night, my Soul, my daughter,
> Cry,—clinging Heaven by the hems;
> And lo, Christ walking on the water
> Not of Gennesareth, but Thames!

But it was another poem that he shouted, a poem with the same meter and the same rhyme scheme. It was a poem that sounded at first like Pentecostal glossolalia:

"'Twas brillig, and the slithy toves did gyre and gimble in the wabe!"

Six or seven men were on the platform now. They moved warily. One of them slipped suddenly behind Peter and locked his arms around Peter's arms and body. Another had pulled the prostrate man out of the lilies and was attempting to revive him.

"All mimsy were the borogoves!" Peter shouted.

His left hand was fumbling the buckle on his belt. With a quick backward thrust, he jabbed his right elbow into the stomach of the man behind him. The man dropped his arms with a loud "Oof!" Simultaneously, Peter's left hand zippered downward and his trousers dropped to the floor.

"And the mome raths. . . !"

He stepped out of his pants. Before anyone could stop him he ran to the side of the rostrum, reached into the fly of his pink shorts, whipped out his penis, and shot a stream of liquid straight at the head of Mrs. Schwatzer, the organist.

"Bullshit!" he roared.

It was at this moment that our choir director, a frail and gentle man, climaxed our amazement. He picked up one of the brass candelabras at the back of the choir loft, lowered it as far as he could, then swung it like a pendulum. One of the center candle holders struck Peter on the left side of his skull with a sickening bonk. The unlit candles dislodged and sprayed over the podium.

Mrs. Schwatzer, understandably, had fled from her seat. Peter pitched head foremost over the top of the console. His body slithered down across the multi-leveled keyboards, producing a burst of discordant, unearthly music. He lay there on his stomach, in a motionless sprawl, head down, eyes closed, his head and chest on the console seat, his naked knees and thighs still pressing the ivory keys. That awful sound, that demonic lost chord, continued to reverberate from the ceiling, from the walls and floor, through the aisles and through our eardrums like the stuck horns of a dozen cars, each horn with a different pitch and timbre. At the spot where Peter's head had come to rest on the yellow plush cushion, a dark pool of blood was slowly spreading.

Two men dragged Peter off the keyboards. They cleared a space for him on the floor. I picked up Peter's discarded shirt and jacket and tossed them down to Edna. She threw the jacket over his exposed front, then I vaulted over the lilies and helped her wrap the shirt turbanlike and tight around his head. The choir director informed me in a shaky voice that he had telephoned Billings Hospital for an ambulance.

I looked at my watch. It was exactly twelve o'clock. High Sunday noon. When I replaced the watch, I noticed that my hand and the white radiance of my waistcoat were stained with blood. Sirens wailed in the distance. Someone had also called the police.

29

Aphasia

Edna rode in the ambulance that took Peter to Billings Hospital while I remained at Midway Community Church to do what I could to restore order and to fend off a thousand questions from inquisitive church members who refused to leave. An intern on duty in the hospital's emergency ward injected Peter with an anesthetic to prevent him from waking while his scalp was being stitched. A few hours later the coma turned into a deep and normal sleep.

On Monday morning Peter awoke in full possession of his faculties, but suffering from an aching head and what the doctors called "motor aphasia"—an inability to speak. Although he understood everything that was said to him, and was able to reply by writing notes, he was incapable of vocalizing a single word. He could hum or whistle a tune. He could even sing the words of familiar hymns. But when he tried to speak he could do no better than produce a few slurred, guttural sounds.

I was permitted to visit Peter on Monday afternoon for a ten-minute period. He was lying on his back when I entered the room, the left side of his head covered by an enormous bandage. His azure eyes lit up when he saw me, then there was a sudden rush of blood to his face as he pulled the sheet over his head in a childish gesture of embarrassment. After the nurse had propped him up with a pair of pillows, he insisted on scribbling long, profuse apologies on a notepad. I did my best to convince him that no great harm had been done, and that the episode soon would be forgotten. It was as much my fault as his, I said, for insisting that he preach when I should have realized the state of mind he was in. The words must have had a hollow, unconvincing ring. Peter started to shake his head, but the throbbing was too painful.

He wrote on his tablet: "Have you heard from Martha or her father?"

I told him I had not.

He wrote: "Please phone Middleton when you get home."

I assured him I would.

A nurse caught my attention, tapped her wrist watch, and ushered me out.

The psychiatrist assigned to Peter had asked me on the phone that morning to stop by his office before I left the building. I had expected an elderly man, perhaps with a beard and a Vienna accent. He proved instead to be a chunky young midwesterner, from Iowa as I recall, with curly black hair and an innocent, dimple-chinned face.

I knew nothing yet of Peter's Saturday night altercation with Middleton. I was not even aware that Peter had preached his sermon without any sleep the night before. The doctor listened intently, making rapid notes, while I gave a chronological account of what had happened in my pulpit the previous morning.

I tried to explain Peter's behavior as a symbolic expression of his disenchantment with Christianity and his growing fear that if he became a Christian minister he would become a hypocrite. Clothing, I reminded the doctor, has always been a popular symbol of religious faith.° Had Peter decided that, like the emperor in the fairy tale, he had nothing on? I spoke of the dream that Peter had described to Edna and me on Saturday, his dream of being naked on a crowded golf course. When I remarked that the golf club was an obvious phallic symbol, the doctor looked up and smiled.

"You think so?"

"What else could it be?"

"Well, it could be just a golf club. Of course it's a typical embarrassment dream—the sense of shame, the watching eyes of the crowd, and so on. But we'll discuss it again after I've had a chance to talk with Peter. Have you ever observed in him any impulse toward exhibitionism?"

"No. None whatever."

°There is no need to belabor this point, but I cannot resist citing Jonathan Swift's *Tale of the Tub*, even though I believe Peter had never read it. In that savage allegory on the history of Christianity, a father (God), in his last will and testament (New Testament), bequeathes a coat (Christian doctrine) to each of his three sons: Peter (the Roman church, after Simon Peter), Martin (the Lutheran church, after Martin Luther), and Jack (the Presbyterian church, after John Calvin). The book tells how each son gradually alters his coat in spite of the will's explicit instructions that such alterations were not to be made. Ingenious loopholes permitting every change are, of course, found in the father's will. As for the symbolic use of clothing in the Old and the New Testament, the reader can check such words as "clothe," "clothing," "raiment," and "garments" in any good Biblical concordance.—H. W.

"Doesn't he enjoy being in front of an audience? Clergymen, you know, aren't much different in this respect from entertainers and actors and politicians."

"Oh, in that sense, yes. I suppose Peter *is* as big a ham as I am. I thought you meant exhibitionism in the sexual sense."

"I did, actually. There's a well-established correlation between infantile sexual exhibitionism and the better disguised exhibitionism of people who like to be on stage. Sometimes it's not so well disguised. The male ballet dancer, for instance, wearing leotards that are tight in the crotch, or the female stripper. But even among legitimate actors, it's not unusual for analysis to uncover repressed exhibitionistic drives. In times of mental stress, or under the influence of alcohol or other drugs, those tendencies can become overt."

"I understand."

"We had a well-publicized instance here in Chicago a year or two before the war. It involved John Barrymore. Did you hear about it? One night he got into a crowded elevator at the Ambassador Hotel—I suppose he was a bit drunk—and proceeded to relieve his bladder."

"Yes, I did hear about it," I said. "I've never noticed such a tendency in Peter. At least not before yesterday."

I have observed that most doctors (and psychiatrists are no exception) become annoyed whenever a layman says anything at all that indicates familiarity with the doctor's specialty. But I could not keep myself from asking the psychiatrist if he was aware that in the purification rites of early religions it was urine, not blood or water, that had been most widely used as the ablutionary liquid. Had he read, I asked, Ernest Jones's *Essays in Applied Psycho-analysis*?

The doctor leaned back and laughed. "You're referring, I take it, to Jones's famous paper on the symbolic significance of salt? If I remember right, he argues that the water of baptismal rites, the holy water of the Roman Catholic church, and so on, derives from the earlier use of what he calls 'vital fluids'—especially urine and semen. Do you really believe that?"

"Well, yes," I said, a bit miffed by the doctor's levity.

"I suppose Jones may have a point, but it's hard to be sure. I met him last year, by the way, at a congress in London. What a funny, conceited, intolerant little Welshman he is! And what crap he's gotten away with in his technical papers!"

He must have seen a shocked expression on my face, because he quickly altered his tone. "I understand Jones is working on a big biography of Freud. That should be interesting. He certainly knows the early history of analysis. But we're wasting time, and I have to interview a patient in about twenty minutes."

He consulted his wrist watch. "I can't see any need to get involved with urine as a purification symbol. Why would Peter want to baptize your organist? It's more likely, don't you think, that his act was one of desecration? After all, church music is as good a symbol of Christian faith as clothing—maybe even better."

"And there's the double meaning of the word 'organ'."

"Yes, yes," he said with an irritated sigh.

"What," I asked, "do you think has caused his loss of speech?"

"Ah, good question. I really don't know. The skull was fractured on the left side of the frontal lobe, rather low. The fracture overlaps part of the temporal lobe." He tapped a chubby forefinger against his left temple. "There's a lot of evidence that this spot in the brain—it's called 'Broca's area'—has something to do with speech. If it's damaged it can cause aphasia of the type Peter seems to have. But the X-rays show only a skull fracture. If there's any damage to the brain tissue it must be slight. It's possible that the aphasia is mostly psychological. After what you tell me about Peter's religious doubts, I'm wondering whether his loss of speech might not come from a belief that he no longer has anything important to say. I suspect, though, the reason's even simpler. His memory of what happened is so painful he just can't bring himself to talk about it yet."

"That makes sense."

"My guess—of course I could be entirely wrong—is that he'll be talking again in a few days. He's young. He's healthy. His mind is clear. He seems not unduly upset, considering all the circumstances. I think he's exploiting—not consciously, you understand—the knock on his head as an excuse for silence. Does he know anything about Broca's area?"

"I doubt it. I never heard of it before."

"Well, the fracture will keep him in bed at least two weeks, maybe longer. I'll be talking to him and giving him tests. We'll see how things go. I appreciate your good assistance, Dr. Wilson. Could you stop by here again, same time, this Friday?"

I told him I could. When we stood up and shook hands I said: "I didn't mean to play psychiatrist. After all, I'm just a clergyman."

"I don't mind," he said. "We need all the help we can get. Sometimes I feel more like a clergyman than a psychiatrist. As for Jones's essay on salt, my advice is to take most of it *cum grano salis*."

"*Pax vobiscum*," I said, raising my right hand in a benediction.

When I got home, Edna informed me that Middleton had phoned and wanted me to return the call as soon as possible. I guessed he'd seen the story about Peter in the morning newspapers.

He had. While I gave him a partial account of what took place (I omitted the final episode), I was surprised by the long silences that followed each of my horrendous revelations. No expressions of shock or sympathy. Just silence. I had the impression he was periodically putting his fat palm over the mouthpiece so I couldn't hear him chuckling.

It was not until I finished that Middleton proceeded to give me a description of what had happened the night before at the Abernathys. Now it was my turn to listen in silence to the incredible details. At several points I actually put my own hand over the mouthpiece so Middleton could not hear *me* chuckling.

Indeed, I listened to Middleton's story with considerable satisfaction. It helped explain Peter's breakdown. Stronger pressures than I realized had been building up inside his skull. There was surely a layer of symbolism in his actions much deeper than the clothing metaphor. Nakedness is an ancient and universal symbol of guilt. Need I remind my readers that not until sin entered the Garden of Eden did Adam and Eve become aware of their nakedness and make for themselves aprons of fig leaves?

As Middleton rattled on, I became convinced that it was guilt, pure and simple guilt, which had motivated Peter more than anything else: guilt over his prayer at his mother's hospital bedside, guilt over the imagined hypocrisy of his approaching church career, guilt over having struck the father of his prospective bride. Above all, he was tormented by guilt over his relationship with Martha.

Looking back on it now, with all the advantages of hindsight, it seems clear to me that Peter's attitude toward Martha had been undergoing a rapid but only partly conscious change. Both of them had begun to realize that something was amiss, yet neither had been willing to bring their suspicions into the open. Preparations for marriage have a way of accelerating in intensity and complexity. Even when a break is mutually desired, it becomes increasingly difficult to initiate. I sometimes think that this must be the underlying, seldom recognized, reason for all the elaborate rituals with which cultures surround the simple decision of two young people of opposite sex to live together and bring up children. It is a clever trick by which a society strengthens its family system, by which it increases its number of offspring and its chances for survival.

Peter's fist had bashed through all those ritualistic barriers. It had, so to speak, solved the problem with one clean blow. Whatever sense of release he may have experienced, however, was overshadowed by his sense of loss and shame. He must have felt that he had deceived Martha even more than himself, that his relations with her had been no more than a cruel masquerade.

The marriage plans had, of course, been canceled. Middleton informed me on the phone that Martha was breaking the engagement. But she did want to visit Peter. Through her father I made arrangements to meet her Tuesday afternoon in the reception lounge on the hospital's main floor.

Martha looked less distraught than I expected. Yes, she said, before we took the elevator to Peter's floor, the ending of their engagement was absolutely final. She still admired Peter very much, though now it was obvious to her that they could never have made each other happy. No longer did she feel toward him the way she once had. I listened sympathetically, occasionally interjecting a diplomatic comment.

Would there be a big emotional scene when Martha and Peter met? My fears were groundless. She nodded solemnly to him when we entered. He nodded solemnly back. I introduced Martha to an intern standing by Peter's bed and to the elderly man who was sharing the room with Peter. The young doctor had been a radioman on a Navy cargo ship during the war, and Peter had been swapping war stories with him by tapping him on his forearm. The intern excused himself. Peter said goodbye by rapping a pencil on the metal bedpost.

Martha and Peter behaved toward one another with inflated good will. It was, of course, an elaborate put-on. Peter still could not speak a single word. They exchanged friendly banalities, Peter by writing notes, Martha by speaking aloud. Neither said a word about what had happened at the Abernathys' home or at my church. Nothing was said about breaking their engagement. It was taken for granted.

They shook hands like old pals. Martha smiled and waved a white-gloved farewell at the door. There were no tears in her wide gray eyes.

The door closed slowly and silently, the way hospital doors always do. Peter looked sleepy and sad.

"Do you think you can patch things up with Martha?" I asked.

He shook his head.

"Do you want to patch things up?"

He shook his head again.

"You'll be getting your doctor's degree in June. Are you still planning to be ordained?"

His lips began to tremble. With great effort, yet loudly and distinctly, he pronounced the single word: "No."

Looking startled and pleased, he struggled to say more. His lips and jaw quivered. There were gurgling sounds in his throat. No words came out. I could see pinspots of perspiration on his forehead.

"Give it up for now, Pete," I said, patting his arm. "I have to leave anyway."

He sank back on his bed, head twisted to one side. When I left he was crying silently into the pillow.

The next morning he spoke several words to the nurse. That afternoon, during a session of tests given by the psychiatrist, he was able to repeat any word after it was spoken to him. By the end of the week he was talking in simple sentences, with only occasional periods of hesitation and stammering. Permission was given for him to leave his bed and walk up and down the corridor, and to sit in a small lounge near the elevators. When he was not taking tests he passed the time by reading popular magazines and paperback mysteries, or listening to a portable radio that Edna had brought him. When the two of us paid him a visit, in the middle of the following week, he was speaking normally.

"He's sure feeling better," said the man in the other bed. "This morning he was chasing all the nurses."

"Correction," said Peter. "*They* were chasing *me*."

Before Peter was released from Billings, at the end of his third week there, my wife and I conceived a plan. Every spring, for the past eight years, we had been going to Santa Fe, New Mexico, for a month's vacation. We had come to know many people there, and the growth of the atomic project on the mesa at nearby Los Alamos had brought to the area a number of Gray City scientists and their wives whom we counted among old friends. Rudolf Carnap and Charles Morris, both members of Chicago's philosophy department, had summer homes there. Taos, a village of artists and writers (now hippie communes!) is not far away. (D. H. Lawrence, who was living in Taos when he wrote the short story mentioned in my footnote to Chapter 27, is buried near the village.) Edna always enjoyed visits to the nearby Indian pueblos, and there were occasional anthropological "digs" in the area where she ran into former classmates.

Both of us had grown attached to Santa Fe. We loved its musical-voiced natives, its spectacular Krazy Kat scenery, its invigorating air, its magnificent sunlight. We believed that Peter would enjoy it there, away from Gray City and its divinity school, away from the professors whose mouths, as James Stephens once put it, "are filled with sawdust."

We planned to go there in June, after the commencement ceremonies, but there was no reason why we could not spend a week or two in Santa

Fe now and take Peter with us. His psychiatrist agreed that it was an excellent idea. I arranged for one of my graduate students to take over my classes, and Professor Haydon, who enjoyed occasional opportunites to preach, agreed to substitute for me in the pulpit.

I mentioned the plan to Peter a few days before he left the hospital. "You've finished your thesis. It's a fine piece of work. As you know, it's been accepted. You can still take your examinations in June and get your degree as you planned. We'll forget about your ordination for the time being. I've already rented a house in Santa Fe. It has a second bedroom. How about it?"

While I was talking, I could see from Peter's expression that he was overjoyed. He gripped my hand and began to thank me while his eyes filled with tears.

30

The City of Saint Francis

Peter did not want to return to his dormitory room where he would have to face his friends in the divinity school. Who could blame him? Edna and I packed his clothes into his trunk and Navy seabag, and his books into about a dozen cartons that we obtained from grocery stores in the area. With the help of the custodian of my church and his station wagon, we transferred all of Peter's possessions to my house where I stored them in the basement as I had done before when he enlisted in the Navy.

Peter stayed with us for a week before we left for New Mexico. During the week he talked very little. When I was out of the house, he spent most of his time alone in my study where Edna would see him browsing through my books and periodicals, or sitting lost in reverie.

Many of the homes in Sante Fe are adobe structures designed to resemble Indian pueblos. We had rented a small pink-walled house of this type on *Camino del Monte Sol*, a dusty little unpaved road that curves along the side of a hill southeast of Santa Fe's central Plaza. After a taxi deposited us in front of the house, Peter stood there for several minutes looking out over the village, enchanted by the mottled, sun-drenched colors of the landscape, the quaint architecture, the brilliant blue of the sky, and the green and purple mountains in the distance. He filled his lungs deeply with the unpolluted air.

"It's like wine," he said.

In the afternoon, each day that we were there, Peter would strip to the waist for an hour or two of jogging up and down the *camino* and shadowboxing in the yard behind the house. One afternoon he walked around the patio on his hands and did a series of three back handsprings. I had not been aware before of this gymnastic prowess. The color returned to his cheeks. The tan darkened on his face and arms.

Edna and I had been worried about how Peter would react to the Roman Catholic atmosphere that pervades so much of New Mexico and that has made Santa Fe a kind of pilgrimage spot for vacationing Southwestern Catholics. To our surprise he showed an unusual interest in the Spanish Catholic traditions, art, and institutions that surrounded us. On the first Sunday after we arrived he insisted we accompany him to High Mass at the nearby Cristo Rey Church. He wanted to see the *reredos* of Our Lady of Light, a famous ornamental stone screen behind the altar—a screen carved by native artists almost two centuries earlier. The Mexican legend of the Virgin of Guadalupe, whose flamelike image is seen everywhere in Santa Fe, fascinated him. He made a special trip to the Guadalupe Church to inspect the tile panel brought there from a spot near her original shrine in Mexico.* He visited the Cathedral of Saint Francis where rests the body of Archbishop Lamy, whose life inspired Willa Cather's novel, *Death Comes for the Archbishop*. A beautifully carved and painted *nicho* of Saint Clare, the friend of Saint Francis who founded the second Franciscan order, the Poor Clares, so aroused his curiosity that he went to the local library to consult encyclopedias on the Franciscan movement.

Santa Fe's original name had been "The Royal City of the Holy Faith of Saint Francis of Assissi." What patron saint could be more appropriate to the area than the happy, gentle Francis with his ecstatic love of nature, sunlight, and Lady Poverty? Where in all of North America can one read his *Canticle to the Sun* in more appropriate surroundings? On the paperback book rack in the lobby of the La Fonda Hotel (we walked to the hotel every afternoon for pre-dinner tequila cocktails), Peter found an edition of Chesterton's *St. Francis of Assissi*, one of the few of Chesterton's better books he had not previously read. He bought a copy and finished it that evening in one sitting.

---

*This shrine, the oldest devoted to Mary in North America, is just outside Mexico City where it is visited annually by millions of pilgrims. The legend is that on December 9, 1531, the Virgin appeared to Juan Diego, an Indian, telling him she wanted a church built on that spot. The local bishop was skeptical of the story, so Juan returned to the spot to ask Mary for a sign. She appeared again and told him to come back on December 12. When he did he found the hill covered with roses, blooming miraculously in midwinter. He filled his *tilma*, a native cloak of rough cloth, with roses and carried them to the bishop. After they had tumbled out, a picture of Mary was found dyed into the fabric. The original *tilma*, inside a silver frame, now hangs behind the shrine's altar.

The painting shows the Virgin in an attitude of prayer. She is wearing a blue-green mantle over a dress embroidered with roses, standing on the hollow of a crescent moon, and surrounded by gold rays. The fact that the colors remain bright after centuries of touching and kissing is taken by superstitious Catholics to be proof that the cloth was painted by God himself. All sorts of papal honors have been bestowed on this mediocre picture. I do not know if any intelligent Catholics today take the legend seriously.—H. W.

"It's a sort of companion to GK's book on Thomas Aquinas," I recall Peter saying. "What a fantastic contrast the two saints make! No wonder Dante, in the *Paradiso*, has Thomas tell the life of Francis."

I hadn't thought of it before, but of course Peter was right. Thomas was huge, fat, slow, plodding. He saw everything through the eyes of his massive, misguided intellect. Francis was small and thin, with quick impetuous movements: dancing, as Chesterton says, like an autumn leaf in the wind. He sought truth not with syllogisms but with abrupt rapier thrusts of intuition. He has always been one of the Catholic saints most admired by Protestants. I could see how his emphasis on faith, unaided by reason, would make him especially appealing to Peter.

Could it be that Peter identified himself with Francis when he read in Chesterton's book about how the Saint, after learning he had been disinherited by his wealthy father, stripped himself of his clothing and, wearing only a hair shirt, walked through the wintry woods, bursting into song with the joy of finding himself free of all worldly possessions? It may be far-fetched, nevertheless I believe that Peter felt a similar emotion of escape when he stripped the garments of Christianity from his faith. Like Francis, he felt free at last; free to worship God in his own peculiar way, unencumbered by traditions that were rooted in doctrines he no longer could accept.

I am trying, as always in this narrative, to be as objective as I can. It would be unfair to the reader if I did not add that my own opinion of Saint Francis is a low one. I can appreciate his lovable qualities—the gay humor, the simple piety—but I cannot see him in the round as other than a simple-minded, badly educated clown, carrying a heavy burden of unconscious sado-masochistic drives. The familiar picture of the Saint, pretending to play a fiddle by scraping one stick upon another, always struck me as characteristic of the man: an amusing bit of vaudeville though hardly productive of substantial music.

One evening I spoke to Peter about these opinions and suggested that sometime he should look into Saint Bonaventure's life of Francis. It was the source, I informed him, of most of Chesterton's anecdotes. The picture it gives of the Saint is not so palatable to modern tastes as GK's carefully screened collection of tales. Who today could believe Bonaventure's story of the sheep which, after hearing a sermon by Francis, trotted to a church and genuflected at the altar?

The Saint's constant display of his humility through mortifications surely betrayed a vast unconscious pride. It is often said that no man ever lived who more successfully imitated the life of Jesus. I cannot believe it. Where do we read of Jesus mixing food with water to make it more insipid, flaying himself violently with a rope, refusing to remove the lice from his clothing because he counted it an honor to wear those "celestial pearls"? Did not Jesus wash the feet of his disciples? Did he not allow Mary of Bethany to wash his own feet and dry them with her hair?

Peter's response to my carping was an impish smile. "My dear Homer, you have me all wrong. I'm not interested in the real Saint Francis. No doubt everything you say is true. Of course the miracle tales are ridiculous. Who knows what caused his stigmata? But can't you feel . . . " Something checked him. "Don't be alarmed, Homer. I'm not bouncing over to Rome."

I have included this dialog because I want to make clear that Peter's interest in Saint Francis in no way indicated a revived interest in Catholicism as a viable religious faith. His attitude was closer to George Santayana's poetic way of viewing Catholic mythology—gorgeous and irrelevant. Peter was far enough away from orthodoxy now to enjoy Catholic art and poetry without having to worry about its truth. None of it was true. He was seeing it from outside. He was seeing it in a way that is easier, I suppose, for an ex-Protestant than an ex-Catholic.

Yet his attitude was not quite the same as Santayana's, for Santayana was an atheist. There still was something in the faith of Saint Francis—even more, perhaps, in Chesterton's way of looking at the world—with which Peter could identify. He was intrigued, for example, by a description in Chesterton's book of the artist who examines a landscape by bending over and looking at it between his legs to see the colors and shapes from a novel perspective. The mystic, writes Chesterton, always sees the world upside-down. He sees everything suspended, as it were, by God's mercy. "He who has seen the vision of his city upside-down has seen it the right way up." The saints are "thankful to God for not dropping the whole cosmos like a vast crystal to be shattered into falling stars. Perhaps St. Peter saw the world so, when he was crucified head-downwards."

I did not argue with Peter when he read those passages aloud. I believe that it is better for a man to stand upright and see the world the way it actually is. Prolonged standing on the head induces a metaphysical dizziness that clouds the vision and distorts the mind's map of reality. But I was too impressed by the speed of Peter's recovery to risk setting it back by argument. Edna and I were taking great care to avoid discussions that might upset him. It was a foolish caution, for it soon became apparent that Peter did not in the least object to talking about the amorphous shape that his faith was now assuming.

The moment came one evening after a brief thundershower. He and I had climbed to the flat roof of our house to smoke a cigarette and enjoy the wet night air. It was cool enough for us to wear our sweaters, and I had thrown some piñon logs into the fireplace to take the chill from the sitting room where Edna was reading.

The sky had cleared quickly after the rain, as skies in New Mexico usually do. Now it was splattered from rim to rim with what Lord Dunsany somewhere called the "old, old, unbought stars." The Milky Way twisted overhead like a luminous celestial path, a King's Highway. The Spaniards called it the *Camino de Santiago*, the Road of Saint James, the patron saint of Spain. It was more clearly visible than I had ever observed before. Peter remarked that he had not seen such a brilliant sky since the nights when he took a lookout's watch on the flying bridge of his destroyer escort. Suspended low in the west was the thin crescent of Sister Moon. We sat on a small adobe ridge that surrounded the rectangular roof, breathing the beautiful air, our cigarettes glowing in the night like giant fireflies. Brother Wind caressed our faces.

Peter broke the stillness. "It's good to be alive."

"Yes," I said. "When you add it all up, the good and the bad, I suppose it is."

"And are you thankful you're alive tonight?"

I had been skimming through Chesterton's book on Saint Francis, so I anticipated the trap Peter was setting for me. "If I say 'yes,' you'll ask me who or what it is I thank."

Peter drew on his cigarette, and in the strengthened glow of its ash I could see the amusement in his eyes.

"It's true," I continued, not waiting for an answer. "It's true that I feel a certain sense of gratitude. I can empathize with Chesterton when he writes about such a mood. I see no reason, though, why I have to give Nature, or the Cosmos, Being—whatever you want to call the totality of everything there is—I see no reason why I have to give it a personality similar in some way to my own. I'm part of nature. I enjoy existing. I don't know why I exist. I don't believe anyone knows. I'm not even sure it's a meaningful question. Anyway, in the process of living I find enough meaning to satisfy me."

"You admit, though, there's a profound mystery about existence?"

"Who could deny it? And it's here, of course, that a humanist can have emotions of awe and humility. One would be a fool to think that science has done more than pick up, as Newton put it, a few pretty shells on the shore of a limitless sea."

"Do you think science some day will discover everything?"

I thought a long time before I answered. "Given man's present brain, the notion is obviously absurd. You can't teach physics to a jellyfish. You can't even teach it that two and two is four. Why should our feeble little brains be the best that evolution can fabricate? If we don't blow up our planet, there may be billions of years of evolution ahead of us. As our brains get better, the reach of our science will get longer. For all I know, this growth of knowledge may be infinite. There may be an endless series of differently structured levels of truth. No, I don't believe science will ever discover everything."

Peter sat for a while in silence. Finally he said: "I'm beginning to understand, Homer, how much we have in common even though we're still so far apart on the biggest question of all."

"Yes?" I said, watching his face. It was in deep shadow, but I could see that his chin was raised. He seemed to be looking off into the sky above the dark mountains.

"We share," he said, "what Otto called a feeling for the numinous, a sense of the *mysterium tremendum*, the *totaliter aliter*."

"I suppose we do," I replied. "But why call it the *wholly*-other? Why emphasize the gulf between what we know and what we don't? Our world is partly knowable to a cat. And beings in another solar system, as far ahead of us in intelligence as we're ahead of cats and dogs, must live in a world that surely is partly knowable to us. Things overlap. Differences lie on spectrums. If by 'wholly-other' Otto meant no more than all the truth that humanity doesn't know at the moment, then I don't object to the term. And if you like, there's no reason why you can't call it 'God.'"

Peter shook his head. "No, Homer, that would be using the term dishonestly. God may be wholly other, but the wholly-other isn't the same as God. At least not the same as Otto's God, or the God of Moses and Jesus. Otto added another attribute, remember? It was the holy."

"I know. And that's where he and I, where you and I, must part. I admit that emotions of awe and fascination, of fear before the Unknown, are primitive, inescapable emotions. Even as cold a fish as Bertrand Russell must surely experience them at times. But to attribute to that Unknown a holiness, a moral concern for human history, is to project our own personality into the darkness, to use ourselves as models for the structure of . . . of what? Of beings in higher space-time continuums? Of the total structure of Being itself? I prefer the attitude that Herbert Spencer had toward what he liked to call the Unknowable. By definition we know nothing about it. I see no justification for describing it with anthropomorphic models."

"Then," said Peter, "you have nothing to pray to. No one to thank for being alive, no one to ask for forgiveness, no one to ask for courage, no one to provide you with a life after death."

"No one."

"Then you shouldn't speak of God."

"I agree. I only meant that I've no strong objection if someone wants to use the term as a synonym for nature. John Dewey said the same thing in his book, *A Common Faith*. But I prefer, like Dewey, not to use a God language."

"Except when you preach on Sundays."

"Yes. I plead guilty. Then, I do use the term. I use it, though, in the poetic sense that Dewey argued was permissible on occasion. I use it because my congregation needs it. But I mean by it nothing more than an expression of natural piety toward the universe."

I expected Peter to seize on these remarks as an excuse to lecture me on hypocrisy, but he let the matter drop. We each took a fresh cigarette from our packs. I located a match folder in a pocket of my cardigan and tried to light several matches. Each time the breeze extinguished the flame.

"Let me," said Peter, taking the folder. He scratched a match then held it between both hands in an unusual way that he had learned on the weather deck of his ship. The cupped hands, with a horizontal circular opening formed by the thumb and forefinger of his right hand, were like a dim flashlight which illuminated his rugged features from below, accentuating the slight twist of his nose. We bent our heads in turn to draw on the flame.

"Belief in God is a funny thing," he said, shaking out the match and tossing it over the roof's edge. "Not believing in God is like believing in the sunlight of Santa Fe and not believing in the sun."

"I'm surprised at you, Peter. Now you're dredging up the old first-cause argument, the argument Kant so completely ripped to shreds."

"I know Kant destroyed its logic. I'm not so sure he destroyed its emotional force."

"I'll buy that," I said. "You started your religious Odyssey with a strong conversion experience in Holiness Tabernacle. From your point of view the universe is still a tabernacle of the holy. Of course it's an emotion. I'm not even sure it's an unhealthy emotion. Freud, you know, considered the possibility that the need for God, for a personal God, is so deeply a part of human nature that only the strongest and toughest-minded can give it up—that the price of widespread atheism might be a widespread cultural neurosis. When the gods go, the demons move in."

Peter laughed. "You're the most honest atheist in the world, Homer. Sometimes I think that deep down in your unconscious you really believe in God, but you won't admit it."

"I don't think so. Even if I did believe, even if everyone believed, it still wouldn't prove that God exists."

"No, I guess not."

"Didn't it ever strike you as odd of God," I said, "to take such extraordinary precautions to conceal himself?"

[This, of course, was many years before the cover of *Time* (April 8, 1966) asked in bold blood-red letters, "Is God Dead?" It was before the death of God became a topic of cocktail conversation, before car bumper signs assured us that God is indeed alive and living in Argentina. It was before suburban ministers read *Honest to God*° and suddenly discovered Bonhoeffer and Tillich, and Paul van Buren's "secular meaning of the Gospel" (*i.e.*, humanism), and that God is "down here" in the muck and grime and carbon monoxide of the secular city instead of "up there" in nice clean outer space where presumably the theists assume he is.

It was before the Right Reverend James A. Pike, ex-Catholic, Ex-Episcopalian, ex-believer in the Virgin Birth and the Trinity, became a convert to Spiritualism after experiencing poltergeist phenomena and talking to his dead son in seances. It was before the dying Protestant liberal churches were given adrenaline shots by the Black revolution and ecumenism and the Vietnam War. It was before Catholic priests began to talk out loud about celibacy and birth control and intermarriage and papal infallibility; before Father James Kavanaugh wrote a best-selling book about his "outdated church," got married, and unfrocked himself; before the Dutch Catholics turned into Protestants.

It was before hip ministers of big-city Protestant churches discovered jazz and folk rock and polymorphism and pot and underground movies and *Peanuts* and experimental plays with four-letter words and *Fanny Hill* and flower power and encounter therapy and the spiritual meaning of the orgasm.

It was before the rise of "play theology" and the introduction of "happenings" into church liturgy. It was before Harvey Cox, of the Harvard Divinity School, staged his famous 1970 Easter celebration in a warehouse discotheque. According to *Newsweek* (May 11), this impressive ritual began at midnight Saturday with "a projector [that] flashed images of Vietnam atrocities in an updated version of the Stations of the Cross. White-clad dancers from the Harvard Divinity School mimed agony, while harsh background music boomed a dissonant Passion of Christ. By 3 A.M., chains of dancers formed, swaying and lifting each other aloft. The crowd swelled to 1,500, and a rock band called The

---

°Any reader who is curious about my opinion of Bishop John A. T. Robinson's flimsy book, *Honest to God* (1963), and the furious controversy it aroused in England and the United States, should look up my long review, "Holy Smoke!", in the June, 1964, issue of the *Journal of Secular Theism.*—H. W.

Apocrypha played 'I Can't Get No Satisfaction.' Then Cox entered, dressed in white satin vestments trimmed in pink embroidery, followed by five other clerics costumed variously in Byzantine and psychedelic robes. The Baptist minister stepped forward to an altar laden with fruit, bread and wine to read the Gospel account of Christ's Resurrection. And when he finished, the silence was suddenly burst by the deafening crash of Handel's 'Hallelujah' chorus.

"Using the highly politicized liturgy of the Berkeley Free Church, Cox intoned the 'Kyrie Eleison' (Lord, have mercy), to which the crowd responded: 'Right on!' Bread and wine were passed around and the congregants reacted by feeding each other. Bright balloons wafted to the low warehouse ceiling and incense sweetened the air. At 5:45, someone pointed to the patch of morning visible through the skylight and the entire crowd rushed outside, chanting, 'Sun, sun, sun'."

Right on, Harvey, my friend! Is Jesus dancing with you, Harvey? Who's your booking agent, Harvey? Have you thought of adding a little juggling and a few magic tricks to your act, Harvey? Do you think, dear Harvey, you'll ever stage a happening that will be more shocking than my own little Easter service happening of 1948?]°

Peter stood up and thrust his hands into his trouser pockets. "No, Homer, I'm glad that God conceals himself. If there were logical arguments, if there was evidence we could see or hear or touch, we'd all *have* to believe. It wouldn't be free choice. It wouldn't be love. Don't you see? The secret of faith is that it doesn't have *any* cognitive support. God wants uncompelled love. I'll even admit that such love may have its origin in unconscious memories of our parents. We live in a patriarchal society, so naturally we project the father's image on our concept of God. But every child has to be brought up by somebody. If the state took care of its children, there'd still be some kind of human intelligence—a nurse, a hospital staff, a school—some person or group of persons to play the parental role. Freud was probably right. Faith *is* the memory of being cared for in childhood. But is that a good argument against it? Why couldn't this be God's way of giving us, his children, a normal hunger for himself?"

In the darkness I hoped Peter couldn't see me smiling.

"There's still a mystery about faith," he went on. "It's not enough just to recognize the natural impulses behind it. You can't live as if God ex-

°Harvey Cox is still in show-biz. During a liturgy he conducted in 1972 at Columbia University's St. Paul's Chapel, in New York City, he took off his shoes to swap socks with a student. Everybody exchanged "things" and "kisses of peace," sang, danced, drank wine, and thoroughly enjoyed the festivities. "Whatever happens," said Cox (New York Times, May 29, 1972), "that's the plan."—M.G.

ists when you secretly believe he doesn't. You still have to decide, somehow, whether your desire, the projected image, does or doesn't stand for something outside your head. And once you make the decision that it does, the decision leads to its own peculiar kind of certainty."

"Peculiar's a good word for it," I said. "If the decision isn't based on empirical evidence, and if it isn't based on reason, there isn't much left to justify it, is there? All you can say about it is that it satisfies a longing."

"That's all," Peter agreed. "There's no other justification. Unamuno said everything. Faith *is* Quixotic. Faith *is* absurd. Who can pretend to understand it? There's a deep mystery about it. It's tied up with the enigmas of God and free will, with the incredible fact that a world exists and we're in it and we know we're in it and we know we'll soon not be in it. Faith *is* a kind of madness. I don't deny it. I can't explain why I believe. I only know I can't *not* believe."

The lights of Los Alamos flickered faintly in the distance. I pointed toward them. "It was over there that our scientists invented a new type of bomb. We dropped one on Hiroshima. We dropped another on Nagasaki. Thousands of good people died in agony. How do you fit their deaths into your theology?"

"It's not easy. The best I can do is trot out the same old tired arguments. You've heard them all before. Moral evil is the price we pay for freedom. Natural evil is the price we pay for a world of natural law. Gravity keeps us on the earth. If someone falls off a cliff, gravity murders him. You can't expect God to cancel a law every time it's about to hurt someone. You can't have everything. You can't have a world with nothing but goodness any more than you can have mountains and no valleys. Human history without evil would be as meaningless as the old square triangle."

"And cancer?"

"Yes, it's also part of the price. Evolution operates by natural laws. Sickness, disease, famine, death—they're all part of the big price. How could evolution avoid them? Our task is to do what we can to overcome them."

"You sound," I said, "like Dr. Pangloss. A young married couple in my church has a four-year-old child dying of leukemia. It would be hard to persuade them that this is a price they have to pay for existing. There's an old Arabian proverb that goes: 'When you see a blind man, kick him. Why should you be kinder than God?'"

"It's not funny, Homer. But you're right. My arguments aren't very convincing. Evil is another dark mystery."

"It seems to me that you're evading all the dilemmas of theism by calling them mysteries."

"I don't think it's evasion. It's just an honest confession of ignorance. Thinking about *anything* has to end finally in mystery. And why not? After all, we didn't make the world any more than the jellyfish did. Why should the human race be easier to understand than time and space and matter and energy? Faith in God doesn't explain an electron. Why should it explain evil? Faith doesn't solve any metaphysical problem. It just eases our anxiety. It makes the pain a little less painful. It makes the truth a little less sad."

He sat down again beside me, on the low ledge of the roof. We listened to the sound of footsteps coming toward us.

"What are your plans?" I asked. "If you don't intend to preach, what do you intend to do?"

"I'll find something."

He flicked his cigarette forward with his middle finger. There was a burst of crimson fireworks when it struck the glistening trunk of a large cottonwood tree. In the wet grass it glowed for a moment then went out.

"You've won," he said.

"No," I said, "I've lost."

Below us, on the *Camino del Monte Sol*, a young Spanish-American girl walked by. She was wearing a tight skirt, and her shapely bottom jiggled in the soft light of a street lamp. Our heads swiveled slowly as she passed. Hypnotized, we watched the ancient rhythms until the girl vanished around the corner of Canyon Road.

Was it possible, I thought, that the canyon between us, between Peter's way of looking at life and mine, was no more than a difference in the use of words? Were we just playing different language games: he with his "God talk," I with my "non-God talk"? Could one language be translated into the other without a serious loss of meaning?

No, I said to myself, it was more than that. The chasm was wider than that. Our respective languages rested on contrary emotional posits. Peter had leaped across the void. It was a leap I could not make now even if I wanted to. Our differences were deep inside our hearts, chained to the hopes and fears of our opposing temperaments.

Across the Rio Grande Valley, in the far foothills of the Jémez mountains, the lights of Los Alamos continued to scintillate. There the thunderbirds of science were carrying on their secret work with Brother Fire and Sister Heavy Water, probing the mysteries of Older Brother, the Eminent Mr. Sun, courting the love of Little Sister Death. To the east, silhouetted against the stars, we could see the black profiles of the mountains called *Sangre de Cristo*. Smoke from the burning piñon wood, with its rich cedar fragrance, coiled upward through the small clay chimney near us and slowly dispersed its atoms into the moist night air.